CLOVER

AN APOCALYPTIC TALE

BOOK 1 OF 4 IN
THE SAVAGE DERANGEMENT SERIES

CRAIG R. SMITH

Clover: An Apocalyptic Tale

This is a work of fiction. Names, characters, places, and incidents are the product of the author's imagination or are used fictitiously. Any resemblance to actual persons, living or dead, events, or locales is entirely coincidental.

Edited by Kat Betts

To my grandparents, Norma Jean and Clyde as well as Elizabeth Dolan and the many others that have inspired and supported my writing career over the years.

I can remember it like it was yesterday. The crusade between the malicious entity known only as the Corporation, an invective entity that thrived on power, corruption and manipulation, and the rebels that opposed their infinite suppression. I don't comprehensively recollect everything that went on during the time the Corporation had complete control, but I do remember humans being a caring species and how the Corporation used this compassion as a weapon against the world's citizens. They didn't deserve the fate they were dealt, but I have become powerless to resurrect their faith in humanity or defend them from their approaching annihilation. The nuclear blasts sent their very existence into a chaotic downward spiral and had a hand in corroding the environment and establishing its diabolical post-apocalyptic condition. The once nourishing planet has become a desert abys, our final punishment for the multitude of transgressions, including our inability to stop the Corporation's malcontent.

– Clover

PROLOGUE

The environment had changed dramatically after the use of the thermonuclear weapons in the so-called final resolution to the Corporation's rebel problem. The planet transformed from its thriving, radiant state into its current fiendish condition. The planet's surface had become arid and infertile, filled with porous sands and radiated soil—not even worth spitting on. Those humans that had survived the cataclysmic event now lived underground in protected hovel-like structures or outside the heaviest radiation zones. They were mainly located in the deadly Wasteland. The war forced the atmosphere to change dramatically, creating massive turret storms and swirling winds that would appear out of nowhere and seemed blow at will.

The intense solar heat that rained down on the planet's dead and dreary surface was slowly cooking it to its final demise. Solar radiation caused massive flux in surface temperature, forcing the inhabitants to deal with everything from nearly unbearable heat during the day to frigid cold at night caused by the ever-thinning layers of the outer atmosphere. Very few things endured the climate change and only the most dangerous species roamed the arid sea of dunes. Only well-equipped humans could venture out for long periods of time.

Most human knowledge had been lost in the war and whatever knowledge remained of the past would soon flee with the passing of any surviving elders. Most human life-forms moved in groups to avoid being ambushed, robbed, raped or even killed. There were small communities that arose after the poisoning surface radiation slowly dissipated to a safe level. But, like most inhabitants of the new world, they did not move about in the dark, afraid of what roamed in the darkness. Many forms of predators roamed, but the humans had a legend that claimed a nocturnal beast in human shape and form hunted in the darkness and all that dared venture after dark would be exposed to this new breed of nocturnal creature. The legend was mostly to keep inhabitants from encountering the real horrors of the night.

The Wasteland, an outer rim of desolation that surrounded what remained of colonial habitats, had many dangers—large scorpions the size of small armored vehicles that fed on smaller inhabitants, gigantic sand worms that acted as scavengers in the Wasteland, and other poisonous creatures that could pull a whole traveling caravan down under the sandy, dead surface. The humans that dwelled in the Wasteland had many other dangerous obstacles than the deadly creatures that roamed among the Wasteland's landscape. Most of the human inhabitants residing in the Wasteland joined gangs like the Outland Rustlers, raping women, seizing goods and murdering in the desolate, sandy tundra.

In the early years of after the war, herds of Outland Rustlers stayed in the barren Wasteland, attacking those that wandered into their territory. Most settlers avoided these areas when looking for refuge or food, hunting and cooking utensils, and drinkable water. The issue now was that the rustlers were venturing into the habitable parts of the world and endangering the lives of the settlers.

Emergence

The lethal incandescent sun started to ascend slowly over the barren horizon. Its reddish-purple illumination obliterated any portion left untainted by the enshrouded cool nighttime. The sun rained down its antagonistic rays onto the surface of the planet announcing a new day of extreme heat and despair was about to begin. The cracked surface made the planet appear as an aging and coarse bystander who had lost all sense of what was happing to their face. Finally, the sun reached its pinnacle and filled the sky and arid terrain with its malicious radiation. Heat emerged instantly from the sunrise and swiftly became too much to bear. The furnace-like heat felt much like living within the sun itself.

Soon after the raging sun rose, a small family emerged from the safety of their hovel dwelling. A father, mother, and a teenage daughter along with her twin brother all stood at the edge of the structure, checking their gear one last time. They had prepared rigorously for their long journey to the town of Sonoma in search of supplies. The father was hoping that an early start would allow them to accomplish their goal and return before darkness fell. It was a long trip to the abandoned town, but even as cautious as they were that day, a set of eyes watched their every move.

Clover observed the family from a distance and watched with extreme inquisitiveness. One of the family members had drawn his focus. In fact, this member didn't make the bioengineered assassin curious, she caused a sense of déjà vu that had him perplexed. This was driving Clover insane. The family was the first sign of humanity since emerging from his hibernating state. It was an amusing sight. Their slow, lumbering movements reminded him of some type of slow tortoise that had no care in the world—not a very good way to survive in this barren waste.

These humans move in a slow and carefree manner, with absolutely no regard for the scent trail they leave behind. It's a wonder they have endured out here this long. They make easy targets for hungry predators. Following their trail will not be difficult at all, he thought.

Clover was the origin of the entire project, and prototype for Reinhart's cadre of assassins, commissioned by the Corporation and commanded by General Reinhart, the project's superintendent and originator. Clover had keen night vision, allowing him to track and observe targets at night. With a heightened sense of smell, the ability to track targets from miles away, and lightning-quick reflexes, he was the perfect hunter. He was created to eliminate the rebel leaders that were giving the Corporation nightmares.

Clover's curiosity exposed the audacious assassin to dangers he had shielded himself from through his extended truancy, but it was too late to retract his pursuit now. Fortunately, those that would be alarmed by his sudden arrival and his reemergence, both intriguing and threating, were too occupied with other things to notice him.

He stared intensely from a safe distance as the family slowly gathered like some exotic flock preparing to head south for winter. His custom overcoat flapped in the ever-increasing wind like a canvas sail pushing through a chaotic storm. He could sense a colossal sandstorm approaching rapidly. His overcoat was designed to move fluidly, allowing him to grab his throwing weapon in a fluent motion. It tapered in such a way that he could retrieve the two Katina's strapped to his back in their sheaths.

Clover had seen human habitation before, but nothing like this human family moving unhurriedly through the traitorous abys before him. The family gravitated toward one another, helping each other across the treacherous terrain. Other humans he had encountered had either burrowed themselves away from any human contact, avoiding confrontation as much as possible, or had been the aggressor, pursuing one another like predators.

Clover shielded his eyes from the sunrise, as each family member slowly disappeared under its delusional halo. Clover was much more efficient as a nocturnal predator but his predatory senses could still track the family through the intense sunlight and the oncoming, thrashing storm, despite the storm's death threats.

Something drew his attention back to the origin of his curiosity, the mother. Despite being burdened by all the gear she wore, she managed to display a maternal sense about her. She constantly looked after her adolescent children who trailed behind her. She kept encouraging them to keep up every time they fell behind. The woman's materialistic mannerisms indicated that she had a nurturing nature, unlike her spouse, who kept yelling for them to keep moving. Shelley Whiteherst's motherly mannerism and eminence was giving the bioengineered assassin a feeling of déjà vu, which left Clover in a semi hypnotic trance and forced him to temporarily lose track of the family's movements for a few moments.

Without warning, a hypnotic voice burrowed into Clover's mind. It was a voice that constantly haunted him but, with his elongated seclusion, he'd not heard the voice in some time.

"Clover," echoed the feminine voice. The voice was soft and warmhearted, much like a mother speaking to a young child. "Why have you become so lost? I have been searching for you forever. It's time for my precious Clover to find himself, his *true self*, not the self he has been portraying for some time. Once you discover the true nature of your being, you can return to purposefulness and fulfill your destiny."

Clover shook himself and, as if he had been daydreaming, the voice dissipated from his mind. The soft voice had affected his ability to follow the family. It had been a nuisance, disturbing his many heightened senses since end of the war. He held his head briefly in agony. "Who are you?" he asked. "Why do you haunt me as you do, mysterious voice? You won't let me be. Give me the answers I seek or let me be." *It just won't go away*, he thought. *And what did the voice mean? Discover my essence and find my true self? Riddles that won't subside. I need to discover things on my own before it drives me insane.*

Clover thought of the woman's movements and her mannerisms. She brought back emotions he had buried deep within. *Maybe I will find the answers I seek in this family, in this human female. Maybe the haunting voice is driving me toward her, but why?*

The weather was about to change abruptly and give Clover more cover to pursue the traveling family closer without exposing his position. His senses had alerted him of the storm's presence long before the humans would ever spot it. It came out of the west, a massive sandstorm that would engulf the entire region. Its sudden arrival had emerged from the direction of the Wasteland, which surrounded the livable parts of this region. This would be trying for the family; they would have to stay close to one another so that none of them became lost in the dense, forceful storm. Even though the family members had become accustomed to the weary weather conditions on the surface, they still struggled to travel through storms such as the one moving on them. The oncoming storm was shielding the sun's position and as they moved farther onward it was going to become more difficult to gauge the time of day.

Clover trailed the family, but not so far behind as to lose their scent. The humans' trail could easily be lost in the oncoming storm with the massive amount of debris now being flung in every direction. He moved as swiftly down the dune as he could, but the loose, sandy terrain made maneuvering through the vast dunes difficult, even for his superior capabilities. Suddenly, something out of his way caught Clover's attention. The object reflected an obscure light just floating above the surface, but he couldn't quite interpret what the item was. He swiftly moved down the dune hill, sending sand debris tumbling down its slope.

Clover reached out for the object laying just at the surface's edge. The object wasn't easy to grab at first, it seemed to be wedged between the sandy surface and the coarse tundra of the underground below. He tugged at the object many times, but its sandy grave wouldn't relinquish it. Clover dug into the sand like canine franticly searching for a lost bone.

It took quite an effort. Clover strained and pulled at the object with all his might and, after what seemed an eternity, he finally reached the object. He started to yank it to the surface, and slowly the object moved, but the dune didn't want to give up its treasure quite yet. The object began to slip back under the surface, but Clover wasn't about to lose his prize after expending so much effort to possess it.

I refuse to lose my cool. This thing hasn't defeated me yet. Clover gave it one last tug and the object propelled from the sandy depths, knocking him off-balance, and tumbled down the concave dune ridge.

Clover landed abruptly, sending sand and debris flying in every direction. He sat up and examined the object in his grasp. It was a human skull, attached to some sort of leather restraints, which the leather had rotten away, must likely over time. The only thing weighing the skull down was the remaining oxidized chains that once attached the leather restraints to the rest of the shackles.

Clover raised the human skull and its decrypted chains to eye level and fondled the leather restraint and rusted chain. He knew the shape well, having assassinated more than his share of human targets. *Human, young adult, possibly mid-twenties to late thirties*, he thought. The assassin rotated his prize from side to side, attempting to analyze it and give him it's sad tale. *Well me friend. Life must have been harsh for you to die so young. Were you enslaved for some devious crime or were you one of Legion's slaves, that crossed my nemesis once too many times?*

Then Clover noticed on the back of the skull, two small cylinders both the size of his finger nail, dangling from the chain. They were both heavy for their size and Clover thought it might have been the reason for his difficulty in retrieving the skull. "Weights on the chains?" He mumbled. "Could this have been a sacrifice and not punishment?" Clover may never find out the answers to this question. He never had tried to question any of Legion's lackeys before ending their worthless lives. It just wasn't in his design to do so. But if he had the opportunity, he might just have to do just that. To gain more insight on Legion's maltreatment of those in service to this horrid tyrant.

Clover had heard rumors of Legion's malcontent for his human slaves. But he couldn't tell what portion was myth and what was real. He knew never to place his trust in human tales, heck they had him being the monster of the Wastelands. But the torrent times only clouded the whisperings that rode the wind.

The skull was well decayed, most likely from being exposed to the sun's horrid rays. It was only a partial skull at that, but he could still make out marks which disparaged the remains of the skull. The marks that covered the surface of the skull seemed somewhat familiar to the assassin, but he couldn't quite remember what made such distinguishing marks. It was missing a portion of its lower mandible and it was heavily cracked in several spots, as well. Clover stared at it for a little longer, examining it in detail, then threw it away like unwanted trash and moved on.

Trying to regain the scent of the family, Clover started to see signs that placed him on edge. Sinkholes had appeared along his trail leading back toward the general direction he had lost the family on. He inspected a few sinkholes a little closer with caution. Each hole seemed to be larger in diameter and depth, like something was trying to emerge from the subsurface, but had failed in each attempt. It concerned him greatly. The sinkholes seemed to be made by something, rather than have a natural cause. Just as he had made it to the top of the dune, the sinkholes disappeared and in their place emerged massive paw prints in the sand.

Clover inspected the prints in detail, much as he had done with the sinkholes. It dawned on him what he had unveiled. Clover looked to the very top of the dune in horror. "A Ranquar manatee!" His heart began to race. "What is one doing this far, this close to human settlements? They usually keep to the deeper parts of the Wasteland where they can hibernate within the sand. This sand is too shallow for them."

A Ranquar manatee was an enormous bearlike creature with a massive head and bone-crushing jaws with needlelike teeth and razor-sharp canines at each corner of its mouth. It had the ability to burrow itself into the sand and blend in until it was ready to pounce on its prey. It had no fur on its body, merely wrinkled skin that was as tough as a walrus's hide. It was quite difficult to take down and it wasn't something he wanted to deal with, but it was apparent to Clover that he might have to be the aggressor if one was stalking the family. He knew the beast had a reputation for brutality and if it did attack the family they stood no chance—the manatee would rip the humans to shreds.

It must have picked up their scent. It must be tracking them. An image of the deteriorated skull he had found earlier came to his mind. *I must move swiftly before it's too late.*

Clover made it to the top of the dune and saw something moving just below him. The ranquar manatee was preparing itself to attack the traveling humans and it was too busy to notice his presence. The family was just now coming into sight and Clover felt adrenaline rush through his body, giving him an extra boost of energy and making him feel a little stronger. He focused on the massive beast below, and as his view narrowed in on the beast he temporarily lost sight of the family. He was quite aware that he couldn't attack the creature head on, the manatee was massive in size and brute strength and he would be shredded to pieces if he took that approach.

Clover prepared himself for his surprise attack and measured his leap with precision. He positioned himself close enough to the edge of the dune's summit so that when he launched his body at the beast, he wouldn't miss his mark. Right when he felt he could catch the beast completely off guard and when the beast had the meatiest part of its wrinkled back exposed, Clover propelled himself at the mountainous mound of muscles and wrinkled skin.

His attack struck home, landing directly on the beast's burly head. The manatee's tremendously thick head had very few places to grab a hold onto. The jolt of the landing was rough and he nearly lost his grip on the creature's large, slippery head. Clover grabbed for anything he could, but felt the wrinkled skin slipping through his grasp. Finally, he grasped onto the beast's horns that protruded from each corner of its enormous head. The horns happen to break Clover's decent off the beast and onto the sandy surface.

The manatee let out a colossal roar, one Clover was sure would echo far beyond their confrontation. The bioengineered assassin hung on for dear life like a rodeo cowboy riding an enraged bucking bull. The manatee switched its focus from the traveling party to its attacker. It launched itself out of its burrow in a desperate attempt to throw Clover off, with several enraged and contorted leaps and throws. He had to hang on for dear life, grabbing anything he could find before he was thrown from the creature's back.

Half dazed, Clover reached for his throwing weapon, a four-pronged weapon with curved, razor-sharp blades tied together to create a circular weapon. Each blade acted to propel the weapon through the air as the weapon turned end over end. The blades were made with a special light-weight material found in the outer reaches of the galaxy known as Teriyllium Magnesium. The blades would never chip, shatter or rust, no matter what type of substance they sank into. Clover could throw the weapon from any angle and the razor-sharp weapon would still get great veloc-ity because of its unique design. He knew he might only get one shot at putting the beast down—he needed to act quickly before the manatee was on top of him, else he would lose the opportunity altogether.

The beast sniffed the air with its long snout-like nose and took in its adversary's scent. It could smell Clover's defiance. The beast roared at the assassin, exposing its malformed mouth and its needlelike teeth. Saliva dripped from the beast's tongue and collected at its front paws which dug into the corrosive sand. Clover positioned his arm in a striking position, readying to throw the weapon. *I have to make this count*, he thought.

In one fluid motion, Clover threw the weapon at the Ranquar manatee. The razor-sharp weapon tumbled end over end with a vigorous speed toward its target. The colossal beast seemed to be frozen by some hypnotic force as it watched. The weapon flew briskly through the thin air, like a knife through warm butter, and sliced through one of the beast's mangled ears. Yellow blood spewed from the wound and the weapon landed a distance behind the beast.

The beast roared in pain and fell to one knee. The attack seemed to daze it just enough that it staggered and exposed a weakness Clover felt he could exploit. He ran at the beast which reared its head just in time to see the assassin raise one of his Katina's. The creature lunged at the assassin, once again exposing rows of flesh-shredding teeth. Instead of grabbing Clover's flesh in its snare, its strong jaws only snapped at thin air. It had missed Clover completely.

It was dazed by the fact it had missed its target. Clover went into a slide beneath the creature's underbelly.

He didn't have time to impale the beast with his katana, because the slide moved him too fast under the manatee's belly. Instead, the assassin sliced through one of the beast's hind quarters with one swift motion, nearly severing the limb clean off. The beast staggered and fell to its hind legs.

Clover emerged from under the manatee and slid to where his throwing weapon had landed. He had done it. He had wounded the beast, something unimaginable when the attack had first begun. He retrieved the weapon, wiped it clean of the beast's thick yellow blood and prepared for another attack. The beast looked his way, as if to confirm what had just transpired, while blood seeped from the wounds. It got up and hobbled as it repositioned itself.

Clover homed in on the beast's massive cranium next. He knew this attack would be more daunting than the last, so the assassin focused all his effort on the beast's thick skull and aimed carefully. Clover threw the weapon and watched it close the gap between them. The throwing weapon moved once again with unabated quickness, slicing through the humid, dry air. This time, the ranquar manatee's reaction was spot on. The bearlike creature's massive jaws snatched Clover's throwing weapon from the air and tried to crush it.

"Now that's not what I had planned," said Clover, giving the beast a slightly mocking smile.

Instead of allowing the creature to throw him off guard by the sudden snatching of his favorite weapon, Clover adjusted his next attack. "Let's see you defend this one."

Clover used his lightning-quick reflexes, leaped into the air and moved toward the beast. With the throwing weapon it its jaws, the creature could only look up at the Katina's bearing down onto it. The weapon slashed through the tough wrinkled skin and ran right through its nasal cavity. The creature lost all ability to breathe and dropped to one side, releasing the weapon in its grip. Clover retrieved his second sword, simultaneously removing the first from the creature's nasal cavity. He rammed the second blade into the throat of the creature, creating a gaping hole. Then, with the other sword, Clover slit the manatee's throat completely, letting its blood flow onto the sand beneath it. The sandy ground turned dark yellow, creating a puddle of yellow sticky film as the coarse sand absorbed the creature's blood.

Clover stared down at the dead beast. "That will teach you not to hunt humans anymore," Clover said. "I think I will leave your decaying flesh for a female sand spider to feed on; it's mating season for them and I'm sure she can feed her young with your corrupt flesh."

Sand spiders were hybrid scorpions that grew as big as a large dog and had twin stingers and four pincers. They were the true predators of the Wasteland.

CHAPTER 1

With the threat of revolution looming on Earth and endangering the Corporation's stranglehold on all forms of government, this suppressive, ruling entity, under the supervision of General Reinhart, a power-hungry military leader hell-bent on world domination, commissioned a secret project to design unique assassins and super soldiers. Each had unmistakable attributes and capabilities designed for each individual's objective—to combat the materializing threat from revolutionary factions that opposed the Corporation and their vested control. The Corporation and its supporters felt it vital to have this project and its test facility kept secret, so it was built off-world, giving them more control over its seclusion.

At this secret off-world base, personnel were hand selected by the general and his staff. Even though he gave the Corporation's board the feeling they had the final decision on personnel hired, this was a façade. General Reinhart had an egocentric personality and had become so paranoid that he feared interference from the board, to the point he swore they were trying to remove him from the project and place their own pawn in his place. The general secretly had spies disguised as board personnel record board meeting conversations to keep informed of their every move, staying one step ahead of these "rich snobs" as he called them.

Project personnel were forced to swear never to disclose information about the project or its secret base to anyone, nor let any detail slip. If they revealed *any* details of the project, the result would be the immediate termination of the employee, and the assassination of their families as a deterrent of future actions.

The fate of humanity, along with the project itself, would be held in the hands of two individuals. Doctor Sergei Peterovitch, the lead scientist on the project, was a dedicated man that took his work seriously. The other, a Machiavellian man named General Reinhart, was the project's lone supervising authority. He reigned sovereign over the entire project and was Doctor Peterovitch's superior. Reinhart's manipulative powers and ambition always seemed to interfere with the good doctor's work, usually causing more problems than it solved.

The research facility resided on a moon in an unclassified star system, far away from Earth. The Corporation feared discovery and didn't want any outside influences to interfere with the project. The surface of the moon itself was desolate and gray with very little vegetation, if any at all. The surface had a gray tint that created an unsettling mood. The lack of solar activity provided a shadow effect, which made it perfect to conceal the secret base.

The moon had a slight atmosphere, which created a halo effect around the surface, as if the place possessed a sacred aura. Humans struggled to live or even travel on its surface without the aid of environmental suits. The atmosphere was just too thin for humans to breathe, causing near death, if they were not properly prepared.

The unclassified moon was void of life, except for its new inhabitants who lived on the base. Nothing could survive outside the base's artificial environment; the air was dense and only the protective walls of the research facility provided the employees with suitable living conditions. The base's location had become like a banshee in the night, only a handful of corporate personnel tied directly to the project knew its true location, while the rest of the base personnel were never told where they truly were or how they got there. Most of the board members of the Corporation didn't even know of its existence. This kept anyone divulging secrets to the public. But you know how it goes, someone always lets their tongue slip and word of the operation rapidly got out. Soon, many were trying to infiltrate the secret base, either by force or by deception.

✝

The surface was dusty and gray. Shadows snuck up like a vicious predator stalking its prey. If there were any air at all, it was dense and hard to breathe. A man in his forties ran along the rocky surface, kicking up rocks and leaving a dust trail as he fled. His coat trailed as he ran, but the distressed individual wasn't quite sure what he was running from, he only knew something was approaching and he was terrified of it. The fleeing man couldn't see much behind him, but he knew that if he stopped then whatever was pursuing him would catch him. The thought drove his desire to escape. His movements seemed weighed down; the harder he ran, the slower he became. He could hear his heart beating rapidly with each step he took.

Screams of agony echoed from behind him, sending chills down the man's spine. The screams reverberated inside his eardrums, causing him to become temporarily disoriented, stumbling along as if he was in the dark. Something was pursuing him, but he couldn't see anything following, nor did he dare stop to find out what it was. Even as the man ran as fast as he could, thunderous footsteps from whatever swiftly approached rattled the ground. A gargantuan, demonic beast pursued him.

A horrific sound reached the dismayed individual, as trepidation grew within and the thump-thump cadence of his heartbeat quickened. The silence between the massive pulses was sending him into a deeper frenzy. The man stumbled, lost his balance and fell to one knee. He looked back, anticipating something horrific, but all he could hear was his own heartbeat, no longer beating franticly, but a rhythm that was quite familiar to him.

Then everything became silent, no sound whatsoever, just the soft cadence of his own breathing as his lungs took in more air and his chest heaved in and out and He was in a much calmer state and his movements started to slow, as if he had entered a euphoric state. The man tried to shake off the effect, knowing he would have to continue his flight.

"Have I been drugged?" asked the middle-aged man.

The air around him became still and he felt the evil presence of his demonic stalker. The panic-stricken man could feel his blood boiling, as if it were on fire, and he could no longer feel the pounding in his head, or the burning sensation in his lungs and his chest, just the excruciating scalding sensation in his veins. He felt as if he were about to combust. He performed a panoramic spin but couldn't see anything at all, just gray empty space-- even the other fleeing individuals had vanished.

His pursuer knocked him off his feet and landed on his chest. The pressure was so great he felt he couldn't breathe. Only the obscurity his demonic attacker loomed over the man, but he still was unsure what or whom had attacked him, he still hadn't seen a damn thing. Face down, the victim couldn't see his attacker, but he could clearly feel the creature's razor sharp talons or whatever it was using to dissect him into pieces.

The creature's form finally appeared to him out of thin air, like it was cloaked by some mysterious trance or cloaking device. Panic-stricken, the man wasn't sure if his eyes were deceiving him. Its eyes were reflective, like a chameleon in the gray thin air, and stared right into his own with a venomous hatred. The creature slid something out of its cloaked attire and rammed it with a jolt into the man, sending a violent rush of pain all over.

Blood slipped from every orifice he had, and he began to choke on his own blood. The man reached out in search of mercy. Mercy he knew he wouldn't receive. The creature leaned in and whispered in his ear as he lay dying.

I'm coming for them all, Doctor Peterovitch. *I intend to murder all your children, and not one of them will survive, not even your pet assassin. I know he's secretly your favorite. Oh yes, that one will endure much pain before I end him, but he will meet the same fate as the rest, like you are now. Tell them that Nightshade is coming for them.*

Slowly, the man stopped breathing.

†

Doctor Sergei Peterovitch sat up in his bead, inside his berthing quarters, covered in sweat and his chest heaving in and out. His heartbeat returned to a manageable pace, but not before the thin-framed middle-aged DNA scientist felt he had sat there a lifetime trying to catch his breath. The room was pitch black, but Sergei could still feel the coldness of the steel box he called his domicile. Despite being one of many like it at the lab end of the research facility, its cold, sterile appearance had a comforting effect on the doctor. It was a place he could collect his thoughts after a long day in the lab. The lab was the wrong place to do this, since there where a plethora of personnel coming and going constantly. Thinking in such a chaotic environment just wasn't plausible. His head was pounding a million miles an hour and Sergei wasn't sure if that was an after effect of his nightmare or the vodka he had consumed before bed.

"Too much vodka before bed," he thought out loud.

Gingerly he tried to climb out of his rack without falling off and landing on the cold, uninviting deck. When Sergei's bare feet struck the cold steel floor, *When Sergei's feet struck the steel floor, his feet nearly cramped at the chill.*

"At least now I have my wits about me," he said.

He attempted to make his way to the washroom to refresh himself; his tired physique swayed from side to side as he walked. His head rocked back and forth like a schooner on the high seas, making the journey to the washroom seem daunting and impossible. Blueish overhead lights illuminated the tiny room embedded in the west portion of Sergei's quarters. He gazed in the miniscule mirror overlooking the steel sink and saw a man his own mother wouldn't recognize. A Slavic male in his late forties, with bags under his eyes, stubble covered his oblong face and what appeared to be wrinkles were starting to emerge. His headache was increasing in intensity, so the scientist reached into the tiny medicine cabinet hanging above the steel sink and swallowed down some pain pills.

Waiting for the pills to take effect he looked straight at the Corporation's logo was engraved into the mirror glass. The three-quarters planet logo was outlined with a white border encased in shadow with a tiny star peeking over its horizon, reflecting a white border, as if the star was illuminating the planet directly in front of it. The logo had The Corporation highlighted in bold letters across the embroidered line.

Doctor Peterovitch gave the mirror a sadistic smile. "Fucking Corporation. It's going to be the death of me one of these days, I can just feel it."

This wasn't the first time he'd had a horrible hangover after working late into the evening, if it even was evening here—who could tell? He'd had his eyes temporarily closed, to catch a few more moments of shut-eye, when Sergei got the impression someone was watching him. He opened his eyes slowly and there, in the mirror reflecting through the corporate logo, was a face staring back at him.

The figure was a younger version of himself with one difference, the face had a large cross tattooed on its forehead.

Sergei attempted to shake off the image in the mirror, but when he opened his eyes again the image was still there, its gray eyes scrutinizing him. "Fuck off! I don't have time for hallucinations."

The figure seemed to intensify its stare. "I'm no hallucination, Doctor Sergei Peterovitch."

"Wait one moment, how do you know my name?"

"I know a great many things about you, and yes, I am real, in an odd sort of way." The face hesitated. Sergei got the impression that this mysterious face didn't want to say too much, like a parent evading some uncomfortable resolution. "You're the lead scientist on a secret project for the entity known as the Corporation."

"Wait a damn minute, how do you know that? That's supposed to be classified information."

"Let's say I know how many things will play out for you and the participants of the project you're currently working on, Doctor Peterovitch, even for your employer, the Corporation."

"What are you supposed to be, some kind of foreteller or something?" Sergei asked.

"You could say that." The face hesitated. "They call me Preist."

"That explains the tattoo on your forehead at least. But what do you want with me? Who are you, really?" Sergei asked.

"I am your son, Doctor Peterovitch, or what you would call your 'DNA replicate'. I don't have time to explain it all to you. You must trust me, you're all in grave danger."

"My son? Heck I'm not even dating anyone . . . Wait is it my lab assistant, Kat? Is Kat your mother?" Sergei could only shake his head.

"No, Doctor. I have no mother, you create me just before your demise. You used your own DNA to design me, like the others. But I don't have the time to discuss this in detail."

"You mean like the project prototypes?"

Preist nodded.

"Shit, you mean it really worked?"

"Snap out of it, will you? Like I told you, you're in danger. Reinhart isn't to be trusted."

"Hell, Preist, is it? I knew that right after I took the job. He is a cynical, coldhearted bastard."

"There is something else stalking you and Reinhart isn't the only adversary you have. There is something much more sinister going on behind the scenes. Even the Corporation's board members are in the dark about it. Just remember to embed all you know into me so I can save humanity from itself before it's too late. No matter what happens during the trial runs, keep pushing forward and don't quit the project. You're the father of us all, Doc."

Slowly the face faded away until only the Corporation's logo looked back at him. Sergei rapped on the glass pane, but the face was gone.

The research laboratory resided on the moon's dark side, which shielded its remote location and allowed the base's security to track unauthorized visitors before they could spot the base. Most of the lab's side of the moon base was built under its rough surface, hiding it from spies and any sabotage attempts. Along with the base's heavy security, an invisible energy shield was installed around the base and access could only be granted by security. All visitors had to be approved by the project's commanding officer in advance.

The soles of Sergei's shoes squeaked as they struck the semi glossed surface of the hallway floor. It wasn't likely he would be able to sneak up on anyone. He could feel his access badge swaying back and forth as he walked through the maze of hallways, toward his lab, which was embedded deep in the complex's interior. The hallway was well lit and even though they weren't visible, Sergei knew security cameras covered nearly every inch of the base. He had traversed the maze millions of times over the past five years—he could have done it blindfolded.

The laboratory split off into three sections, the research side, the berthing side and a third side; that was a place he knew very little about, it was Reinhart's little secret. Doctor Peterovitch ventured deep into the structure's interior, toward the secret lab where he had worked for more than five years developing what he hoped would be something to secure his name in science history forever. Each new corridor exposed him to more strict security measures, both seen and unseen. The farther Sergei moved, the more scrutinizing the security measures became. He had become accustomed to them. Security monitors carefully observed everything the employees did, but couldn't transfer sound to on looking security personnel due to confidentiality agreements—the security budget had been stretched to its limit for the project.

Each hallway led to a specific location. If an employee wasn't authorized access to a certain part of the facility, they were denied access to that section. The access was programmed into the employee's badge and when access was denied, a buzzing sound would emit from the access panel and a silent alarm would go off in the security control room.

As was the usual security protocol for Sergei's daily walk to his lab, an overweight security guard halted his progress. "I'm sorry for the delay, Doctor Peterovitch. But security has been tightened of late. I'm supposed to inspect every lab personnel's clearance with a fine comb. You understand, right?"

Sergei nodded his understanding. "Of course, Clarence, I understand. We all have a job to do."

The security guard looked down at Sergei's access credentials. The guard squinted his eyes as he read the detailed description on the access badge. His forehead scrunched, making his head look like a dried-up prune. The guard continues to scrutinize the credentials thoroughly, not making any sound as he did his due diligence. It made Doctor Peterovitch even more anxious to get through this checkpoint. Sergei waited for the guard to finish his job, not allowing himself to become agitated by being detained for so long.

What good would it do me? he thought. *Becoming agitated and bursting out at my detainer will only make things worse.*

The guard, still not feeling at ease, referred to his digital security device, looking for the access codes that matched Sergei's security clearance before letting the scientist continue. The device was acting up this morning and kept cutting out on him. The impatient guard shook the device franticly.

"Damn technology, what a piece of shit," the guard mumbled under his breath. They had not updated Sergei's access form and under new authority protocols his high security clearance wasn't easily accessed by the guard. It wasn't giving him the authority to let Sergei pass, either. The burly guard, with the flat face, large stomach and tidy uniform looked him up and down, as if he could see through Sergei's usual professional wear.

Doctor Peterovitch smiled at his detainee. "How's your day been going, Clarence?"

The guard flipped the badge once again, like he had missed something in his initial scrutiny of the badge's detailed information and glanced at its shiny exterior. The guard started to make a gnawing sound, like a beaver carving up tree bark. The man's breathing was deep and unnerving. It was clear from its cadence that at some point he would develop emphysema.

"I'm not finding your access codes, Doctor Peterovitch. I know you have the authority to move into the lab, like you do every day," said the guard.

"You're quite observant, big fellow. It would be odd not to give access to the lab to the project's lead scientist, would it?"

Sergei passed two more checkpoints and overheard guards discussing the tightened security. "Ya, Charlie. There are rumors of spies trying to infiltrate the facility. Can you imagine trying to get through the tighter security the Corporation has implemented?"

"That's the whole point, Frank. There must have been some of them getting through, passing along corporate secrets, or they wouldn't have increased the security protocols without warning."

"That's impossible," responded the other guard. "Our protocols are tighter than a fellow comrade's posterior Do you think it's an inside job?"

The other guard only shrugged.

As Doctor Sergei Peterovitch walked into the observation room, the lab logo, imprinted on the cold steel door, scorned him with its malcontented essence. Sergei impatiently rushed by the symbol that had reigned down on him since joining the project. The imprinted logo was a sinister-looking skull, missing its lower mandible painted black with a red border on the ring surrounding the symbol and a gold three-pronged star embedded into the skulls fore skull. The painted portions stood out on the steel surface, giving it an even more malicious nature. The words Fusion Biodiversity Genetic Engineering Labs were embedded across the logo.

The lab, indeed the entire facility, was a subdivision under the Azmarth Research Umbrella, which was owned in partnership with the Corporation as its sole client. It was the price Sergei had to pay if he wanted to continue his lifelong work under the new government structure.

In the far west wing of the laboratory lay two bodies on inspection tables. Separating the observation room, the place where lab personnel did most of their work, and the lab itself was a thick pane of glass from where the doctor could observe the subjects. The room was silent and its only entrance was heavily guarded. There was only one way to gain access to the lab—through the observation room, where Sergei now stood.

Both the observation room and the lab itself were immaculately clean. The biggest difference between the two rooms was all the machinery and digital equipment that filled the observation room. Sergei looked around and realized how technological the room had become. With the ever-growing progress they had made over the years, more equipment had emerged in the room. The only other difference between the two rooms, apart from their machinery, were the two subjects the machines monitored.

The observation room seemed to light up like a Christmas tree display with red, green and blue lights from lab equipment illuminating the glass of the room. The lab and testing center was separated by one-way mirrors which kept the scientists safe from any accidents that might occur inside the lab. Sergei hadn't realized it before now, but it felt like they were the ones on display, not the subjects lying in the other room.

Sergei's reflection stared back at him for a moment. He was a tall, lanky man, with a square jaw and long fingers. He always walked with purpose, causing his white lab coat to flap behind him like a cape. Many had thought

Sergei's dress sense slightly odd, but they didn't know his type. *Come to think of it*, he thought, *I do have an unconventional style of dressing.*

The project's lead scientist always wore the same style of trousers, , and a nicely pressed shirt. It was peculiar because he always donned the lab coat, which concealed anything he wore.

Nothing was conventional about Doctor Peterovich. He found unique ways to get lab results, but he never failed to achieve them no matter the circumstances, despite criticism from his colleagues. Sergei wasn't much for conversation and hated to be forced to be present at fundraising events—he wasn't much of a social man. Sergei didn't understand what their problem really was, he was there to work, not to become a socialite. Despite the isolation he placed himself in, he hadn't done better work in his professional career. He preferred his work and a glass of vodka to the company of others.

Before proceeding with the day's activities, he looked down at the paperwork from the previous day. He reflected on how he had got to this point in his life and specifically the longevity of his scientific career, which all seemed too surreal. As a child, he could remember looking up to the stars, daydreaming for hours, always quite unmindful of his own surroundings. *Maybe*, he thought, *that's where my ingenuity and creativity come from.* He was the most intelligent child among five children and graduated at the very top of his class from the Kiev School of Natural Science. He was, at one point, considered the very best in genetic science and knew physics quite well also, to the point of being arrogant.

Doctor Peterovitch looked out into the lab through the reflective glass at his creations and smiled with satisfaction. "How are my boys doing today?" he asked the prototypes through the pane of glass.

Joy resonated within Sergei every time he thought of what he was accomplishing with the project, no matter who his employer was. He always got a tingling sensation and a feeling of pride when he looked at the prototypes themselves. Despite the impression his body gave, he was like a proud papa on graduation day. His professional demeanor didn't express the elevated excitement he felt. *I have finally done it!* He thought quietly. *I have accomplished something that no other colleague will ever achieve. I have been able to create life from nothing! This must have been what Doctor Frankenstein felt after seeing his experiment come to life.*

He returned his attention to the previous day's lab results. Blood tests, cardiograms and other biological data that had been gathered on the project prototypes. It all seemed like a success. He wasn't just proud of what he had accomplished, he was starting to get the sensation deep within that he was like a god, a magnificent creator, an artist of some magnificent piece, a genius on biology.

Then Sergei remembered the conversation he had had this morning with the image of Preist and the jubilation he felt quickly dissolved. Something began to eat at his mind. *I can't make anything out that the image said. What did he mean by warning me of imminent danger?*

The silence of the room was interrupted with an explosive happy demeanor. It was Sergei's lab assistant, Ketrina Dooling, better known as Ket by some of the lab personnel. Her entrance interrupted his scanning of the reports, but it was difficult to stay mad at the young lab assistant. She had a way of lighting up the room with her presence. Ketrina was a tall thin brunette with maternal attributes, always kind and always full of life—that was her charm. She could always be found cleaning either room or bringing in some baked goods she had prepared the night before. She always chewed gum and popped bubbles at Doctor Peterovich, which tended to get on his nerves. Her vivacious personality, along with her long eyelashes and green eyes made her a favorite with all the male lab personnel.

If Sergei was the typical antisocial, Kat was the total opposite. She was lively and full of joyful glee with an expression to match.

"How are you today, Doctor Peterovich?" she asked joyfully.

As usual, Sergei didn't look up from his charts. "I'm doing fine, Ketrina, how are you?"

Ketrina smiled at Sergei. "Peachy as always, Doc." She blew a large bubble and popped it in Sergei's ear.

Sergei turned swiftly to his lab assistant with a displeased look. "Haven't I asked you a million times not to pop your bubbles in my ear?"

The few lab techs in the room snickered.

Kat gave him a sad and nearly innocent look. "Sorry about that, Doc."

Sergei turned back to his work and without looking at her said, "We have a lot of work ahead of us today, Kat. The sooner we begin the quicker we will complete our daily tests."

Ketrina batted her eyelashes at her boss, smiled at him to lighten the mood and nodded as she smacked her lips. She could always tell when Doctor Peterovitch was in a tense mood. And today, he seemed to be in state that permeated unrest. He wasn't in a foul mood, but she understood something was amiss.

Without warning, the lab door swung open violently and Sergei's boss, General Reinhart, entered. The room's loose and relaxed atmosphere dissipated instantly. Reinhart was a large, round-shaped man who walked with a stiff limp. He used a support cane and reminded Doctor Peterovitch of a decrepit old troll from some childhood story. He could ruin any mood, whatever it was. He had a round face with a full beard, and large hands to match the rest of his body. He wore military attire with medals draped across his chest that clattered together as he walked.

General Reinhart ran a very tight watch and didn't take well to horseplay or foolishness. From Doctor Peterovitch's experience, he didn't think the general would ever appreciate a joke, even at Sergei's expense. The rumor was that he would reward those who failed him in unfavorable ways, like hanging them. He would watch with great pleasure while they strangled to death.

Ketrina now understood why Sergei wasn't in the best of moods. All she could do was stare with dread at the lab's new visitor.

The floor creaked under the general's massive weight and Doctor Peterovitch's feeling of being like a god disappeared with each step the large man took. Even the men Reinhart had accompanying him gave off a bad vibe. Reinhart's men were never to be trifled with and had shady and dark pasts, from what Doctor Peterovitch understood. Reinhart chose men with unstable personalities and no immediate next of kin. Sergei assumed this made it easy for the general to control them. They were Reinhart's hit men, handpicked from assignments the general had commanded. Their eyes gave off the sense of chaotic complaisance, and Sergei never knew if they might leap up and attack one of the lab personnel or ransack the observation room.

Reinhart carried a very old briefcase which he used on anyone he didn't receive results from. It was wrapped in old, worn leather and had what Sergei believed to be bloodstains on portions of its surface. What bothered Sergei the most, however was when Reinhart would purposely crack his massive knuckles, it was an action that drove Sergei crazy. Reinhart's presence always gave Sergei chills, but this was even more unnerving for him—this was an unscheduled visit and the doctor hated unscheduled inspections.

The general sat down and gave Doctor Peterovitch a sinister smile. "Good morning, my dear Doctor."

Reinhart's sadistic smile made Sergei more nervous than usual. His palms filled with sweat, his throat quickly became parched, and his normally clear vison started to become fuzzy. He even struggled to hear anything that was going on around him. It was like he had been drugged and all he could concentrate on was his agitation. He stuttered a greeting to his employer. "Hello, General. How are you today?"

The general sat his large briefcase on the table and managed to knock one of the vials of DNA over. The vial started to make its way to the edge of the table. The specimen approached the edge of the countertop, and Sergei envisioned the vial falling off the table's edge and tumbling to its impending doom. The thought of the irreplaceable specimen smashing into pieces on the clean observation floor made Sergei even more anxious than he had already become. Fear crept into his mind, like an incurable plague. Without any hesitation, the doctor moved as quick as a cat and snagged the vial. He held onto it with a death grip.

"Watch it. You almost spilled this sample onto the floor!"

Reinhart looks over at the vial Doctor Peterovitch is coveting and notices the vial serial number, XB-245. With his usual sinister smile, General Reinhart made an inquisitive gesture like he was clueless to the vial's content, but he knew more than he let on to the good doctor.

Reinhart bates Sergei into explaining himself, even though the general already knew what was embedded in the DNA. You fool. I already understand the importance of the vile and its content. Who did you think ordered the collection of the sample? You better be able to deliver on your promise or I might be replacing you sooner than you would even expect.

"Why the worry, Doc, what's in it?"

Sergei replaced the vial in its proper place, with its contents still intact and away from his fat, irresponsible boss. One of his assistants came over to check if the doctor and the specimen were unharmed.

Sergei waved off the lab assistant irritably and looked furiously back at Reinhart. "It's alien DNA, from a deceased demon from a far-off star system. But what do you care, you big clumsy oaf?" Hesitating, Sergei questioned his employer. "Why are you here, Reinhart?"

General Reinhart leaned back into the chair, and gave a chuckle as he stared at Sergei with interest. "Why did you use demon DNA? Sounds like a risk to me." The large man sighed, then removed a cigar from his left breast pocket. "To answer your question, Doc, our employer, the Corporation, has become seriously agitated with the lack of progress and wants immediate results."

Doctor Peterovitch shook his head. *He doesn't remember any of the conversations we have had over the years*, he thought. Sergei took a deep breath.

"You don't understand, Sergei," Reinhart continued. "They are talking about shutting you down for good this time." The general looked like he might break down and cry, but Sergei knew that wasn't his boss's style. The old man looked back at Sergei.

"We've heard this all before," Doctor Peterovitch said. He hesitated, almost expecting to be struck for his insubordination. He looked maliciously into Reinhart's glassy, bloodshot eyes. "You said you wanted a prototype that could morph its skin into a suit of armor, and this alien DNA was the toughest we could find to accomplish what you desired. The monster had a tough exterior unlike anything we can access on Earth. Plus, there was genetic code missing from the second subject that we could never hope to recreate. And why the rush, Reinhart? I thought you were going to remind the board that this is a time-sensitive project? Rushing evolutionary design takes time."

Doctor Peterovitch looked at Reinhart intensely before finishing his explanation. "He has the strength of a thousand souls, this prototype."

Reinhart's expression transformed to one of pleasure. He had the look of a schoolchild learning something was real that he had always thought was a myth.

"Missing code?" Reinhart asked as he took a drag from his filthy cigar. "What does the other one have for DNA coding?"

Sergei felt his comments had ignited the general's interest. He started to wonder what Reinhart's hidden agenda was. Sergei looked past Reinhart, trying to imagine what the general was doing when he wasn't hovering over Sergei. He licked his lips. His raging desire was to explode out of his skin and tear the old general to shreds, but that would have its own consequences. Looking at Reinhart's bodyguards he thought there would be no way he could reach out and murder the old fool before they would be on top of him. *I'd be dead before my body struck the ground.*

"Among other things, a wolf's scent, a hawk's night vision and, above all else, my own DNA. By the way, General Reinhart, haven't I asked you before not to light that cigar in here? It contaminates my lab."

The general removed the cigar from his mouth and looked at the doctor. Annoyed, he put out the cigar. "Is that DNA in both test subjects, Doc?"

Sergei shook his head. "No, absolutely not. Only the super solder test subject, per your instructions."

Reinhart looked at the doctor. "So, Doctor Peterovich, are these two almost ready for some trial runs?"

Sergei looked back at the two bodies lying in the lab. The god sensation that he'd had before the general arrived returned. *No matter what happens to this project or myself, I know I have done something amazing.*

Sergei wiped tears away and pretended to read from last night's reports. "The last of the lab reports tell us they are stable enough to do some testing. I just think we need to take it slow."

Kat interrupted the power struggle between the two men with her bubbly and flirtatious way. She bounced between them and fluttered her long eyelashes at the general, distracting him from her superior. She gave both men her infamous smile.

"Just be gentle with my Clover," she said.

Both men turned to the lab assistant. "Clover?"

Ketrina leaped around like a ballerina, bouncing all around the room. "Yes. He's my good luck charm. I look into his mesmerizing eyes and I feel he's my four-leaf clover."

The general coughed and looked at the young lab assistant. "Is she a kook or what? Which one of them is she talking about?"

She gave both men a flirtatious bat of her eyelashes. "I think I'll go clean them up now. Excuse me, gents."

After Ketrina left the observation room, General Reinhart leaned in and whispered to Doctor Peterovich. "Is she always like this?"

Sergei looked at Reinhart as if to say, *you know the type, I'm sure.*

"You better hope these test trials go well, Doctor. We have invested a lot of money into this project and the Corporation is eager to implement the assets as soon as possible."

The general picked up the tube of alien DNA and fondled it in his large hand. "Am I making myself clear to you, Doctor?"

"Crystal, General." That menacing euphoria had returned. He wondered if the general had hired an agent to murder him after the initial trials. Was that what Preist had alluded to?

General Reinhart looked out into the lab. "Clover, huh? Well I think a good name for the other one should be Legion, don't you think?"

"Why Legion?" asked Doctor Peterovitch.

"Like you said before, good doctor. He has alien DNA inside him. He has the strength of a thousand souls," responded General Reinhart.

Legion had been created the same way as Clover, though he was much larger than most humans. They were considered kin, since they came from nearly the same DNA pool as was in Doctor Peterovitch's vial. Legion was created as the model for General Reinhart's super solider. Armor was built into his DNA, so when he went into battle his skin changed to protect him.

Ketrina made her way toward the two subjects, carrying her supplies and wagging her imaginary tail.

Ketrina set the objects down and prepared to do her work. She looked at Clover lying on the table. "Hello, my dear. How are you this fine morning?" She gave him one of her pearl-white smiles. "Oh, Clover. How I always wait in anticipation to come to work to be close to you and gaze into your amazing, unusual eyes."

Kat pulled on protective gloves and retrieved a few objects. She returned singing. Her voice was soft and soothing and she danced as she worked. Ketrina tossed back her hair and started cleaning Clover. She had never felt so alive before. She dabbed a sponge on Clover's face and worked down one side of his body. His face glistened and made his skin look fresh and clean.

She understood she had onlookers, but she didn't care. It wasn't the voyeurs that excited her. Kat gazed at her patient and *spoke to him as she went.*

"My dear Clover. I know we have onlookers, but just ignore them. They don't understand our relationship."

She turned and drained the sponge out, then washed the dirt and grime from her subject's face. She glimpsed Doctor Peterovitch's and General Reinhart's silhouettes as they spoke to one another. She ignored it but on returning her concentration to her subject, she caught the glimpse of a shadow, not coming from the scientific room, but from the hallway outside the lab. Kat shook it off, her imagination was playing games on her.

Clover's eyes snapped open and he stared at Kat. Her reflection bounced off his glossy eyes and she tossed her sponge in the air, startled. She grasped her chest, feeling her heart beat heavily. "Oh, Clover, you scared the life from me!" She leaned in and touched his skin. "Can you hear me, Clover?" There was no response so she returned to her work.

"Kat, are you okay?" asked one of the lab techs. "I thought I heard you scream."

"Yes, I am fine. Clover just opened his eyes and was staring directly at me."

The lab tech looked down at the monitoring equipment. "It must have been an impulse response. Maybe it was from your singing." The lab tech started to laugh.

Kat scrunched her nose up at him. "I'm a fabulous singer. My soft voice soothes them," she responded.

A flash blinded her.

"I think that came from the hallway!" The tech yelled.

Somewhere in a distant office, far from the secret moon base's location, a classified conversation was *taking place*. The airtight door was locked and no one was permitted to enter the cold, steel room. Only one source of light shone directly in the middle of the small structure. A lone figure was just out of sight, working at a small desk, just within the shadows of the room. No recording devices were allowed and a sensor had been run to prevent anything that could record the conversation.

On top of the desk was a plaque that read Cliton Rassputin – Recruitment Agent. A hologram glowed with an orange tint and flickered from the poor reception the room received. Mr. Rassputin spoke to the individual in the hologram with his back turned.

"I take it that the asset has failed in her mission?" queried the hologram.

The agent turned around, sipping on a cup of tea. His lips were stained a reddish-green. "That would be correct, Shadow Lord. We were unable to retrieve what you asked of us."

"I assume," said Shadow Lord, "that your asset didn't disclose anything that would lead back to us?" The hologram flickered. "If she had that would be unfortunate for us and all those that were involved. I would have to unleash an asset of our own to eliminate such targets."

"I don't see that being necessary. We had an agreement with our asset that if captured she wouldn't expose anyone involved with the operation. Your secret and your connection with the board is safe. If she had said anything, the contract states all family members would be subject to . . . penalties."

"That wouldn't be necessary, Mr. Rassputin. We could carry out a job like that on our own."

The agent dropped his cup of tea and rushed to clean his trousers. "I—I wouldn't be exposed to that, would I?" He looked up at the fading hologram.

"It isn't all that important. We have enough intel on the project to move forward anyway. Her capture is enough to confirm the suspicions of my master, and to allow us to move forward with our plans." The hologram had nearly faded away. "Your services are no longer needed."

"What does that mean?"

"You have been paid in full. We will not speak again, Mr. Rassputin. Goodbye."

The figure in the hologram faded away completely, leaving the soundproof room still and quiet.

CHAPTER 2

After the first trials were run on the prototypes, Clover and Legion, the project rapidly picked up momentum. Mass production began and these designed assassins and super soldiers appeared just like products coming off an assembly line. Each commodity's mutation was unique, designed to execute a specific programming. Some could throw razor-sharp claws like daggers, while others had internal gifts, like being able to utilize sound waves as weapons or manipulate matter with their minds.

The differences between these later specimens from the original prototypes, despite being unique onto themselves, had drawbacks. There was deterioration of the DNA from the original subject's; even though the code was similar to the prototype's, it had become less refined because the scientific teams were forced to copy the DNA for mass production. Impurities in many of the subjects—which the scientists had overlooked—and the overall corruption of the original host DNA made Clover and Legion still far superior to the rest, in nearly every aspect.

The entire project was kept secret as long as possible. Only the Corporation's CEO and his must trusted colleagues knew of its existence. Even then, no corporate associate understanding all the fine details of Reinhart's project, not even the CEO himself. Those directly involved felt that having less-superior assets would make them more manageable in the long run. But this would lead to even greater animosity among the subjects, forcing some to reject their overall programming.

Soon the facility had become vastly overpopulated. It didn't take long for conflicts to arise between those supporting and those rebelling against their human masters. The base became overcrowded and the living conditions dire, as space for living quarters and training was further truncated. Despite this, the general had become immensely gratified over the success of his project and picked Legion as his enforcer and future successor. Reinhart observed from a distance as each group of soldiers and assassins began their rigorous training.

Individual and group training began immediately, according to the subject's gifts. Some, like Clover, were trained in the far corner of the facility to be assassins. They were trained in the arts of deception, throwing weapons and other ninja and ancient samurai methods making them proficient killers for their masters. Swordplay was part of this training and since Clover was the first prototype for this skill set, he thrived in this training—it was embedded in his DNA. He quickly became known as the wielder of the sword, the shadow assassin, for his stealth and ability to never be seen.

The super soldier training happened in a secluded courtyard with restricted access to essential facility personnel only. Outside of a small handpicked few, including Reinhart, Legion and his so-called hit men recruits were being trained as a special force of elite soldiers. The training had become so secretive that no one outside their small group knew of their training methods.

Legion leaned in toward his mentor and was forced to bend down because of the immense height difference between the old man and himself.

"I see that you are pleased, Master." Legion nodded at his mentor. "When will we collect my brothers and sisters and lay siege to the planet your people inhabit?"

Reinhart peered into Legion's dark, shadowy eyes. Legion's appearance would spread fear into the hearts of those that opposed him. But they weren't the only ones Reinhart wanted to cower. Some of those board members could use scaring as well. *What did Comrade Nikolai say?"* Pondered Reinhart. *"Oh yes, now I remember. He would take care of the board, was that it? Well, just in case, I might send some of these assassins to make sure the job was completed, I don't trust politicians or corporate tycoons one ounce.*

"Patience, Legion. I want to make sure everything is ready before we make our presence known on Earth. Then we will sweep through all that oppose us like a sharp knife through warm butter." General Reinhart looked at Legion with a daunting and devious smile, as if the old man could read his protégés thoughts.

Legion returned the gaze. He wasn't sure whether to loath the old man or love him. If it wasn't for the general he might not even exist, but on the other hand Reinhart was still human and Legion had a wretched hatred for all humans and their precious humanity. His heart raced out of control every time he thought of the exuberance the humans around him expressed for one another, but which was counteracted by inflicting so much pain on one another. It churned his alien blood into a raging pit of fire. *They don't know how good they have it when they are belligerent toward each other. Looking down on us like some type of pet with human admiration.*

Reinhart returned his gaze to the training in front of them. "Speaking of ready, have you checked on our special unit lately?"

"They are on track with their training, Master. I can guarantee that," Legion said.

General Reinhart smiled his small wrinkle-infested lips. Time had not been kind to the general, but he could still command presence, even from a figure as daunting as Legion. "Very good. When they are ready, I want you to take them and test their skills. Take Clover along to assist you, but do it in the most secret way possible. I still want them to be my little surprise to the board."

"Clover!" cried Legion. "He isn't a soldier, he is a cutthroat, nothing more than a shadow in dark places—and that's where he belongs."

Reinhart looked back at his protégé disapprovingly. The old man's gaze was cold and uninviting. It was like Reinhart had nothing inside that gaze but death and deviousness. It was a stare like no other and sent chills down Legion's spine. This would be the first and last time Legion would allow his mentor to force Clover into his missions, unless Legion deemed it necessary. Clover was good at one thing, killing targets with minimal attention drawn to himself. But he was far from a solder. The others under Legion's command followed his orders without challenging his command. Clover, on the other hand was as insubordinate as they come.

"Fuckin assassins." Mumbled Legion.

Legion glared down at his mentor with vexation in his stare.

"I will have my time old man and when it comes, neither you or anyone else will stand in my way. But for now, you can undermine my authority and treat me like a child, for now." Mumbled Legion.

"I don't appreciate you questioning my command, Legion. Clover is just as capable as you are, carrying out missions. Remember, he is the origin of the entire project. In any case, he is more capable than most of those under your command. That will be the end of this debate. Am I clear?"

Legion glanced down at the old man with contempt. *My time will come, old man. And when it does you had better check yourself, or you might end up like your human companions—crushed beneath my weight.*

Deep underneath the visible facility, Reinhart's special commando team were in intensive training. They were kept separated from the rest of the trainees, since they were the elite force of Project Annihilation. Reinhart and Legion felt it imperative to keep the team's existence secret from the general population of the project as long as possible; the trainees' concentration was paramount to the project's success and they were just at the beginning of the process, far from ready for action.

Isolating them developed skills that would aid them in seclusion and enable them to execute their programming with flawless precision. The underground part of the base was built into the moon's core. The secluded part was cold, dimly lit and parts of the hallway walls had crusty layers lining it, giving it a dingy, uncomfortable feeling. The only light came from artificial lighting installed throughout the underground passages.

Grunting sounds and the sound of metal clanging against metal, echoed along the secluded courtyard, as weapons were forced against one another. Their intensive training escalated. Each subject learned a different style of hand-to-hand combat to aid him or her in their assigned missions. The echoes vibrated throughout the enclosure as the unique commandos honed their talents.

At the far end of the isolated training area, a group of trainees were engaged in a three-on-one exercise, supervised by human trainers. A skirmish broke out among a few of the trainees. The humongous figures stood toe to toe with one another and their shadows engulfed their human instructor, as if the sun had been blotted away. Zeus, a massive gorilla with powerful shoulders, towered over eight feet tall and possessed dark fur that engulfed his entire body. His huge hands were clenched into fists, ready to battle his opponent with a rage that mounted inside of him.

Opposing Zeus was a creature of similar magnitude named Deselation. This creature had the ability to mimic many forms of darkness, which included clouding human minds, creating bewildered emotions in humans and producing nightmarish hallucinations. His physical form never truly metamorphosed, but the simulacra he could project did.

His main attribute was the ability to cloud minds and get them to do what Deselation wanted them to do. But once Deselation got inside of human minds, he could steal memories, thoughts and information, like a thief cracking open a safe. But this didn't work on Legion or any other subject connected to the project, they simply weren't human or at least they didn't believe they were.

A trustworthy servant of Legion, Deselation's true form was only known to a handful. The form he used most was a troubled shape which mimicked the Minotaur from Greek mythology. His bull-like features made for a daunting sight. Deselation walked on two hoof-like feet and gargantuan horns much like a ram's that protruded some three feet out from his high forehead. His eyes were a void, the quintessential essence of death.

Fire expelled from the monstrosity's nostrils like a fire-breathing dragon. He also possessed the ability to cloud human minds and make them believe they were in a dream state while he commands them to do his bidding, an echo from his own twisted, warped mind. His last trait was the ability to foresee events by reaching out with his mind, much like a crystal ball.

Zeus ground his teeth in anger as he stared intensely at Deselation's deformed figure. A high-ranking human trainer, contracted by the Corporation, had her training garb torn, exposing her body as she lay on the ground in shock. She had a small stain of blood on her ripped uniform from biting her attacker and a trickle of her own blood at the corner of her mouth. Neither behemoth was looking down at her. The two adversaries stared at one another.

"I think your friends owe the young lady an apology," Zeus said with rage. He gashed his teeth together and tightened his fists, inflating them to twice their normal size.

"Can't the lady relax a little? The boys were only having a little fun," Deselation said.

"Her breasts are so soft. I have never felt human breasts before." Quartz smirked at another trainee.

"Females aren't toys for you to play with, even if she is human," declared Zeus, puffing out his massive chest. His forehead moved back, displaying the shape of his enormous skull. Each trainee understood how angry this confrontation was making Zeus. His fists tightened to the point of exploding and Zeus's body tensed, displaying his strength as his muscles rippled.

"You're so high on giving orders, Zeus, you need to be taught a lesson for once," replied Deselation. The beast moved forward and raised its formidable horns in Zeus's direction.

Zeus responded forcefully. "Watch your tongue, trainee! It's Master-at-arms to you. That disrespect will get you thrown into the brig."

Zeus and Deselation charged one another. The ground shook and they locked themselves into a powerful struggle. A deafening *boom* reverberated as the two leviathans clashed with one another. Zeus held Deselation at bay, making the minotaur shake profusely and stagnating him with his own powerful arms. The struggle moved back and forth, as one gained control of the other for brief moments at a time. But Zeus was only toying with him. He could easily have destroyed him at any time, but this was Zeus's game, he made his opponents feel superior than they really were, only to break them in the end.

Deselation breathed on Zeus, a breath so horrible and rank it could melt metal.

"You fight like your breath smells, Deselation. Poorly, with tragic results in the end." Bellowed Zeus.

Deselation head-butted Zeus with his horns, forcing a slight tear in the ape's skin. Blood trickled from Zeus's forehead, staining his dark gray fur. Zeus growled at his adversary, flashing his flesh-ripping teeth. Deselation was stunned by this reaction and couldn't move to defend himself. He had never experienced such an abominable display of rage, especially from Zeus.

Zeus's growl made the trainees back away a few steps, sensing further collateral damage oncoming. Then the massive beast grabbed Deselation's protruding horns with all his might and built-up fury he raised one arm and struck his opponent in the upper jaw, sending Deselation flying into an adjacent wall. The collision shook the entire courtyard, sending its occupants seeking cover. Deselation recovered slowly; he wiped the blood dripping from the corner of his mouth and gave his opponent a shocked expression.

"You still have a lot to learn before you will ever reach my level, Deselation," said Zeus.

Deselation looked over at three of his comrades. They surrounded Zeus.

"Oh, *now* you want to continue the training, do you?" Zeus looked at each trainee, one after the other, measuring them up. Each one seemed scared out of their wits and he knew it. "It's time for me to show you all who is really in charge here."

The trainee in front of Zeus leaped at him like a toad leaping from its perch, but the sergeant-at-arms slammed into the trainee to meet the attack and knocked the trainee backward. A second trainee wrapped his slim arms around Zeus's shoulders, not even able to completely encase the gargantuan ape in his frail grasp. Zeus grabbed the trainee around the waist and tossed him in the opposite direction like a rag doll that meant nothing, knocking the trainee into a near-unconscious state.

While Zeus had his attention diverted, the third trainee struck the side of Zeus's ribs and pulled his hand back in pain. The pain in Zeus's side was excruciating, it felt as if a thousand needles had been placed into his abdomen. But it was nothing compared to the trainee's sprained wrist and shattered hand.

"My hand!"

"I'm going to hurt more than your hand," Zeus growled. "You shouldn't have done that, boy."

Zeus's expression hadn't changed and his deep monotone voice boomed and didn't miss a beat. He was either as tough as the trainee had ever seen him, or he was excellent at hiding his pain.

He grabbed the trainee by the throat and started to choke him. The trainee turned pale and passed out. Just in time to save his friend, the first trainee leaped up and struck Zeus in his back, forcing him to release the trainee he was choking. Zeus spun around to face his attacker. Now the apelike creature showed the same anger he had displayed with Deselation just moments before.

"Do you have any last words before I destroy the last essence of your worthless life?" Zeus mocked.

The trainee backed up a few steps, but it wasn't far enough out of Zeus's reach. He grabbed the trainee like a twig, lifted him over his head and flung the trainee's body like a wet towel against the wall.

Before he could do any more damage, and with Deselation still not reengaging in the battle, the lone male human trainer stepped in. "That will be enough from you today, Master-at-arms Zeus. If you persist down this road farther, I will be forced to report your insubordination to Legion himself."

Zeus bowed to the human trainer. "Yes, I will recant my emotions for the time being."

The conflict had ended, but neither Zeus nor Deselation had a desire to let it be. The hard feelings would endure.

†

In another part of the secret training facility, underground where there was even less access, two human personnel—one a lab tech and another high-ranking military adviser to General Reinhart—oversaw an imprisoned figure, half drugged and restrained on a chair. The human figures are housed securely behind safety glass. The military adviser leaned over and whispered into the lab tech's right ear.

"So, what do you think?"

The lab tech could only shake his head. He was only half paying attention to the officer and concentrating on the subject on the other side of the glass. "It beats the hell out of me. This situation has me more confused than you are, sir."

"Well what the hell is he? You can't tell me you have absolutely no clue, you people created him," the adviser said. The tech could sense his superior's despair. It was in his eyes, his voice, even in his actions. It was like the adviser was afraid to do anything at all. The adviser looked from the tech to the figure drugged in the other room. His eyes were frozen in a bewildered state and his muscles tense. He saw sweat rolling off the adviser's cheek; the tech wouldn't be able to get a definite discussion from the adviser in his current state of mind.

The lab tech plugged in something to the viewing screen and the display started to fill with data streams. Data files moved rapidly down the safety glass that separated the observers and their hostage. The large amount of data gave the adviser a headache. He held his head and moaned. The lab tech shook his head in frustration.

"Make it stop, why don't you," bellowed the adviser.

"It doesn't make any sense at all." The technician scanned the mounds of data flashing by. "There is nothing in the files that explains this condition. He's a freak of nature, in a place where there are more than enough freaks to go around."

"Are you saying he is a freak among freaks within a massive freak show? Isn't that an oxymoron?"

Before the tech could respond, the door to the observation room flung open and a shadow loomed over them. The shocked men froze. Legion entered the room, towering over the human onlookers. The floor moaned from his weight—he was like a god among children, both in stature and in presence.

"I hope I haven't interrupted your conversation, gentlemen," Legion said in his dark and menacing voice.

The adviser responded in a shaky, low monotone. "We were only discussing the detainee's condition, Master Legion."

Legion glared at the human officer with a disgruntled and cynical stare. "So, tell me, why was I called down here? What is so important about this detainee?"

The lab tech swallowed before answering Legion's question. He was shaking and could barely convey what they had discovered. "It's an improbable occurrence, sir." The tech's voice continued to waver from a normal but shaking tone to a low whisper. "Science can't explain this phenomenon." The tech moved slowly to the glass and touched it with his shaking hand, enlarging the data stream. He opened another file and placed it next to it, so everyone could see the two files simultaneously. "He, or better yet *it*, calls itself Quasar, and seems to be an anomaly of nature. We have . . ."

Legion interrupted the tech by raising a bulging fist to silence him as he would to a nagging dog and read the file for himself.

Transcription:

Data Input: Subject 1A creation of sub particle inertia required. Desired effect, subatomic energy field.

Input Test results: Negative.

Data Input: Subject 1B creation of subatomic energy weapon. Desired effect, pulse cannon array; subject should be able to eliminate any energy shield within 1000 kilometers.

Input Test results: Negative.

Legion looked up from the display and his jaw tightened. "That doesn't make any sense. By your data, you weren't trying to create a bioengineered subject at all. You were testing high-energy shields and weapons. One like a shield generator might produce. But why would a bio lab create something like this? It's amazing," Legion said.

"It must be the doc trying to upset the entire project. You realize he hates the fact the general oversees the project, not himself," the adviser said.

"Instead of creating a weapon in one form, we have created one in another. This guy can rip apart people, plants, rocks, entire planets and stars with his bare hands. Energy resonates from Quasar's hands and when he sets his focus on a target, he launches this energy at it and the energy moves faster than the speed of light toward the target. The subject ignites into a ball of energy before exploding. Its particles superheat to millions of degrees until they reach their threshold and ignite . . . And his brother is worse." The tech claimed. "He can destroy things with his mind. He rips the atomic structure completely apart and, if it was in the mood, could reconstruct it in a different pattern."

"Interesting," said Legion. A smile protruded through the shadow that draped his face. "This fellow could be quite useful to us."

They looked back at Quasar. He had his head down and a humming noise was coming from him. Then, without any warning, he looked up at his tormentors and gave them a dead stare that sent chills down the humans' spines. It was even creeping Legion out a little, but he stood his ground and Legion and his prisoner stared each other down. The safety glass started to shake. It shook so hard that eventually it cracked.

Legion touched the cracked safety glass.

"Did you see that?" asked the tech. "He cracked the safety glass without touching it. Has that ever happened before?"

"I think I'm going to like this one," Legion said. "By the way, whatever happened to his brother?"

The adviser looked at the data file and took a deep breath before responding. "It says he escaped a while back and his whereabouts are unknown." Sweat rolled down his neck.

†

Implementing the entire program took more time than planned. Six months after the initial tests were run on the prototypes, Clover and Legion were completed and declared operational. Thousands of other assassins and soldiers were completed and training began to prepare them to execute their programming.

Over time, some of the assassins and soldiers struggled with their initial programming. Some of these designed killers started to become self-aware of their own humanity and slowly stopped accepting orders from their superiors. Their new fear wasn't judgment of their actions, but the fear of Legion's deadly stare. Many of these malcontents were rounded up. Some were executed for their treason, but some were thought to be able to be rehabilitated or reprogrammed and were placed into prison camps scattered throughout the moon base.

It was early morning at the main prison camp and the prisoners were just getting rounded up for the morning muster. Legion's first task after the initial training of his special commandos was to show the general his ability to lead. He was assigned to manage the main prison complex, before the first wave made their way to Earth.

The camp was poorly constructed; the walls of each prison berthing section had huge indentations made by the settlement of the rocky, unstable ground beneath them. With the surface ground constantly moving and buildings not being secured properly it usually led to structures occasionally falling in on themselves. Even worse were the conditions in the berthing areas, where prisoners shared cramped living spaces and had no privacy. Little light illuminated the cells themselves and the cramped cells housed up to four prisoners. Male and female prisoners were housed together, which caused even more tension between prisoners and occasionally riots broke out.

Several of these rejects had become ill from malnourishment, poor living conditions and many other ill-fated factors but they were still treated without dignity or respect. Instead of receiving treatment for their ailments, they were forced to work alongside their healthy inmates. The prisoners were overworked in many areas of the prison and the lab facility itself. Those that either couldn't work or refused to work were beaten harshly.

Each morning they were lined up for work detail. A work detail officer would choose prisoner details. This morning the detail officer's voice boomed through the west wing as the lights came alive and the prisoners struggled to rise from their bunks. The bunks, like the rest of the prison camp, were hard, poorly built and non-conforming. A lot of grunting and complaining could be heard throughout the wing as prisoners lined up.

Through the only doorway leading from the berthing area, came a short and round figure. He had a round face with a pig like snout and stubby arms and legs. This figure wore a clean pressed jumpsuit which held his rank insignia on his right shoulder. Every guard saluted him as he passed by. He had a bull horn announcing his arrival and yelled that if they didn't get up that instant and form a line he was going to have their hides for breakfast.

"Attention, scum. Time to get your lazy asses out of the sack and get in a straight line," the officer announced.

Prison guards hurried the remaining prisoners out of their racks and rushed them to the mustering line for the morning inspection, which seemed to be more a scrutiny of their failed character than anything else. Some of the prisoners that who were shoved toward the mustering line stumbled and fell. This only made the guards even more mad. The short stumpy detail officer glared at these poor individuals with contempt. To enrage their tormentors even more, some of the sick prisoners threw up right where they stood and that drew the attention of the work detail officer.

The officer walked up and down the prisoner line carrying a steel pipe to keep them in line. He slapped the cold metal pipe against his palm. It kept the prisoners on edge. The floorboards creaked their discourse as his polished military boots maneuvered onward.

The prisoners exposed to the living quarters and the environment that surrounded them seemed to not only create displeasure in them, but to also aid in their final destruction. Widespread starvation and disease killed off a large majority of the prison population, with the outside environment leaking in constantly. Most of the remaining population were fatigued, sick or beaten to the point of near death. There were prisoners that had bruises, permanent scars or had missing limbs from the guards' abusive behavior led by the detail officer. The officer walked toward the end of the line. A prisoner bent down and threw up in front of him; the vomit splattered on the officer's polished boots.

He rushed up to the sick prisoner, lifting their head so he could glare his contempt for what the prisoner had done. Saliva and blood fell from the prisoner's mouth. Some residue remained on his lips.

"Did I give you permission to throw up on my deck and make this ungodly mess? Now you're going to have to clean this shit up with your tongue, because I can't have your filth on my immaculate floor."

One of the prisoners, Tigerous, was a very thin woman with leopard-tattooed skin. She had the ability to throw her razor-sharp claws as weapons. If they struck the right nerve they could paralyze their victim with a poison embedded inside. Tigerous had an aggressive and sometimes naïve attitude, especially toward authority figures. She leaned down and whispered to the sick detainee.

"Get up. Don't show these assholes any weakness or they will exploit it. I have heard the punishment for not going out on work details can be ruthless."

The guard walked over to Tigerous, slapping the metal pipe in his hand. She quickly straightened, trying to hide the fact, like she hadn't moved toward the sick prisoner. She could hear the guard's boots strike the flimsy wooden foundation of the barracks as he approached her. She could see the guard staring at her in a way that made her feel dirty.

"Is there a problem, Tigerous?"

She shook her head in response without looking up—it would only serve to get her more beatings and bruises.

"Maybe I haven't given you ample attention lately, is that it?" he said, still slapping the pipe in his meaty hand. "Maybe you like the way I touch your delicious, exotic skin." He leaned in closer and whispered, "You're a little too feisty for your own good. I think I need to tame the animal in you and I know just how to do it." He backed away from her. "Isn't that what you really want? For me to give you what your animal instincts desire?" He looked around and the other guards who had started to chuckle.

The officer motioned to a few guards close by. "I guess he won't be going out to work today. He looked back at Tigerous who was still standing stiff at attention. He pointed the steel pipe in her direction. "We will resume this another time. Don't worry, I won't forget about you, my feisty kitty."

"Not if I get my claws on you first," she said under her breath. "I'd rip that fleshy throat of yours and watch your life force dissipate from your nasty flesh, you fat piece of dung." Animosity and coldness shone in her eyes as she traced the guard's steps without moving her head.

The guards grabbed the prisoner and dragged him off the mustering line. The sight is a sorrowful one. Dragged by his arms, the prisoner had the appearance of near unconscious.

A prisoner in the muster line watches his colleague being dragged off, instead of keeping his head straight forward at attention. This gets the attention of the detail officer who slammed his steel pipe into the inattentive prisoner's abdomen.

"Keep your hands and eyes forward at all times. We don't want any unnecessary accidents, do we?" the work detail officer whispered in his ear.

All the guards started to laugh, but the prisoners stayed still and quiet.

The officer stood up and walked into the middle of the open area of the berthing section, smacking the pipe against his bare hand like before.

"I know all of you hate my guts. I hate to inform you, but that is just music to my ears. I do this for your own sanity. See, if you would only accept the nature you have within you and do your job, you wouldn't have to deal with me in this way."

The officer's boots echoed up and down the berthing hall. He looked each prisoner square in the face and smiled his crooked snooty smile which reminded many of the prisoners of a distorted swine, with his fat puffy face, circular cheeks which made it seem like he had no eyes.

He continued his malicious assault. "I do this all for you. I'm making you understand the grave mistake of your ways. We are not human, so why act human?"

He motioned to the guards to start escorting them out to their work detail.

†

Somewhere in a dark and secluded dimension, the Shadow Lord had an audience with his own deity. The room was dark, desolate and menacing. No light could penetrate the ruinous powers that lay in front of the agent of darkness. The Shadow Lord's master was a dark, cataclysmic entity, hell-bent on total tyrannical control over all living things. Most constructs neither scared nor aroused emotion from the Shadow Lord, but his master sent fear deep within his dark, misshaped form.

A deep and rancorous voice bellowed at the Shadow Lord. "What news have you brought to me?"

"Master. Our contacts within the Corporation have reported back. Your devious plan has been executed as you have instructed them. Deterioration of the donor DNA from the original subject's code, is occurring as mass production continues. Future project commodities will become more flawed with the continuous copying of the donor DNA. They will, however, be easily controlled or eliminated."

"What of the prototypes? Will they be so easily manipulated to join us?" asked the menacing entity.

The Shadow Lord swallowed hard and hesitated before answering his godlike master. "Unfortunately, no, Master. We didn't have time to corrupt their DNA. Theirs is the purest form from the donor. I'm sorry to have failed you." The Shadow Lord knelt in front of the dark, uninviting cloud that was his master.

The shadow lord was the Darkness's most reliable servant and acted on its behalf. The Shadow Lord could glide across the floor, influence minds and was the direct contact for the shadow agents of The Darkness.

The menacing entity bellowed a scream that shook the entire construct. Black blood gushed from the Shadow Lord's head. "Wait, Master," he cried. The pain subsided temporarily. "I was able to place the device you instructed for one of the more intellectual humans to discover. With the right manipulation, they will think it's a discovery of their own doing. It will be like a ticking time bomb that will, if used as you have envisioned, be a way to cripple the two prototypes, making them vulnerable to our own creation."

"The rock of unimaginable power created by my own hand."

"Yes, Master. It will deceive them and bring them to ruin. You will have your conquered empire yet."

A mass prison escape attempt was in progress and the prison wing went into lockdown. Legion, along with Clover and some of Legion's specialty guard, are assigned to recapture the prison escapees or execute them for their escape. Mass confusion scattered the camp as, one by one, the fleeing prisoners were apprehended. Prisoners ran in fear of being misidentified as escapees. It was either die trying to escape the camp or die living inside the camp walls.

The camp security can't gain control of the escapees and many of the interior prison guards give up the pursuit easily. The prisoners wouldn't last long outside the base without environmental suits. One escape attempt, which had happened weeks before, led prisoners to an abandoned cave, but only their prison garb was found, none of the escapees' bodies were ever recovered.

A group of escaping prisoners led by Tigerous and Quasar broke for the protection of the shadow of the moon, hoping that it would shield their escape attempt. That was a mistake. Their hunters, including Clover, could sense their movements by their very scent. Clover could see the prisoners moving in the shadows, making their escape attempts futile.

The escaped prisoners led by Tigerous stopped to catch their breath. Tigerous looked behind them to see if they were being followed, but she couldn't see anything over the dust mound. Everyone's breathing was sporadic and uneven. Tigerous's chest heaved in and out as she tried to catch her breath. The two leaders looked at each other with uncertainty.

"We need to keep moving," said Quasar. "We don't know if they saw us run in this direction or if they will split up their search party."

"I agree with you, but don't you realize we had help from the inside? I think he will lead them away from us. He is good at forming false trails."

Quasar looked at the rest of the escaped prisoners. "It's a long trek to the shadowy part of the moon. Looking at our traveling companions, I'm uncertain everyone will make it."

Without looking behind them, Tigerous started to climb again. "Then we best be on our way."

Clover, along with Legion and his prison guards, pursued the three escapees who made their way through the shadow of the moon. They let the standard guard capture the others. With his hunting ability and superior speed, Clover led the tracking party, like a scent dog leading a pack of hunters. The scent of the three escapees drew the tracking party closer, as Clover maneuvered over moon rocks and the fine granite terrain, much like the desert climate back on Earth. He left Legion and the three guards behind as he rapidly gained on their targets.

Clover soon spotted one of the prisoners and waited until he reached striking range, then he threw a four-sided throwing weapon with razor-sharp edges designed with lightweight material and with an advanced aerodynamic design, at his target's feet. The weapon whirled toward its target, tracking the escapee even more rapidly than he had on foot. With a forceful impact, Clover's weapon struck the escapee with precision.

The escapee tumbled to the ground, stirring up moon dust, marking the spot where he fell. The escapee smacked his head on the grainy surface as he fell, opening a wound and started to leak blood. The attack left him unconscious, lying in the shadows, and allowed Legion and the tracking party to catch up. Clover was standing over his victim, less like a vulture admiring his conquest, and more like a mother wolf trying to decide how to move her cubs from their den. He made sure his escapee wouldn't get away as the party approached.

The two other escapees were brought before Legion, their hands bound over their heads. They were forced to their knees, as the guards jam their weapons into the prisoners' lower backs, sending pain throughout their bodies. They cried out in pain. This seemed to delight Legion and his followers, but not Clover. He seemed to sympathize with their prey, instead of relishing the conquest. He could only manage to shake his head in disagreement.

Legion walked over to one of the detainees.

"Captain Legion," responded one of the guards. "We have captured the last of the prisoners."

Legion looked down at their captives. "Good. You may execute them now."

"As you command," the guard said.

The guards executed the two prisoners. Clover turned to his brother in a rage.

"What the hell are you doing? We are only supposed to detain the escaped prisoners, not murder them. They have not warranted execution."

Legion turned to Clover with fury in his dark eyes and contempt for his brother's outrageous behavior. "Brother, we are gods to these minions," Legion said. "They are worthless, almost as much as the humans are. We must display our dominance over them before they have a chance to challenge our authority."

Clover tossed his cloak aside and faced Legion. The rest of their hunting party looked on in anguish, shocked by his defiance.

"That doesn't mean you should kill them, especially execution style," returned Clover.

Legion stepped toward Clover's captive, and pushed Clover aside like a toy. He stared deeply at the scared detainee, then returned his gaze to his brother.

Legion grimaced at Clover. "Be that way then, if you must. If you won't execute the prisoner, then I'll have to do it for you."

Legion removed his heavy great sword and started to lower it to strike the prisoner on the neckline. All his concentration was on the execution, and he doesn't see his brother move to defend the prisoner. Clover struck Legion's sword with his own. The clash of their swords caused sparks to fly in all directions and the effort kept Legion from killing the downed prisoner—for the moment.

They struggled to overtake one another. Legion's weight gave him the advantage over his smaller brother, and Clover struggled to keep control of the duel. Their faces met each other, close enough that Clover could feel Legion's breath against his own face. Legion quickly started to overpower him.

Legion stared into Clover's face and raged angrily, "I will have no insubordination of any kind from them. They have lost dignity for themselves and for their own kind. But the hell if I will ever take it from my own kin."

"I guess you're going to have to live with disappointment, Legion," Clover said.

Clover forces the two swords apart, sending Legion falling to the ground. The ground shook temporarily from the mass of Legion's body colliding with the surface. Clover took the opportunity to strike Legion; he moved into position and struck Legion first in his face, but only managed to piss his brother off. When that did not suffice, he struck their mammoth leader in his armored chest plate.

The force sent Clover tumbling backward to the ground, dazed.

Legion looked down at his chest plate to see if any damage had been done. "I guess the Doc did one hell of a job on my armor, boys."

Legion's armor. was embedded into his skin, in his very DNA, and nothing could penetrate it, no matter what was used or how strong his attacker. As far as Legion was concerned. All he had to do was concentrate and his suit of armor would materialize and replace his skin. Legion rarely used the armor, only one certain occasions and this seemed to be an ideal time to use it, or as Legion thought, to display it for a wow affect.

Clover leaned on one knee and attempted to strike Legion once again. He grabbed a dagger from his boot and threw it at Legion. The dagger made its way toward Legion, but it didn't reach him fast enough. It bounced off Legion's armor leaving no damage whatsoever.

Legion gave Clover a sly smile. "I give you credit, brother, your effort is valiant. Unfortunately, your results are unsuccessful, as always."

Legion grabbed Clover by the throat and struck him in the center of the face. This sent him flying high in the air and he landed against a large boulder not far from where he had been. "Brother, you need some assistance. Blitzkreig, please assist my brother, will you? Help him understand the magnitude of his insubordinate behavior."

From behind the tracking party came Blitzkreig, an extremely tall creature with a disfigured face. He had one black eye and one colored. His long arms seemed to drag on the ground and he was dressed in rags which made him look poor and homely. He used shock waves that generated from his entire body and culminated in his hands.

Blitzkreig raised his arms in Clover's direction and struck him with his shock waves. The attack made a loud echoing sound and the *whomp-whomp* could be heard miles away. The severity of the attack sent Clover up into the air again and he landed on his back, unconscious.

His body lay there as the posse gather around his body.

"What do you want to do with him, boss?" Blitzkreig asked. "Shall we end his life now?"

"Kill him?" Legion asked. "No, he has his own destiny to fulfill. Death isn't meant for him, not at this moment." Legion leaned over and whispered in Clover's ear. "We will have our time to battle, then we can truly find out which one of us is superior."

Legion motions for them to carry his body back to the barracks. "He will have significant memory loss. I will have to assist him in remembering the past."

CHAPTER 3

During the time between the rise of the Corporation and the war with the human rebels which led to the apocalyptic destruction of human society, the Corporation was on the brink of losing its manipulative grasp. Rumors arose of a revolt within the Corporation itself and many members of its board have questioned the loyalty of its leader and whether he is competent enough to lead them through the turbulent seas they now found themselves in.

The news reporter was dressed in a professional manner; her snugly fitted suit had been professionally pressed at the cleaners just hours before. The suit hugged her curvaceous body, but Nikolai hadn't noticed how much he was attracted to her at the time of the interview because of her aggressive and demeaning line of questioning. Her mic was stationed directly beneath her chin as she gave her report. The wind blew her hair and thin overcoat erratically. She was nothing like the women the CEO dated, but later, high in his corporate office suite, that's what made one of the most powerful men on the planet so turned on.

The other women Nikolai pursued all required lavish and expensive clothes, jewelry and exotic vacations to make them happy, but what did they do for him? Well, nothing much but act as arm candy, as far as Nikolai was concerned. This woman had a much more honest and sophisticated persona, one that arose more than physical attraction. This same essence about the reporter also placed Nikolai in a particularly foul mood, despite his physical arousal.

He began to grind his unblemished, pearl-white teeth, making a sound like sandpaper dragging across a course, jagged surface. The palms of his hands sweated profusely. He would receive less than immaculate exposure and this made the powerful CEO very uncomfortable. He wasn't accustomed to women making him feel uneasy, but this bitch next to him, with her smart clothing and aggressive style of reporting, made him feel he wasn't in control, a feeling that sent the ulcers inside him churning.

Nikolai gave a false smile to the reporter and the mobile news camera. Nikolai could feel his facial muscles frozen in that false smile and his body tensed to the point of exhaustion.

Smoke billowed in the background, something had been burning for a while. It had turned into smoldering smoke, not a blazing inferno with charred black smoke, more like a hazy weather cloud dancing too low to the surface. The field reporter looked straight into the camera without much expression, but something was on her mind and her audience could see it written on her face. Nikolai Volkov was too busy with the smoking building to notice.

Her eyes were focused dead center on the TV screen. She had a tense demeanor which gave her an annoyed expression. Her grip on the mic was strong and tight, as if she were about to explode with exasperation.

"This is Karen Kornobber for Action 24 news. Today there was another food riot in the downtown market district. This is the twelfth riot of its type in the past ten days," she said. The reporter brushed hair from her face and didn't sway one bit, keeping her professional demeanor as she continued her reporting.

A shaky video replayed the morning's riot for the audience to witness. Food rioters climbed over each other, trying to retrieve the scarce volume of food. Volunteers backed away from the invading citizens. The representatives of the Corporation stopped handing out the food rations for the day. It left many families starving and the food shortage ignited rage within the people in the food line and sparked many to rush the food handlers.

The reporter returned to the TV screen with a solemn expression.

"We talked to the Corporation's CEO, Nikolai Volkov, about the riots that have been rapidly multiplying of late." The reporter turned slightly to introduce Volkov.

The CEO stood in front of the camera with an equally smart and professional demeanor, allowing himself to be interviewed by the reporter, as he looked sternly into the camera with a forced smile. Nikolai was rarely available for an interview. He had an arrogance about him that he was more than aware of, and his sinister smile seemed to be a blend of disdainful hatred for the female reporter and sadistic, be-lucky-you're-interviewing-me-because-I-am-too-busy-for-you look. He didn't need any extra hatred for this reporter, all he had to do was remember all the women of his past. But the Corporation's CEO wasn't about to miss a beat when answering the reporter's questions; he had done interviews like this one too many times to become flustered.

Nikolai's slender frame and square jaw made him look much younger than his midforties age showed. The scar that ran across his forehead reflected the camera lighting. He loosened his expensive fine silk tie, which matched his expensive tailored Armani suit. He always had to keep his professional demeanor, he never knew who was watching. There were certain individuals within the Corporation that would leap at the chance to seize his high-ranking position and dispose of him.

His ambition was to control the world's populations and force citizens across the globe to depend on his company to supply their every need. Unlike General Reinhart, he didn't want to destroy humanity, only rule over it.

The reporter turned to him and forces her mic in his face. "Well, Mr. Volkov, how does your company feel about the multitude of protests and food riots that have been happening?"

Nikolai refocused his attention halfway between the reporter and the shooting camera, trying to look like he was interested in what she was asking. He didn't want to show the anxiety he felt deep inside—like a deer staring down the barrel of a loaded rifle. He had nowhere to hide, but the hell if he was going to let the simple people know this.

"Well, we feel that there are more peaceful ways for people to express their ideas on the food shortages around the world. Violent acts only fuel more violence," he said calmly.

The reporter's hazy green eyes looked on Nikolai with detest. Everyone could tell she knew he was attempting to shun her line of hard questions. "But doesn't it say something about the condition of humanity and the manipulation of citizens your company is portraying?"

The reporter glared at the CEO with even more contempt, as he answers her half-heartedly.

"Well what do you say when your company cuts starving people off? Those people that have starving kids and are unable to provide for their families? Those people with menial employment or no work at all and shortages in food that are handed out every day?"

Nikolai gave the reporter a look he had used many times. It was the look of disbelief mixed with immense shock, and he used this look to shield his emotions. It was the same expression he used to give his own mother when he was forced to eat something he disliked, but she was long gone now and no one forced him to eat anything he didn't like. His eyes became sorrowful and he gave the camera the impression that he cared for the starving population.

"I think you have been misinformed. We give out all the food we have, and give it to the public, we don't horde supplies from anyone. The raging war with rebel groups has caused food supplies to dwindle considerably. Maybe it's the rebels you should be criticizing, not the entity that supports the masses."

The news reporter grasped the mic firmly and the muscles tightened on her face, her cheeks raised and her jawline stretched to the point of snapping. Her contempt for the CEO was all too obvious.

"So, your company doesn't horde food supplies then?"

Nikolai shook his head. "Never." Nikolai, through his personified, business-minded expressionless face thought, *I'd like to grab that mic from you and bash you fucken head in, you bitch!*

The news reporter grimaced as the Corporation's CEO continued to pile on the lies.

"So, the rumors aren't true then, according to you and the board?" she asked.

"No! We are a very generous company and only want what's best for the community. That is propaganda used by rebels to aid their revolutionary tactics and bring citizens to their lustful cause."

"And those causes are misaligned to your company's greedy agenda, are they not?" retorted the woman nastily.

"I'm sorry. I am not able to discuss those matters, at this time." Nikolai smiled back into the camera.

The reporter glares at Nikolai with so much contempt that her producer starts to scream in through her earpiece to end the interview.

The reporter turns back to the camera and smiles. "Well, there you have it. Live from the source himself. Now you can judge for yourself who is in the right. Back to you, Jan."

Looking down on Metro City from his top-story office suite, the CEO of the mighty Corporation, Nikolai Volkov, reflected on how detestable the occupants of the city below were. As he watched the ant-like figures, cars and other vehicles passed by, all busy in their worthless lives, he felt like a god.

"This is the culmination of my assiduous ascension to power. As a young boy living in Russia, I aspired to be like those businessmen walking along the streets in

Saint Petersburg with their expensive suits and outlandish ties rushing off to their important jobs. Now look at me, I'm the one that is on top of the world—literally! These minions are now under my very feet. They depend on me and the Corporation just to exist."

He detested them and only saw them as serfs on a plantation required to serve his every need. It seemed like an entirely different place to the one he lived in. But this metropolis was something more, because it was the home of the Corporation, which had manipulated its way into every industry and every governmental structure on the planet. They controlled food supplies, transportation, housing, jobs and, among many other things, the security of the citizens under their power. An uprising began against this mighty entity as they started to manipulate and keep consumer goods and services to a bare minimum. The uprising caught the Corporation off guard.

In the struggle against global superiority, the lone governmental body, the Corporation, was losing the battle against the somewhat inferior rebel forces that seemed to fuel the uprising against them. This created friction between the Corporation and those they were suppressing, giving the citizens a glimmer of hope. The leadership of the Corporation knew they would have to crush that hope if they intended to continue its monarchal presence. The rebels made every effort to prevent the Corporation from taking over completely, using every tactic in their arsenal.

The Corporation, in retaliation to the uprising, with the support of its CEO and confidence of General Reinhart, activated the first stage of their secret project.

Clover, Reinhart's most revered and skilled assassin, would sneak into rebel hideouts, hide himself in dark receding corners and wait for the right moment to strike. Then, when the time was right he would pounce on his target, usually a leader of the resistance while they were alone, and devastate them until they could no longer breathe a word about their attacker. Even though Nikolai found Clover intriguing he was always fearful—a character like Clover was very dangerous. *What if this assassin of yours ever went rogue or became a turncoat?* he would constantly ask Reinhart.

Nikolai was getting heat from the board for more concise results, as usual. They could only process results, not progress. *Those grebannyye stariki can't comprehend the hard strife that comes from an operation like this. They only see results, but it's the details of the operation that generates the results. I would be better off if they were all dead.*

Inside the office, the decor was designed especially for the CEO and his outlandish and luxurious tastes. The office walls rose high, like a fortified castle wall, and the side of the office that wasn't plated with clear, tinted windows had an elaborate earth-tone pattern, with ghostly images of women contorted with one another imprinted in it. The images matched Nikolai's perverted appetite. Ever since his childhood, where he constantly took beating from his sadistic stepmother, he resorted to treating women like playthings, but no matter how perverted he got, he knew he would never be as invective as General Reinhart.

The south side of his office overlooked the skyline of downtown Metro City and at the height it sat at, dwarfed every building in the city. It stood at cloud level, like some mystical realm far from the street level below. Nikolai had his office this high above everything else to remind every-one in Metro City who the big dog was. The view could be breathtaking on a clear day, and today was one of those days, with the sun radiating through the panes of glass. Volkov's silhouette reflected off the dark tinted windows and gave the impression that someone was looking back at him.

†

Nikolai was standing directly over his desk, the ho-logram of his computer desktop flickered as the limited light passed directly through the holographic image. His desktop was tied directly into a secure server which stored classified documents that only high-end officials of the Corporation had access to. The main screen on Nikolai's computer had the unmistakable corporate logo. He had to type in a security code to access the next screen with more data files. The next screen appeared and there was a number of icons on them. Each icon represented a department within the Corporation. The ones Nikolai was most interested in had even deeper security embedded into the access code, including voice recognition. Before he was allowed to access them, he had to enter his twelve-digit access code.

Once he obtained the secure screen, the Azmarth icon appeared, bright white with its name embedded inside the solid brackets. Azmarth was the umbrella division for all the Corporation's research labs. He double tapped the icon and it exploded as if his touch had some type of chemical reaction with the holographic icon. Once the screen recovered six new icons appeared in front of him. Each icon was a similar bright fluorescent blue. In the top left corner of the screen, inside an octagon icon, was Dark Matter Physics Labs. The top right corner of the screen was the Proto Ion Labs icon, shaped like an old twentieth century refrigerator that faded out during the period. In the far bottom corner, shaped like a cyclone, was the Echoen Black Hole Research Labs; they did interstellar research and vehicle design.

There were three other icons. The Prototype Mass Star, a group that simulated star collapses and designed artificial stars and, at the far bottom right corner, the Abyss Quantum Physics Lab. But the one he was most interested in was right in the middle of the screen. The Fusion Biodiversity Genetic Engineering Lab, with its sinister-looking skull logo, missing its lower mandible, painted black with a red border on the ring surrounding the symbol and a gold three-pronged star embedded into the skull's forehead. Nikolai double tapped the icon and he gained access to a mass of data files attached to the Reinhart project.

Nikolai looked over some documents on the project that the board wanted more clarification on. To this point they had been kept in the dark by the general. Some of the files in front of him included biodiversity testing, early genetic lab results, how the Corporation obtained the alien DNA, even some logs from the crashed cargo ship. Everything that was attached to the project, every subject that had been created to this point, including the project's prototypes, was missing. Nikolai slammed his fist down on the expensive, wooden desk, making the desktop hologram shake and fade for a moment before returning.

"Damn it, Reinhart. Why are you keeping me in the dark on the meat and potatoes of the project? There is nothing here on the subjects themselves. What are you hiding from me?"

Nikolai's secretary, Denise Mc Carver, walked the down the hall toward her boss's office; her high heels stuck against the floor making a thumping sound as she moved. The sound was unmistakable and even in his vexed mood, Nikolai couldn't miss that sound. She approached carefully and entered her boss's office with a grace of a swan. All the men on the top floor loved to watch her sway her hips and maybe she even enjoyed it a little bit. The side-to-side motion her thighs created drew a lot of attention as she made her way through the floor's open space to her boss's office.

She coughed to get his attention. "Mr. Volkov, I'm terribly sorry to disturb you." Denise hesitated in fear of angering her boss. Nikolai constantly lashed out at her when she interrupted his work and today he seemed quite distracted.

Nikolai responded in an annoyed tone. "What is it, Denise?"

"You have a visitor. It's General Reinhart, sir, as you requested."

Nikolai responded in a condescending manner, without leaving his position at his desk. "Denise, send in the good Comrade General, don't make him wait. Go about your business hastily, my dear."

General Reinhart might be a portly old man, but he commanded attention when he appeared and Nikolai was not immune to the general's influence. The presence of the general always put Nikolai on edge, not in the way the reporter made the CEO nervous, but in a friendly awkward way. The general had a way of making Nikolai feel inadequate to the point of feeling like a young boy still living in war-torn Russia. It wasn't that Reinhart looked down on him, but he seemed to talk *at* him, instead of *to* him. Maybe it was the way the general would look at him or Reinhart's condescending mannerisms. The general knew that Nikolai was at his mercy; relying on the project as much as he was forced Nikolai to give the general too much power.

Reinhart had ambitions to control the world and was using Nikolai and the board to access the resources needed to accomplish those goals, but Nikolai knew. Reinhart took extreme pleasure in making corporate suits like Nikolai squirm. Keeping the board in the dark about the project gave him even more pleasure and generated more power for himself. Reinhart knew that the board looked down on him as a lesser being, almost to the level of the people they were swindling out of liberties. No, make that *less* than them. He was a leech crawling on their backs and sucking them dry.

Denise escorted the general into Nikolai's office. Her red hair draped down her thin tall shape and swayed as she walked. Her clothes clung tightly to her curvaceous body and the general was still admiring her form as he hobbled into the office.

The general watched as Denise's hips moved from side to side. He hadn't seen a woman such as her since his wife passed. He thought, *This woman could give a man like me a new vigorous stride in my loins. I don't think even Sergei's assistant—oh, what is her name?—could touch this creature.*

Reinhart was one of those men that always sought out the company of gorgeous women, no matter where he was. He saw them as playthings, a tool to meet his sexual needs; even his own wife had started out as a desire, nothing more.

Reinhart gave his close friend a crooked smile. "Comrade Nikolai, it's been a long time, it's so good to see you, my friend."

The two men embraced each other.

Nikolai motioned for the general to take a seat. "You shouldn't make yourself so scarcely seen, my friend. We have so much to catch up on. How was your off-world trip?"

General Reinhart took his place in one of the leather chairs facing Nikolai's desk. The leather squeaked as air rushed out from the cushions as the large old man wiggled into a comfortable position. It was like watching a walrus positioning itself to mate. The old man looked at Nikolai with slyness only the general could convey.

"Same as usual, my friend. These trips always wear me out and the scientists always give me the third degree when I show up unannounced. Anyways, it's really good to see you, Nikolai." The general pulled out a cigar and sniffed it like it would give him an energized feeling.

The general pointed the cigar toward Nikolai. "What one, old friend?"

Nikolai waved him off dismissively. Reinhart placed the cigar in his wet, salivating mouth and lit it up. "So, I hear you have a new place in the country and that you're seeing someone new. Is it serious or just one of your many flings?"

Nikolai swallowed his vodka and set the empty glass in the center of his desk. "I'm not seeing anyone serious. When have you known me to commit to a serious relationship with a woman?"

Reinhart blew a smoke cloud from the cigar up into the air and waited for it to dissipate. "Oh, that's right. You have mother issues, I almost forgot."

"And my new place is cozy enough, even though it's an awfully spacious pad with lots of room to do whatever I want. Did I tell you I have two world-class hunting dogs?"

"You hunt, Nikolai? I didn't know that," Reinhart said.

"Nothing like that, just something to keep me company. The house is so large it echoes when I come home. It's only the dogs that fill the void. But it's definitely an upgrade from the old place."

"Oh yes, I remember that shack. It was truly a dump and I'm glad you decided to move."

"Well you must visit some time, you and your lovely wife. By the way, how is her health these days?"

Reinhart stopped smoking and gave Nikolai and sharp detest-filled stare. "That old witch? She's still recovering from lymphangia Cancer of the *lymphatic system* She can't die soon enough for me." Reinhart stubbed out the cigar. "But please spare me the bullshit, we both know you wouldn't have summoned me all the way down here just to socialize and see how my family is doing, Nikolai. You need something from me."

Nikolai responded in a solemnly. "Very well." He retreated to his office chair and peered down at his desk. He paused for a moment and without looking up, he began. "General, we have an urgent matter than needs your attention." Nikolai looked back up. Solitude and despair had replaced his social demeanor. He looked as if he hadn't slept in days and his face looked like it was starting to sag, his eyes had become bloodshot and solemn. He went from looking youthful and alive, to looking like an elderly CEO near wits end.

"The Corporation is losing its hold on the government across the globe, you know this, right?"

Reinhart sat without uttering a word; they had been friends too long and Nikolai understood the general knew this already. Rumors were floating around about the Corporation losing its grip, that they may lose the war against the rebels.

Nikolai took a deep breath before he resumed. "Resistance groups are winning the battle against our segregation efforts. We could lose the power that we have worked so diligently to gain. If we lose this war with the insurgent factions, the people will take back control of the government and the Corporation will cease to exist. The board has granted me temporary power to do anything required to stop this from happening."

General Reinhart reached for his walking cane and slowly maneuvered himself to the edge of the leather reclining chair. With one arm, Reinhart leaned on Nikolai's desk and the two men's faces were just inches apart. Nikolai could feel the old man's breath, a distinctive musky smell, as if he had been living in some dingy place, not including the cigar aroma he now wore as cologne.

General Reinhart had a smile on his old worn face. An expression that always sent chills down Nikolai's spine.

"Comrade Nikolai, let me assist you in your time of need. Let my . . ." Reinhart hesitated for a moment, then continued. ". . . children do what they have been designed to do. Don't waste billions of the Corporation's dollars, let the project be your solution to this troubling issue."

Nikolai hesitated, as he looked into the general's old and deceptive eyes. All he could see was his own reflection, without even a glimpse of his old friend present in those tired eyes. *Reinhart would be one hell of a poker player. Maybe that's why he was put in charge of the project in the first place*, thought the young CEO. Being able to be calm in all circumstances was the general's gift. He had climbed the ranks quickly and was not about to relinquish his command for anyone.

"That's the entire problem, General. You haven't given me or any of the board access to your pet project. You have omitted reports on the subjects created by your scientist. I need something concrete to take to the board. You need to give me access to your project directly."

General Reinhart looked deeply into Nikolai's golden eyes. It was the same discomforting look Nikolai's father had given him before his disappearance when Nikolai was still young. "You told me I'd have total control of the project, Nikki."

"You have," responded the CEO. "More than I or the entire board feel comfortable letting you have."

"And in the process of giving me total control, you also agreed that there were things you didn't want to gain knowledge about. What little you don't have access to is for your own safety. Anyone trying to steal secrets can't threaten you because you don't have total access to the project. I'm doing this for your own safety, it's a danger-ous project to be associated with."

"I didn't realize that meant keeping me in the dark. The board is giving me flack about the lack of access to the project. I'm trying to keep us both from breaking rocks in a manual labor camp."

"Fuck the board!" responded General Reinhart. "They are all decrepit old men with little left to hold on to. This will be the project we all gain godlike status from when it's all through. We will be gods, Nikki. I like to think as myself as a father figure to you and I'm watching out for the best for you. For the best for both of us! Can you understand me?"

"Very well, Comrade General, do what you think is best. Since this is your department of expertise," proclaimed Nikolai.

A crooked smile displayed on Reinhart's face. "You won't be disappointed, my friend. My boys will come through for you, you will see."

Once the general left his office, Nikolai leaned back into his office swivel chair and issued a deep sigh of frustration. *Between the riots, the general's manipulations and the badgering of the board, I may not live to see fifty,* he thought.

Nikolai looked to the gray and placid ceiling of his office. He was becoming tired and slowly drifted into a semiunconscious state. A euphoria had come over the CEO and he started to hear voices. In his dreamy state, he remembers a conversation he had a few days ago.

☩

Nikolai picked up his office phone's receiver and depressed the private button on the phone. He waited and a loud click rung in his ear, the filtering device had come on and it was safe to speak. "Hello," he said.

"Hello, Nikolai," the deep voice said. It had a deep and ominous tone to it.

The expression on Nikolai's face rapidly changed to one of unease.

"It's been a long time, hasn't it?" the voice said, not wanting to give away who he was.

The man on the other line and the Corporation's CEO never exchanged names, it seemed much safer that way, to keep them both anonymous and avoid any extortion attempts from outside sources.

"I guess it has," returned Nikolai. "What do you want? I am quite busy now."

"Hostility . . ." said the voice on the other end. "I expect a more respectful tone from you. You're treading on thin ice these days, Nikolai."

"You don't have to deal with the day-to-day operations as I do. Once again, what is the purpose of you calling and harassing me?" the CEO asked.

"Right, enough of the small talk. I forget you aren't much for that these days. I am calling to get the status of your project, since you have neglected to update the board on any detailed information, to this point. As you are quite aware I am the last resort for the board and I extract data that can't be retrieved any other way."

"Ya, I know. You're the enforcer hired as the board's muscle." Nikolai shook his head. "You know I can't divulge that information to you."

The voice gave a deep and unsatisfied sigh. "That's quite disappointing. I was hoping for more cooperation from you. I expect defiance from Reinhart, but not from you. There is going to be an emergency board meeting and the board will be voting on the fate of your secret project and its fate with this company."

"How have you come about this information, enforcer?"

"I have my sources. It was the board that collectively decided for me to be the one to contact you. But let me warn you, Volkov, you and your friendship with Reinhart will also be in jeopardy and your very future with this company may go down with your pet project. The general's time has come. He will be terminated. Goodbye."

The phone connection was interrupted with a click that rang in Nikolai's ear.

†

Nikolai awoke with a sudden urgency about him. He became panic-stricken as a headache began to come on and adrenaline rushed through his veins.

"I must do something and quickly. "Mumbled the CEO.

Nikolai picked up the receiver again, pressed the private button and dialed rapidly.

After several rings, a husky voice answered the phone. "Hello."

"Yes. We have a situation that needs your delicate touch."

After a moment of silence that seemed like an eternity to Nikolai, the voice responded.

"Who's the target?"

"The entire board, Shadow Agent," returned Nikolai.

Silence on the other end for a moment, then the husky voice returned.

"That will cost you extra, my friend." said the voice on the other end.

"Fine. But there is one stipulation, it has to be attended to immediately."

"An accelerated timetable?" The voice became silent for a moment then, as calmly as the call had been answered, the voice responded. "We accept your additional mission parameters."

The phone went dead.

"Okay, that was sudden. Now let's see how many threats you and your cohorts can manipulate me with when you're six feet under," Nikolai said.

CHAPTER 4

The night sky was dark and clear with only a slight illumination coming from the moon overhead. The conditions were perfect for hunting, and Clover's nocturnal talents heightened when it became dark. Like many nocturnal predators, he hunted better when his prey couldn't see him approaching. The only things visible when the bioengineered assassin moved through the night were his glowing red eyes. The rebel hideout would be heavily guarded—Clover knew this well because he had done this many times before—but none of them would be able to see quite like he could in the darkness. This would-be Clover's fourteenth assassination mission, and each one was getting harder to swallow. Killing these poor souls had become an adrenaline rush, but his mind kept nagging at him after each mission. He wondered after each kill, *Am I killing a little piece of myself after each assassination?* He could never shake the lingering thought from mind, no matter how hard he tried.

They moved methodically through the devastated brush, making only the slightest of noise, only occasionally hearing the crunching sound of charred bark underfoot. It sent a ringing sensation that played havoc with his heightened senses and with each branch that broke, Clover cringed. He never liked making any sound, he was an assassin by design and stealth was his only friend. It was these abilities that gave him a reputation that wondered from rebel hideout to rebel hideout, one that legends were made of. But each time Clover heard his own mythical legends, he had a hard time believing they were about him, rather than some fictional character made up to scare young children. The noise didn't bother Legion or their guide, it was like neither could hear the noise they were making. That, or they didn't fear the consequences of it.

Their guide led them through the tunneling path encompassed by half-destroyed forest trees, keeping them hidden from the hideout security as they approached the secluded base. Even if Clover had become separated from either of them he could still manage to smell their bodily scent—another attribute of his superior design.

Their guide was a well-known human tracker who was very well paid by the Corporation and knew the area like the back of his hand. He had a reputation for aiding corporate raids on local rebel hideouts which forced the

Corporation to keep his identity and whereabouts hidden from the public. Their guide's dark skin and odd mixture of modern clothing and ancestral weapons made for an unusual blend. He was covered from head to toe in leather and fur, another combination that struck Clover as odd. The tracker wore a shawl to shield his identity, which could come in handy when sneaking up on the security gate. He played the espionage game well, on both sides of the war. Oh, the Corporation felt that they had him under their wing, but at times he made friends with local rebels, giving and taking intel to use for his own purposes.

The assassin had never encountered a human as unique or well adapted to his environment as their guide. The tracker had been hunting in the area his entire life.

I can't see his eyes and that makes me nervous, thought Clover. *Is he leading us to our destination or into a trap?*

The fighting between the rebels and the armed militia of the Corporation had all but cleared the former wooded forest of its majestic beauty. This was once a vast eco-system of gargantuan Sitka spruce trees encasing a small riverbed that slit the region into three pods. The upper Washington State region had been a breathless wonder but now many of the trees stood bare, while others lay on their sides like a mammoth giant had fallen over, knocking the trees and their branches with it. Large bare patches in the canopy let in what light there was from the full moon.

Clover could only shake his head in disgust. *Look what our war has done to this once amazing place.* He took in the aroma of the burned forest which seemed to resonate with death. He felt that the entire region looked broken and beaten, much like the human spirit had become since his kind had arrived on Earth. The distinct aroma smelled to him like someone had come into these woods and set them ablaze. It wasn't like the aroma was fresh with the smell of green grass and leaves drying in the fall sun. It was the smell of death that had heightened his awareness. It was everywhere and Clover knew the scent of it, since he had been designed to kill. He wasn't sure which was worse, the burning sensation coming from the charred forest or the decay of rotting flesh emitting from the earth.

Clover saw the remains of battles which had been fought over this land, with the residue of smoke still rising from the burned wood. Burned equipment, military field packs, leftover ammunition shells from massive guns, as well as blast trenches that created pockets all over the area. As they passed over charred tree limbs that had fallen, it was apparent that all the nutrients had left the woodland, as most the debris littering the forest was dead. There were other signs that displayed both human resistance fighters and General Reinhart's super soldiers had been through this area not too long ago.

Clover reached down and touched a footprint in the mud. *Human boot print,* he thought. The print seemed to have been embedded in the ground as if someone wanted them to discover it. *This track isn't freshly made*, he thought. *This appears to be from a military-issued boot. Is this from the battlefield or as we get closer to the rebel hideout will we discover more?*

There were several other boot prints surrounding the human ones. This was another one of his valuable traits. Clover knew these others quite well. Clover had done too many missions not to be able to distinguish human tracks and the ones Legion's followers left in their wake. He closed his eyes and touched the foreign footprints.

"We know one another, don't we?" The bioengineered assassin whispered. A wave of emotions struck him full force. Some enveloped positive energy, but too much was horror stricken and torment.

Some of Legion's spies had been in the area recently. Clover could tell by the trail they had left behind, and their scent as well. He didn't just know familiar human scents, but his own kind as well. If the humans were horrible about covering their own tracks, the agents of the Corporation seemed to be worse at it. *Was it arrogance or blind disregard of the trails they leave?* Clover wondered.

Legion looked back at him and could only manage to shake his head, as if to tell Clover to keep moving. Clover smiled crookedly, mocking his sibling.

Their guide told of wolves that used to roam the wooded lands. "In this area, before the rise of man, the timber wolf used to hunt and prowl. Now their spirits trek these lands as its guardian. You can see spirits of these deceased hunters traveling through the now-dead forest when the moon is right."

"They and myself seem to have a lot in common," mumbled Clover. "The timber wolves, being nocturnal hunters, not the natives."

The guide smirked. "Yah. I can believe that."

He senses my wolflike presence. He truly is of this land, much more essence of the spirit people and less human, Clover thought.

Legion turned. "That's enough talking from both of you. We don't need any unnecessary attention brought on us."

†

They finally arrived just outside the rebel hideout, on the west bank of the dried-up riverbed. Legion, followed closely by Clover, treaded the muddy, empty riverbed.

Their guide turned to them. "This is where we part ways. The entrance to the base is merely two hundred yards and I don't have the desire to get any closer. Good luck to you both." Their guide pointed in its direction. Once he had directed their path, the guide turned around and reentered the charred woods, disappearing as the leafless forest engulfed him.

"We have to walk across an open field. I want us to keep our cloaks over us to conceal our identity," said Legion.

"Are you insane?" responded Clover. "They will spot us for sure. The burned woods supply us with no cover at all. This isn't very stealthy."

"It's our only access point. Any other direction we try will surely spark their suspicion," Legion said. "Keep your head down and let me do all the talking."

They walked across the war-torn field. The field had large artillery pits. Fire and smoke receded from every portion of the devastated ground, much like the charred forest. It was obvious it had been from a battle between the resistance and the general's army. Despair and desolation crept into Clover's mind as they passed the ruined field, the same feelings the charred forest had on him.

It wasn't the devastation that disturbed Clover, it was the thought of the people that had died in the fighting. A chill ran down his spine. Their path was just as distraught as the area around them, with only artifacts of the past left behind. Broken-up asphalt littered the ground, like a melting pot with a multitude of ingredients. A broken street sign was buried in their path, half telling them that Tacoma, Washington, was only fifteen miles away.

They finally reached the front gate. The place initially didn't look like much. Outside the heavily guarded security gate, which looked quite out of place, the rest of the compound seemed run-down from their vantage point.

Clover wondered if Legion's intel had been mistaken. They had never had any assignments in such a pathetic place as this one was. The security gate was made of thick iron and was rusted all over, but especially at its structure points. They couldn't see the rest of the rebel hideout; the height of the gate concealed the hideout's secrets. They were met by two heavily armed security personnel and were questioned aggressively. The two guards had an exasperated look about them. Neither guard appreciated the sudden appearance of their new visitors, not one bit.

The entrance of the hideout was an old warehouse attached to an abandoned mill. The mill had stopped producing lumber from Washington State's rain forest, long before the uprising.

Clover could sense the inhabitants moving inside the hideout, beyond the reaches of the gate. He could sense their fear and doubt. He closed his eyes and visualized the inside of the hideout. He could see it all, despite its fortification. It was like he had an eagle eye view, soaring high above the entire complex. With his animalistic senses, he moved throughout the camp, without even taking a step inside.

The fortified perimeter was surrounded by mountainous hills to the east and by the charred forest to the south and west. The mountains stretched high in the sky, a fortification in itself. Clover felt it must have been strategically chosen for its seclusion, but the burned field facing its main entrance played a vital role as well. It kept would-be spies from getting too close to the hideout before they were spotted.

Before they reached the security gate and faced the guards, Legion stopped. Legion pulled Clover close and spoke so that only the two brothers could hear. "Don't fail us, Clover. We are all brothers in the same struggle, no matter our differences. Many eyes are upon the success of this mission. If you fail, I fail as well." He jabbed one of his massive fingers into Clover's chest plate. "And you know I hate defeat."

Clover gave Legion a look that told Legion he had done this many times. He knew who was watching them. Soon he would not be able to keep his mounting anger from getting the best of him. He felt that sooner or later they would have to duel once again and this time Clover didn't intend to get his ass kicked. *When the time comes, it will be just me and you, and this time none of your goons will interfere with our quarrel. Then we will see who gets the better of who*, Clover thought.

Legion and Clover finished walking to the gate and were rudely greeted by the two visible security figures. They knew there were others watching them.

The first security guard held out his free hand. "Hold it right there. What is the nature of your visit here?" The security personnel looked them up and down, scrutinizing their appearance. "Do you have documents to tell us who you are, so we may confirm?"

The second security personnel responded rudely. "Remove your hoods so we may identify you both."

Legion looked around the outer portion of the hideout, scoping potential weaknesses in the rebel's hideout. A smile protruded through the shadows of his hood. He flipped it off, exposing his exceptionally large head and astronomical features to the guards standing in front of them. He gave his normal glare at the two guards. The spine-chilling glare expressed a sinister look, one that scared humans in to seeking cover. His dark eyes had a red tint to them, and his jaw muscles forcefully cramped against each another. It made his appearance even more daunting. He looked like a child's Halloween mask, except it was skin, not latex. It was truly a demonic gaze that he gave the two guards in front of them.

"We are here to see Juan Luke. I have a messenger here that has vital data that I think he might want to possess," Legion said.

Juan Luke was a senior captain in the rebellion and had great influence with many junior commanders. Reinhart felt the captain's assassination might break the resistance and his plan was supported by the reluctant board. In addition, Juan Luke had won many critical battles, managing to keep the Corporation from overwhelming the rebels.

Both security guards raised their automatic weapons, one being an American M-16 while the other guard held in his dirty grasp a Chinese copy of the Russian AK-47. They waved their weapons in their visitor's faces. The second guard was grasping the trigger of his rifle aggressively. Clover sensed the tension in the man's mind and the anxiety that ran through the man's body. The second security guard spat on the ground, close to Clover's foot and violently wiped his mouth clean. The residue was a murky, brownish-white color that foamed even after exiting the man's filthy mouth.

This man acts like a barbarian, even for these chaotic times. He is unruly, rude and reeks like a wild beast. Has humanity lost its self-worth and dived back into its primordial stage?

"Give us the message and we will pass it on to him promptly," the second security guard demanded. "No unscheduled visits are permitted. No exceptions will be made." The guard had a more scurrilous look about him than before and his grip on the rifle intensified.

The second security guard jammed the nozzle of his rifle into Clover's ribcage, trying to get him to lift his head. He tried to peer into Clover's hood, but failed to see even one detail of Clover's hidden face. His frustration was mounting to the point of exploding. Losing his cool was the last thing the man really wanted to do. Clover, too, needed to avoid losing his temper. It would cause him to leap into action and expose Legion and himself before gaining access to the rebel hideout.

"I really think that he needs to hear this for himself," Legion said, averting the frustrated guard's attention. "I feel only the messenger can convey the message in its proper light. No offense, I just don't have confidence leaving with this type of information to security personnel. I'm sure you understand me, don't you?"

Clover looked up at the security camera. Its red, ominous eye scanned over the scene attempting to gauge the severity of the situation and trying to identify their new visitors at the same time. Clover's eyes glistened as the moon's illumination reflected off the camera lens and into his nocturnal pupils. He didn't need to see who was watching them; he could sense their agitation. It was like Clover was mockingly communicating to the people on the other end.

The first security guard glanced over at Clover, then moved his attention back to the gargantuan Legion. He wasn't sure how to proceed and was dumbfounded by the situation he found himself in. He'd lost his train of thought completely. He was just as agitated as his partner and the security personnel watching them on the other side of the rusty gate. The difference was that he was seasoned enough to be able to keep calm, unlike his trigger-happy partner. He knew an overreaction could get them all killed in a blink of an eye.

The first security guard said steadily, "He hasn't seen many visitors lately. The paranoid rumor of the Corporation creating assassins to kill off rebel leaders has him boarded up nice and tight. Since then he doesn't come out for anyone."

The first security guard lowered his rifle and relaxed his defensive stance.

Clover glanced at the first guard, noticing his relaxed state. *He lowered his weapon,* thought Clover. *Why did he do that? Have we gained his trust already? If it were me, I'd be suspicious as hell to have two strangers show up in the middle of the night, wanting to see my leader.*

The guard's partner didn't share his friendly sentiments and still had the tip of his rifle planted in Clover's ribs. The guard dug the tip even deeper in agitation. The pain felt like someone ramming a thousand blades into his side, but Clover kept his focus on the task at hand and refrained from reacting.

"I say let's take these two into the woods, take what we want and put them out of their misery. If we can't coax the message from their lips, then it wasn't that important anyhow."

The second guard looked Clover dead in the face. "What do you think about that, partner?" In even more frustration from not obtaining a response from Clover, the angry guard snapped at Legion. "Your friend doesn't talk much, does he? How is he supposed to deliver any message if he's a mute?"

That's when Clover spoke up. He used a low and calm tone, one directed toward the angry guard. "I only speak to those who have the ability to understand the message that I have to deliver. I seriously doubt your simple-minded, ego-driven persona could understand anything that my lips would convey to you." Clover's red eyes pierced the cover of his cloak, exposing themselves to the agitated guard. This made the guard weak in the knees and he was speechless in response. He loosened his grip on the rifle and removed the gun tip from Clover's side. He wasn't the only one who had gazed into those scary eyes. It was a common response.

"Okay now, let's allow cooler minds to prevail on this," the first guard said. "I'll make you a deal. I'll take you to our leader and let him decide if he wishes to speak with you. I can't make any promises to you, okay?"

The first guard motioned to his partner that everything was under control and that their visitors were not a threat, that they weren't even armed. Little did they realize what Clover had hidden under his cloak. Clover's razor-sharp weapon, cold to the touch, would easily slice through both guards' meager flesh. Clover enjoyed the touch of this concealed weapon. Those in the complex would soon know who he and Legion really where and what they came to do. Escaping would be a feat unto itself.

The guards lowered their weapons and the first guard motioned for them to follow him.

┆

They moved swiftly past the main gate and into the interior of the hideout. The guard led them through the rebel complex, which was more than it seemed to be, but Clover already knew this already. There were many hidden passageways which could take a person beneath the surface. Clover caught a glimpse of many of these passageways that led into dark stairwells. But Clover didn't even need to venture into these dark passageways or even peer into them to know where they might lead, he had been inside several rebel hideouts and this one, despite its remote location, wasn't any different in design than the others he had been in. The difference was that he had snuck into the previous ones, and this time they were being escorted through it like tourists.

The low portion of the hideout was draped in thick concrete. It kept the dampness and dewy smell underneath the complex, but also protected the occupants from any potential attacks. It shielded the actual number of rebels living in the hideout as well as how many supplies the rebels possessed. The concrete wall was pitted and weatherworn, a testament to how the elements had treated the complex. There was a dripping sound coming from somewhere deep in the underground passage. Each passageway was connected to the hallway they were traveling down. It was a maze. They passed by a group of militants preparing for an assault. *The soldiers seem well equipped,* Clover thought as they passed a few areas that were presumably ammunition lockers. He could see the outline of assault and heavy artillery in the shadows. *Where are they getting the supplies to continue their campaign?*

"I'm just curious, I have been in many rebel HQs and never seen rebels so well equipped. Where do you get your supplies from?" Clover asked.

Legion looked back at Clover with an uninviting glare.

They stopped for a moment and the guard looked around to make sure no one was listening. "You're awful curious for a mere messenger."

"Like I said, I've been inside many rebel hideouts," responded Clover.

"Well the weapons are stolen from raids on Corporation armory warehouses, while the food supplies are meant to go to corporate militia and their allies near campaign battlegrounds. We distribute the food to those that choose to live outside our protective reach." The guard motioned to Clover and Legion to keep moving.

They moved on through a section of the hideout that housed civilian refugees. It was obvious to Clover that the rebels wanted the refugees and the military supplies separated, with massive steel walls constructed to split the two areas. Clover could only assume it was in case the hideout was attacked, it would be easier to evacuate the civilians because the focus would be on the supply section, allowing the civilians a hidden escape route while the rebels fought off invaders.

The inhabitants were moving around cautiously as the group approached. Clover sensed hesitation from many occupants living among the rebel hideout. They feared the newcomers who had invaded their living space. Most of the civilians fled their path and into some underground sections of the hideout, shielding themselves from view. Clover turned just in time to notice Legion glaring at the fleeing refugees. Clover didn't need to see the snarl Legion had on his face, he could feel the hatred building deep within his brother. Something he cared for less than his hateful reaction.

A group of youngsters stuck their heads out and stared at Clover as they passed by. He returned their gaze with one of his own, his red eyes glaring out at them. It caught the youngsters by surprise and they playfully stuck their tongues out at him. He smiled and returned the gesture with his own tongue, longer and darker than their own. The children giggled and ran off screaming and laughing, covering their mouths as if Clover had told them a dirty joke.

The guard guides them past a room, where an elderly woman carried a pot, steam rising from its top. Clover looked to the room with interest and realized it was a kitchen and food storage area all in one. There was canned food and other non-perishable foodstuffs, as well as a small room adjacent to the main one that appeared to have frost on its door window. Clover thought it was where they kept the perishable food like meat. He was starting to get the impression these rebels were more well equipped than he had originally thought.

They climbed a metal staircase that rattled as they ascended. It shook wildly and creaked nosily as they moved along its rusty surface. It swayed side to side as they moved, telling Clover of its advanced age. Their footfalls echoed loudly, announcing their arrival. Clover lifted his hand off the railing and noticed his palm was covered in rust. He looked up the side of the rusty railing that seemed to lean off to the side on an angle. It was apparent to him that this railing had been there for many years, between the rust-filled surface of the railing and how it no longer provided the support it was originally intended for. There was a vast gap between the aging stairwell and the rusted-out railing.

I guess stealth mode would be thrown out the door crossing this thing. Good thing we are being escorted to my latest victim, thought Clover.

They reached their destination at the top of the railing. They passed through two steel doors that creaked as much as the stairs shook and approached a similarly built closed door. It was a large chamber, boarded up tightly, as if the occupants were fearful for their lives and desired no company. This was the spot where Legion and Clover would part company.

Legion turned to Clover, before they parted.

"Remember what I told you, brother." Legion jabbed a large finger into Clover's chest. "Don't let your family down. Accomplish the task at hand."

Clover returned Legion's warning glance with one of his own. "Fine, Legion. I'll do this one last job. But I'm tired of all the pressure you, General Reinhart and the Corporation places on me. I have more than earned the respect I should be receiving. It's time for me to go rogue," whispered Clover.

Legion laughed at Clover's threat. "Very well. I guess your suppressed memories have made you forget all the dirty little things we have done in the name of the mighty Corporation."

Legion turned and walked away. This would be the last time they saw one another, face-to-face before the war. Clover had no regrets leaving the security of the Corporation's wing. The question looming was whether Legion would just let him go.

The security guard knocked on the chamber door. The room beyond the door echoed a hollowness that announced their arrival. The door was thicker and much sturdier than Clover expected it to be. The look of it was quite misleading. Clover mistook it for a door that could be knocked down by force. This would be good, when the rebels came to aid their leader, it would give Clover time to escape and not have to fight every rebel in the fortress. By the sounds of their banging, he could tell the room was spacious.

From within the boarded-up room, Captain Juan Luke answered without looking up from the charts. "Enter."

Clover and his escort entered the chamber swiftly, so as not to keep the captain waiting. The hall was gray and partially cloaked in shadows, since they used very few lights to illuminate the hall. It had a musky smell, like a pair of wet socks left in a plastic bag. Candles lit the dark room and the aroma of burning wax lingered in the stagnant air. The floor was as rusty as the stairwell and made of a similar metal, as well. A brisk coolness filled the place, coming from a draft blowing from beneath them, possibly from a deeper underground shaft. Most likely he would find the pathways from this place connecting to one another, even the ones they had passed on their way here.

The captain was a frail and aging man. It was apparent this leader hadn't eaten well for a while, or even slept well. This frail figure was graying quickly and his arms and face were worn with wrinkles over his pale skin. Clover could hear the captain wheezing, each breath elongated. The rebel leader's clothes, including his fatigue jacket, were a size or two too big. Tired eyes reflected the charts he was working on as they entered.

There were four other figures in the room. They hadn't said a word since Clover had entered and he could see the distraught looks on their faces. He had just interrupted an important meeting, one that the rebel leaders were unwilling to continue while he occupied the room. The four men took a few steps backward, trying to utilize the shadows in the corner of the room. Clover gave a slight grin at this. *Little do they realize I can sense their presence, even in the shadows*, he thought.

As he waited for a proper introduction, Clover thought, *I don't even need to eliminate this old man. He will die soon enough on his own from exhaustion, fatigue and old age.* Then he looked toward the four men trying to use the shadows as cover. *These other souls aren't in much better shape than their leader. They will never see the battlefront again if I have anything to do with it.*

The captain stood in the middle of the hall overlooking a chart on a flat table half covered in shadows.

The security guard escorting Clover hesitated. His silence made for an awkward moment, but he then interrupted the proceedings.

"Captain, you have a visitor." The guard paused for another moment before continuing. "It's a messenger and he claims he has some vital information that he wants to convey to you personally."

Captain Jean Luke looked up without much of an expression on his face. "Very well. We are finished here anyway." The captain nodded to the other men in the room. "Leave us alone."

"Yes, sir," Clover's guide responded.

The men left the room.

Clover scanned the room waiting for the last of the captain's men to exit. He was looking for a way out of the stronghold chamber. *There must be another way out of this dilapidation.*

Then the bioengineered assassin noticed a drainage trap concealed under an access panel in the metal floor. He understood faculties such as this one had ways to rid of waste and this one was expanse enough that he could escape through. *There she is. The instrument of my evading dash. The drainage most likely will take me just outside the fortress walls and with the darkness of the oncoming night, they will never be able to track me.*

Then the feeble voice of Clover's victim, one that made the assassin nauseous inside, broke his distracted silence.

"What news do you bring me today?" Queried Captain Jean Luke.

Clover didn't respond to the Jean Luke's request immediately and this irritated the captain. He started to become nervous and jittery.

"Why don't you remove your cloak and show me who you are, my friend," the captain ordered.

Clover gave the old man another moment of silence.

In his deepest and most sadistic voice, Clover began. "My dearest Captain, I wish you to pay close attention to what I'm about to tell you, because it will most likely be the last thing you hear before you and your kind perish in a rain of fire."

The captain's elderly gray eyes shot to life and the wrinkles on his aging face merged as he scowled. Clover's jest had apparently taken him by surprise and Captain Jean Luke gave his full attention to his new visitor.

"What do you mean survive? You're being extremely vague, friend, you're treading on the edge of my suspicion and make me question the true meaning of your visit today," the captain said.

Clover ignored him. "Humanity is on the brink of disaster. A war is coming to your doorstep and it's up to the leaders of your society to help you all endure the hell that is attached to it," Clover said.

"If you haven't noticed, we're in a war already." The captain gestured at the map laying on the table. "It's with the corporate mongrels that keep normal citizen's poor and hungry."

"You're about to be blindsided by a force that, to this point, has been cloaked from your view," replied Clover. "Something so massive your species may never recover," the assassin reproached.

From beneath his cloak, a shiny object was revealed to the captain. It took Jean Luke's breath away. It was a cold, steel-looking weapon with four razor-sharp edges encompassed in a circular device which retracted, exposing the four blades. It was aerodynamic for quick, stealthy flight. Clover grasped it by a circular handle designed especially for his strong grip.

The captain hadn't expected his uninvited guest to be armed and he froze for a moment, not sure whether to flee or call for help. The walls were thick and well-fortified. Even if he could call out for assistance, it would take the rebels within earshot time to rescue their captain. The weapon briefly hypnotized the captain, more from shock than anything else. Clover's target pointed to the object with a shaking hand.

"What the hell is that?" the captain cried out.

Clover looked down at the weapon. He started to laugh.

The captain moved backward and reached for his pistol but fumbled with the strap and struggled to retrieve the weapon, costing him precious time. Clover reached for his weapon and launched it at his victim. The blades sliced through the air between them creating a horrid, high-pitched noise.

The razor-sharp weapon sliced the captain's shooting hand, cutting it clean off and sending it along with the sidearm it had finally grasped. Jean Luke fell to the rusted, dirty floor and made a *thump* as the man cried in pain. The old captain could only manage to lie there bleeding and shaking profusely in shock. Clover knew he could leave the man be and he would bleed to death eventually, but that wasn't his MO. He would much rather stick the old man and watch his life dissipate right before his very eyes. Jean Luke grabbed his wound and tried to scream, but could only manage a faint "eck."

Clover bent down to retrieve the weapon. He watched with pleasure as his victim squirmed in agony. Clover's animalistic nature was seeping through, but he had to shake it off, there was no time for this. He held the throwing weapon in one tight grip and leaped into the air like a predator pouncing on a new meal. He landed on the man's chest with such force that it nearly pushed all of Jean Luke's breath from his body, preventing him from screaming for help. Clover leaned in, removed his hood and stared into the man's eyes.

"Pipe down, my poor man. Be a distinguished gentleman and die with some dignity," Clover said forcefully.

Clover inserted his weapon deep into the captain's body and blood flew out of him rapidly. The captain's blood ran thick, covering Clover's entire arm with blood.

†

It was late, on the far side of town in the *Dvoryan* district of Metro City. A senior board member lay in his bed drowning on his own vomit and blood. The elderly businessman tried to grab at his neck as he bled to death.

His speech was gurgled as blood flowed down his throat. The wet, sticky blood ran down the man's chest and onto the satin sheets. He tried to sit up, but he had lost too much blood to even do that. He turned to a light seeping into the dark room. He thought he had seen a shadow flash by just moments ago. He felt for his wife's body, it seemed cold and dead lying next to him. He tried to awaken her, but there was no movement from his spouse of forty-five years.

The elderly board member tried to call out her name but it came out as one big gurgle. "Ma–ar–agery." There was still no response.

Something moved out of the shadows and into the slight light coming from the window next to the bed. The board member could only see a flicker as the individual drew near. The dark figure leaned down and whispered.

"It is a pleasure watching you die in such agony, old timer. It gives me a euphoric high I just can't explain," the figure said.

The old board member's face contorted with fear. He started to shake a finger at the dark apparition in front of him. "What are you?" he stammered.

"You could say I'm your death, come to collect your soul for all the foul things you have done in your life."

The elderly man reached for his wife. "My Margery, please don't harm her." The board member felt the coldness in his wife's body.

"Oh, you have nothing to fear, old man. She died in her sleep, I made sure of that. She felt absolutely no pain. But you, on the other hand, will die a painful and excruciating death. I have orders to make sure of that and I intend on following through on those orders." The Shadow Agent laughed sinisterly. It sounded like a banshee's cry, screeching through the board member's eardrums.

The old man cried out one last time.

After the board member's death, the Shadow Agent retrieved a communication device from his cloak.

"Shadow Agent to base."

"Go ahead," said a voice on the other end of the communication device.

"The assignment has been completed. All the Corporation's board members are dead. Only one remains, CEO Volkov."

"You know what to do," said the Shadow Agent's commander.

"He is as good as dead."

✝

Nikolai Volkov was at his new estate just south of the city limits, but he didn't notice his uninvited guest. As the CEO was downing a glass of vodka, something struck his shoulder blade and forced him to drop the glass. The glass shattered at Nikolai's feet. He looked around but could only see darkness in his spacious home.

"Wh–who's there?" demanded Nikolai.

The only response he received was a sinister giggle no louder than a whisper. Pain arced through his right shoulder. He had been cut by something, the same something that had forced him to drop his evening glass of Yuri Dolgoruki Vodka. He had imported it by the crateful from Moscow itself. A feeling came over him, something was coming for him. The hairs on the back of his neck stood at attention. Breathing and something warm at his side alerted him that someone was standing directly next to him.

The Corporation's CEO ran for the kitchen's back door. The sound of a razor-sharp object sliced the granite tabletop, leaving a gaping hole next to the sink. The invisible assassin wiped Nikolai's blood from its four-bladed, razor-sharp weapon.

Nikolai burst into the spacious backyard of his brand-new estate barefoot, nearly propelling the backdoor off its brass hinges and ran for his life. Nikolai hadn't had time to slip shoes on, but protecting his bare feet was the least of his concerns. He nearly stumbled a few times and his breathing had become quite labored from fleeing his own demise.

A sharp pain ran through one side of his body, like he had been mysteriously stabbed repeatedly. Volkov reached down and came away with a handful of blood on his hand. He could feel the gashing wound oozing blood. His head started to spin and he began to stumble through the spacious backyard. The CEO stumbled and fell to his knees. He was panting like he had been running for miles without any reprieve. He turned towards the mansion's backdoor waiting to spot his attacker at any moment.

I need to keep moving or whomever attacked me in the kitchen will catch me for sure. Nikolai thought.

The Shadow Agent pursued the CEO, following the trail of blood left behind by his victim. Volkov had been injured. The dark assassin wondered if the CEO might die before it got the chance to slice Volkov's throat. The blood trail encased the estate, from his den to the spacious grounds. The Shadow Agent knew the CEO of the Corporation wouldn't last much longer, he had struck a vital organ and the trail was becoming darker. He could sense Volkov's agony.

"Keep fleeing, my friend. I can do this all day, but you have the sands of time running against you," the Shadow Agent called.

Nikolai stumbled into the assassin's view, holding something in his unbloodied hand, then vanished behind a group of bushes. The CEO spoke into a metal device. "Initiate Protocol 75."

A digital voice responded but the agent couldn't make out what it had said in response. Nikolai turned toward his pursuer. The CEO still held the area where his liver was, and he was still bleeding out. Then the dying CEO whipped around with an object in his grasp. He held it tightly. "Go fuck yourself!" Shots fired in rapid succession, but none of them found their target.

"That's the spirit I like to see," called the Shadow Agent.

Nikolai leaned against an old well basin with half its wall missing. It was no longer used to retrieve water and had no pulley at its top. His blood had already coated the weather-stained stones that remained.

The cloaked assassin threw a razor-sharp dagger at his target. End over end the dagger flew in search of its victim It seemed to move much quicker than Nikolai could flee. His face had become contorted and he didn't notice the dagger slam into his forearm until it was too late, forcing the pistol from his hand and becoming defenseless. The momentum of the attack sent the CEO rolling over into the well. He disappeared into its darkness. The Shadow Agent leaned over edge of the tiny well. He couldn't see or hear a thing.

"Nikolai, are you down there? Don't think this will end my pursuit of you," the assassin called. *If he does reach the bottom, he will most likely be dead. I can't possibly climb down into this tiny well. I must report the mission a success and hope the bastard bleeds out; if he manages to survive the fall, that is.*

Metro City's skyline transforms from dark and quiet, into a furious rage of fire and ash as the nuclear fireball lit up the night sky. Warheads ignited all around the world, ending life as it was. Aftershock followed by aftershock struck the people of Metro City, and it was accompanied by heat, fire and smoke. The fire moved down to the bottom of the city, leaving nothing alive in its path. Screams could be heard, but they quickly became silent.

The skyline disappeared and the scene darkened again. Everything had died—or at least it seemed that way. Society had fallen at the whim of its greatest entity, the Corporation. Protocol 75 had been enacted and the apocalypse had come.

CHAPTER 5

The harsh and menacing sun crept over the range of dunes on the deserted edge of the Wasteland. The reflection of the sun's rays turned the outer rim of the desolated land a reddish-orange color and illuminated the dark ocean of sand under its vigorous span. Only a few isolated shadows remained on the surface, as anything left in its wake succumbed to the rising sun's immense power. Emerging from the safety of their protective hovel, soon after the sun made its accent, moved a human family. They were about to begin their journey westward to the township of Sonoma.

Clover had followed the family across a good portion of the outer rim and several times had come extremely close to the Wasteland's borders. He had never experienced humans traveling so eagerly or who were so willing to place their own lives at such risk. He had ventured into and out of the Wasteland numerous times, but that was because he was hunting prey and had become used to the harshness of the barren Wasteland. That was one of Clover's key traits, adaptability. These humans had no reason to venture so close to the horrid Wasteland border, not unless the leader had felt Clover's presence. *But that is impossible*, thought Clover. He was so diligent at keeping his distance and being nearly invisible to the naked eye. He knew of no human that possessed the ability to sense his presence. No, he was merely being paranoid. Clover was so accustomed to using shadows that he wasn't used to walking so boldly in daylight, but this expedition was far from normal for him.

The trip was long and hard for the family. It possessed many hazards scattered along the way. No family member was ever permitted to venture off on their own; there were innumerable dangers. The dangerous conditions, the increasing heat and multiplying storms on the plains, unwanted guests stumbling upon their hovel—these were just some of the dangers lurking among these lands.

The leader of the family was the father, Calieb Whiteherst. He had a physical appearance that was unusual for a human male. He was tall, maybe approaching six foot four, but lanky with lean muscles that were stronger than one might expect. His surprising strength was the result of spending a hard life in this post-apocalyptic world. He moved with a slight hindrance from prolonged exposure to the harsh elements. He could always be found wearing his famous tan surface gear that made him look like something out of a steampunk novel, small tight goggles smudged and full of sand, a leather environmental suit designed to traverse the arid and harsh terrain, a large backpack and his surface terrain boots.

Now that he was older and had a family, he knew the dangers that lay out here, so close to the edge of the Wasteland. He had experienced enough death to last him a lifetime. His knowledge gave him and his family an edge against potential traps set by others who wanted what they possessed, but his family struggled to comprehend these dangers—they hadn't experienced what he had.

Calieb would always call out to his trailing family. "Everyone keep it tight. We don't need anyone to get lost in the heavy wind current or a sandstorm." His actions made him seem like a wicked dictator, but he knew that by keeping them on edge allowed the family to survive.

Then there was Calieb's wife, Shelley Whiteherst. She had become hardened by the harsh environment, but that didn't eliminate her nurturing and caring persona. She had to be strong-willed and witty, as well as quick on her feet. She had teenagers who loved to run off on adventures, even when they were warned of the dangers they might encounter. She would double check the family's clothes to make sure each family member was on track when they set out for every voyage, especially when they came so close to the edge of the Wasteland. Shelley's main duties as the caretaker, outside of the family's overall well-being, was to make sure the children stayed out of their father's way as he scoped the areas for dangers or led them through hazardous portions of the land. She was a good house-keeper, cook, and nurse and she had become resourceful at making do with the things the family found.

She was always concerned for her family's well-being, and always kept an eye on them. She would often yell out to them as they went off on their dangerous and adventur-ous expeditions. "I only have one set of eyes and I can't keep track of everyone's whereabouts." The twins paid no heed and would take off, ignoring their mother's warning.

Doria, like many girls her age, was a dreamer and pre-ferred having her head in the clouds than pay much attention to what she was doing or where she was heading. She was a slender and frail girl, who was easy to bruise. Her mother would constantly catch her dreaming of dressing up in beautiful evening gowns and going to extravagant events, meeting handsome men from all types of lifestyles, not that she had ever seen any extravagant events personally, at least not in this wretched place. She would be the one her mother had to keep her eyes on the most, especially if they explored towns which had shopping malls and elegant clothing stores.

Doria would gravitate to these places and disappear for hours, ignoring her duties to the family. After picking up a fancy dress she would spin around and say to her mother, "Have you ever seen such elegant of a dress mother? I feel like one of those models that you told me about, the ones you saw when you were a little girl."

Then there was Doria's twin brother, Straus. He was always coming up with unique schemes to get into deep trouble with their parents. When he wasn't off exploring the ruins of the towns or designing his own brand of mischief, Straus found ways to annoy his sister. Despite it all, he had a kinship with his sister, a link. He always knew where she was—normally.

Straus would always say, "Don't tell Mom, but I'm going off to explore on my own."

His sister would say, "Mom's not going to like that one bit."

Straus would swiftly turn to her and give her a glazed stare. "You better not, if you know what's good for you, Doria."

As Clover got closer to the family, he noticed more intricate details. They tried to walk single file to cover their tracks, but humans were always sloppy and could never do it well. This family wasn't much different, no matter how hard they tried. He could even tell whether the footprints were an adult's or child's just by inspecting the print itself. He could tell the father had some experience making long distance runs because the family attempted to make zigzag patterns, trying to confuse any pursuer they might have. Clover, however, was designed to track and their efforts only amused him more.

The family was covered from head to toe to protect them from the harsh environment of the outer Wasteland. Each family member wore protective headgear with goggles designed to keep sand out of their faces and to block the UV rays cast down on the planet's surface. They all wore heavy, weather-resistant coats made to withstand the harsh winds and excess radiation in the atmosphere. The coats were made with extra linings sewn into them to help insulate the family members from the harsh environment of the Wasteland. Everyone wore footwear which had been created to endure walking through the Wasteland all day and to keep radioactive decay and insects from entering them unexpectedly.

The father was at point, leading his family through the treacherous outskirts of the Wasteland. He had an old rifle slung over his shoulder. He had carried it, 'just in case' he always claimed, but was never seen using it. Calieb carried a larger pack than the rest of the family. The other family members carried their own packs tight against their bodies so that they might collect supplies on their journey. Each family member carried a different size pack, one that wouldn't impede their travel. The father usually ran point and kept his rifle ready. He had trained each family member to shoot the rifle, just in case the family needed defending, but he was the primary user of the weapon, prepared to meet with any trouble that came their way.

He would always warn them: "We never venture off alone because of the dangers that await us in the Wasteland. If any of you come across Outland Rustlers, alert the rest of the family and run as fast as your legs will carry you. They are not to be trifled with."

Sonoma was the closest town to their residence and the family had ventured there many times before for supplies. Other townships were farther away, but the drawback to going to Sonoma was that it took them along the edge of the dreaded Wasteland. The other townships would be safer, but it would take days to reach those towns and they could never know if the towns had been raided already. It would have been a waste of time to travel for days to reach these other locations and still not get what they needed. The family had to deal with the constant sandstorm that came from the Wasteland territory and bombarded local communities.

The wind blew heavily, throwing sand and debris all over, camouflaging anything approaching the family's position from the east and directly from behind. It was a sandy blanket draped across the entire region. The family was forced to move at a very slow pace, both because of the gale winds and the uncertainty of whether anything was following.

Clover was designed with the ability to hunt at night, and the oncoming storm would only give him more cover to pursue the family. He had the ability to see into the darkness like a wolf and his eyes glowed because of his night vision. Clover wore a black hybrid trench cloak, one that mainly was a trench coat designed to conceal his throwing weapons, hide his twin Katina's and allow the assassin flexibility in his movements. The hybrid cloak utilized a hood attached to the trench cloak to conceal himself, while the rest that covered most of his body. Made of synthetic leather and stained with blood, it concealed his identity and helped hide the weapons he had in his possession. The cloak blew in the wind as the sandstorm grew in intensity and moved ever closer. Underneath his cloak, he wore a high-strength armor suit which gave the assassin even more protection. The suit was lined with durable material that prevented it from tearing, had large plates made of a hybrid protective armor that protected the assassin, while giving him maneuverability, like his trench cloak, to protect his chest and separate plate sections allowing Clover to maneuver swiftly without restraints. It meant the armor could be penetrated, but that was the price he had to pay if he wanted to superior movement.

There is a legend among the humans that began as a mere myth but developed into something outrageously wild. It goes something like this: One moment the air would swirl in your hair and lightly brush against your skin. Then everything would go dead silent, no wind would shuffle the leaves on branches, no animals could be seen scampering away. Then you would see the redness of his eyes and you would know your luck had run out—you would be dead in a heartbeat. But a more modern tale, one told especially to young children to keep them from venturing off into the darkness of night was that the bogeyman had no face, that he had razor-sharp fangs and claws that ripped flesh from bone and lingered over children's dead bodies as he suckled at their souls and entrapped them forever. He would use any tactic in his arsenal to enslave them; sweets, child benefactions and empty promises. This bogeyman went by the name of Clover.

Even the Outland Rustlers dared not cross paths with the predator he was known as, in fear of igniting his rage and defiance. One time he was rumored to have taken apart an entire gang of outlanders with nothing but his razor-sharp fangs and claws. But those were stories told by parents to keep their children close to them.

The legend was continuously told by storytellers to a more adult like audience of how Clover and his cohorts would ravage human settlements and even murder their own kind. This ignited fear and hatred for Clover's kind and developed animosity between the Corporation's creations and humans. They were thought to be heathens of the time, the time before the Great War, a time before humans torched the sky. Then, after the fire in the sky nearly wiped out all living creatures, Clover disappeared and went into hibernation.

Clover wanted to get a better look at the family, study them, watch them interact with one another. He knew he must not converse with them or interfere in their affairs for that would send them in a rage of panic and his opportunity to learn from them would be lost. He kept his distance so as not to alert them to his presence.

The father stopped and glanced in Clover's general direction. He didn't think the human male could see him through the debris field created by the oncoming storm, but Clover wasn't entirely sure. He had seen humans with the ability to sense things without seeing them. *What did the humans call it? Oh yes, premonitions.*

✝

As the family made their way across the dunes, they were forced to stop several times because of the humid and dry air which kept the family dehydrated and worn out. The father turned, his rifle positioned aggressively as he scanned the horizon. Calieb held the rifle in front of him with a tight grip, ready to defend the family. His muscles were tensed to the point of exhaustion and the grip he had on the aging rifle made his arm feel like it was a thousand pounds, as if he had carried it for days without re-linquishing his grip on it. It wasn't slung over his shoulder like a marching platoon member or dangling loosely at his side, in one hand. No, experience had taught him that acting nonchalant in this harsh environment was only asking for trouble.

"I have this feeling something is following us from behind, but I can't see shit through this sandstorm," Calieb said as he looked back at his wife.

He turned his gaze up to the late morning sky, but couldn't see very far for the sun was high in the sky, not yet having disappeared under the cloud of sand vastly approaching. He shielded his goggles with a hand, but the sun still penetrated through. Even though he was well protected from the elements, he could feel the burning rays of the hidden sun. It felt like his skin was burning from the inside and he could still feel the sand scraping his face, like sharp fingernails running over his skin.

Calieb Whiteherst removed his goggles from his face, shook out the sand debris coating them and, for just a moment, looked southwestward. He squinted his eyes to improve his vision, but the oncoming sandstorm made visibility to their rear hazy at best. Calieb could not see far beyond the stormy horizon, nor far from their posi-tion, so he gave up any attempt to fight the morning sun.

He replaced his goggles over his sweat-covered face and continued onward, leading the rest of the family.

Clover looked skyward. *What is he looking for? There is nothing but sunrays driving down on him.*

The family continued to make their way to the summit of a dune. From there they could see the town of Sonoma in the distance. Both parents looked at each other, giving each other a confirmation nod to proceed. The family started down the steep sandy dune with caution.

As they made their way down the dune, being less cautious than before, sand started to fall from their path and slide down the dune. Sand fell all around them, an avalanche barreling down on them. The descent became steeper as they proceeded onward. The mother called out to Calieb, who had gained significant ground. "Slow down, we can't go as fast as you." But her husband didn't hear her plea through the sandstorm's gaining wind.

The teenage daughter slipped, losing her balance, and started to tumble dangerously down the dune. The girl's momentum moved her rapidly toward the base of the dune, not knowing what might lie waiting for her. She could crash into giant rocks or into the sandy depths drowning in a sea of sand or even into the jaws of a predator waiting under the sandy surface.

Clover tensed. The impulse to leap to the falling child's aid was immense, but that would expose his position and he was too far away to rescue her anyway. He was helpless to aid her and could only watch as the scene unfolded.

The father leaped after his only daughter with a swiftness that astonished Clover. Calieb used his boots to guide him down the steep slope like a surfer. His descent took him side to side as he gained speed. Calieb's control over his body's momentum allowed him to move purposefully after his daughter in a direct and sufficient intercept course. Both family members descended quickly towards the sea of beige sand below, as they moved closer with each breath they took. The father reached out and grabbed his daughter's arm. He struggled to use his other arm as a competent brake to slow their descent.

Clover's watchful gaze intensified as the two humans drew closer to what seemed to be a harsh and sandy doom for them both. Slowly, Calieb and his daughter's descent slowed until they rested at the base of the dune. Clover relaxed a little. *That could have been bad for the them both. Crashing at the speed they were descending into the sea of sand below would have been quite messy and most definitely attracted unwanted attention from all over.*

The daughter grabbed her father and hugged him forcefully with gratitude. "Thank you for saving me, father. I thought I was done for." They stood there, for what seemed forever, until the rest of the family reunited with them at the dune's base.

The family approached the outskirts of Sonoma. In the time before the war it had been a small southwestern township. It was filled with a grocery store, an arcade shop, a gun shop, a shopping mall and, among other buildings, a comic book store.

The family had to watch their step—shards of broken glass littered the streets, along with the interior of each building. The sound of glass shards breaking under their feet echoed as they walked and each footfall sounded as if they were breaking the skeletal structure of the town itself.

"Watch where you step, I don't believe the cleaning staff has come by yet." the father called.

The glass shards were the result of blown-out windows which hadn't disintegrated in the original blast during the final stages of the war between the Corporation and their rebel nemeses. Calieb looked around to see if anything had changed since their last visit. Birds perched on the broken window sills. Calieb remembered the windows being intact, but with the debris surrounding them couldn't be sure how long ago that was.

Several buildings still had blast markings on their exteriors. It made the town feel dingy and desolate, a ghost town of the modern age. The war had taken its toll on the town, despite it having survived the blasts. Between exposure to the new harsh climate, and the littered remains of raiding parties and scavengers, the town wasn't recognizable any longer.

Straus snuck up behind his twin sister, Doria, and let out a loud scream in her ear. Startled, she became disoriented and tripped over her own feet. She landed on the shard-littered ground, sending broken glass everywhere. Doria looked around at the glass surrounding her, then raised her hands. A few pieces of glass were stuck in her hands; cuts filled with blood that trickled slowly on her palms. Tears formed in the corners of her eyes. She wiped them away with the back of her hands.

She looked up at her brother, giving him the evil eye, but before she can scold him Straus yelled out. "What the hell is that?" He pointed to the limp body lying next to his sister. "I never noticed dead bodies lying in the streets on our previous trips."

The town's narrow streets connected to the main road. Each street, each back alley, was littered with corpses. There was no need to cover their mouths from the stench of the dead, the aroma of death had long since left these poor individuals.

The family hadn't visited Sonoma in months, but Calieb couldn't remember seeing even one dead body lying out in the open, let alone a whole slew of them. Someone had dragged them from their resting spots and into the open.

The mother stepped forward. "Whoever did this was looking for something, I would say."

Calieb remembered a similar scene—he and his now-dead brother had experienced something like this. It was a trap, and this had the feel of a Rustler's MO, if he remembered correctly. *This seems quite bold even for them. There are too many bodies for just a mere trap.*

"They had to be to do something this heinous," replied Calieb. "Be cautious, they might still be here, whomever they are." The father raised his rifle before proceeding.

Distraught, Shelley looked at her husband. "Outland Rustlers?" she asked.

"No, my dear, I don't think so." He knelt beside one of the dead. "These dead bodies are deteriorated enough for me to know they weren't killed here. Rustlers would have never taken the effort to do this. This is something far more sinister, if you ask me."

Even though he moved with a businesslike purpose, the father had to hold back his emotions when he came across scenes like this. He had a feeling they were not alone. It had less to do with the string of dead bodies they had found and more to do with an eerie scent that electrified the air. Calieb's heart started to beat a little faster as they walked along the deserted street. Perspiration drenched his grasp on the rifle while his mouth became cotton dry. No one could see any emotion on his face, but he felt quite anxious.

His focus intensified and his demeanor changed from a man looking for supplies for his family to a predator on the prowl. *Where are you hiding, you sons of bitches?*

Squawk! Calieb turned quickly down an empty alleyway, aiming his rifle. He was sure he was ready for any confrontation that might occur, but he knew he was a mess inside, trying to hold back the apprehension now flowing through his veins. His heart raced and he was like a bottle rocket, ready to explode and lose control. Nothing seemed to move at first, which only fueled his unabated anxiety. Then, from a group of damaged trash cans emerged two enormous vultures, bigger than he had ever encountered before. The vultures passed overhead, flying out over the main street and toward the west.

The father responded with panic, his breathing became elevated and his grip on the rifle's trip became even tighter, almost firing in the direction of the noise. "That was a close one." He released the tension on the rifle's trigger. He turned to his wife to confirm everything was okay.

In the stir of confusion, Straus ran down the street, yelling and making a lot of unwanted noise.

Calieb wanted to turn and yell at his irresponsible son in frustration, but his wife touched him softly on the shoulder as their son disappeared down the street and out of sight. "I'm sure he will be fine," Shelley said in her usual compassionate and gentle tone. "You know the boy is growing up fast and it can't be helped. He's so curious and wants to explore."

Calieb shook his head. "You know as well as I do that splitting up isn't something the family should be doing, especially after discovering bodies littering the streets like this."

Calieb's wife smiled tenderly. Her smile could always melt his heart. It was like sitting next to the sun, just without the radioactive decay that went along with it. At times, he could see the vibrant woman he had married all those years back. Her beauty could light up a room and the way she handled their children and her maternal touch always made her seem goddess-like. Nothing could touch her dimpled smile. There were times, like these, though, that made her appear worn and void of energy altogether. It always seemed to him it was these long voyages that took all the essence from her. It took nearly all the family's energy to travel across the sandy terrain to reach Sonoma, not including scavenging for usable supplies, which seemed to be depleting quickly. Soon they would have to find a new place to replenish their supplies. This town would soon become void of anything useful so the journeys would become longer.

Calieb watched as Shelley entered what remained of the town's grocery store to collect the dry goods they needed. He waited a moment before heading off to find battery packs for the electric stove.

As she entered the abandoned store, a stench stretched out to her which made her hesitate. Despite having come into this store many times in the past, she hadn't been able to get used to the smell of rotting meat. The sensation always made her nauseated, but she knew that they couldn't afford her getting sick, they had precious little time for any of that.

She moved to the closest storage shelf and started to fill her and the children's backpacks that the family would use to collect canned goods. She inspected each can carefully before placing them into her pack. She retrieved a can and flipped it over. The Corporation's infamous logo struck her with malice. Seeing the shadowy planet image with the star appearing in the background like a peeping tom made her feel unclean inside. Antagonism filled her veins, her cheeks flushed and her hand began to shake.

"Fucking Corporation!" she screamed. "If it wasn't for them, none of us would be in our current predicament." Despite her frustration she tossed the can into one of the food packs.

Shelley reached down to touch a set of dusty prints close to the shelf she was picking the food from. *Fresh tracks*, she thought. *Possibly from a large canine . . . A dog, or worse a wolf or jackal made them. They can't be more than a couple of hours old.*

She now turned toward the exterior of the shop and scanned it the best she could, like her husband had taught her. *We need to get the supplies and go quickly. The appearance of these tracks just complicated things.*

"If my family would listen to me for once," Shelley said to no one out loud, as if she expected the rest of the family to hear her. "We wouldn't find ourselves in extreme situations. We'd be able to avoid troublesome hoodlums like those outlaw rustlers."

Then Shelley turned to her side. "Doria, my dear, help your mother finish gathering the supplies as quickly as we can."

But Doria wasn't at her side, she wasn't even in the shop itself, she had vanished much like her brother had. Shelley's lips pressed together tightly. She was steaming mad and gave the empty shop a venomous look. Her eyes welled up and she wanted to ball her fists.

Calieb emerged, tossing his pack to the ground. He knelt for a moment and tried to catch his breath. "Damn these battery cells are getting heavier each time I retrieve them. They may become the death of me someday." He spots his wife's shadow and looked up with a loving smile. "Dear, I have found the correct battery cells for the stove. These ones were in a cellar and were tougher than hell to get out, but I managed it." He showed the massive batteries to his wife. "This should be efficient enough to get us through the upcoming winter." Each one fit snuggly into his pack.

Shelley's expression didn't change, in fact her arms were crossed against her padded chest and a scowl had emerged on her drained face. Calieb had seen this expression before and it was never one that made him comfortable. "Okay, I have a stupid question," Shelley said. "Where is Doria?"

Calieb stared back at his wife. "Where is Doria? I don't understand the question, my love."

"Yes, where is your daughter? Has she run off again? She was with me before you left and now she has vanished."

He swallowed hard. "Disappeared? This is becoming an awful habit of hers."

Shelley sighed and shook her head. "I can give you a hint on where your daughter has run off to. I know our daughter like the back of my hand."

"Where? Tell me my love," responded Calieb.

"To the most logical place for her in to be in this town, the mall."

⸸

The inside of the abandoned Sonoma mall was dark, damp and possessed several shadows and dark crevasses, even in the robust energy of the midday sun. Wiring hung from the ceiling rafters, exposing the mall's internal makeup. Sand had built up in the corners and in the metal railings that had once supported cheap ceiling tiles. Years of neglect had taken its toll on the mall's interior with no one to perform routine maintenance or look after its well-being. The missing ceiling tiles exposed the heartbeat of the once vivacious mall, with its crawl space and rafters now laid bare. As dark as the mall was now, it would be impossible to tell if something was lingering inside the rafters or in the other dark hiding places within its interior.

Doria searched through the numerous dresses still on their hooks, not giving a care or proper attention to who or what might be watching. All those astonishing dresses were just hanging there for her to sift through them. Each designer dress, every exquisite evening gown, each prom dress—they beckoned her to inspect their fine design and topnotch material. Despite being faded and heavily coated with dust and dirt, they all had a glamorous feel to her. *Have you ever seen such beautiful designs in clothing? I wonder how long they have just been sitting here, waiting to be worn by a woman like myself?*

She picked up one of the dresses, placed it against her chest and spun around like a ballerina, allowing the elongated dress to fan out in the process. Her heart was racing a million miles an hour and she felt elated by the gowns and dresses that waited for her to pluck them. Doria examined herself in the shop's cracked and decayed mirror with a jubilant gaze, imagining she was on Broadway wearing the glamorous purple evening gown as she walked down the runway, littered with celebrities on each side.

The tall thin redhead spun side to side to get a feel how the purple, fringed dress would look on her. She thought about the glamorous actresses that her mother had spoken of. Doris Dalila, Rada Snigir, Alice Naminkovsky-Stone—women she imagined would look amazing in one of these dresses, despite never seeing any of these women for herself.

She imagined herself standing on stage after a play like *Oklahoma, Les Misérables* or even *South by Southwest.* "My dear sir, it's a privilege and an honor to meet you today." She pretended to blush to an invisible suitor. "Why certainly you may escort me to the ball." She let out a fantastic laugh. "But of course, your flattery is appreciated."

She continued to admire herself in the broken mirror and doesn't notice someone approaching from behind. The shadowy figure stopped and watched the girl admire herself in the old broken mirror. Watching her daughter made the mother remember when she was Doria's age, dreaming of exotic places—a time right before the war broke out and the world as she had known it had ended.

Doria was startled by her mother's sudden appearance and spun around to face her vexed mother. Shelley had exasperation written all over her face. Her eyebrows had stretched up toward her sand-filled, disarrayed hair. Doria spun quickly in a moment of dumbfounded surprise, grasping the dress she held against her teenage body.

"Doria, haven't we discussed why you shouldn't wander off by yourself? If I can recollect, about a thousand times already. Just because your brother does it doesn't give you the right to do it also, it's way too dangerous to be playing these games. We never know who may be watching us."

"I know, Mother. We shouldn't be wandering off on our own, but it's been so long since we have come town and look at all these pretty clothes, have you ever seen so many in one place? And all not being used." She sticks her hands out, offering to show her mother the dress she found on the rack.

Shelley grabbed her daughter's hands firmly to agree with her that they were a sight to see. She knew that her daughter would look amazing in one of them. "I'm not saying that any of these dresses would not look fabulous on you, Doria," her mother responded. "Especially the one you have in your arms, it must have taken the maker a long time to create it." They looked back into the mirror and admired the dress one last time. "But we must be going."

A musky smell emerged at both ends of the mall's hallway. The mother recognized the stench; it could only be Outland Rustlers. It wasn't a strong smell, but she would recognize it anywhere. The stench was a filthy, dirty human sweat smell, not the decrepit, decaying metal and plastic of the devastated mall. With no time and nowhere to hide, Shelley knew the only chance she stood was to stand her ground and defend herself and her daughter.

Outland Rustlers were renegade bandits that roamed the desolate plains of the Wasteland. They were known to travel long distances when stalking groups, only to slaughter, steal and rape.

The mother leaped up and pushed her daughter back into the clothing store, yelling at their uninvited guests as she did. "I can smell you from a mile away, it's like you haven't properly bathed in a month." She withdrew a dagger hidden inside her belt loop and held its jagged, cold blade out toward the darkness of the mall's hallway.

"I don't know what you want or what devious things stir inside your mind, but you need to leave immediately. We have an escort party waiting for us that will shred you apart if you harm us in any way," she said. Shelley swallowed hard, realizing how dry her mouth was. She wasn't sure if her bluff would be called or if it might deter the bandits from attacking.

Laughter issued from the darkness of the mall's hallway, like a jackal crying into the night air. A voice bellowed out at the two women.

"That's a very interesting story, missy, but we have been following your party for a while. We know that there is no one else except the man you travel with, the two children and yourself. I don't think anyone will be coming to aid you today," called the rustler's invective leader.

The rustlers emerged from their shadowy hideout. There were three to the left and two others to the woman's right. All of them wore rags and a few still had their own teeth, but all were unshaven and carrying weapons of many different varieties. The men move a little closer to the women, approaching cautiously as if to avoid an ambush emerging from the mall's shadows. Each rustler member exposed their weapon of choice. One carried an Uzi submachine pistol, another had a large machete, while another carried assault rifles. One approached the mother with a lead pipe and the man next to him fondled a set of throwing knives in each of his hands.

Shelley shielded Doria from the approaching rustlers in anticipation of the attack. A few of the rustlers attempted to lunge at Shelley. Doria let out a loud scream.

Meanwhile, outside the mall in the desolate street, the father argued with Straus at the comic book store. The two stopped what they were doing and rushed to see what the commotion was about. While still cradling his rifle, Calieb and his son ran toward the screaming.

Straus said, "That sounds like Doria! I would know that scream anywhere."

They ran into the dusty and deserted building; a figure emerges from a crawl-space panel and out the side of the cracked mall foundation. The young girl ran at full speed toward her family, waving her arms wildly and screaming hysterically. They stopped her and the Calieb set down his rifle and embraced the teenage girl. He pulled her away and tried to calm her.

"Where is your mother?"

"Where did you come from?" Straus asked.

The girl continued to sob, unable to talk without shaking profusely. Her father looked up from his daughter, toward the mall's demolished entrance.

With a sob Doria said, "Men attacked us! Mom pushed me through hole in wall. I ran hard to daylight."

Calieb and Straus stared at the mall entrance a moment and then ran to the entrance as swiftly as they could.

One of the rustlers lunged at the mother with an aggressive stab of his weapon; it missed her shoulder by mere inches. She felt the blade as it nearly caught her shoulder. she slashed the man's wrist with her dagger, forcing him to drop the knife in his hand. Blood trickled from the man's wrist. A second rustler moved in to test the woman's skills. He didn't fare any better than his colleague. This one got his face sliced by Shelley's dagger and he dropped to his knees, yelling and holding his bloodied face.

Shelley retreated, hoping to discover an escape route. Glowing eyes appeared from within the dark corner behind her, merely feet from the fighting.

The Outland Rustler behind her struck the back of her head with the butt of his weapon, forcing her to the mall's dusty floor, unconscious.

Fifteen minutes before the family had entered the mall, from the south loading dock where the old overhead door had fallen in on itself, Clover was hiding behind an old trash bin, watching the ruthless gang readying themselves to corner the two females. He had picked up on their scent as soon as they had entered town. He knew intercepting them would be necessary, but he didn't want to draw undue attention and reveal his presence to the family. That would be bad for his recon mission.

The stocky leader was engaged in a conversion with one of his foot soldiers. "I don't want any harm to come to the adult female. She appears to be healthy and of breading age. She will fit in well with the other childbearing captives we have," the Outland Rustler leader said.

"What of the teenage girl?" the other man asked.

"She is of no concern. You may do with her as you please, just don't make so much of a mess so that it hinders our operation in the region, understood?"

The foot soldier licked his dirty lips. "My what fun we could have with a tasty morsel like her." The soldier saluted his leader and ran off into the darkness of the mall.

Under his breath, Clover responded. "I have to react swiftly if I expect to save the human females. Using them as bait may be the safest course of action for everyone. Well, except for these bandits, of course."

Down the dark corner of the hallway, directly behind the two females, a voice echoed. "It isn't a good day to be a bad guy, at least not in your case," said Clover.

Clover reached into his cloak and retrieved his razor-sharp, four-sided weapon, the same one he had used many times in his assassination missions from Clover's past life. In one fluid motion he threw it in the direction of one of the rustlers engaging with the human female.

One man reached for his automatic weapon with multiple magazines installed. Just as he was about to spray bullets into the new figure's direction, Clover's weapon slices through his wrist. The weapon fell to the mall's dirt floor with a 'thud'. The sound reminded the mother of striking meat with a flesh-pounding hammer. The second man behind Clover approached and started swinging a large machete at the newcomer. The man missed by inches each time and Clover tumbled away on the ground. He recovered quickly, returning to his feet in a fighting stance, ready for the next attack.

The rustler yelled out. "Damn it. I missed him." The man cleaned grime and dust off his already stained clothes.

"I see someone in this mob has some skill, that is good news. I need some practice with live targets, it's been too long," Clover mocked.

The bioengineered assassin threw off the hood of his cloak and brushed the body of his hybrid cloak to reveal his hidden figure. He was relatively stocky and had a muscular physique compared to the Outland Rustlers. Clover stood approximately six foot one and had a broad chest. He wore protective armor on his chest and arms with an assortment of weapons attached to him that included a pair of Katina's. He drew the swords in unison and readied himself to take on any attacker that dared engage him.

"I'm ready for your pathetic attempt. Are you?"

Clover arched one arm, holding one of his Katina's back like a fighting scorpion. With the other he balanced the stance, standing at an angle which allowed him to defend any attack coming toward his front or sides. His back was to a half-collapsed wall, giving Clover some protection from behind.

The rustler with the large machete lunged at him with great force, but it was nothing Clover couldn't withstand. Their weapons clashed together, making a loud sound that echoed all the way down the opposite end of the hallway. The steel of each man's weapon met as the they struggled against one another. While Clover's attention was on the rustler with the large machete, another gang member attempted to attack the assassin. Clover, sensing the surprise attack, reared his powerful back leg and kicked the second attacking man in the chest, which sent the attacker flying down the dark hallway and toward the Rustlers' on looking leader.

The man with the machete tried to use his weight against Clover but all that did was make the assassin mad. "Is that the best you got? You're going to have to make a better attempt if you're want to strike me down." He threw his weight into the man and with his inhuman strength forced the machete away from the rustler, leaving the outlaw defenseless. The rustler looked at Clover, dumbfounded.

Clover holds the blade of his sword at his opponent. The edge of the blade was merely inches from the man's flesh. Even in this dark, dismal place, the well-crafted sword reflected what little light penetrated the cracks in the failing ceiling. The man took a few steps backward and acted defenseless. "Haw man, I didn't sign up with this gang to get myself sliced up."

Clover relaxed his grip on the sword, and motioned for the man to get lost. The scared rustler took a few more steps backward and ran for the exit.

"Come back here, you stupid shit!" The leader watched with an angry look his face as the man flees the scene.

Then the leader of the band of rustlers looked on with unease. He nodded to a rustler in the dark corner adjacent to Shelley's position. With Clover's attention averted, the soldier could sneak up on her. The last remaining rustler got behind the woman and pointed a shotgun to her head, readying the trigger. In one fluid and swift motion, one of Clover's sword blades passed through the back of the man's skull, leaving the soldier limp. He fell to the ground.

The leader started to back into the darkness, trying to flee Clover siege, but something made him stop, Clover wasn't for sure what made the Outland Rustler decide to commit suicide, but it was all for the better of the family, he was sure of that. The leader retrieved the machete laying on the ground and ran in Clover's direction, swinging the weapon wildly. Clover knocked him away, grabbed his throwing weapon and threw it at the man struggling to reach the unconscious woman lying on the floor.

With one final attack, the last remaining rustler moved in on Clover. With his other sword, Clover sliced the rustler from the bottom up, cutting in one motion. The soldier's body split in two and fell to the floor. It was at this moment the woman's family stormed into the dark hallway of the shopping mall. Clover grabbed his cloak and disappeared into the dark.

†

Calieb ran down the dark hallway and saw the carnage. Straus pulled a comic book from his pocket and showed it to his father. "Look, Dad, just like the comic."

Straus showed his father the drawing of Clover fighting off demons and Outland Rustlers at the same time. The sides of the book were charred and somewhat faded, but the artwork was in good condition. Calieb shooed the boy away as he tried to revive his wife. She slowly regained consciousness and he smiled gently at her.

"Welcome back to the land of the living, dear," he said.

CHAPTER 6

On the outskirts of the township of Demure, Deselation moved with awkwardness toward his master's abode. Deselation possessed the ability to cloud human minds, like a dream state from his own mind. He could also see present events by reaching out with his mind.

The inhuman creature reached Legion's lair still panting from his all-out sprint to reach his master in time.

Deselation forced open the heavy steel doors, ones that had been attached to its now rotted, decayed frame. It took great strength to move the mighty double doors but and they creaked as the interior was exposed. Deselation stepped his hoofed feet into the darkness of the hallway before him. A set of red devilish eyes emerged from the shadows and a creature grunted in displeasure. Deselation halted his progression into the dark room for a moment and gathered his courage. Legion wasn't the type that you could go to unprepared; Deselation had learned that the hard way. The shape-shifter had encountered Legion's wrath on more than one occasion and the experience had imbedded itself in his brain.

A deep voice bellowed from the darkness. "Who dares disrupt my meditation?"

Deselation bowed to the darkness. "My master. Forgive my intrusion but it is I, Deselation. I have urgent news for you."

Legion approached Deselation. His behemoth structure overwhelmed even Deselation.

"Go on, instruct me. Tell me what you have seen, Deselation," Legion said.

Deselation rose from his bow and gave his report to Legion.

"Sir. There is a rumor going around that some commotion is occurring in sector seven. In the east corner, the town of Sonoma, sir."

Legion grumbled, displeased. His reptilian-shaped eyes glared down on his servant with fury. Deselation could feel the steaming emotions emanating from within Legion's very soul. Despite his long service to his master, he would never get used to Legion's rage.

"Go on."

Deselation took a deep breath. "Master, he has returned. Or at least that's what the rumors suggest."

Legion emerged from the darkness and grabbed Deselation by his thick, muscled throat.

"What did you just say?"

Legion tensed and lifted Deselation. Deselation couldn't breathe.

"It's Clover, sir, your brother. He has returned from hibernation. But as I said before, they might only be rumors."

Legion released Deselation who slowly recovered from his master's unexpected attack, rubbing his throat and trying to regain his breathing. He looked up at his master's gleaming red eyes.

"Scouts are reporting seeing a human family moving westward, away from the township of Sonoma. It is rumored that Clover moves closely with them."

Legion's giant footsteps could be heard walking back to his throne-like chair. *Little do they realize there is a more sinister shadow waiting in the Wasteland. One that could end all my troubles if I allow it to.* Legion shook off the notion and looked back to his servant.

"Do you anticipate our little trap worked?" The behemoth smiled slightly as he thought of the trap his followers had laid in Sonoma. "I want to know why the family left the town so abruptly."

Deselation nods his massive bull head. "Yes, Master."

"Who do we have in the region?" Legion demanded.

Deselation moved into what little light the doorway let in and unrolled a topography map. He looked it over carefully before responding. Legion leaned over and watched the minotaur-like creature process the information the map offered.

Deselation shook his head, not quite sure how to answer his superior.

"We don't have any assets in that exact region, but Sand Crawler and Blitzkreig are close by."

Legion grunted again, sending chills down Deselation's spine.

"Send them to intercept the family and scout the area. I want to know if these rumors are true."

Deselation bowed his bull head, partly in respect and partly in acknowledgment of the orders.

"Yes, my master."

The disoriented and distressed family made their way for home with the supplies they had gathered from Sonoma. The return journey was just as stressful as the journey there. Darkness was starting to settle in and with the ordeal the family had just encountered with the rustlers and the stranger at the mall, the father kept looking back behind them to make sure no one was following. It slowed the return journey. His wife was shivering and trying to comfort their daughter. Everyone was in shock; they had never experienced such an ordeal in any of their trips to Sonoma before.

Clover pursued the family, but as before he kept his distance. The oncoming night would give him cover to follow the family closer than he had on the way to Sonoma. Night was when Clover did his best work, prowling through the night and stalking victims with cunning and stealth. No other creation of the mighty Corporation did it better. Even after vowing not to assassinate with a thirst for blood, he couldn't stop himself from stalking through the night.

Clover sniffed the hot, arid night air that coated the edge of the deserted Wasteland like a blanket, smothering them. The night might seem vacant, to the naked eye, but Clover knew better. He could smell others roaming around after the sun had set. Despite the near suffocation, Clover could smell each family member's scent. Each one was distinct and it irritated the assassin's noise. He could see them through the dwindling sunlight as dusk made its rapid descent. He had become so accustomed to using his nocturnal senses that it was second nature to him these days. Unlike the time before the fall of society, before the launch of nuclear weapons, Clover relied less on his nocturnal senses and more on his instinctive nature.

Despite the anxiety, he sensed coming from the family, there was one, Straus the young adolescent, that puzzled Clover. Clover had experienced a long range of emotions from his countless victims, but the boy's enthusiasm and playful nature had the bioengineered assassin confused.

He had never seen any human talk to absolutely no one and from watching the child, Straus expected a response from no one in return.

It seemed the boy was speaking to someone, from the bits and pieces of conversation Clover could pick up drifting to him on the air. But Clover couldn't see or sense anyone else among the family. Straus seemed to be talking and conversing with no one. The child even seemed to be having physical confrontations, no matter how playful they might seem, with an invisible entity who Clover couldn't see, hear or sense at all. *Humans. I will never understand them, especially this young child. Who could he be possibly talking to, if not one of the family members in his traveling party?*

Despite their close call with the Outland Rustlers, Straus was filled with excitement and seemed to their pursuer ready for even more. He bounced around like a jackrabbit, kicking up sand and dust as the family retraced their path home. He and his imaginary brother, Yellon, who appeared when Straus was either stressed or excited couldn't keep either of their imaginations from playing tricks on them. Living so close to the edge of the Wasteland and the dangers that came with it, Straus had slowly developed Yellon to cope with the many anxieties that he had to wrestle with.

Straus and Yellon had been on many adventures together, real and imaginary. From all they encountered while in Sonoma, normally an uneventful place to visit, they imagined something was following them home. Back and forth the two adolescent boys kept up their horseplay, shielding Straus from displaying his anxiety. Yellon struck Straus with an open fist and playfully leaped back in to defensive position ready for Straus's retaliation. This was a game they had played ever since Yellon started to appear to Straus.

"Come on, you wuss. Let's see what you got," Yellon mocked. "You wouldn't stand a chance against one of those thugs, so quit trying to act tough."

Yellon lifted his chin, daring Straus to strike him back. Straus raised his fists, but something within kept him from striking. Yellon danced around and played the jester, mocking Straus. Straus gave the imaginary Yellon an angry and irritated look. His eyes became like daggers, sharp and deadly, his jaw muscles frozen in such a way that it looked like he was snarling. Despite his animosity, he couldn't bring himself to attack the unseen member of their family.

Straus's colorful language interested Clover. He had never experienced such colorful terminology before. Of course, he had never followed a human family home either, and had yet to experience the tribulations of adolescents. *The youth and whomever he is traversing with seem to be bouncing around and exposing the family's position, even in the darkness. If I were a predator on the hunt, it wouldn't be difficult to track them with the commotion they are stirring up.*

The commotion Straus was making finally drew the mad glance of the boy's mother. She was already shaken up by their encounter with the Outland Rustlers at the mall, and now the antics of her son were eating away at her last remaining nerve. Her menacing stare made Straus feel miniscule and frail. She rarely got mad at him, despite the teenager's behavior.

Straus staggered away like a drunk, rubbing his arm. In his frustration, he was eager to retaliate, but he hesitated, fearing his mother's wrath. He looked steadily at her, waiting to see her reaction. Despite his growing curiosity of the world they lived in, he ultimately feared angering his parents. His father would be the enforcer, delivering physical punishment for his behavior, but Straus's mother, despite her nurturing nature, could be emotionally draining on him. Once an incident was over, however, he and Yellon would be back to their horseplay, forgetting the punishment their last outburst had caused.

While Straus resisted any type of retaliation, Yellon got another shot in. This time the shot landed on the meat of Straus's right arm and Straus started to rub the area even though it wasn't really bruised at all. Straus fell to the sandy ground and gave a cry of pain. He rolled his protective jacket back, despite knowing that he would get the third degree for doing so and glanced at the make-believe bruise. Once again, the boy's antics drew attention, but this time the entire family had noticed. *I know if I hit him back in retaliation Mom will skin me alive. She isn't in a particularly good mood after the mall incident*, he thought.

Instead Straus cried out, "Oh that was a savage shot, Yellon. You know you're such an ass wipe."

Straus struggled to one knee and that's when the pain shot up his arm. He held it like he had been shot unexpectedly. "Damn that hurt, Yellon. You're such a fucktard sometimes!"

Yellon took Straus's attention away from the horseplay. "Damn bro, did you see all those dead bodies, it was like some sort of nightmarish scene."

Straus looked up at his imaginary brother with disdain. He pulled the comic out and looked at it once more. "Ya, I saw it alright. It's like a scene from the comic. Do you think the legend is true?" He turned to page ten and pointed at a scene with a drawing of Clover and his red glowing eyes with hatred in them, fighting a band of Outland Rustlers.

Yellon shrugged his shoulders. "Beats me. If so I bet Clover killed those people. And maybe he's leading victims into that ghost town."

Straus stood up still holding his arm. "Clover would never do such a thing. He's a good guy, remember?"

"He's a bioengineered assassin, douche!" Yellon went to push Straus over.

Clover's face contorted as once again the adolescent's behavior baffled him. *Why would this child allow such behavior influence his own attitude? What's really going on here that I can't see?*

Straus moved to avoid the attack and fell off a small dune cliff. He rolled a little way down the sandy hillside. Still dazed, he looked up at the family moving onward without him.

The continued commotion finally drew Shelley's wrath. She was still in shock from the attack at the mall, and she couldn't concentrate on where they were or the direction they were headed. Somehow, the fury penetrated through her stoic mask. She removed her sand-coated goggles and shook them off. Her eyes were normally bluish gray but, in her rage, they had become the eyes of a Wasteland demon, ready to pounce on its unwilling prey.

"That's all I can stand!" the mother yelled, making threatening gestures with her exposed fist. Her face contorted and Straus's loving mother was replaced with a demented witch. "If you persist with this horseplay, I will have your hide. Mind me, when we return home you will be working on extra chores until you're an old man."

Straus looked at his brother with rage in his eyes. "See what you have done now? We are both in hot water."

Yellon stuck his tongue out from his dehydrated mouth, then turned around quickly as if he had heard something. Shaking it off, he continued after his family.

Straus continued to watch behind them as they walked closer to home. He had the impression they were being followed.

Yellon tried to get Straus's attention. "What the hell are you doing?"

Straus only shook his head. "I don't know, bro. I keep getting this eerie feeling." He looked back into the fading daylight and watched as the shadows crept up on them.

"Feeling, like what?"

"Like I said, I don't know. But ever since we left Sonoma, I've been having this feeling that someone or something has been following us."

Both teenagers stop and stare into the abyss of the darkening edge of the Wasteland as it slowly disappeared into the abys of darkness. Neither boy can see anything with their trail being conquered by the oncoming night. Yellon shook his head. "I think you're imagining things. The sun's heat must be making you delirious," Yellon said.

"No, man. I'm dead serious about this. I keep thinking something is tailing us and closely."

"Well, we won't be able to tell until this storm blows by. I must admit I have grown to trust your instincts," said Yellon.

Clover had become quite close now. He could clearly understand the adolescent Straus, but still couldn't pick up on whom he was speaking with. Clover continued to mirror the family's footprints, so that he wouldn't be detected or if others had followed the family's trail. They wouldn't know he was following them. Even though the boy kept looking back, Clover managed to stay unseen. Clover's advantage was his ability to see through the massive storm allowed him to keep back without losing their scent.

The family finally arrived at their home, tired and famished from their journey. Clover stayed beyond the home's sight.

Everyone had gone inside except the boy, who had started attending to his chores assigned by his malcontented mother. Stacking wood in the woodshed and preparing to carry back fuel for the evening.

Little does the family realize Clover had followed the family home. It wasn't out of curiosity anymore; he felt that danger was coming. He wasn't sure how he knew this, he just did.

"Man, this shit sucks," Straus said loudly. "See the trouble you've gotten us into?"

He threw a handful of wood into the pile already there.

"Me? It was a mutual decision," Yellon said defensively. "I didn't see anyone twisting your arm."

A frustrated and offended look formed on Straus's face.

"Excuse me, cheese nuts?" Straus said. "It was just as much your actions as mine. See what horseplay always gets us into?"

Yellon threw down an imaginary stack of wood, ready to fight. "Hey, fuck off! You don't need to be belligerent. I don't need any of your shit, are you hearing me, Straus?"

Straus looked around. "I think something is out there. I heard something move over the ridge, in the distance."

He pointed to the southwest corner of the family's property. Yellon walked to stand behind his brother and looked out over his brother's shoulders. He surveyed the scene carefully, but after some searching he only managed to shake his head in frustration.

"I don't see anything, man. I think you're getting skittish on me," Yellon replied.

Straus removed the comic book from his half-empty pack. He flipped throw the comic franticly and then when he reached the page he wanted, he pointed to the graphic drawing of a hooded creature staring back at them with malicious red eyes. It was an eerie drawing, but it seemed to fit the situation and Straus's delusion. The character had red wolf-like eyes, a razor-sharp sword blade, fang-like teeth and saliva dripping from its mouth. The hooded character had his sword leveled at his nemesis.

"Do you see red devilish eyes out there anywhere? Maybe he's come back to finish the job." With a vicious smile, Yellon laughed.

Straus stepped out of the woodshed and headed in the direction he swore the noise had come from. His brother grabbed his arm.

"Are you going crazy or something? You know it's forbidden to venture out after dark," Yellon cried. "Or are you looking for a beating? I get it, you have no fear of the death that lies just beyond the ridge of dunes."

Straus glared over his shoulder at his imaginary brother. "I won't be alone, unless you're scared. Are you coming?"

Yellon followed Straus, a nervous expression plastered on his face.

The two boys approached the area where Straus believed the first noises had come from. They peered into the darkness of the night, but struggled to see anything.

Yellon whispered into his brother's ear. "Can you see anything?"

Straus brushed him off and acted as if he were alone. Inside he wished he was.

A whistling soared toward them from the west and something passed by at a velocity quicker than their eyes could catch. The object that had made the sound sliced through the air, splitting the space between boys and its intended target. A gasp was heard in the opposite direction and a death-defying cry rent the air, unbearable for their human ears. The boys turned toward the direction the object had flown from.

A voice bellowed from the direction they were looking. "I think it's time you went inside now," the voice said.

Clover emerged from the darkness of the night in a phantasmagorical state, with a haze encasing the assassin's physical form—at least that's how Clover appeared to the boys. The boys froze in shock. The figure moved next to them, but was looking in the direction he had thrown his weapon. A loud scream emerged from the darkness, startling the boys.

The boys hastened off towards their home. They turned around one last time, checking to make sure this was real. Clover approached the entity that had let out the banshee cry. A trail of sticky blood ran along the sandy surface and Clover used it to track his injured target. He came across a creature holding its bleeding arm and panting with exhaustion. The creature tried to shield its face from the hunter without success. Clover knew the creature before he saw its face, its scent gave it away instantly.

Clover looked down on his victim with a satisfying smile. It was one of Legion's minions, Sand Crawler. A mutant soldier, Sand Crawler could mutate his arm into a paralyzing stinger, much like a scorpion's tail. Once the stinger pierced its victim it injected poison that acted as an acid. He was disfigured, with one wounded eye—a result of having one too many encounters with Clover in the past.

The two adversaries had battled on the secret moon base with Legion's encouragement. Legion had known Sand Crawler would lose. That fight had caused the injury to Sand Crawler's left hand; it had been lopped off after Sand Crawler had submitted to Clover and, while the assassin's back was turned, he had tried to stab Clover in the lower back. Clover's ability to sense Sand Crawler's movements had resulted in Legion's goon losing a good portion of the hand. The eye was a result from an attack after many of the bioengineered subjects had come to Earth. He wanted to test Clover again, thinking his improved skills might win him Legion's favor.

"Sand Crawler. I knew it was you. I sensed your heat signature and your stench is all too familiar to me," Clover said. "As one of Legion's goons you have a knack for causing havoc along the outer territories, but aren't you a little out of your patrol territory?" Clover leaned down and tossed warm sand on Sand Crawler's wound. "You might want to fuse that arm before it gets infected. You might lose it for good this time."

Sand Crawler gave Clover a jaded, half-hearted grin, one that Clover understood was more for show than purpose. His victim was in extreme pain, but he knew not to trust Sand Crawler; he could be sneaky and conniving, and before you knew it would have you in his grasp.

"Clover. I see you have finally come out of your hibernation to hunt once again," Sand Crawler responded.

Clover brushed off the sand remaining on his cloak. "I haven't had the need to come out, since scum like yourself roam the planet. There's no room for decent individuals like myself any longer."

Sand Crawler laughed and looked down, remembering the nasty scar the assassin had left during one of their many encounters.

"Well, this time things are different, I guarantee you that, old man." Sand Crawler tried to move but bellowed in pain and sat back down. "Soon Legion will control the entire Wasteland and then there will be nowhere for you to hide."

Clover bent down, retrieved his weapon and wiped the green blood from its razor-sharp edge.

"I've heard that many times before, why would this time be any different?" Clover asked.

Sand Crawler looked around for his partner and noticed a shadow moving in on their position.

"Okay, Blitzkreig, let him have it."

Blitzkreig's freakishly huge body appeared out of the darkness. His large frame moved slowly, like a tortoise on hot pavement. The sand sank beneath his massive weight as he moved in to attack Clover.

Clover stood to face the behemoth as it slowly approached his position. Sand Crawler was a decoy, he realized, and the real attack was meant to come from one of Legion's oldest and most reliable soldiers.

"Oh, I see you brought a friend to assist you this time," Clover said.

Blitzkreig removed the lanky black gloves that covered his long bony hands. They had withered to nearly nothing since their last encounter. He used shock waves which generated in his body and accumulate in his hands. A shock wave struck Clover in the chest, knocking him over, onto the sandy ground. After shaking off the effects of the attack, Clover noticed a shadow closing in on him. His sight was still blurred from the attack, making him vulnerable to another strike.

Then, in a surprise moment, a claw was catapulted towards Blitzkreig and struck him in the side. The sound of the claw striking its target echoed in Clover's ear as it thudded into Blitzkreig's side. Clover looked in the direction of the attack with his blurred vision, but all he could make out was a silhouette.

Tigerous emerged from the darkness of the night and approached the slumped Clover. She moved with a grace of a gazelle and the speed of a cheetah. A combination rarely seen even in civilized days. She helped Clover to his feet and gave him a flirtatious smile.

"I knew you would need my assistance eventually, you always have," she said.

Clover's lightning-fast reflexes and his ability to sense the attack just before it happened saved both their lives. The injured henchman had recovered, but still moved with slowness—not that he had ever moved swiftly. Clover removed one of his swords from its sheath and the two adversaries faced each other.

Sand Crawler, still ailing from his wound didn't expose himself totally to Clover. He covered his ailing side and hid his missing arm, the one he used to strike his victims with, afraid he might lose his life for good this time.

"I've been waiting for this opportunity for a long time. I will have my victory dance once and for all when I kill you, Clover."

Clover lowered his sword a moment and with a crooked smile mocked Sand Crawler. "Beware what you wish for. You might regret it in the end."

Behind Sand Crawler and Clover, Tigerous prepared to engage in her own battle against Blitzkreig. Blitzkreig had recovered from Tigerous's initial attack and challenged her head on. The behemoth stood with a slight slump. He pulled out the claw, tossed the bloody weapon to the ground and massaged his wound.

He looked at Tigerous with vengeance in his eyes. "That hurt, bitch."

Tigerous licked her lips with her pinkish tongue and smiled. She batted her eyes at her opponent and placed her hands on her hips. "Next time I'll give you more than a love tap, darling."

She pushed her long dark hair to the side and slipped out another claw from her feline paw. She held it in her hand, poised to strike Blitzkreig again, but this time she was determined make it a death strike. The two engaged one another. Blitzkreig unleashed his chaos weapon, vibrating the ground. Tigerous leaped out of the way just in time, missing the shock waves by inches. Blitzkreig's attack bounced of several rocks nearby and dissipated.

Tigerous countered with grace and quickness, kicking Blitzkreig in the back of the head. He tumbled head over feet. Dazed, he lost his bearings and Tigerous's location for a moment.

Meanwhile, Clover and Sand Crawler continued their duel. Their weapons clashed against one another, creating a god-awful sound in the darkness of the night. Clover slid his sword down Sand Crawler's weapon, shearing some of his opponent's weapon away. Metal shavings littered the ground. He gained enough leverage on Sand Crawler to push him out away, sending the wounded creature to the sandy ground with a hard thud.

Clover hovered over Sand Crawler smiling. "It seems you have failed as usual, Sand Crawler. I have no desire to offer mercy to you except by ending your life."

"You call that mercy, you coldhearted son of a bitch?"

Tigerous and Blitzkreig reengaged one another, squarely facing each other. Blitzkreig released his fury and Tigerous maneuvered out of his weapon's trajectory, another near miss. With one swift motion, Tigerous threw a claw with full force. This one struck Blitzkreig in the meaty part of his throat. The claw dug deep into his windpipe and he fell to his knees. She walked up to her adversary and looked down at him.

"Darling, don't ever taunt a scorned woman. And never call me a bitch."

She took another claw, held the behemoth's head steady and rammed it into Blitzkreig's skull. The monster fell. A gaping hole replaced the claw she had thrown into his throat and creamy goo leaked from each hole in his head. When she was satisfied that the behemoth was dead, she retrieved the claws and wiped the blood from them. She licked some of his blood from his face. It tasted bitter.

"You have too much iron in your diet, hon. Your blood tastes too thick." She walked away from the body.

The battle between Sand Crawler and Clover was approaching its climax. As Sand Crawler lunged at Clover, he tried to use his injured stinger. It was a mistake. The combination of his slow movements from the injury and Clover's swift movements ensured Sand Crawler missed Clover completely. Unbalanced, he fell to his knees, like a man offering his own life to the executioner. He was exposed and at Clover's mercy. A sharp pain spreads across his neck as Clover's blade slices through Sand Crawler's flesh—dead, his body falls.

"Are you hurt, are you okay?" Clover asked.

Tigerous batted her eyes at him. "I'm just peachy, king sugar. Now don't you worry your pretty head on my account now, okay?"

Clover shook his head to clear his thoughts. He was mesmerized by Tigerous's sudden appearance. He hadn't seen her since before he had gone into his so-called hibernation. "Tigerous, what are you doing here? I thought you were prancing around the Wasteland with some of those thugs you hung around with."

"I knew you needed my assistance. But now isn't the time for small talk, we have pressing things to attend to." She passed by him and rubbed his cheek softly.

Searching through the dead's things, not far from the place they had just fought, they discover something unexpected. One of Legion's human slaves was attached to the sandy ground by a chain. He was crawling around to find an escape route, fearful that Clover and Tigerous might murder him.

Tigerous looked over at the human slave who had been left unattended by the Legion's goons. Legion used humans to do menial duties like run intel operations, or as slaves in Demure.

With a sly smile on her catlike face, Tigerous poked at the slave, mocking its predicament. "Now what do we have here?"

Clover flipped the slave onto his side and revealed a recognizable marking on the human. Memories flooded Clover's mind: tattoos on prisoners he was forced to hunt on the secret moon base, before being shipped to Earth—the horrid actions they were forced to do made Clover weak at the knees. The mark was a hexagon with two lines running through the middle of it and two dots on each side. Clover hesitated but attempted to shake off the déjà vu.

"He's one of Legion's slaves. He and his followers use humans to do manual labor and other undesirable work. I can only assume this one is a tracking slave. I have seen other such humans provided to Legion's goons. They are disposable if their masters encounter something that might normally devour their host in the Wasteland."

"I have seen Outland Rustlers use human captives in the same manner, out in the Wasteland." Tigerous gave the human a look like she was pondering killing the slave where he lay. "Let's kill him now so he won't give away our position."

"He might have valuable resources, we need to hang onto him for a bit," Clover said. He looked over at the woodshed; the lights still on.

"We can tie him up in the shed. For interrogation later," he said to Tigerous.

Tigerous grabbed the man by the throat and ignored the man's extensive trembling.

"Come on, turd, we are going to make you quite comfortable for your stay. I think you're going to enjoy our vivacious company."

She dragged the human into the shed and tied him up in its rear. There he wouldn't receive much light at all, but during sunrise the morning rays would rush over the lip of a small window near the front of the shed to wake him.

"Sweet dreams, sugar, don't have any bad dreams, because no one will hear you—or care, as a matter of fact." Tigerous lightly slapped the slave on the cheek.

†

That night Clover had a reoccurring nightmare, one he has unable to rid himself of. The difference between this one and the many others was he knew who the killer was this time.

Inside an enclosed and remote laboratory, on the secret moon base, two bodies lay on separate examination tables. The lab is quiet with no one around except the two bodies. It may or may not be the same lab that Clover and Legion were first created in, the details were too uncertain and the lab too bright to be sure. All the base labs looked the same. White, clean and nearly deserted.

In the distance a soft feminine voice echoes inside Clover's head.

"Clover, it's time to awaken, my dear." Echoed the tinder voice.

Clover opened his eyes for the first time. The light above penetrated his retinas and his sight was blurry. Besides his blurred vision, everything around him was foggy. He had never used his eyes before. Double vision affected his sight and the entire room spun as objects started to merge together. It was difficult for him to make out what was happening inside the lab. He couldn't move, his unused muscles didn't want to comply as he struggled to sit up.

The feminine voice echoed deep in his mind once again. The beautiful brunette in a white lab coat was cleaning his face. Clover looked to his right and into her mesmerizing hazel eyes. She smiled and her attractiveness entranced him. He had never seen anything so wonderful and gentle in his life. But then, had never seen anything before he saw her. He closed his eyes once again and imagined they were in a faraway place.

The room started to spin and the lights that illuminated the lab blended together. Clover passed out.

A good amount of time passed by before he woke. As he adjusted to his new surroundings, his vision became steadily more coherent. He lay on the examination table again, like he had many times before.

A loud scream shook Clover from his dreamy state. He sat up on the inspection table, which amazed him, because he hadn't been able to sit up before now. Two figures struggled across the lab. Legion held the lab assistant from behind, his humongous hands draped around the woman's neckline. She was putting up a fight, but dramatically losing the battle. He truly was displaying his dominance over the human female.

"My brother, we belong together, not with these worthless frail creatures. Join me and we can become gods to these worthless things. I do have to admit though, brother; this one smells sweet. I don't blame you for liking her," Legion said.

Legion smelled Kat's long brunet hair. She tried to pull away from him but with no luck. Legion forced her back to him. Her body slammed into Legion's massive chest.

"Unfortunately, we can't allow them to coexist with us. We will need to eliminate them so they won't be able to halt our progress. We are the evolution they could never hope to achieve," cried Legion.

Legion reached from behind and thrust his fist through her chest. Ketrina Dooling screamed in horror as her blood spilled, then her body went limp and fell to the floor like a rag doll. Clover screamed as he rushed to Kat's body lying on the lab floor. Everything went blurry and quickly went black.

Clover woke quickly from his nightmare in a pool of sweat. He could only lie there; his body was stiff and frozen. The woodshed was still dark, but the sun was slowly starting to rise. He was still trying to catch his breath from the nightmare. He attempted to sit up after what seemed forever to him. Aches extended throughout his body, it was like he had been lying there all his life, but it had only been a few restless hours of sleep. He grunted as he rose to a sitting position. The aches slow subsided and he regained control of his body.

Clover stood up, walked to the entrance of the wood-shed and gazed into the brisk morning air. The sun's early morning rays reflected off his face, illuminating his animal-istic features. No one could see them; he always roamed the plains at night and always wore a hood to conceal is identity. Deep in thought and entranced with his emotions from the nightmare, he did not notice as Tigerous approached him from behind. The night sky dipped below the horizon and dawn began to rear its ugly head in force. She slipped on her soft undershirt, the one that protected her skin from the aging leather pack used to carry her vital supplies. She wrapped her arms around his neck.

She could feel the tension in his neck muscles and leaned her head onto his chest, listening to his steady heartbeat. The rhythmic thumping soothed her and she closed her eyes for a moment before opening them to the rising sun.

Tigerous whispered deep into Clover's ear. "Having more nightmares?"

Clover nodded but said nothing.

"How long has this been going on, Clover?" she asked.

Clover shook his head as if he didn't really know the answer. "Way too long. Longer than I care to admit and I can't seem to get them out of my head."

Tigerous looked at Clover, her face filled with contempt and concern.

"Tell me about this one."

Clover shook his head. "I'd rather not, Tigerous."

Tigerous squeezed his arm tighter. "Was she there? The woman you keep dreaming about?"

Clover gave her a look of uncertainty. Then he realizes who she was referring to. "Yes, she was."

A voice echoed in the back of Tigerous's head. It was the voice of Ketrina Dooling. *Tell him, Tigerous. He needs to know the truth about us—about you, me, everything that happened.*

Tigerous shrugged off the voice in her head. *Go away, Ket. I don't need your reproach persecuting me, at the moment.*

"Did you say something?" Clover asked.

Tigerous looked deep into Clover's eyes and produced a counterfeit smile.

It's time, Tigerous. You can't hide the fact any longer that we are always going to be part of his past. You must be honest with him if you want anything to develop, Kat said.

Tigerous walked a few steps away from Clover so he couldn't hear her mumbling to herself. "Shhhh will you? I've had it up to here with your belligerent behavior. I have enough sorrow to fill the both of us."

Mark my words. If you don't confront your demons and confess to Clover who we are, it will isolate you two even more than you have done so far. You will be made to pay a heavy toll for your atrocious procrastination.

"Ha! This coming from a dead woman."

Not as dead as you will be, if you keep this act up.

Tigerous spun toward Clover who hadn't moved a muscle since she had stepped back to confront her own demons.

"Who is she? Where have you seen her before that you keep dreaming about her?" she asked.

Clover closed his eyes again as the sunlight from the rising sun invaded the space they were standing. He shook his head in response. "I have no idea who she is or what these dreams even mean. I guess it must be from a time I have long forgotten."

Tigerous moved in closer, until their lips are inches apart. "Maybe she was a past flame?"

Clover shook his head. Their conversation was starting to irritate him. "I don't know where all this stuff is coming from, Tigerous. The nightmares, memory lapses, the connection with Legion, it's all a mystery to me. I have so many questions that need answers." He took a deep breath.

Tigerous refocused her attention on his eyes. She was as attentive as a school girl with a crush. She looked down, away from Clover. In a soft and almost low voice she asked, "Will we ever be able to fix us? I mean, I would love to be what we once were for each other. It was something I have never felt since."

Clover gave he a cold and emotionless response. "You know the answer to that. I'm an assassin, even in this thankless hell. I'm a nomadic loner and can't see myself dragging someone through my hellish lifestyle, Tigerous. All we would do is hurt one another again. Take you, fleeing for the Wasteland without even a goodbye. It's those actions that drive the dagger into our hearts and prevent anything going further."

Sadness descended on over her face. "I understand. We were frightened. Heck, I was frightened myself and needed to get away. I knew you would never be held down by me. So I took a chance in the Wasteland."

Clover returned his gaze to the oncoming dawn and the slow-moving daybreak. "I'm sure there is someone that has the answers. We must find this individual or at least find someone that can point us in the right direction. But one thing has become clear—of all the years I have been having these nightmares, Legion is the cause of all the evil that has happened. He is the puppet master behind everything, including the monstrosities against our own kind. He must die, and I'm the only one capable of doing it."

Then it dawned on them both. They looked to the area they had tied their human prisoner. Clover could make out the human form with his infer red sight; the slave was quite smaller than they were, it seemed to be almost childlike.

Tigerous nodded in the direction of the half-asleep human slave. "What about him? I'm sure he knows something."

They moved swiftly toward the semiconscious prisoner. He was tied securely to a wood beam that acted as a support for the old shed. Dried blood covered his lip from when Tigerous had struck him.

Tigerous threw a bucket of cold water on him and he woke abruptly. He struggled to gain full consciousness, still half dazed.

The slave looked up at his assailant, and gave Tigerous a gruesome and twisted expression as he responded to her rude awakening. "Why did you do that?" He covered his head in anticipation of retaliation.

He looked up in the direction of his assailants. Clover and Tigerous emerged from the shadows of the shed and directly assaulted the human to retrieve the information they sought.

Tigerous grabbed the man's throat and started to poke one of her claws into it. "We have questions for you and how you respond to them will determine whether you live or die. Do you understand me, my friend?"

Their prisoner mumbled incoherently and waved his hand wildly in the air. His speech came out garbled and neither Clover or Tigerous could understand him.

Tigerous acted venomously, mocking their prisoner. "What is that? I can't understand you, you're going to have to speak up."

Clover grabbed her hand and released the pressure from the human's throat. "How do you expect him to talk when you won't give him even a little air to breathe?"

Their prisoner started to choke on his own vomit and spat up some blood. He grabbed his throat and rubbed it. Clover looked at their guest impatiently. If he didn't get the answers they had wanted, this could be a very short day for the slave.

"Okay, my friend, it's time for you to start talking. I can only hold my confidant at bay for so long."

Clover took a deep breath and wiped the sweat away from his eyes.

"I have questions and I'm sure you either know some of the answers or know someone who can answer them."

The man looked up and nodded his understanding. "Okay, I'll attempt to answer you as best I can," the slave responded. "But I can't guarantee that I have the answers you're searching for or if I even have the answers you want."

Clover gave him a deadly stare for what seemed an eternity to the human.

"Where does our species come from? I have a need to know this and you need give me this information—I am certain you have this information."

The human slave started to get nervous. He wasn't sure if he could answer Clover's question. He shook his head. "I don't have the answer to that question."

Clover drew nearer the human and a stern look appeared on his face. "You better answer me, slave," Clover demanded. "I don't have the patience for game playing. I will ask you one more time."

Clover took a few steps backward and the slave saw Tigerous sharpening one of her claws.

"Then answer me this. What is Legion and why is he so drawn to me?"

The slave looked up at Clover, frightened. Once again the human slave could only shake his head. "I don't have that answer, either. I don't know any of these things that you are asking of me. I am merely a slave." He shook his head in disbelief at his captor's questions. "What makes you believe that I have these types of answers?" the slave asked.

Tigerous leaped at the slave and furiously grabbed his face.

"You little fucker, we know you can access resources to answer our questions. We know slaves get close to Legion and his goons, despite your lowly status."

"You must have overheard your master talking about our origins, how we became who we are. I know he has this knowledge, I feel it within him," Clover said.

The slave started to tear up, afraid for his life once again.

"Man, I don't know anything of the sort. The only individuals that have that type of knowledge would be Legion himself and the one they call Master Reinhart."

Tigerous and Clover look at one another.

Tigerous grabbed the slave's face and started to squeeze. "Who's that supposed to be, my little pet?"

Their prisoner grabbed for his head protectively, like a child trying to avoid being beaten. Tigerous let go just long enough for the slave to speak.

"He's human, if that's what you want to know. I have no idea who he is, but he seems to have Legion on some sort of leash. It's like he has something over Legion that he can't break." The human rubbed his head for a moment. "Come to think of it, there might be one other that can answer your questions."

Tigerous glared at him. "Well? Spell it out, little man, we are waiting. You must think we have all day to sit around and tell stories." She turned to Clover. "Let me rough him up a little. That will loosen his tongue."

"The only other person that might be able to help is a scientist," said the slave. "Legion and his goons call him Preist. He lives within a research laboratory on the outskirts of San Francisco."

"Where exactly is this scientist?" Tigerous demanded.

"I traveled with Legion and his goons a couple of times to visit him. Preist has assisted Legion on several occasions. He's the only one that Legion doesn't threaten, at least not physically—that only makes Preist shut Legion out, which is the last thing Legion wants."

Tigerous's fury started to mount.

"With what? How does this Preist assist Legion and his goons?" she asked.

The human slave got to his feet slowly, wobbling like a drunken sailor. "He does several things. He is currently assisting Legion, repairing his DNA. A portion of his DNA is slowly morphing and he may never be able to shape back into his original fleshy state once the defunct portion of his DNA overtakes that part of it. This comes from conversations I have heard on the many expeditions they have used me for. I can break into many types of places—they decided to enter my DNA into the archived databases so I know can access many places Legion's goons don't have access. His DNA has a defense mechanism, and over time his transformation damages the structure of his DNA. You do know that he can turn his own skin into a samurai suit of armor, right?"

Clover inched closer to the slave.

"That's something that we didn't know," Clover said. "You said you have access to all the secured databases but Legion doesn't?"

"No, he made sure he did, but some places were encrypted before the fall of humanity. Only Preist could encrypt my DNA into some of these older structures. Many of Legion's lackeys don't have this access."

"How can we trust this little twerp? How do we know he isn't lying to save his hide?" Tigerous said.

"He also built an energy shield for Legion, so that none of your kind can invade the town he runs. He manipulates all those mutants under his control."

"Why are you telling us this? Can you really take us there?" Clover asked.

Straus appeared from the shadows of the barn doorway. His thin frail frame reflected the new day approaching. He held something in his hands and smiled at the slave. He passed Tigerous and Clover and knelt beside the prisoner. He placed a bowl of food he had stashed away from dinner and a water skin next to the recovering man.

"This is for you, eat up. I know you are starving, I can see it in your eyes."

The slave rummaged through the food Straus had placed in front of him while still staring at the adolescent child.

"What is your name?" Straus asked.

The slave hesitated a moment then said, "Schmidt, Joachum Schmidt."

Straus offered his hand. "My name is Straus, nice to meet you." Straus turned to Clover and Tigerous. "I knew you were following us." he said with a quirky smile.

"You're not scared?" Tigerous asked with a soft tone.

Straus shook his head. "Nope. I'm a big boy. I have adventures all the time. Well, me and my brother."

The slave looked at Tigerous and Clover, then back to the boy standing between him and his captors. He wouldn't be harmed if the adolescent boy was present. He straightened himself and wiped crumbs from his shirt.

"Ya, I suppose I could take you to him, but he isn't keen on seeing people. He's kind of on the shy side and dislikes surprises," Schmidt said. "Hell, what else do I have to lose?"

The slave stood up and shook his limbs from their numb slumber.

Tigerous leaned over toward Straus. "Straus, that's your name, correct?"

The adolescent nodded.

"I need you to do something for us. You need to convince your family it's not safe to live here anymore. You have to convince them that we are here to help them and we are going to take them to a safer place, do you understand me?"

The boy smiled at Tigerous, but gave her an untrustworthy grin behind the smile. "How can I be sure you're telling the truth?" He looked at Clover. Clover nodded back at the child. Straus looked at Schmidt. "Okay, but I have to warn you, my parents aren't the trusting type. It will take some time to convince them to just pack up and leave our home. They won't totally understand the reasons behind your assumptions. They don't know you like I do."

Straus ran off to the family hovel.

The slave's attention drew back to his captors. "You do realize, by helping you Legion will kill me for sure this time. Heck, I realize If I don't help you, you're going to end my life as well, correct? What wonderful choices I have to decide from."

CHAPTER 7

It was about six months, before reuniting, in their battle against Sand Crawler and Blitzkreig, Clover and Tigerous had departed and traveled their separate paths. In an act of impulsiveness, Tigerous decided to attach herself to a renegade group that was hunting down Outland Rustlers in The Wastelands. These renegades were more scavengers than mercenaries, searching of Rustler to intimidate and exterminate.

These renegades were a small outfit, mostly with little or no combat training or experience. The other members, excluding Tigerous, had only been on the receiving end of the Outland Rustler's incursions. Many of Tigerous's scavenging comrades had been victims of these raids, with a few them losing wives, children, friends and others close to them. Then there were the few loners in the group that had obtained the skills to survive in the Wasteland. These individuals possessed the skills to fight with bladed weapons and on the rare occasions they stumbled onto firearms.

A few of these encounters they had with the outlaws of the Wasteland had turned lethal and bloody. These encounters had had alerted the Rustler leadership of their presence in the Wasteland, which led to the Outland Rustlers now beginning to prepare for them. There was even a hit squad of Rustlers tracking them down. Poorly if you asked Tigerous. She could always smell them when they became too close.

Tigerous and her band of 'unique individuals', as she liked to call them, had come across an abandon Outland Rustler's camp in the west region of the Wastelands. Tigerous and her newfound friends began to scavenge through the remains of the Rustler camp. The rag tag group had been hitting some of the outlaw camps along the *Barron Crease Ridge*, leading up to western most plains of the Wasteland, attempting to cripple their attack efforts on human settlements.

They had been quite careful not to leave any traces that would lead back to them or evidence that would point towards their involvement. This was going to be a safety issue, if they started to become sloppy in their sieges. The last thing their little group needed was a concentration effort from the Rustler's elders gathering their forces together to trace them down. Then their efforts would truly be in vein.

In the process of raiding these mobile Outland Rustler camps, Tigerous and her band of merry men scavenged for anything useful. Recently they had come across many of these abandoned camps, as if the outlaws had just decided to leave everything behind. They had left no trace of where they had gone or why they had left in such a haste, without packing up their gear, it wasn't like them at all. The outlaws left no scent to track or trails to follow. Camp tents were in good condition for being out in the Wasteland, with the normal wear of sandstorms beating against the hide tarps of the tents. There were no signs of disturbance. The weapons were stacked in a uniform style, seemingly undisturbed.

A single trail of smoke appeared in the distance. Tigerous had spotted it first, since it was easier to smell the smoke from the distance than for her companions seeing it from a far. The intensive Wasteland wind was blowing in the opposite direction and it seemed to be a lesser factor. Tigerous took three scavenging companions and moved toward the origin of the smoke, leaving the others to the scavenging effort. They took a careful approach, as Tigerous was trying to visualize any ambush that might occur along their path.

Tigerous sniffed the dense, stale air to pick up any scent to lead her in discovering the origin of the smoke, but the wind coming out of the west gave her nothing to go on.

Tigerous's animalistic senses were warning her to stay away. But even with paranoia settling in and she wasn't sure why her senses were bombarding her, she hadn't seen any signs of danger, to this point. The group continued onward. Still Something just didn't seem right and, to be honest, *I should listen to my senses. They're driving me insane.* She looked back at the three men following her lead. *Something is warning me that danger seems close at hand, but nothing appears wrong at all. Not even my sense of smell is picking anything up, so why do I fear what we are about to unleash in our discovery?* Tigerous's head began to pound and her limbs began to receive a tingling sensation, something she thought was bizarre. She readied my claws as her muscles tensed.

The source of the smoke was the dying embers of a fire. A strange, cloaked figure sat with its back to the approaching guests. Tigerous had never seen the likes of the figure in all her time scavenging throughout the Wasteland. Warnings were ringing ever so loudly and from this unknown figure, as all her senses were in alert status. The unknown figure refused to face the newcomers or even acknowledge their arrival. These bizarre actions warned Tigerous even more and she removed one of her claws and held it tightly in the grip of her feline hand. Tigerous took a deep breath and thought, *I am ready for anything.*

The scavengers slowly approached the figure, but still their presence didn't stir the figure one bit. The figure was humming a god-awful tune and just sat there, crouched next to a now-dead flame. Without turning around the creature spoke in a sinister, mocking tone.

"It's about time you came to me. I have been waiting for you for a while, my dear. I was starting to wonder if you would ever get here," the cloaked creature said.

One of Tigerous' traveling companions responded with a, "What?" and looked at the rest of us with a perplexed expression.

Before they were aware of it, the cloaked figure leaped from its crouched position, faster than anything Tigerous had ever seen before. *Not even Clover's speed seemed to compare*, she thought. In one fluid motion, the ultra-fast figure reached beneath its cloak and retrieved a throwing weapon, one that seemed familiar to Tigerous. The figure propelled the weapon at one of the scavengers. The aero-dynamic weapon soured gracefully though the air, slicing through the dense air. All Tigerous could do was track the weapon's path of destruction with her feline hearing. The whirling sound the attack weapon made as it spun end over end towards its intended target.

The weapon managed to fly over Tigerous' right shoulder, just missing her by inches. She felt the weap-on's blade pass over, as a slight surge of wind from the weapon's aerial oscillation. It sundered the scavanger's head clean off. His head plummeted from the scavenger's shoulders and toward the figure now facing us all. All the scavengers, including Tigerous, were shocked by the sudden attack. Suddenly, everything became disorientated and silent to Tigerous, she couldn't hear a thing.

Before any of the scavengers could retaliate, the figure disappeared into thin air, like some magician, leaving only a small indication behind that he had even been there. They all stood around dumbfounded by the chain of events, not knowing how to respond or what was going on at all. Emotionally, Tigerous felt as if it all had been a bad dream, but her feline senses informed her differently. Little did we realize we were being set up to be slaughtered.

They looked to the north, but the disappearing figure wasn't there, then to the south, but again there was no sign of their silent assassin. It had a familiar style and flair, that Tigerous knew all too well, but she instantly knew it couldn't have been the infamous Clover. She knew for a fact that Clover was prowling the western dune slopes in the South-Western quadrant of the Wasteland. Too far from their current location, for it to be Tigerou's friend. She also knew that Clover didn't have the ability to suddenly disappear into thin air. Tigerous sniffed the air. *It can't be Clover, I would be able to smell his presence and I've got nothing to go on.* It was like their silent assassin just didn't exist. But she knew better. She looked down at the dead scavenger's body and chills ran through her entire body.

Then, as the numbness was fading away from her, the dark assassin reappeared behind one of the remaining scavengers. It thrust its arm straight through him like he was a Paper Mache doll. Blood and organs started to fall from the extensive wound. The assassin's victim fell to one knee as Tigerous watched his essence flow from him rapidly. The scavenger's hazel eyes slowly turned dark and grey.

Tigerous' heart nearly halted, as her altruism reach out to the dying scavenger. A tear formed in the corner of her eye, making her feline vision blurred. Screams resonated from every direction snapped her back and Tigerous wiped the tear away. She concentrated her attention on their disappearing assassin, but still struggled to track him, as he faded in and out of sight. *I will avenge you. Your death won't be in vein.* Tigerous proclaimed.

Tigerous prepared one of her throwing claws, aiming just above the assassin's frontal lobe, then she got a glimpse into the assassin's hood. There was no face, just a darkness where the face should have been. All the same, Tigerous could still feel the figure smiling back at her, despite having no mouth to do it with or at least none she could see. *I must do this as swiftly as possible, before this assassin decides to disappear again.*

She hesitated for one moment, then released her clawed weapon.

Tigerous' razor-sharp claw soared through the air like an ICBM, cutting through the air, without wavering one bit. It all seemed to move in slow-motion for Tigerous as her weapon moved expeditiously toward its intended target. She held her breath in anticipation. *It's going to do it!* She screamed inside her mind.

But just as before, the figure vanished, leaving only its hazy residue behind. The claw sliced through the cloud that the assassin had left behind. Tigerous could only stand there in her astonishment. "Damn it I missed." She mumbled to herself.

Tigerous spun around in disorientation, unable to react to the continued slaughter. She watched in a panic, horrified by the scene that played out in front of her.

One by one, each party member was murdered in the same gruesome manner. Tigerous wanted to intervene, but she seemed to be helpless to prevent the total annihilation of her scavenging companions. She had become engulfed by her anguish negligence. *I am aghast at this malevolent assault on my scavenging companions.* She wasn't sure what to do next. Heck she couldn't even track his movements outside when the invisible assassin would appear to kill his victim

Tigerous' heart began to beat profusely and her head started to spin out of control. Then her heart began to beat faster. She questioned the reasoning behind the maleficent assault. *Why is this mystical being doing all this? What have we done to deserve such an abominable fate?* Then the mysterious voice of the assassin snapped Tigerous out of her semi-hypnotized state.

"You don't realize how long I have been awaiting this moment, Tigerous. You have truly made a reputation for yourself out here in the Wasteland, haven't you? It will be sad to see you die under my blade, but all good things must come to an end."

Without giving the assassin an opportunity to strike her dead, Tigerous made a split-second decision and sprinted for a sandy hillside close by. Her hope was that it might provide a glimmer of shelter if she could reach it in time. Tigerous' agile advancement, kicked up sand in her flight to safety. She didn't dare look back, but she could sense that the disappearing assassin was in pursuit. The closer she came to the hillside the more she felt the doom advancing on her. *I have to make it to the hill or my life will end as abruptly as my travel companions 'lives have.*

Just as she had reached the dune hillside, she felt the presence of the shadow assassin at her heels, but refused to look back into its desolate form.

Then, from somewhere above, a burst of energy exploded from the hillside with a loud eruption, as if the hilltop had opened and in a rage of disapproval struck the assassin dead in the chest. The strike sent shards of the assassin's chest plate in every direction, exposing his location. Tigerous' noticed, as the assassin tumbled back down the dune hill, he had been right on her heels.

She had peeked out of the corner of her eye, and witnessed the assassin's dense semitransparent chest plate explode for herself. The dark exterminator gave an agonizing scream, one Tigerous would never forget. The assassin's scream was so terrifying it would echo in her head unopposed for a very long time.

Once she had reached the very edge dune hill, she saw a lone figure staring down at her with astonishment in its bright eyes. He held a staff in one hand and was dressed in a dingy smock, which seemed no more than pieces of shredded cloth crudely threaded together. It covered the individual like a priest's smock, but the difference in the figure's smock was it protected him from the harsh living environment.

His voice boomed as he spoke. "Come out of from the open, you will be safe inside."

The tall hooded figure motioned towards an opening in a rocky mountain side, covered in sand.

Tigerous took one more look back at the place where her attacker had once stood. The cloaked assassin had vanished once again, but something inside of her felt the assassin hadn't died in the energy strike and she would no doubt see him again.

†

Tigerous entered the cave, despite her apprehension. It was surprisingly warm despite the lack of a heat source. It was obvious to her that her savior had been living there for some time. There were a few things scattered throughout the visible portion of the cave. There wasn't much light, apart from the light entering the cave's entrance. It was dark and dismal inside the cave, but there wasn't a sense of malcontent that you might think from such a gloomy dwelling. Instead there was a feeling of melancholy surrounding the place.

There wasn't much to the cave's interior, outside of it being rocky and uninviting. Outside of the darkness of the cave the deeper you moved into its interior, only light that existed was illuminating from Tigerous's host. These was something unusual about it that Tigerous just could put her finger on. It looked foreign, not from this world.

Why does that staff seem so much out of place? If this staff isn't made from human hands, then where did this individual get it from? She wondered.

The individual set his staff down against an adjacent stone wall. With her excellent night vision, Tigerous looked past the flickering camp light reflecting off the surface of the staff. Even though the object wasn't in the range of the camp fire, she could see the staff as clear as day. The staff seemed to be made of a composite material—not quite metal, but something similar. But even the material of the staff seemed more alien than not. It was peaking Tigerous' curiosity even more. The shaft of the staff seemed to be smooth, but with a sturdy design. The surface of the staff seemed to be worn, with many scrapes and indentions along the shaft. The staff head came to an oblong tip made and an addition loomed lower than the tip of the staff.

The tip end was still glowing, like all the energy hadn't dissipated from it totally.

"The energy blast must have come from that tip, because nothing else makes any sense. Hell, that doesn't make much sense either." Mumbled Tigerous.

All she could do was readjust her eyes and shake her head.

Then Tigerous' host sat down, turned and faced Tigerous with a gentle smile. He had turned back the hood of his smock and that's when she looked into her host's tragic, sad eyes. Her host stared at her with a simple smile. It was her long-lost friend, Quasar! She was in a state of total shock. Quasar offered her something to eat that smelled and looked like fish, but she knew better. There were no longer any major water sources on Earth to house any fish species.

"'My dear Tigerous, how have you been? It's been such a long time since we have seen one another," he said.

Tigerous swallowed whatever he had offered her swiftly, which tasted harsh but salty all the same. She was still astounded by his impeccable timing. "Quasar, I haven't seen you since we arrived on Earth, after the prison break. How have you survived so long alone, out here?"

He gave her little emotion in his expression, something Tigerous remembered being a characteristic of her long-lost friend. She had become accustomed to before their abrupt departure from one another. "I get by. Speaking of getting by, how have you come to find yourself so far out here? It's a dangerous place even for the likes of us. You're fortunate to have survived the Shadow Agent's attack," he said.

"Shadow Agent?" She asked.

"Yes. The Shadow Agent roams these parts, creating terror among the Wasteland's inhabitants, but I think ultimately he is searching or waiting for the final battle."

Tigerous couldn't quite believe my ears. What was her long-lost friend telling her?

"Quasar, I'm not following you."

"'There is a storm coming, Tigerous. One that will not only place the humans' existence in jeopardy, but our kind as well."

Quasar paused for a minute, as if recollecting his own thoughts.

"Legion is mounting an attack against the humans to wipe them out." He continued. "He is also believed to be mounting a similar campaign against those that oppose him. But he isn't the only threat to our kind. There is another, a much more powerful entity observing from a distance. Most likely the Shadow Agent's master."

"Tigerous dropped the remaining food in her feline hand. 'How do you know this?'

"I have spoken to Preist on several occasions."

"Preist?" She gave Quasar a blank stare of confusion.

"Yes, Preist. He is one of the most intelligent and reliable of our kind. He will be one of our biggest assets, and a close ally in the coming war." Quasar reached over and lightly touched Tigerous on the shoulder, like a parent to a lost child. "There is only one way to defeat Legion and his quest. Clover is the only one strong enough to defeat him. In this, he will need reliable allies like you, myself and Preist."

Tigerous stood up and brushed herself off. "So, you will join us in our fight against Legion?"

"No. My time for intervention has not yet arrived. There will be a time for me to emerge and join the fight. But it isn't for me to intervene in this fight between brothers. Trust me when I tell you this is your place to make a stand. Mine is yet to come. Now go and seek out your former mentor. He will need allies, and quickly."

Tigerous stared out of the cavern entrance into the dying sunlight.

"Very well, Quasar."

Mount Vernon, Washington
While Tigerous was combating the Shadow Agent in the Wasteland, a band of Legion Followers including

Zeus, Quartz and Black Widow hunt down the last remaining members of the wanted Wolf Pack. The Wolf Pack had fled up the Pacific Coastline blending into the mountains. But one by one the allegedly last of this renegade gang had impeded Legion's authority and executed their leadership's objectives flawlessly, perished in their ditch effort to flee. The dwindling numbers of the Wolf Pack each died alone, in their own separate confrontation with Legion's bounty hit squad.

The wind had picked up, while Zeus led the squad into the rocky layer. The behemoth gorilla waddled up a rocky ridge and looked out from behind a partially devastated boulder. His enormous gorilla eyes transfixed on the entrance to the mountainside hideout. Two Wolf Pack guards blocked the squad's path in collecting their bounty.

Quartz leaned out from their camouflaged position and hastily scans the situation.

"This will not be any cause for alarm, comrades. I will touch these poor souls and toss them aside."

Quartz started to leap out from behind the boulder, but Black Widow seized his arm before he could compromise their position.

"I'm in charge here or have you forgotten?"

Zeus gave a monotone grunt and looked back at the two guards with steadfast stare.

"Legion left me in charge and we will go about this in a stealthy manner, not drawing more undue attention on ourselves than is necessary. Am I understood?" Bellowed Black Widow.

Zeus didn't bother looking back at her.

"Neither of you are combatant trained, neither of you should be in charge." Mumbled Zeus. "Screw this, I'm tired of procrastinating."

Zeus let out a ferocious roar and leaped out at the two Wolf Pack guards.

The sudden attack took the two Wolf Pack guards by surprise and they hesitated for just a moment. Zeus struck his gargantuan fists against his even greater chest, in a display of rage. He flashed his primordial canines as he let out a second roar. Legion's loyal sergeant launched at the wolf pack guard, soaring into the air with his colossal arms spread out wide and slammed the wolf pack member into the rocky wall behind them. The attack knocked the spear weapon out of the wolf pack member's grasp and shook the very ground beneath them both. Zeus's larger-than-life strength nearly killing the guard in one swoop striking his gargantuan fists into the wolf pack's chest.

The guard's eyes turned upward, as Zeus grabbed the wolf pack guard with both hands and started to choke his adversary.

The other guard responded, raising his weapon to strike the gargantuan Zeus down.

Quart leaped to Zues's aid just as the wolf pack member was about to strike the humongous gorilla down.

Quartz screamed, "Die Wolf Pack, die!"

The guard stopped in mid-attack and met Quart's surprise attack with a 'Clash'.

"You idiots." Mumbled Black Widow.

Quartz and the second wolf pack guard struggled against one another, with the wolf pack member winning majority of the struggle. Quartz slapped away the pointed edge of the guard's weapon and freed himself from the wolf pack member's vicious attack. Quartz stepped closer to his adversary and the guard's razor-sharp edge of his weapon slashed into Quartz's side. Blood started to flow from the wound expeditiously. Quartz grabbed his wound and nearly fell to the ground in a sharp, agonizing pain.

As the wolf pack guard raised his weapon for the killing strike, something punctured the guard's canine flesh from behind. The guard's canine eyes rolled up and foam started forming in the wolf pack member's sagging mouth. The guard fell to the ground, dead before he hit the rocky surface. Black Widow was wiping canine blood from her stinger, when Quartz looked up at her with an enraged scowl on his face.

"To inform you, I had that completely under control. I could have beaten his ass without your assistance." Quartz said with a forceful tone.

Black Widow gave him a sly smile. "Sure, you would have darling." She patted him on the side of his bronze cheek.

Zues had the first guard down on his knees.

The wolf pack member slapped at Zeus's humongous forearms as Zeus continued to choke him.

"Do it Zeus!" Screams Quartz.

"Do you mind finishing your duty asap big guy. We have more paramount things to accomplish." Huffed Black Widow.

Zeus turned to Black Widow with a ravenous expression on his primate face.

"Shut up Black Widow." Returned Zeus in an angry manner. "Neither of you have honor within you. You wouldn't understand respecting your opponent or giving them an honorable death."

"Whatever. Just get it over with." She sniffed at Zeus.

A cracking sound.

Zeus lays the wolf pack member's head softly on the ground and a sorrow expression appears on his solemn face.

"I am truly sorry."

"Good, you are finished. Now can we get on with our duties." Mocked Quartz.

The inner dwelling of the subterranean hideout was surprisingly lit. The three visitors moved with caution deeper into the dwelling. Torch flames were lit all around the chamber walls, making the environment warm inside, not just well illuminated. The three visitors see a man well siting on a make-shift throne made with wood, stone and other material. Three Wolves of War sit around the base of the throne. He is lightly stroking one of the wolves' heads, as it stays subdue.

"Wolves of War." Mumbled Zeus.

"I thought they were just a myth." Whispered Quartz.

"Apparently not." Returned Black Widow.

Quartz. Sized up the three colossal wolves. He gave a mystified stare that told Zeus that Quartz was shocked by the mammoth size of the creatures. Quartz especially seemed mesmerized by their exceptionally prodigious heads, which could engulf Quartz's upper torso inside their substantial canine mouth. Then there were the razor-sharp teeth enveloped within their mouths. The substantial size of its paws, which nearly matched Quartz's own hands. Let alone the vastness of the rest of the Wolves of War body, which Quartz had no measure to judge at all.

The human host also witnessed the bewilderment in Quartz's inhuman eyes and gave the hesitant visitor a devious smile.

"Impressive, aren't they?" Bellowed the human. "They are excellent trackers and they can smell a scent from miles away. But my favorite attribute of theirs are their gargantuan size, making them excellent protectors."

"Where in the hell is King Rue?" Shouted Quartz. "Legion is far from thrilled with the Wolf Pack and there is a price on the King's head."

Zeus noticed the wolf closest to the human, the one the man stroked its head, ears stood erect, as if it heard something that grabbed its undivided attention. The colossal wolf was growling at Quartz under its breath. Zeus could sense its protective nature and it understood the visitors may become hostel towards their master.

"Tone your voice down." Hissed Black Widow. "Do you want us to be torn to shreds?"

The human glared at Quartz and his companions with a sinister smirk on his face. None of them could see the human's eyes. They were shielded behind a set of dark Gargoyle shades.

He looked down at the wolf lying at his feet.

"The wolf pack use to use them to track down prey. But that was when they were servants under the tyrant Legion's command. But his treachery against them exposed Legion's malcontent, even against his own kind. King Rue then finally understood what was coming for the wolf pack. If he had sought us out before hand, he would have known way before then. Pity."

Quartz pointed a finger at the human. "Where in the hell is the good king. Tell us now and quit stalling."

All three wolves stood up and were in an aggressive stance.

"Oh, be very careful my friend. They sense your aggression and might thrall you at any moment." The human looked at each visitor with interest. "King Rue is far from any threat. I am here to…" The human thought for a moment before answering in a condescending manner. "Entertain you."

"Who are you?" Questioned Black Widow.

The human took off his shades and exposed his glazed over eyes. He smiled at their exasperation.

"I am a seer. I was born this way and I'm neither human nor your kind. You could say we are a freak of nature." The seer started to giggle softly. "We witnessed Legion's treachery long before it ever happened, but the good king didn't want to heed out warnings. I saw you coming while you exterminated many of King Rue's people. He is no longer your alley. An asset Legion can no longer manipulate."

The three of them stood there looking at one another, unsure what was being told to them.

"Enough of this riff raff. You're going to tell us what we have come all this way to discover." Boomed Zeus.

At Zeus's bellowing, the closest Wolf of War launched itself at the enormous gorilla. Closer the oversized wolf came towards Zeus, with its mouth wide open, exposing its razor-sharp teeth, as Zeus stood his ground, bracing for the confrontation. Zeus snatched the gargantuan wolf's super-sized snout, with its mouth wide open. Zeus used his primate hands to separate the wolf's mouth, before the hulking wolf could take a bite out of him. Zeus had one hand on the top of the wolves mouth and the other at the bottom, preventing it taking a humongous chunk of flesh and fur from him.

Zeus struggled against the Wolf of War's jaw strength, keeping the wolf from closing on him and swallowing a portion of his hands.

The immense power of the wolf pushed Zeus backwards. The wolf lunged at him, with its powerful paws as it attempted to force Zeus's leverage from him. Zeus would pull the wolves' head one way, then it would flip its head back in the opposite direction, trying to wrestle free of Zeus's mighty grip. Each time the enormous wolf would lunge at Zeus, as if it was still trying to get to him, even in the predicament it was in.

Zeus pushed the gargantuan wolf back in the opposite direction, keeping himself from being pinned against the rocky wall and the mighty wolf itself. Zeus grunted and shoved the wolf's mouth away from his primate body.

"You have foul breath, you mongrel." Bellowed Zeus.

The Wolf of War attempts to snap its jaws shut, chopping his hands clean off. But Zeus and his mighty strength halted the beast. Zeus gave the barbaric wolf's mouth a harden jerk and ripped the wolf's upper and lower mandible apart, killing the creature instantly. Zeus tossed the limp, dead wolf's body to one side.

Quartz was struggling with another wolf. He was pinned to the ground by the Wolf of War struggling with him. Black Widow had dispatched the third wolf with ease, its dead body bleeding on the rocky surface. Black Widow was wiping the wolves' blood from her stinger as she made her way to rescue Quartz.

Quartz's wolf was clawing at him and its helpless victim could do very little to defend himself. The wolf cut Quartz on the side of his midsection and Quartz let out a massive cry. The bronze man lie their ready to be dinner for the gargantuan wolf. *I must help Quartz, despite his annoying mannerism, he is still under my protection. But I'm too far away to assist. He'll be dead before I reach him.*

Then the wolf started clawing Quartz again and the Wolf of War moved on him. Just before the wolf was about to have its meal, it stopped its pursuit and fell onto Quartz. It was dead. Blood poured out of every hole in its colossal head. Black Widow wiped more blood from her stinger, like it was a daily routine for her. Quartz struggled to lift the heavy body of the Wolf of War off and Zeus decided to lend a hand.

"Your welcome, little man." Black Widow snorted.

Zeus turned violently to the human and snatched him from the throne and lifted him so that they were eye to eye. Zeus squeezed the human's windpipe but not hard enough to choke him to death.

"Tell us where the hell is King Rue. He will pay for his insolence."

Zeus shook the human.

Despite having Zeus's large hands wrapped around his neck, the human could speak quite clearly.

"You, me poor Zeus have been duked into this crusade of Legion's. You a good sole, I can see the goodness within you."

The it dawned on Zeus. The voice wasn't even coming from the individual he held. It almost seemed like it was an echo behind the voice. Like it was coming from a far-off place.

The human looked over at Quartz and Black Widow.

"Now, these two on the other hand are true agents of chaos. They will do anything that Legion commands without questioning the reason."

"Shut you hole up!" Screamed Quartz.

"Do it. Kill him Zeus. He has nothing to offer us." Recanted Black Widow.

Zeus let the man down gently.

'No, I cant. I wont. We don't kill humans." Bellowed the gargantuan gorilla.

"But he isn't even human." Returned Black Widow.

From behind, Quartz struck Zeus in the back of the head and sent the behemoth to his knees.

Before Zeus could recover, Black widow slapped energy cuffs around his thick wrists and a surge of energy ran through Zeus's body, making him scream out in pain. Then Zeus became silent, but still his barrel chest slowly heaved in and out.

The human stumbled away from the stunned Zeuas.

'Where do you think your going?" Mocked Quartz.

The bronze servant of Legion grabbed a hold of the man with his head pressed in between his bronze hands. Slowly the man turned into a bronze statue. Quartz slammed his forearm into the remains of King Rue's deceiver and the body shattered into pieces.

Quartz spun to Black Widow.

"Great, now how are we supposed to get his body back to Legion?" Questioned Quartz.

"He's not dead, merely in a sleep state. He can walk with us without giving us any trouble." Black Widow replied.

"Like he was sleep walking?"

Black Widow nodded.

"Great. Now how do we explain all of this to Legion. He's not going to be happy what transpired."

"Leave Legion to me." She returned.

CHAPTER 8

On the outskirts of the decimated town of Demure, many miles from the action of Sonoma, an undisclosed human messenger moved swiftly as possible toward the town. The unnamed messenger was camouflaged from head to toe, but he was still quite visible to Legion's unseen roving patrols. He brought the news of the failed attack on Clover. Waiting for him on the outskirts of the town is Black Widow, one of Legion's trusted right-hand assistants.

Black Widow is one of the apostles of Reinhart's, known as the Omega by his disciples of the new world order. She is a sly and devious creature, who sticks her victims with a paralyzing poison before she taunts and kills them slowly. Black Widow had soulless black eyes which reflected the scenery around her. She could always be found wearing black leather from head to toe and had long silver and black hair that seemed to always move on its own, as if it were as alive as she was. Her relentless pursuit to please Legion and their godlike leader, the Omega, drove her purpose and every ounce of her blood. At times, it could make her unbearable to deal with. Her fear, along with her admiration and respect for their leader, drove her to submission and that is how Legion liked his followers.

She greeted the human messenger by grasping his throat and squeezing it. She glared at the messenger with contempt as he started to shake profusely, his teeth chattering. She could smell the fear running through the messenger's body and it pleased her. She pressed her elongated fingernail into his throat, just enough to puncture the skin, but not enough to inject the deadly venom than ran through her veins. Blood trickled from the wound and down Black Widow's thin arm. It seemed to dissolve into her leather attire.

"It is unfortunate that you would bring back word of failure. Legion will not want to hear this." She slapped the messenger across the face, causing a red mark that covered his entire right cheek. The messenger spat a substance out—blood seemed to be mixed in with the foreign fluid. Black Widow watched with interest as the messenger tried to recover from her love tap. She relished in the human's pain and savored it before she continued. "So it will be your job to break the news to him," she said.

The messenger's jaw dropped. "Me?" he stuttered. "Why do I have to give him the news?"

Black Widow only gave the messenger her soulless stare, not uttering a sound.

"I have heard rumors of the master's tirades when he receives bad news." He looked down, beaten.

Black Widow grabbed the human's jaw forcefully. For such a petite creature, she had surprising strength. She lifted his head and brought him close enough to her that he could see his own reflection bouncing off her black eyes. Death approached inside of those eyes.

She responded with a touch of malcontent in her voice. "Because it's your news to deliver and it's your duty to receive the punishment for it as well."

Black Widow dragged the messenger along with her—a predator dragging its kill back to its burrow. They made their way through the heart of Demure, allowing the town's occupants to watch as they passed by. She liked making a spectacle when taking victims to her master. Legion, on the other hand, disapproved. She never understood why, maybe it had to do with it giving her the illusion she had more power in the community than she really did.

As Black Widow dragged the messenger through the town's center, she looked up at the charred and burned corpse loosely tied to an old and cracked lamppost. An example made by Reinhart's 'lead by example' philosophy. It was still burning and smelled like pig fat dripping into a fire pit. Skin, then muscles and finally ligaments slowly deteriorated in the fire until nothing was left except a charred body. Chills ran down her spine as she could still hear the victim expel a horrid and deafening scream as he slowly died. And that was hours ago.

Now the corpse hung there in silence, but Black Widow had the unsettling feeling it was following her moments as she passed by. Challengers to Legion's authority and any disloyal followers were banished to the Wasteland to die.

Black Widow knew how intimidating Legion could be. She had experienced his wrath and punishment before. He had placed her in a pit of boiling worms that kept her skin from healing. The pain seemed to come to her as she thought of it. She wanted to touch the aching sensation just below her shoulder blades, the place the boiling worms had festered and left a scar on her nearly unblemished skin. A cold shiver ran down her arms and spine, and she had to shake the memory from her head. With some hesitation, she pushed hard against the old heavy doors. They were overused and decrepit, and led into the main foyer. The doors slowly swung open, issuing a creak that echoed loudly in the darkness of the hall, announcing her presence.

They reached their destination. Legion's quarters were a run-down version of Demure's town hall, with broken hinges on the doors, and windows with no glass remaining. Dust covered the walls and floors and the place had an ominous echo about it as you walked on the old, creaky floors. It had a dark and gloomy interior, one that had a foul odor to it. Legion's presence was always daunting, but coming to their leader was made more dreadful by their surrounds.

Black Widow thought she could feel every soul that had never left the darkness of this dark abyss staring at her. They called out to her to halt her progress and hightail it away from this place. She knew if she ever ran from Legion the consequences would be quite severe. Desertion was not acceptable. She was loyal to Legion though; despite his cruelty, he had been good to her. No, she had to continue, she had a job to do and was dedicated to that job.

Acting like a medieval ruler he would hold his post-apocalyptic court when the town's occupants desired his attention on subjects they felt important—such as living conditions and food rations. When one of their own defied his leadership, Legion would gather everyone in the town to and would pretend to allow them to judge the traitor. Only one made the final decision in Demure, and his words were law.

But Legion hadn't drawn the support of everyone in Demure. Allegiances were made for and against Legion's tyrannical rule. It had split the town in half between Master Reinhart's followers and Legion's. Legion gathered new followers every day, possibly from his ruthlessness or maybe they saw his leadership as the future of their own kind. Master Reinhart and Legion were aware of each other's desire to lead Demure's inhabitants, but Legion had assets outside the town, especially in the Wasteland.

Legion's intimidating personality kept the inhabitants of the town subdued and manageable. It prevented his incompetent subjects from undermining his leadership and kept any notion of revolt subdued. Only a few had dared challenge his authority and each incident had resulted in the death and humiliation of the perpetrator.

In Black Widow's fear and anguish, she tossed the human aside. Her prisoner landed against the cold, uninviting floor. The messenger was still recovering from his earlier ordeal with his captor when he felt the harsh cold foundation collide with his face. Blood fell from his mouth and nose, streaming onto the pavement and staining it.

She looked down at the helpless human. "I would stay right there, if you know what's good for you," she said. She gazed into the darkness, knowing somewhere in the shadows Master Reinhart and Legion waited. She took a deep breath and proceeded forward.

Deep in the darkness of the former municipal building, her fear multiplied the closer she moved toward her feared leader. Her heels echoed in the emptiness of the building. The *thump-thump* resounded in her nearly numb mind. The sound couldn't chase away her terror. Shortness of breath followed an unsubdued sense of anxiety.

Her breathing increased rapidly and her nocturnal senses kicked in. In the far-right corner of the room, hidden by shadow, sat on old decrepit man. He was slouched over, looking like a large pile of horse dung hanging from a suspended hook. She had never seen their leader look like this before.

Black Widow stuttered as she called out to her master. "Master Reinhart, forgive me for my intrusion. Unfortunately, I have disappointing news for you."

She hesitated a moment, took a step backward and then froze. She had the feeling that a set of eyes were watching her from behind.

Out of the bleakness of the shadows came a small, croaking human voice, one that she had come to know well. "Yes, my child, what is it that you have to convey? Speak what's on your mind and in your heart, don't be bashful."

Black Widow hesitated. The inhabitants of Demure believed that Master Reinhart ruled over them and that Legion was his leading puppet. Master Reinhart had always made her uneasy. If the actions of Legion were considered cruel, then Master Reinhart's were grievous and atrocious. Black Widow never understood why her fellow inhabitants called Reinhart the Omega, as if he were some type of god.

All Reinhart is is a frail old man. He doesn't have abilities like the rest of us, he is truly an outsider. Master

Legion is the true god that we should worship. He will be the one to lead us to a new beginning, Black Widow thought.

✝

There she was, in the deepest part of the secret moon base. Peering through the glass Black Widow could see Ketrina Dooling cleaning Clover, the person she use to be before Reinhart got his hands on her. She couldn't believe her eyes. This was before she had even been created, but she understood the spy she was before had seen too many things to escape her predicament and only spotty memories had remained. *Reinhart's technicians had done a horrible job eradicating the spies' memories from my head. I can't get these last moments out of my mind.* Black Widow looked down. She was wearing a janitor's uniform and a voice was screaming in her ear through a telecom piece. Loud voices echoed up and down the bright hallway.

A siren sounded above her, penetrating every room on the wing.

Black Widow looked like a deer in headlights. Hurried steps came from every direction. She peered down the east hallway, then down the west hallway. She was trapped. Black Widow reached into her uniform pocket and retrieved a small object. It was a film chip of some sort, she swore it was.

"Halt! There is no escape, so there is no use in flee-ing," a security guard called as he drew his weapon.

Quickly security personnel surrounded her. One of the guards attempted to grab her by the arm, but she wasn't having any of it. Black Widow swung around and kicked a guard in the crotch, sending him to the floor. Another guard grabbed her by the hair, but only managed to pull off her wig.

"What the . . ."

Before she knew what had come over her, Black Widow smacked the man in the face, sending him into the wall directly behind them. He fell to the floor, unconscious.

A foreign woman's voice came out of her mouth. "Don't ever lay your grubby hands on me!"

She dodged a third guard with a swiftness and ease that seemed familiar to Black Widow, but she understood it wasn't her moving around. The janitor stuck her tongue out at the guards making a mockery of them all. Black Widow didn't feel in control at all, it was as if someone was moving her body for her, like she was a marionette. From directly behind her, someone cracked her on the top of her head with a blunt object, knocking her to the ground. A figure slowly walked up and straddled her body, but she couldn't see who it was; her head was spinning.

"Your full of spunk, aren't you my dear?" Black Widow recognized the voice of General Reinhart. He looked at one of the security personnel. "Take her into the next room. I'll be in there in a moment."

The remaining guards took Black Widow into a private room with thick walls and no windows. They were isolated inside the room—privacy would be guaranteed. Blood dripped from the corner of her right eye and another guard had given her other eye blurred vision as well. As far as she could tell there were four guards in the room with her. They stripped her down to her underwear. The room became cold and Black Widow's nipples began to ache. She could feel them rubbing against the material of her sports bra. The breeze from the air vents felt good against her hot, sweat-covered skin. The guards strung her up by her hands. Blood dripped down her face, falling to stain her undergarments.

At least none of them touched her yet. But she was sure that if given permission they would gladly place their filthy hands all over her near naked body.

The general walked into the secluded room and looked at the lead guard. "Well?" he asked.

"Sir, we checked her and her garments. We have found nothing to identify who she is or who she is working for," the guard said. "Her fake credentials are top-grade, fooling our entire system."

"So, she has someone working for her on the inside. She must be well funded to go through so much trouble," General Reinhart said.

The guard grabbed her cheeks and squeezed them in his powerful hand. "Who do you work for? What is your mission, your directives? How did you get access to the facility?"

Black Widow looked at the guard with her black, swollen eye. She spat blood in the guard's face and smiled. "Fuck you, monkey man," she said in a high pitch.

He struck her in the gut and she folded over, setting herself swinging. The guard raised his fist to strike her again, but the general interrupted him.

"That's enough. We don't need to kill her, we need answers." He looked at the abused woman. "Hon, I can make them stop. Just tell us the information we need."

Black Widow laughed in the foreign woman's voice and the lead guard struck her in the face, nearly knocking her unconscious again.

"Answer the general and don't be cow about it."

She started to laugh again, but this time it sounded closer to a cry, but without the tears.

"You all are a bunch of fucked-up individuals. No, you're not men at all, you're all overpriced redneck pigs with shiny badges and credentials."

"Bitch, tell us who hired you to spy on us, or pain won't be the only thing you experience," said the lead security guard.

"No matter what you do to me, you will never break me," she screamed back.

General Reinhart walked up to the battered and nearly naked woman. He lightly touched her skin with his cane. "You have spirit, I must admit I definitely admire you for that my dear. Maybe if I had more people like you working for me we wouldn't be so far behind schedule."

"Sir, I don't think we are going to get anything out of her," the guard said.

"Pity, I was starting to enjoy this," General Reinhart replied. "You may do with her as you like. I must depart, my dear, but I want you to know I really enjoyed your company."

The guards untied her and escorted her out of the room.

Black Widow would never forgive or forget what he and his security personnel had done to her that day. Or better yet what they had done to her when she was a spy gathering intel on the project, before they turned her into what she was now. Not that she was complaining much at all. She was alive and the spy was dead. She had a vendetta to settle with the old man and she knew just who she could count on to carry it out.

†

A voice boomed from behind the old man and shook Black Widow from her trance.

"The attack on Clover has failed once again," Legion said, agitated. "Sand Crawler and Blitzkreig have failed to eliminate him. Once again Clover shows his superiority over our soldiers, Master."

Legion's connection to Clover's soul and the rest of their kind, gave him insight to many things, including his brother's emotions. He could feel the fear resonating from within Black Widow. He fed off intense moments like these.

Black Widow knelt and started to plead. "Clover is a strong adversary and we can't seem to overcome his abilities, but he isn't invincible, my lord. We will find a weakness and exploit it, if I had more competent assets, that is."

Reinhart leaned forward. "Are you suggesting Blitzkreig and Sand Crawler were incompetent in their duties, child?"

Legion grunted loudly. "You know they were, Master."

Legion stepped forward into the dim light, allowing Black Widow to see his massive frame. "We know Clover can be harmed, but not by any one of you. We never meant to kill him, it was merely a tactic to force him out of hibernation and in that we have been successful."

The old man beckoned to Black Widow. "Rise, my child. You have nothing to fear from us, you have many things to accomplish. Killing you would not be beneficial to our cause. And it would be a waste of such a beautiful creature, too," said Master Reinhart.

In his contempt for another failure and for Reinhart's loyalty to the imbeciles, as he called them, he leaned in and whispered to his master.

"We do need to make an example to the masses or they will think we are weak. They will see us as unable to maintain our power or dictate orders."

Master Reinhart nods his agreement. "Bring us the messenger, Black Widow," he said.

She stood and went to retrieve the human. Master Reinhart looked at Legion with his normal calm and fatherly demeanor. Legion understood what must be done. He thrived on dealing out punishment. He no longer led a massive army, where he could create despair and destruction on a massive scale, so he accepted this as a consolation.

The messenger was pushed through the hall doors and stumbled into the darkness. Panting heavily, he tried to catch his breath. He didn't realize what stood directly in front of him. Legion grabbed the human by the throat, lifted him and began to choke him.

Still shielded by the darkness of the inside of the building, Legion spoke. "Your failure is unacceptable. It is a black mark on our society. Your discouraging news threatens our desires to make this world more livable for our kind. Relinquishing your life will give our troops hope for the future. You understand that, don't you?" Legion said.

Suspended by Legion's muscular grasp, the messenger shook with fear. Legion broke the human's neck in one easy motion and threw the body against the aged hardwood floor, sending dust everywhere. The human's head bounced repeatedly off the surface and Legion watched as blood leaked from the dead man's nose and mouth.

Legion called in Black Widow and another servant to retrieve the body.

"Display his body to show our displeasure. Impale his corpse like the rest. Get our point across to the others—failure is not an option," Master Reinhart ordered.

Once the messenger is moved out of the room, Legion led Master Reinhart into a more secluded portion of the room to discuss their next move.

"You know they will seek out Preist," Legion said.

"I know. Things are moving along like we planned they would. There is nothing he can tell them that will help them now," Master Reinhart said.

Legion gave his master a grim stare that reeked of disapproval. "You continuously forget about the Monoarc Stone, old man. It is the one thing that will make me immortal. The one thing that will make me a god," Legion said.

Reinhart looked deep into Legion's eyes, as a parent would when they were trying to teach their child a valuable lesson. He places his hands on his son's ridged face.

"Legion, you need to place your energies in things that will help our cause. Instead you go on about being immortal and waste time on mystical ideas," he said. Master Reinhart started toward his quarters, but stopped and turned back to his protégé. "Legion, we are close to dominating the globe and we have humanity on the brink of annihilation. We can't have any of your misadventures."

"I despise humanity. Humans are weak, Master, and they shall perish beneath the force of my boot. In the future, no one will recall humanity even existed, except as mystical creatures in fairy tales."

Legion wrapped Master Reinhart's robe around the elderly man.

"I'm going to wipe all humans from existence."

"Well I hope you can spare my soul and keep this old man around." Reinhart said, his voice cracking. Master Reinhart started to laugh as he disappeared into the darkness of his living quarters.

Legion made sure his mentor had disappeared before a sinister smile appeared on his daunting face. He flexed his fist. "Old man, your usefulness to our cause has just about run its course. Soon I will show our followers who is really in charge. As soon as I gain support from your followers, my reign will officially begin and yours will end."

A noise sounded from the shadowy entrance of the building. Legion looked up and from the dark end of the structure emerged Deselation. He bowed in respect.

"Did you summon me, Master?" Deselation asked.

Legion turned around slowly.

"Yes, Deselation, I did. Have we heard from the scout you sent out?"

"Yes, we have the human family's position fixed. They are being tracked from their previous location."

Deselation handed Legion a note from the scout. After looking at it a moment Legion smiled.

"Very good work. Prepare the troops, we're going after them."

"How many shall I gather for the journey, sir?"

Legion looked at his servant sternly.

"Only as many as we need to accomplish the mission. We are going to kill all the humans, even the ones at the refugee camp. We can travel faster in small numbers and be stealthier as well. We will also kill those that aid the humans."

Deselation looked shocked but bowed to Legion.

"And what about Clover, sir?"

"What about him? He chose his path a long time ago. He will die with the rest of the scum. We have something special for in store for him."

Deselation stood there at attention, taking in his master's orders and not daring to show any disrespect.

"We will get him in San Francisco. I have some guests to retrieve at the refugee camp," said Legion.

Deselation started for the door, but Legion stopped him once again.

"One more thing, Deselation. Let's keep this between us, shall we? You're the only one I feel I can trust. We wouldn't want Master Reinhart to get wind of our plans and perish before it's time, do we?"

"No, sir. We wouldn't want that," Deselation responded.

Legion laughed sadistically; a sound that seemed a mixture of a banshee's screams and of a demon taunting its prey before devouring it.

✝

One hour before Legion's hunting party left for the refugee camp, he gathered the inhabitants of the town Demure. The ruckus quieted as his massive frame stepped onto the deck of his quarters. He looked out at the hundred or so inhabitants of the town with a confident, but stern expression.

"My fellow Demureites. I have come to you with an urgent matter. I will be taking control of this town and beginning my campaign against all humans who stand in our path. Any humans and their allies not aligned with us will be annihilated. All those that have previously sided with Master Reinhart can choose to join us or step aside. No harm will come to you if you choose the latter, but no aggression will be tolerated. Extreme measures are to be taken against the remaining human settlements. They created this hell on Earth, so it is about time we finish taking out the garbage and make this world officially our own."

The crowd roared, and a chant of "Legion, Legion" ran through the center of town.

CHAPTER 9

Preist slowly opened his eyes. The bright artificial light burned his eyes and everything around him was blurred. He could sense someone else in the room with him, but with his lack of sight he couldn't make out who it was. He could hear them moving about as he lay on his back. He was disoriented and couldn't understand why he was struggling to focus his eyesight. He went to rub his left eye and a voice boomed from the other side of the room.

"Don't rub your eye," said a male voice.

The figure moved over to him and looked down on Preist.

"Hello there." The individual smiled down at Preist, but his hazy vision made the face undiscernible, as if it were the reflection in a fogged-up mirror.

It dawned on Preist that he didn't need to see the individual—he knew the voice from the time he had spent in the lab—it was Doctor Peterovitch. The doctor smiled down on Preist. He had always found the doctor's intoxicating smile soothing and, despite his foggy eyesight, it seemed to warm his soul. Sergei was wearing a surgical headlamp, which made Preist a little shaken and perplexed. His stomach knotted and his mouth dried. He looked around the lab but it only caused his head to spin.

Preist groaned

"Relax, my friend. You have had an antagonizing day," Sergei said.

"Doc," Preist started. "Why am I on the examining table?"

"You had an infection in one of your eyes, Preist. I was working on it when you awoke. You should recover soon, don't worry." Doctor Peterovitch patted him lightly on the shoulder.

Then a different type of light flooded his sight. Across the room, housed inside a glass case, was the most breathtaking jewel he had ever seen. It was only just small enough that he could have placed it in his hand. Its bright greenish-yellow illumination was mesmerizing and made it difficult for Preist to take his eyes off it.

"What is that?"

Doctor Peterovitch looked over and smiled. "That, my friend, is the Monoarc Stone. One of the most powerful objects in the galaxy." Sergei sighed. "Unfortunately, because it has such immense power, it is more a weapon than anything else. I keep it hidden in plain sight, so that the wrong hands don't get hold of it."

"How did you come to have it in your possession, Doctor?"

"That is another tale in itself. We discovered it while looking for something else entirely. It was like it had been placed there for us to discover. One day you will understand the tremendous burden this rock affords. One day you will be forced to decide to destroy it or be destroyed by it. The one thing we have discovered, through testing, is that it clings to cellular structures and eradicates their properties."

"Eradicates, Doctor?" Preist asked.

†

While traveling through a small portion of the Wasteland, a desolate space that splits the Habituated Zone, which was once considered the American Southwest and the main portion of the Wasteland, Clover and his new colleagues made their way toward what they considered a safe place for the human family to live. Escorting the family across the land would be treacherous for their human companions.

The family had never been forced to endure such ruinous conditions. Between the mutinous killers that roamed the desolate plains, the predators of an outlandish nature that used the Wasteland as their hunting grounds, the lack of food, water, shelter and the scorching heat from the sun, it was a deadly journey. Even Wasteland rustlers roamed these treacherous plains.

Walking up a dune which overlooked the entire valley of arid, mountainous range of dunes, Clover looked back at their human traveling companions. His expressionless face didn't display his concern for their well-being. He looked at Tigerous as she walked up to him, then went back to looking at the family who constantly struggled to keep up.

The trip through the Wasteland was a hard and tumultuous journey and on top of all that, the humans had no experience traveling through the Wasteland's treacherous environment.

Tigerous grabbed Clover's arm firmly and she could feel the businesslike motion of his muscles beneath his cloak. He stopped moving like a machine that had its emergency stop button pressed. He didn't bother turning around to see what she wanted and Tigerous had become accustomed to his cold, distant reactions. She knew she had his attention, but she wasn't sure for how long.

"I think we need to stop for a while," she said, looking back at the family. They were bent over gasping for air, like they had climbed to the peak of Mount Everest. "They are exhausted and need some rest, Clover. The journey over this dune range is destroying them."

Clover looked back at them with much less sorrow in his eyes than his counterpart had shown. They needed to hurry before the sun set or they would be in a world of hurt. There were only the two of them and they couldn't possibly defend themselves and their human companions. Humans weren't welcome this side of the Wasteland and they couldn't see in the darkness like he or Tigerous could.

"Okay, we can stop for a little while, but we need to keep pushing forward soon." He looked toward the setting sun. "They're not going to make it at this pace, Tigerous."

Tigerous looked at the struggling family, overburdened with the few possessions they had chosen to take; she felt frustrated. "We should have never convinced them to come with us. It is a journey most humans would perish from. The family isn't used to traveling on this side of the Wasteland, and they still don't trust us."

"Can you blame them? If it wasn't for the adolescent boy, they would never have agreed to let us escort them to the refugee camp, not after all that had happened," Clover said.

"Straus said it was the bodies of Blitzkreig and Sand Crawler that convinced them to leave. I don't think they had much choice," Tigerous said.

"If they hadn't, Legion would have eventually sent more men and we wouldn't have been there to rescue them. It was the right decision, no matter the cost to them."

Tigerous attempted to tell the family that it was going to be alright and that they could rest a bit. She moved with grace, despite the unforgiveable terrain under their feet, and Clover admired her for it.

He hesitated for a moment, watching how she methodically moved about, assisting them, taking their packs off and checking on the children. *She is good with them, maybe she would be a good mother; something I would have never guessed or could ever offer her.*

"You were right about them becoming a hindrance. Their frail bodies make us a target in the open plains," Clover whispered. Tigerous had warned him that the family would slow them down; despite how she cared for them, she still didn't trust their kind. Clover knew her history with humans hadn't been the best, yet despite that she still felt responsible for this family. It was placing them in harm's way. They were human, no matter how Clover and Tigerous spun their vulnerability. But Clover knew they couldn't be left for the slaughter that was coming, not after the incident with Sand Crawler and Blitzkreig.

Clover turned to Tigerous whose attention was still on the humans. "Are you ever going to tell me why you and those thugs were so far into the Wasteland?"

She looked at Clover solemnly. For a moment, he swore that she would ignore his request altogether. *That's not like her to brush me off in such a nonchalant manner.*

What has gotten into her? She has been acting odd since we took on our human companions.

Tigerous looked back at her mentor. "Very well, but I must admit they toe the line between piracy and doing good and honorable things for others."

"Tigerous," Clover said. "I believe you have changed, I mean for the better. What happened while you were away?"

✝

"That's when I made my way to find you and you know the rest," Tigerous said. "So where is this refugee camp at, anyways?"

Many human refugee camps had been set up to house and protect humans living along the borders of the Wasteland. This was where Clover was taking their traveling companions, since their home had been compromised by the arrival of Legion's spies. Clover had traveled the Wasteland many times, mostly under the cover of night and usually undetected. Traveling over the plains during day was a whole other thing. He knew it was going to be difficult to spot the camp. They were designed to shield from any predatory attack, in the daytime or at night.

The party had been traveling the outer Wasteland for days, but it seemed much longer than that and fatigue was starting to set in, first for the humans and then for Clover and Tigerous. Their reactions had begun to be affected by the heat of the furious sun and the environment's extreme dryness.

Clover scanned the horizon to gauge the direction they were heading. During the day, the luminous sky tended to blend with the sandy landscape, but now the sun was dipping below the horizon. Clover hoped his nocturnal senses would help more than they had during the daytime. Even with his superior eyesight, he couldn't penetrate the furiousness of the daytime's residue, which still illuminated the horizon. He shook his head in frustration. They were truly alone out in the Wasteland.

Clover shook his head once again. "I don't know, Tigerous. I can't see anything for miles. The refugee camp should be well in sight by now."

Tigerous went back to the group and grabbed the human slave with her catlike grip and with a lot more strength than he expected from her. Her grip closed on the slave's windpipe. Her toned thin muscles contracted as her agitation increased. She stared right into the slave's fading eyes. He started to bellow.

She ignored his cries and dragged him to Clover. The slave tried to shield his face, not sure what might happen to him next.

"Okay, scum, I thought you told us this refugee camp was out here?" she screamed in rage. "So where in the hell is it?"

The slave ducked into a ball trying to avoid being slapped in the head. When he thought, it might be safe, he looked up, shaking in fear. When he noticed, she wasn't going to strike him like before, he relaxed a little.

"I'm not sure, I haven't been out this way in a while," Schmidt said.

This time he was struck. Tigerous's attack came with such speed that he couldn't defend himself. She struck him across the top of his head, creating a sound like a piece of raw meat had been struck with a mighty force. The blow sent the slave to land flat on his face, swallowing hot sand in the process. The warm grains of sand scraped down the slave's throat, setting his throat aflame. For a moment, the slave just lay there, his face in the grainy sand and dazed to the point of becoming unconscious, yet aware of where he was. He was afraid of standing up too rapidly and engaging Tigerous's wrath. Eventually, he recovered and spat the sand out.

Tigerous glared at him with her snarling, catlike expression exposing the inner portions of her mouth. Her pinkish gums and cat teeth displayed as she snarled at the slave. Schmidt ve could tell any compassion she had for the family hadn't transferred to him.

"You better start remembering quickly, or they're going to find your corpse right in the spot you are kneeling." The last part she whispered into his ear. "Do you catch my drift, little man?"

Schmidt held his hands up to shield himself from being struck once again, like a child afraid of being punished. Schmidt's reaction drew Clover from his thoughts and Clover took a couple of steps forward, as if he was going to deal with the slave's uncooperative behavior personally, making Schmidt even more nervous. Clover stepped into something soft in the sandy soil. He peered down at his feet in amazement. He couldn't believe his eyes. *The atmosphere must be playing tricks on me.* He reached down and picked up some of the sandy ground, sifting it in his hands like he was searching for something embedded in the dry ground.

Clover looked in the opposite direction of where they were heading. He tried to peer out over the deserted landscape and thought he saw something in the distance. He definitely saw something out there. Yes, he was sure—but he couldn't decipher what it was. He seemed he saw something that the rest of them couldn't. Clover bent down, scooped up more sand and sifted it through his hands again, much slower this time, paying attention to the texture of the soil.

He lifted his hand up and watched the sand fall to the arid ground. "This sand is moist," he said.

Schmidt looked at Clover with a slight hesitance, fearing Clover's wraith. The slave shook his head in disbelief. "Must be from nomads. They travel across these plains all the time."

"Are you sure about that?" Tigerous looked at Clover with uncertainty on her face.

Clover peered down at his prisoner with a disdain.

"No, this isn't the work of humans at all. Humans don't know how to irrigate arid, sandy soil like this. It's not just moist under my feet. It appears to be some sort of irrigation system that surrounds the entire region, I bet."

"How do you know it's not the work of humans?" asked Schmidt.

Clover tossed the remaining grains of sand away from him, toward the dunes. The soil underfoot was heavier than normal and when the glob of sand landed, it made an indentation on the top layer of sand.

"You forget," Clover said with a self-assured tone. "I was created as an assassin and I know what signs to look for when it comes to human civilization. This is something I have seen before, but not from any human I have ever encountered."

Clover swung his head to the east. Once again sensing something amiss that the others couldn't comprehend. He turned to Tigerous and attempted to get her to look in the direction he wanted. He didn't want to frighten the family, but a scent had struck Clover like an out-of-control freight train. It was familiar to him, but the rest of the party couldn't sense the intruders' arrival. The scent drew his attention first to the party's left, then from its right.

Once he realized they had been surrounded, it was too late.

He had a look in his eyes that she knew quite well. It was his be-on-your-guard look, but the humans could only see his normal expression which rarely seemed to change. To them he had a look of no-thrills excitement that ran all the time without any hint of sadness, disparity or glee.

"Heads up, we're not alone," Clover said.

Tigerous turned toward the family. "Okay, enough rest. We're on the move," she ordered.

Clover looked west, then quickly to the east. The intruders had lured him into believing they had come from behind to surround them, but Clover realized his mistake. He hadn't seen this maneuver since . . . since . . . *I have a feeling of déjà vu now. I haven't experienced such tactics since* . . . Clover sniffed the air a few times to confirm his suspicion.

"Okay, I can smell you now. The wind no longer hides your true scent, Wolf Pack."

Screams were heard coming from the rear of the group. It was too late to react. The family's attention had drifted too far from their escort's safety and now they were paying the price for it. Suddenly, from all around them, several canine-like creatures with many sorts of heads surrounded the party with their weapons drawn. A closer look at the creatures indicated they were men with the heads of different canine animals; dogs, wolves, hyenas and many other sorts. Clover knew them well, maybe too well.

The Wasteland warriors had their weapons, which ranged in type, concentrated on each member of the group. Ruphus, the group's leader, stepped forward. He had a golden retriever's head, with large eyes that constantly surveyed the surrounding environment as if he were searching for something.

"Clover, it's so nice to see you after all these years," Ruphus said.

Clover replied with a mocking gesture that only Ruphus could comprehend. To the humans, it was more like an angry snarl of protest. "Ruphus! I thought I smelled a rat." Clover took a step forward and Tigerous tried to hold him back, afraid of what their captors might do. Clover ignored her and came close to Ruphus. "I see your tactical skills have improved. Using deception to mask your actual approach and numbers—a tactic I once taught you."

"You were always an excellent teacher, Clover. Too bad you chose to leave us. Now you're my prisoner, instead of the reverse."

"You *can* teach old dogs new tricks then." Clover gave Ruphus a slight smile of approval.

Tigerous turned swiftly to Clover, confused. "Do you know these creatures?"

Clover nods his head. "I do, Tigerous." He looked from Ruphus to Tigerous. "These mangy creatures are part of the Wolf Pack. They roam the rim of the Wasteland and terrorize humans and our kind alike. I once was one of them, before I realized the things they were capable of." Clover gave Ruphus a dead stare that would send most creatures, even ones with no souls, scurrying away. "Isn't that right, my bloodhound friend?"

The Wolf Pack was an ancient breed of canines designed specifically for General Reinhart as scouts to flush out rebel leaders hiding in seclusion, before the apocalyptic war. They had a heightened sense of smell that could pinpoint nearly any target at almost any distance. After the war, they had fled to the Wasteland where they ruled over most everything that wasn't tied to Legion's tyranny.

"You got us wrong, as usual. We don't do evil things like before. That was a time of unrest and the monstrosities that were committed were done by all involved. We have payed dearly for those indiscretions. Your legend included," Ruphus said.

"We could smell you as well," barked one of the dog-headed creatures. "We sensed your presence long before you realized we were here."

"I guess I am getting senile in my old age then. My senses must be slipping." Clover winked at Tigerous.

Ruphus smiled. "I'm glad you still have a sense of humor. It is something our kind has sorely been missing of late." He displayed the jagged canine teeth in his mouth. It seemed comical on him, and unnatural. "Come now, my leader would like to have you in his company. He insists on it."

The group was led across the arid plains and to the underground hideout of the Wolf Pack. As they approached the underground entrance, they could finally visually see the refugee camp in the distance. It appeared small, but the camp was large for its purpose. Clover and Tigerous were split from the humans and led to the Wolf Pack's leader while their human companions were led toward the refugee camp, fed, and allowed to refresh themselves.

†

Clover and Tigerous were led to King Rue's chamber. The two of them are escorted through a maze of torchlight chambers in the underground hideout. His lair is built deep underground and had a steady breeze that blew through it. The chamber was filled with shadows and only Clover's night vision allowed him to make out their host's figure.

King Rue had a human body and a jackal's head, a lot like the Egyptian god Anubis. He wore a tunic, and a sapphire ring around his neck. He oversaw the Wolf Pack clan and their mischievous behavior and claimed himself king of the pack, the alpha dog.

King Rue sensed their approach and opened his eyes. His elongated snout had sort of a grimace on it. It seemed to resonate with sarcasm. It appeared that their host was always laughing, even when he was furious. A small cackle emerged from the jackal's snout.

"Well, can my eyes be deceiving me? Is this the infamous Clover that approaches my throne?" King Rue asked.

He leaned forward to see his guests better. His dark, beady eyes reflected the golden tent of the torchlights that illuminated the chamber. The torchlights led them right up to the king's golden throne. *Where did he get that thing he's sitting on? Knowing Rue, he probably forced the Wolf Pack members to drag it through the Wasteland. It suits his personality.*

King Rue stood from his gold-plated throne, which was staged on a set of cobblestone steps to elevate it higher than Rue's subjects. For such a large creature, the king seemed to glide toward them, Tigerous thought. He gave Clover and Tigerous a good looking over, sniffing all around them before he returned to his throne. He slouched in the large chair and stared at his guests.

"Your highness." Announced Ruphus. "We found Clover and his companions on the outer terrain. They were perusing our newly installed irrigation system." Ruphus turned to Clover and wiped clean his eye lids with his elongated, canine tongue. "We just started piping in fresh water into the refugee camp for the humans. They aren't adapted to harvesting crops in the Wasteland like we are."

Clover gave Ruphus mystified expression. One that said he wasn't sure what exactly they were trying to tell him. "Irrigation, growing crops in the Wasteland?"

King Rue chuckled.

"Yes Clover." Responded King Rue. "We have been running water from my fresh water pond underground, into the refugee camp. Humans don't do well without it. Unlike those of us accustom to living in this horrid place."

"Growing crops in the Wasteland? Its unheard of." Interjected Tigerous.

King Rue bellowed out laughter that echoed in the secluded chamber.

"It has been a long time, Clover." King Rue smirked. "Yes, a very long time since we saw each other and had our last argument. Tell me, are you having a hard time re-membering the past? Because the past is clearly imprinted in my mind."

Tigerous looked over at Clover. "Argument? What argument did you have with him?"

Clover hushed her and stepped into the light to see the king better.

"It is true, I have had some memory loss. But I still remember you and your band of cutthroats, and the mischievous deeds you've done while in the service of Legion—including murdering your own kind."

King Rue bellowed with spine-chilling laughter. "Oh yes, those were the good times, were they not?" The king blinked his oversized eyes and sighed. "But I'm not the only one in this chamber with secrets, now am I?"

King Rue looked over Tigerous, as if he had a joke to tell and wondered if she had heard it or not. It made her uncomfortable.

"I bet he hasn't told you the last time we saw one another. He didn't lend a hand as Legion hunted my family down after my refusal to join his hell patrol. Legion eventually forced what was left of the Wolf Pack underground." King Rue returned his gaze to Clover. This time he wasn't smiling. "You forced us to live this life of solitude."

Clover stepped in abruptly. "That's stretching the truth, Rue. You sought me out and I trained your ragtag group in how to survive out here. You demanded that no one dictate how you live. I reluctantly joined you, so briefly. But you did not inform me of the raids on human settlements."

Rue shook his head with disgust. "It was all a misunderstanding. We saw what Legion was up to and was trying to convey to the humans that we could protect them."

"Imprisonment isn't a choice," Clover snapped.

King Rue looked at Tigerous sadly. "I regret some of our past indiscretions. Now we only support humans that come looking for a haven from the Wasteland and its horrors."

Tigerous stepped into the light, allowing the flames to accentuate her tan, striped skin as if she was glowing.

"Aren't you afraid of Legion coming out here and ruining everything you've built? Why do you live among the human refugees anyways?" she asked.

King Rue, now seated back on his throne, tapped his elongated finger on the chair's arm. Clover and Tigerous waited in anticipation for his reaction.

"My dear, we have treated the humans well. We teach them how to survive in the Wasteland environment. We teach them to hunt for food in the Wasteland. Heck, we even provide protection to the refugees," King Rue said.

"But you still didn't answer me about being fearful of Legion. All of our kind have to band together so he can be defeated," said Tigerous.

King Rue looked in Clover's direction then back at Tigerous with some satisfaction. "Young lady. He has no desire to come out here. We are Wasteland folk and he is attached to his own created society, not this pile of rocks and sand. We pose no threat to his domination nor he to ours. We keep to ourselves and that's the way he likes it. We have no alliances with the humans, only those that seek refuge, nor do we befriend Legion's cause." King Rue looked back at Clover. "Why not join us? We could benefit from each other and we could reign supreme in the relentless Wasteland and leave Legion to conquer the plains," he said.

"Sooner or later it will catch up with you—living like this, like a nomadic madman." Clover announced.

King Rue glared at Clover again, but this time without his sadistic smile.

"You're going to see him, aren't you?" Rue said.

Clover stepped very close to King Rue's face.

Clover whispered, "Who are we going to see?"

Tigerous burst in, cutting them off. "We are on a quest seeking knowledge of our kind and a human is escorting us to someone who may be able to help."

Clover and King Rue separated, giving each other their due space. King Rue uncovered a mystical ball that had been hidden under a blanket next to his golden throne. Many different colors were inside of it like a laser light show. He turned and faced Clover.

"You're going to see Preist aren't you? Don't lie to me, I know you too well for you to deceive me."

Clover and Tigerous looked at one another and Clover nodded his head.

The king looked intensely into Clover's eyes. "You know there was a time when you could have been the leader of the Wolf Pack, in my stead. You would have been a great leader to them but, instead, you choose a life of solitude and abandonment. Now you ask for our help." Rue looked away as if he were about to get too emotional and didn't want them to see his face any longer. "I have foreseen this," he said sympathetically. He lifted the colorful ball from its perch. "The journey of enlightenment will cost you the life of a traveling companion. Having this knowledge, will you still proceed to do it?" Then he stepped off his throne and slowly approached Clover. He turned to face Tigerous.

"Clover was always meant as our savior, but none of it surfaced until he left the constraints of the Corporation." He turned his focus to Clover. "Tell me, why do you wish to discover the origins of our species? What then will you do?"

Clover shook his head and looked intensely into King Rue's eyes. Colors, the same as those within the crystal ball, shifted through them.

"I will end this nightmare once and for all. No matter who we are or where we come from, Legion must not succeed. I only want the nightmares to stop, that's why I need to know what we truly are. I now understand why we once existed, but that is in the past," Clover said.

"You have to be joking me. Do you really think that by going after your brother, you can stop him?" Rue asked.

Clover and Tigerous gave each other a look of bewilderment. Clover tried to respond but all he could manage was an "eck."

Rue looked over at his crystal ball.

"I've seen your destiny, comrade. You will place all your lives on the line and the choice will be to join Legion and help him conquer all of humanity, or die trying to stop him. Either way your mission will fail. If you join him, both of you will wipe out our species as well, not just the humans. I have foreseen it. That means all our deaths."

Clover moved toward King Rue. "There is one problem with that prophecy. The future isn't set, things can change."

"Ha, now you're just being foolish," King Rue said.

"You're wrong, I do remember the past. I haven't always had full cognitive memory of my past. It has just always been filled with fuzzy, suppressed memories of the monstrosities I was forced to do as an assassin for the Corporation. This is the fuel that burns inside of me. I will stop this madness. I know what I must do, over all else, even discovering our species' origins. Legion must die. I'm going to end all the torment and anguish he has caused."

King Rue moved back to his throne and relaxed deep into it, no longer tense or aggressive toward his guests.

"Then things are already in motion. You truly then will need Preist's help."

Tigerous called out, breaking the tension between the two men. "I beg of you, do you have a way we can freshen up for the remainder of our journey?"

"Of course. We have an underground spring. Lynx, show our guests to it so they may refresh themselves before continuing their journey."

CHAPTER 10

Clover stared at his reflection. He hadn't seen himself in a while and thought the image looked an entirely different figure than the one he had known all those years ago. The look in his eyes was one of bewilderment. His reflection displayed a stone-cold expression that even he thought seemed alien. Two creatures seemed to live deep within him; the one that he was designed to be, the bio-engineered assassin who fought to surface every chance it was allowed, and the one who had brought the family safely to the refugee camp—the one that he tried to force-fully be, the individual he truly believed he was. Clover had become the very thing he had sworn not to, something so distant that he had become truly lost to what he was doing or where he was heading. That was the real reason to seek out Preist. His goal to kill Legion had just given him the motivation to do it.

His body and mind were becoming drained from years of battling Legion and his quest. His hibernation had not relieved him of any emotional fatigue nor any physical ailments. Clover peered down into the fresh pool of water and gave his reflection a hard but uncertain stare. His face showed fatigue, his skin appeared grayer than the offset peach color of the human family. He tried to shake it off, knowing he was tired, despite being used to traveling so much. *I have been running all my life and this is the first time I feel time is a great nemesis, instead of a useful tool. Where will this journey take us, in the end?*

No matter how hard he tried to force back his demons, the bioengineered assassin Clover had buried deep within wouldn't stop his fight to overtake the version of himself Clover was trying to live as. Clover's red eyes stared back at him, mocking his very existence. The other, more sinister version, the one Reinhart had relied on in the Corporation's attempt to subdue the revolutionaries with, kept chanting inside his head. *You can't get rid of me, Clover. I'm the real you and you can't just erase me because you have gone soft*, the belligerent assassin said.

Clover slammed his fist into his watery reflection, sending fresh water everywhere. He stared at the disturbed water as the surface slowly regained its tranquility. Clover's reflection returned, still with the same coldness as before. The assassin in him laughed. *I told you, Clover, you can never get rid of me*, it mocked. *Do you truly believe you're not who they made you? You're not this humanitarian, the savior of mankind. Come to grips with yourself, Clover! Look around you, humanity has fallen and it's a direct result of your past indiscretions—the real you. I pushed the humans to the brink of annihilation. Can you live with yourself thinking you're not their enemy?*

Clover continued to gaze at his reflection, lost in a trance. With his protective armor off, and his battle-worn skin exposed, he now saw his real age, the one that, from underneath, seemed much younger than it really was. He touched a long scar that stretched three-quarters across his broad, muscle-rippled chest. The scar had never really healed properly and was a reminder of what could happen when miscalculations were made in Legion's presence. The scar was like a road map of where the assassin had lived. The unique memorabilia made him recall the fight that had caused the scar. It was the first time he and Legion had fought. His brother had etched the scar onto Clover's chest so that he would never forget who was superior.

He stared at his reflection quite a while. The image was crystal clear to him and it seemed nearly lifelike. Clover had never seen himself in this condition before, outside of the dreams he had. He had the look of a man that had been on the run for a long time. His eyes appeared to as weary and tired. His face was drawn in and seemed the hard life living like he had been, was draining the very life from him. Then he remembered the look in King Rue's eyes.

We did hunt them down. That's my fault for not stand-ing up to Legion, as he was building him empire of hatred and desolation. Clover could only shake his head. *I must make things right or the tyranny Legion is subjecting everyone to will not seize.*

He seemed to be something different entirely and it was hard to take in what you looked like on the outside. He cringed at the at the sight of his physical form. He hadn't seen himself in a long time and he wasn't sure he liked what he saw.

Tigerous approached the assassin from behind in her usual stealthy way. She advanced with caution and saw he was in a trance, staring at his reflection in the pool of water. She whispered into Clover's ear. "Watcha staring at?" This startled him just a little.

Clover shook off his dazed state. His eyes slowly transformed from their glazed look to his usual predatory gaze, one that implied everyone was a suspicious target. First, he looked at her reflection bouncing of the clear glassy surface. Her reflection, unlike his own, was as soft and breathtaking as her appearance was in person. He had always felt an affection for Tigerous, one could even say it was on the verge of attraction. With her soft bright-orange skin and her catlike features she had the appearance of a much younger species, where he felt much older.

"Nothing," he mumbled. "Just refilling my skin."

Tigerous looked at his reflection and softly rubbed the scar on Clover's chest. She didn't say it—she didn't have to, her expression said enough. It spoke to him in a sorrowful manner. *You look like you're being drained of life with each step we take. I don't want to watch you shrivel up and die. I couldn't bear to see that happen to you.*

She gave him her soft smile which reflected in the water. "Having a moment of déjà vu, are we?"

Clover stared at her reflection intensely. He wasn't about to let her know he was letting his guard down, even for one moment. He wasn't sure how she would take that.

"No, of course not. I already told you, I was refilling my water skin."

His tone was much firmer now, as if he was agitated with her. She backed away a few steps to give him space.

"I was just checking up on you," she said.

Tigerous gave Clover one of her with her catlike smiles. The ones he had seen time after time when she was struggling to force herself in and confused as to how to react toward him. Fear mixed with confusion usually accompanied the forced smile. She was treading lightly, trying not to have him shut her out again. It had happened before, at times, when she became pushy and tried to pick his brain, which was the last thing he wanted anyone to try to do, let alone force their way into his thought processes.

"Is it true?" she questioned.

"Is what true?"

Clover knew exactly what she was asking him, but he wasn't ready to divulge his entire past.

"What the king said about you and Legion hunting them down."

Clover took a deep breath and refused to look at her directly.

"It's true. What he said about me." He stopped for a moment and took in a deep breath, like it was too painful recollecting those moments.

"Tell me what happened." She placed her hand softly on his shoulder.

"It was a time, just after the war, when the radiation had subsided enough to traverse the land. I had gone into hiding and when his agents found me, I was reluctant to aid them. Legion finally guilt tripped me to assist and said that he wanted to unite all our kind. I should have realized this was just his first step in his rise to power and his reign of tyranny that still exists today."

Clover screwed the cap onto his waterskin.

"At first the Wolf Pack assisted us in hunting down what Legion considered undesirables. Those, he swore would impede his utopian vision. It wasn't just humans we hunted down, it was our own kind. That's probably where my unfavorable reputation came from. Anyone that stood in his way was eliminated. As soon as he deemed the wolf pack as expendable, he had us go after them as well. That's when I had enough killing so I returned to my seclusion, but this time I went where they couldn't find me."

Tigerous was stunned, not sure how to respond.

She looked down at her hands, shaking a bit. Dejection was wrestling in her stomach, sending it in knots.

"I am sorry that it happened that way." She looked up with a shed of a tear in her eye. "But you're not that Clover anymore, that's what matters."

Tigerous then stood up from her crouching position, brushing her hands clean.

"We are ready to set off when you are,"

Clover placed his skin beneath his cloak, in its rightful resting spot, still looking at her feminine features.

"Fine. I'll be there in a moment."

She turned and started to walk away, then spun back around and hesitated just for an instant, as if she had one more thing to add, but she knew better than to push too much on Clover. Finally, she disappeared back beyond the rock incline.

Clover returned his gaze to his reflection. At first, he had a look of disgust. It was like looking into someone else's soul. His eyes darkened with mad fury, but he wasn't sure why. His jaw sharpened and his muscles tightened. He knew he shouldn't have snapped at her, she was only trying to help. But his emotional state always changed when reminiscing, especially when he remembered the monstrosities he engaged in with Legion. The angry, frustrated look transformed into one that was quite familiar to him. One that saw strength. It was a look that was like he met someone he hadn't seen in a while.

"We have come a long way, my friend, haven't we?" Clover said, not sure which Clover he was referring to or talking with now. He could feel both entities pulling at him in a twisted tug-of-war game.

Clover slowly drifted into a trance, one that included the feeling of euphoria. He had felt this before when dreaming of the past. A flashback came to him of his training days on the moon base.

†

An alert siren sounded in the west wing of the prison. The prisoners of the moon base were mustered quickly and without any explanation. Today was their section's inspection and their section leader wanted everything to be right. The section leader ran around as if he were ablaze, trying to prepare for the arrival of the inspectors.

"Hurry up! Get in line, you damn worthless scum," screamed the section leader.

Legion, the guest inspector, entered the berthing area, followed closely by a few of his escorts. Clover trailed behind. The sound of the cheap floor creaking under the weight of their feet announced their arrival. Soon, they noticed the inspection detail had arrived. "Attention! Inspection detail on deck," one of the officers yelled.

The section leader called out to the inmates. "Attention! Officer on deck."

The prisoners stiffened. No one dared move a muscle or let out a breath of air, afraid to incur Legion's wrath if they did. The section leader approached Legion and his entourage with due care, slammed his recently shined boots together and saluted Legion smartly. Clover could hear the section leader and his booming voice. The voice, followed by the thump of each inspecting member's boots, caused the floor to vibrate. Clover couldn't see the inspection line, nor the entire berthing section and was only able to fully take in the entire scene when he finally walked through the doorway.

The smell of sweat instantly reached Clover's sensitive ears. It, mixed with piss and the rotting materials the section was constructed of, overloaded his senses. It was as if he had walked into a sweatshop where none of the factory workers had been given a break in weeks. The smell wasn't the only thing that rained down on Clover's senses. He could sense fear, anxiety and hatred from prisoners in every corner of the berthing section. It wasn't just coming from those lined up for inspection—it was radiating from those that were unable to get out of their makeshift bunks, also.

"West Wing Section Leader Lieutenant Gurunge reporting, sir. The west wing is ready and eagerly awaits your inspection, Major Legion!"

Clover looked at his brother just in time to see a sinister smile emerge on Legion's hardened face. Legion motioned, dismissing the section leader, indicating he would take control of the inspection. The section leader moved swiftly back in line and stood at attention with the rest of the men.

Legion looked slowly around the section before moving toward those who were about to receive his judgment. Clover already knew what the judgment was for these unfortunate souls. He could feel the hatred and contempt resonating from his brother.

Legion and the inspection detail walked up and down the inspection line, scrutinizing each prisoner meticulously. Nothing would escape Legion's ridicule. As they moved along, the creak of the floor supports made chills run up his spine. The creak was followed by the heavy thump of Legion's enormous boots, followed by the rest of the inspection detail. Clover's footfalls made the least noise of all, with his light-as-a-feather maneuvering across the most poorly constructed floorboards.

All eyes stared straight. None dared peek, fearing Legion's wrath would turn to them. Standing at attention was starting to get to some of the inspection attendees. Some could barely stand, while others grunted with frustration from standing stiff for so long. Legion glared at each one with an intense hatred and contempt as he passed by. Clover had seen his brother's hatred toward those of their kind that didn't share his contempt for humans and insubordinates. Clover knew how Legion felt and had heard his brother say, "These degenerates present a dark spot on our species. That they live and breathe is disrespectful to those that choose to accept their designed programming and execute it with perfection."

"I run a tight ship here!" Legion's voice boomed through the berthing section, making sure all heard the contempt in his voice. Legion puffed his chest out and walked with a sense of pride as Clover watched him put on a show for all to see. "I expect each one of you to abide my strict standards. It seems discipline has eluded you before, but it will not escape you here, at this very moment of your worthless lives."

The party continued down the inspection line and Clover watched in horror as Legion stopped occasionally to torment a prisoner. Legion messed with his victim's clothing, then pointed it out, as if he was disappointed in their appearance. "If you comply with my high standards, you will find life with me to be very bearable, maybe even slightly enjoyable."

The party laughed at Legion's jape. Clover felt the joke was all in line with a predestined script, one that had been rehearsed many times over. The rest of the inspection detail were like marionettes led by Legion himself as the puppet master.

They finally reached a young Tigerous. Her tiger-tattooed skin shone in the dull artificial lighting. Her worn-out and somewhat torn prison attire flaunted her exotic figure, including her ample bosom. The outfit didn't leave much to the imagination. Legion looked her up and down with a smile that sent chills down Clover's back. Legion's gaze was filled with desire, his eyes following every curve the tight-fitting clothing had. Her body made a statement to the males in the wing, and Clover felt a warning should have come with her that said Dangerous Curves Ahead.

"What do we have here?" Legion said, giving one of his shit-eating smiles. He used the stick he held to open her worn prison blouse to gain a better view of her soft, Ginger toned tattooed skin. It made her uneasy and put her on edge, but she tried to keep her gaze forward, and tried not to offer Legion a reason to strike her. As he walked around the young Tigerous he inspected her backside, and slapped her on the behind with his stick. She jumped in response and rubbed her ass without shifting her focus from the air in front of her. Clover could sense that Legion's victim was starting to size him up; her intense gaze was meant to challenge his authority. She was done playing the good prisoner.

Clover saw her begin to tremble, as did the other members of the inspection detail. Fear and anguish were both present in her emerald feline eyes. She then made a fatal mistake—she made eye contact with Legion. Her reflection was mirrored in them and the two stood challenging each other. Excitement that ran through Legion's loins and he pushed himself against his sultry female prisoner. It was obvious she wasn't subordinate to any male, not even the powerful Legion himself.

Legion peered over at his escort party and smiled deviously. He liked the challenge, and had accepted it with open arms. "I think this is something I could become quite interested in, boys." He looked back to Tigerous. "Wouldn't you like that, my precious thing?" He went to lightly caress her chin, but before he could touch her she slapped away his massive hand and looked up at her tormentor without fear.

She snarled. "Not ever on your dead corpse, asshole."

Legion turned to his inspection party with a look of displeasure and they began to laugh. Well, except for Clover. Clover had noticed Legion wasn't laughing; in fact, he saw his brother wasn't taking it as a game any longer. Legion's entourage stopped laughing as they, too, saw Legion's playful demeanor replaced with seriousness. Legion turned back to Tigerous, aggressively grabbed one of her breasts and caressed it firmly, exposing her skin to the crowd of men. He massaged her tan breast like he was kneading dough.

Tigerous struck Legion in the face with one of her razor-sharp claws, leaving a deep scratch that bled down the side of his face. He touched the wound and tasted his blood. The seriousness in his face was once again replaced with a playful grin. "I say, we have a lively one here, boys. She has spunk in her. I think I'm in love and I think she likes it rough. Let's give her what she wants, shall we?"

Legion grabbed Tigerous, engulfing the surface of her entire throat with his massive hand and lifted her to eye level, leaving her to dangle in midair. Tigerous struggled in Legion's grasp as the two of them stared at one another. She clawed at his grip, attempting to pry Legion's hand free. Neither attempt worked. She was losing the battle as her body slowly lost energy.

Tigerous gasped for air, then her eyes closed and her body went limp. Clover knew he had to act or the young Tigerous wouldn't survive her ordeal.

Legion shook her limp body. "You need a little discipline in you, that's all."

Clover intervened and stopped Legion's tirade. "Legion, can't you see? She can't breathe!"

Legion spun toward Clover with a furious look on his face. "I'm not finished with her quite yet, so stay out of it."

Clover couldn't take his brother's actions any longer, he had seen more than enough.

"I think you are." Clover rammed Legion forcefully, knocking him off-balance and sending Legion to the floor. Tigerous fell to the floor as well but, unlike Legion, her body collapsed, limp. She was nearly unconscious from almost being choked to death.

Clover rushed to her side. "Are you okay? Can you stand?"

Tigerous coughed as she struggled to breathe. "Ga, Ga," noises came from her golden, feline lips. She was still too dazed to speak coherently and Clover couldn't make out her warning.

He tried to assist her, forgetting his ill-tempered brother. Tigerous looked up as Legion came for them, but Clover didn't respond to her.

When Legion's shadow overtook them both, Clover finally realized the danger and turned around.

"You shouldn't have done that, brother," Legion said.

Legion lifted Clover over his head and tossed him against the nearest wall. His collision knocked a giant hole in the unstable partition and Clover dropped to land roughly on the prison floor on the other side.

Clover lay there a moment, limp and covered with dust and debris, as he tried to gather his senses.

Legion walked over to Clover and hovered over his half-dazed victim. Satisfied that he had become victorious over his sibling yet again, Legion spun back in Tigerous's direction, not paying his brother any mind.

"Now, where were we before we were rudely interrupted?" Legion asked.

Tigerous removed her hand from her ailing throat. It was still hard to swallow but she could speak now. "I was about to kick your stupid ass."

Legion laughed. "Hell, you're not only gorgeous, you're a comedian as well."

Clover recovered and got back on his feet slowly. Every muscle ached as he stood up. It was like he had taken a beating from a mob, he had never felt so sore before. He knew he couldn't rest long, he needed to use the element of surprise. He retrieved a piece of wood from among the debris, most likely the remnant of a broken support structure from the damaged wall and threw it at Legion. The wood struck his brother in the abdomen, knocking Legion over and onto one knee.

Clover limped across and hovered over his brother's body. Their roles had been reversed.

"You never could take it in the gut, Legion," Clover said.

He helped Tigerous to her feet, then looked to the others in the inspection party. They were speechless stone statues.

Legion slowly rose and grunted in displeasure. "You're going to pay for that, little brother." He rubbed his abdomen.

Legion sprinted toward Clover and swung with all his might. He missed Clover completely—a testament to Clover's lightning-fast reflexes, despite his being injured.

Legion's momentum knocked the behemoth off-balance again. This was Clover's one advantage over his much larger sibling and was what made Clover dangerous in any face-to-face duel. His ability to outmaneuver any opponent was unparalleled. He could almost sense what his opponent was about to do.

Clover struck Legion's lower jaw. Bone cracked against bone, sending his brother to both knees, exposing Legion completely. In one fluid and lightning-quick motion, Clover struck Legion's barrel-shaped chest, Legion's point of strength. The muscles in the behemoth's chest shook and spasmed from the attack, making Legion cry out in pain. Clover struck the side of Legion's ironclad jaw.

Still dazed and with a muffled tone Legion mocked his smaller kin. "You still hit like a pussy, Clover."

Legion stood, temporarily recovered from his injuries, and grabbed Clover by his throat. He struck Clover in the chest, knocking him to the ground. This time, Clover wasn't given time to recover. Legion retrieved Clover's seemingly unconscious body and lifted the bruised figure above his head. Legion struck Clover across the face. The momentum from the strike sent him crashing through the kitchen on the other side of the berthing section, tearing the door completely off its hinges. Metal and other debris flew from the desecrated door and, when everything settled, there was nothing but a gaping hole where the door once stood.

"No!" Tigerous yelled.

Legion looked back with a sinister smile. "Don't worry. I'll be back for you soon, my dear."

Legion walked into the kitchen and looked around but couldn't see Clover. Apart from the destroyed door, there was no evidence that his kin had even been there.

Legion shouted in anger and balled his large fists up. "Where in the hell are you?"

Clover's voice echoed from behind him. "Right behind you."

Clover came from behind, ramming Legion with all his might. They collide with the countertop and their momentum crushed the metal sink embedded within it. The pipes sprang a leak, sending water everywhere.

"You will regret challenging my authority, Clover," Legion said.

Clover stood up and wiped blood from a wound. "Well, maybe someone else should be in charge. You're a bad leader."

Legion launched himself into Clover and the two of them fell back onto the floor like two young siblings fighting over the TV remote. They wrestled with one another briefly. Clover kicked the heavy Legion off him, retrieved a skillet that had been knocked off its staging perch and waited for the chance to strike.

Legion got to his knees and Clover struck him square in the face, knocking the behemoth unconscious. Jubilation mixed with empathy as he looked half-heartedly at his sibling.

"I win this round, Legion." He tossed the dented skillet onto Legion's chest and looked up to see Tigerous and many other inmates peering into the devastation of the kitchen. He smiled at her before passing out.

Clover, Tigerous and Schmidt left the refuge and set out westward for San Francisco. A storm had started to form in the distance and rapidly moved in the direction they were headed. The wind had increased and soon sand was being flung in every direction, making it difficult for them to keep their bearings on track. Traveling became almost impossible.

With the wind swirling, Tigerous pushed her long hair out of her face. "I can't see anything at all. The wind from the storm is too great," she said.

Schmidt turned to Tigerous and Clover. "If we don't find shelter quickly, we will be caught in this storm and perish."

Clover pulled out a set of binoculars and searched the horizon. Anguish filled his face. He scanned the horizon from top to bottom, but only saw a sand-filled landscape. "I can't see anything in this storm. There is nothing in this desolate place," Clover said, handing Schmidt the magnifying glass.

"See what you can find. You said you have traveled across the plains with Legion before."

Schmidt searched the area with the same result. He magnified the glasses more and did one last sweep of the area. Thinking he saw a glimpse of something, he retraced his movements. There was something out there, east of their position.

"Wait a minute, I thought I saw something, but I can't be sure."

He magnified the glasses even more. Something came into focus. "There seems to be something we might be able to use as a shelter over in that direction."

Schmidt pointed to the southeast, into the heart of the oncoming storm.

In the distance, through the raging storm, a gray building appeared. It was still difficult to make out, but it was clear that it was something they might be able to use as shelter.

Clover ripped the glasses from the slave's grasp and peered in the direction Schmidt had pointed. He tried to show patience, but struggled.

You want us to travel into the heart of this storm?" Tigerous asked.

"Do you want to find shelter or debate whether we should walk into the oncoming storm? Either way, it's your choice but make it snappy—before we are buried," Schmidt said.

"I don't see anything. Are you sure you didn't hallucinate it?" Clover asked.

"Magnify it to 250 percent. It's half covered by a sand drift," Schmidt said.

Clover refocused the glasses and discovered something camouflaged by a large mound of sand. Its gray exterior protruded from the sand drift.

"He's right, I see it now. It might be just what we need to wait out the storm," Clover said.

They slowly descended the dune, careful not to tumble down the steep side of the dune. It was a balancing act between not being knocked over by the power of the storm and the unstable footing down the dune. Sand slid all around them but, somehow, they managed to avoid an avalanche and make it to solid ground. They moved swiftly toward the shelter.

They struggled against the violent wind and the vastly accumulating piles of sand. Between the storm, the slippery footing and the strain of their gear, reaching the shelter was a bleak prospect. They didn't even know if they could get inside once they reached it.

Finally, they reached the shelter's entrance. Its gray, rusty door was half covered by the sand drift. Their hopes diminished a little more. The door looked unusable, as if it hadn't been moved in decades. Clover tested the door and its hinges.

"The door and its frame are somewhat weather-beaten. I think we can open it with minimum effort," Clover said. Tigerous and Clover looked to Schmidt.

Schmidt looked back, shocked. "Me?"

Tigerous and Clover looked at him sternly.

"Fine, I'll be your pin cushion."

The slave tossed his pack to the ground. He grabbed the shelter's door handle and started to pull. It didn't budge. He put his back into and pulled at the door with all his might. He grunted and strained but still the door didn't shift. Schmidt looked down at his rust-stained hands.

Clover set his stuff down and together they tugged at the rusty door. Harder and harder they yanked, without any success. Each one grunted their displeasure, sand mounting in their mouths. They stop a moment, panting from exhaustion. Between breaths, they try to remove sand from their mouths.

"We are bound to suffocate in this storm," Schmidt said.

Tigerous intervenes. "Wait a minute. Try moving some of the sand away from the door. I thought I saw something glow."

Tigerous started digging the sand away from the door. The men followed her lead and soon they were all trying to get as much sand from the doorframe as they could. But they were fighting against the wind, which only deposited more sand in its place. Finally, they removed enough sand to try again.

Tigerous spun back to the men. "That should do it."

Schmidt and Clover pulled on the door again with no success.

"There has to be something we are doing wrong," Schmidt said.

Tigerous moved her hand along the sand-covered wall of the shelter and past the doorframe. At first, she had as much success discovering anything on it as the men had pulling the door open. Her patience endured, and she discovered something buried under the sand drift, right next to the doorframe. She brushed sand from the object to uncover a scanning pad. Tigerous looked at it a moment and when she placed her hand on the pad, it scanned her print, let out a noisy buzz and illuminated with a red glare.

Tigerous looked at Schmidt. "You said before we left on this journey that Legion placed your handprint in the corporate data system? Do you have access to any building owned by the Corporation?"

Schmidt shrugged.

She grabbed the slave's hand. He tried to yank his hand from her grip, without much success.

"Hey watch it, lady," Schmidt said.

Tigerous gave him a stern look. "I'm no lady, remember that."

She placed his hand on the scanning pad and after scanning the handprint the pad hummed a steady noise. The pad turned green. The door unlocked and a *shush* of air escaped as the door swung ajar.

"And that's how we do it where I come from, boys." She curtsied to them both.

✝

Inside the shelter, it was dark and musky. Sand covered what little furniture was left in the main room, right next to the entrance. Tigerous pulled an object from her pack and lit the room. It was as dismal as it appeared in the dark. It looked like it had been abandoned a long time ago. There were cracks that let a little light in, along with flying sand. In the main room, there were a few tables left, some of which were knocked over along with chairs that surrounded them.

"It appears the inhabitants left in a hurry," Clover said.

The walls had a rusted, tanned look to them, like a metal cave. Fallen items littered the floor. Tigerous shone her light onto the adjacent wall and the Corporation's infamous logo was embedded in the metal structure. Next to the logo read Concordia Prisoner Holding Facility.

"This must be an abandoned military outpost used to house prisoners before the war," Clover said.

Schmidt moved to a map painted on the wall. "They used to have an underground training facility in Cold Springs, Nevada. Or at least, so rumor has it." He looked back at Tigerous and Clover. "I wonder if there might be supplies there for a return trip. I bet no one has visited it in decades."

"Are you insane?" Tigerous said. "That's well over a week's traveling."

"This will suffice for the night, while we wait for the storm to pass. I don't think we should venture too far in, we don't know what traps its last occupants left." She looked over at the slave. "I suggest that none of us go exploring late at night."

Clover agreed.

After trying to get comfortable, they all fall asleep. The storm had slowed to a soft hum and they couldn't hear clumps of sand striking the side of the shelter any longer. The room they slept in was dark and the cracks that let in the light and sand had become silent. Schmidt awoke from a nightmare, sweating and trying to catch his breath. He reached down for his water skin and took a sip.

"That dream was so vivid that, if I wasn't sane, I would swear the noise from it was real." He took another sip from his skin and tried to shake off the memory of his nightmare.

A sound echoed abruptly somewhere deep in the interior of the building. It startled him, and he nearly dropped his water skin. Schmidt looked over at Clover and Tigerous to make sure they hadn't been awoken by the abrupt noise. Neither had woken but he knew he had to investigate the noise.

He snuck over to Tigerous's pack and quietly removed the light device. The noise persisted, and Schmidt thought it sounded like rattling chains against a wall. He crept close to a doorway. The old wood planks of the floor creaked. In fear of arousing his captors, he looked back at them, but there was still no movement.

Once out of the room, Schmidt tried to turn on the device, but it refused to cooperate. He slapped it in his hand, trying to wake it from its slumber. It finally lit up and showed the corridor's contents.

The place looked as old and weather-beaten as the shelter's exterior. There were several empty rooms down the corridor that Schmidt thought might have been used as offices. He had been in several corporate buildings during his service with Legion and these spaces seemed familiar to him. He came to a flight of steps and slowly descended into the shelter's interior. There was no real smell to the place, and that was odd to the slave. *Even an abandoned place such as this should have a dusty smell to it*, he thought.

Schmidt finally reached a large, spacious room, the place he believed the noise was emanating from. The room had several empty cages, each a different size. All of them were empty except one. Rusty shackles hung on the far wall of the room. Bloodstains littered the floor, but most of them had started to fade away.

The middle cage was much larger than the rest. It could have housed the rest of the cages in it. Inside was a large gorilla-type beast in chains. The creature was chained to the wall with an enormous thick collar.

The beast eyed him intensely. The slave moved closer and shone his light on the beast.

"This must be what's making all the ruckus," Schmidt said under his breath. He approached the creature, getting right up against the bars of the cage. Flakes of dust fell from the rusty bars.

"Don't worry, friend. I'm not going to hurt you," he said.

Tigerous dreamed she was standing in front of a full-body mirror. She admired her curvaceous figure, but her reflection didn't last long. It quickly dematerialized and Ketrina Dooling stood in a long black dress, staring back at her. Tigerous's alter ego was staring right back at her. Her human reflection had a stern and disappointed look upon her face, as if she were disappointed in Tigerous. Tigerous shook her head in hopes that the apparition would disappear, but Kat still stood in the mirror.

"Tigerous," Ketrina said. "I am quite discontented with your actions of late. You promised you would tell Clover about us, but you haven't. He deserves to know the truth."

Tigerous waved the apparition off. "In due time. I have been quite busy, if you haven't noticed, and just haven't found the right moment to do it. I will, trust me."

Kat's reflection stiffened at Tigerous's pompous attitude. Tigerous's apparition reached out and grabbed her by the throat. Tigerous couldn't breathe and the way her apparition held her throat seemed familiar. Kat's kind, loving eyes transformed into pitch black sockets, devoid of life. Her form melted away and, in its place, materialized the figure of Legion. There was no expression on the behemoth, he only squeezed tighter.

"You and my brother can't hide from me. No matter where you run or where you hide, I will find you. Your death will be by the stroke of my hand. You will not steal my glory a second time, my sweet."

Legion squeezed tighter until her eyes bulged and her jaw collapsed beneath his massive strength. Everything went dark. She heard someone singing a soft melody. Tigerous recognized the voice singing; it was her former self, Ketrina Dooling.

Tigerous awoke in a panic. She sat up panting, her chest convulsing in and out. Her heart raced and the palms of her hands were filled with sweat. She looked over to check Clover. He was staring at her, concerned.

"Is everything alright, Tigerous?" he asked.

She turned to where Schmidt had been laying. His bedroll was a mess. She turned to Clover. "Schmidt's gone!" She turned to Clover again and placed her hand on his arm. "Clover, there is something vital I must tell you and I have been holding it back for a while now."

A loud roar echoed from deep inside the structure, drawing their attention. "It can wait, I think our guide may be in trouble." Clover grabbed his katanas, one in each hand.

The beast in front of Schmidt growled and launched itself, catching the slave off-balance. The beast snagged Schmidt by the throat, its massive hands preventing him from breathing. The slave dropped his light and it fell to the ground. The slave nearly blacked out—all he could hear was the beast's cries.

Suddenly, the gorilla loosened its grip. Standing in front of the cage was Tigerous and Clover. Clover had one of his blades leveled right under the beast's chin.

"Let him go or I'll cut your throat clean off, my friend," Clover said.

The gorilla released its grip on Schmidt and slowly moved back to its perch. It looked down, as if a great sorrow weighs on it.

Tigerous slapped Schmidt across the face. "Didn't we tell you not to go wandering off?"

Clover looked at the prisoner in chains with curiosity. It was a sorrowful look, one he had used on his own reflection at Rue's underground cave.

"Who are you and why are you chained up like this?" Clover asked.

The gorilla looked up at Clover, still with a sorrowful look.

"My name is Zeus. I used to be a great commander in Legion's army of thugs. Now look at me. I have been reduced to this." Zeus puckered his dried lips, trying to wet them in his frustrated state.

Clover and Tigerous looked at the human slave. "What do you know about this?" she asked.

Schmidt could only shake his head. "I don't know who he is or anything about why he is here, but I had heard that Legion was taking those who didn't share his vision to Earth encampments such as this."

"Encampments? This looks like a zoo. I have heard humans say they used to imprison creatures in cages like this," Tigerous said.

Zeus leaped up at the Legion's name. "Legion and his goons are nothing but thugs. They will never know the true meaning of the honor that comes with battle. All they understand is death and destruction. As soon as I opposed him as a leader, he placed me in these shackles."

Zeus looked solemnly at Schmidt. "I mean the boy no harm. I thought he was one of Legion's lackeys come to deal more punishment."

"Punishment?" Tigerous asked. She took a closer look at the prisoner chained up. There were bare patches in Zeus's fur, and deep scars laced his skin, as if he had been pounded persistently by a sharp object.

"Yes. From time to time humans came in his name to inflict punishment on the prisoners. They stopped moving us around and I haven't seen anyone in a long time. It was a natural reaction to seeing the boy right in front of my cage."

Clover placed his sword in its sheath. "We are going to hunt down Legion and his gang. If you like you may come with us, you're more than welcome."

Schmidt couldn't believe his ears.

"I detest everything that Legion and his goons stand for," said Zeus. "Especially Deselation, he is the worst. I will be honored to join your brigade and defeat them."

That was it, the last of the misfit brigade that promised to take down Legion and his wayward gang of thugs. A wolf like assassin, a cat woman with an attitude who threw claws like daggers, a worthless human slave who was a liability and a renegade soldier, formally under the command of Legion.

CHAPTER 11

The night air was cool and brisk at the refugee camp. Many of its occupants had already gone to bed inside the tents provided by the Wolf Pack, while only a handful stayed up. The camp had its usual security detail, King Rue's guards who patrolled its perimeter. The guards weren't skilled at being friendly to those that roamed the campgrounds after dark. The humans and their guardians had an understanding, as much for their own protection as it was for the convenience of the half-breed security personnel.

Groups of tents are scattered around the camp acting as family homes. Most were just large enough to house a small human family, but some came with larger accommodations for the bigger families. The tents were made of special material which protected them from the harsh solar radiation cast down on them during the day, as well as the massive sandstorms that bombarded the camp constantly.

Those that aren't privileged to live under the shelter of the tents had burrowed into the ground and would have cloth thrown over them for protection from nighttime winds and the other nocturnal hazards that loomed at night. They tended to die painful and horrid deaths.

The camp had been overpopulated for some time—more and more humans had been migrating in from the deserted territories. A rapidly moving rumor was spreading about a great whirlwind sweeping over the Wasteland and those not sheltered would perish in the open Wasteland. The storm was heading in their direction, and it came in the form of Legion's mighty fury.

A campfire in the center of the refuge illuminated majority of the camp. The inferno-like fire provided enough light and heat to keep the camp's inhabitants comfortable. No humans were seen out roaming in the night air, only an occasional sentry patrolling the areas within the camp. The combination of human and Wolf Pack members' shadows made the center of the camp an eerie place to be. The only sounds in the camp were the crackle of the fire, the occasional coughing from the tents and the patrol members making their hourly rounds.

One of the Wolf Pack guards whispered to his cohort. "Did you hear something out there?"

His colleague looked out, into the darkness of the night. "Out where?"

"Hell, I don't know. I keep sensing something's out there, something so rotten it fouls up the air. Something that makes me feel the shadows are watching us."

The other stared out into the darkness, sniffed the air and turned to his partner. "The only foul thing I smell is you. Didn't I tell you not to eat too much jerky for supper?"

✝

Legion and his crew approached the camp from the southeast and stopped near the camp to prepare their assault. The invading party stayed low, preventing themselves from being discovered. One of Legion's sentries crawled up from behind.

"All is clear, Master," he whispered into Legion's ear. "They don't expect us at all. The attack will take them by surprise."

Legion turned to the sentry. "Did they catch a whiff of you or see you moving about?"

The sentry started to shake nervously and stuttered. "No, Master."

Legion felt his operative was lying. He could sense the Wolf Pack sentries moving with extreme caution. He felt their anxiety and agitation. The surprise attack on the camp was in jeopardy. He motioned to two members of his siege party and they grab the spy by his arms.

"You will pay for endangering our mission." Legion nodded to the sentries. "Take him far from this place so that when he screams it won't warn their sentries of our raid. Extinguish his worthless life."

Legion motioned for Oracle to get ready. Blind, Oracle was a human who used animals to see long distances, like a set of binoculars.

"Release your seeing-eye bird. Have it scout the camp and tell us what you find," Legion said.

Oracle nodded and reached for his companion, a Northern Rockies hawk, a bird that was all but extinct. He whispered softly to the bird, then released her into the night air.

The hawk soared over the camp's perimeter undetected. She flew over the center of the refugee camp and let out a scream that was difficult for camp's occupants to hear. She was now flying high above the camp, still undetected by the refugees or King Rue's men. As she scoped the camp, her view was sent to Oracle. He described what his pet was seeing.

Oracle's eyes had changed from their normal color to a dark, hazy shade. They reflected nothing. He reported the images of the sentries and their locations to Legion. The man and bird were connected as one, and nothing escaped their field of sight. The camp's occupants came to Oracle as blurred images without faces, statuesque shapes of energy. He could see the number of tents that littered the camp and an estimate on how many human families were housed within the camp's borders. He described to Legion the entire camp's layout in exquisite detail.

"No one moves around the camp's interior, except the roving patrols which are few and far between, separated by large unprotected portions of the camp's perimeter. The human portion of the camp is split in two. One is on the east side of the camp and the other is on the west. The security tent faces the east entrance and it's at the far end of the camp. Nothing will come to their aid in time," Oracle said as the images flashed by him.

With a wide smile, Legion motioned to the party to split up into smaller groups, each consisting of three or four siege units. Legion believed using smaller units would allow them to go undetected until they struck like a viper. The north and south sections of the camp would be hit first. Legion wanted to make as little noise as possible, and allow his militia to take out the patrol areas and bring the rest of his troops into the camp without detection. His plan was to swarm the camp like bees and then extract the humans from their tents. Other units would attack sleeping guards quietly to prevent alerting the camp and bringing the entire Wolf Pack force down on them.

Legion didn't believe the security force could overwhelm their attacks, but it would slow their entry to the camp considerably. They would have to engage in an all-out fight that would consume time; it was possible that a good portion of his soldiers would die—not that he cared for them. The outcome was all he desired, but finding new members of his army was difficult enough. The Wasteland was a vast place, it would take weeks to recoup major losses, so he had to be stealthy.

The tactical team engaging the north gate security used one team member to get the guard's attention. The team member had a high-pitched whistle only the sensitive canine hearing of the guards could hear. He whistled repeatedly, irritating and disorienting the guards. The canines held their ears, unable to call for help or assistance. Both guards fell to their knees, incapacitated. The team signaled that the north gate was secure and Legion gave Deselation confirmation to proceed. The refuge guards were slaughtered.

Legion and Desolation watched from the distance as the invasion continued. The plan's execution was nearly flawless. The siege goes as planned and the guards are quickly disposed of by the first wave of attackers, opening the camp for Legion's raid.

Confusion erupted as the rest of the invasion teams struck the camp at full force. The remaining members of the Wolf Pack assigned to the surface team were slaughtered like cattle as they ran to defend the humans. Blood splattered the ground, the side of tents and many other places as the invasion ended the lives of the Wolf Pack personnel. Wolf Pack bodies lay stacked on the ground.

Screams could be heard from everywhere in the camp, as the raid forced itself into the tents.

Each invasion team watched with a different reaction to the carnage. Some took great joy in watching the humans die right before their eyes, while others neither took pleasure nor felt compassion for those they murdered. Most of the militia had stone-cold expressions on their faces and went about their duties. Black Widow and Quartz led them, pointing team members to specific tasks and making sure each tent had been cleared. Once they confirmed each tent was devoid of human life, they instructed those under their supervision where to take the condemned humans for slaughter.

Legion pulled Black Widow aside as she was completing her duties. She took pleasure in forcing family members to watch as their loved ones were killed, right before their own lives were stolen from them. "I want Clover's young friend found. We will use him to draw my brother away from his comrades. Then I will have my final satisfaction, eliminating my brother once and for all. I don't want any harm to come to the child. Do you understand me?"

Black Widow nodded. "Yes, Master."

As Legion's entourage traveled from Demure to the refugee camp, a message had reached him about each human family member. Legion had spies scattered everywhere from the safe zone where humans migrated to inner-most of the Wasteland itself. He had sent out several of these droid spies to infiltrate human settlements and homes and gather intel. This was one way Legion could gauge where humans had migrated to, and it allowed him to mount his mass extermination. Legion had found several of these relic, mechanical pets in underground storage containers, left behind by the Corporation.

Legion gave Black Widow a stern glare. "If one of our troops harms him, they will have to answer directly to me. Understood?"

Black Widow and Quartz, a hybrid with golden hair and dark eyes, searched from tent to tent. They dragged the occupants of the camp into the open. When Quartz touched a person, he could crystallize his victim's body, turning it to stone. He was one of Legion's favorite weapons.

Humans were split up and King Rue's servants were slaughtered in grotesque ways. The Wolf Pack's blood was spilled all over the camp to scare the humans into giving up loved ones and neighbors in fear for their own lives. Many of Legion's goons were splattered with blood.

With many looks of despair and shock, the humans are questioned about the whereabouts of the teenage boy. They force an adult male to his knees. He shook with fear. Legion's men didn't allow him to look at their master. The man seemed to be in a daze, and wouldn't be able to identify the ruthless leader even if he knew Legion's face.

"Where are the family that came here last night?" Black Widow asked. "We are searching for a teenage boy that came here with his family and the assistance of Clover."

The man attempted to spit at Black Widow, but two large creatures held him down. His saliva landed on Black Widow's boots and trickled down, as if it wanted to get off her footwear in a hurry. It left a slimy residue behind.

"Go fuck yourself, bitch!" he screamed without looking at her black eyes. "No one's going to tell you shit. We know what you are."

Black Widow struck the human across the face and blood sprayed from a newly inflicted wound. She inspected her hand, as if she had thought she had sprained her wrist in the process. Black Widow looked angrily at the prisoner.

"Do you feel like discussing what you know now, human?"

Black Widow grabbed the man by his greasy dark hair and pulled his head back violently. He tried to resist her violent attack and spat in her face. She released the man and wiped the mucus from her face, disgusted by the act. She detested humans, they were a plague. This time she was more than upset at the gesture; she was outraged. The man started to laugh.

Quartz grabbed the man by the throat. The human's skin began to change color as sounds of pain and agony protruded from his body. The man waved his arms, hoping it would grant him empathy from his attacker. When his body turned completely into quartz, Quartz smashes the statue into pieces, sending shards of crystalized human all over the ground.

Black Widow turned and slapped Quartz's face harder than she had slapped the human's. She looked at him furiously. "Why in the fuck did you do that? Now we can't get anything out of him."

"We weren't being successful in extracting info from him anyway. Maybe purging his life force from his shell of a body will encourage the rest to be more open with us and cooperate."

Black Widow stared at him, steaming mad. "You're not here to think. I'll do the thinking for the both of us." She stormed off.

Legion turned to Momentuim, a large creature who looked like Frankenstein's monster in Mary Shelley's novel. He had a square shape, dreaded eyes and large extremities. Once he got started he could not be stopped. His body generated so much torque that the energy released was unrivaled.

"Momentuim, I want you to seek out King Rue and the rest of his men. Make sure that they don't leave their burial tomb."

Momentuim grunted his understanding and moved away to fulfill his master's wishes.

Legion walked into the middle of the camp, where the humans were being forced into a circle, and onto their knees. It had the appearance of a séance gone wrong and that pleased Legion. He smiled at them in his sinister way, giving each human an chill that spread down their spines.

"Dear humans, we are not here to kill you, we don't want anything of the sort. Give up the teenager Clover brought to this camp and we will leave you in peace."

He circled the humans they had captured. He had his hands on his hips, taunting his captives. He received no acknowledgment of his friendly offer, which fed his rage and increased his determination.

"Did I not make myself understood? I will leave you all in peace and no harm will come to anyone in this camp. All I want is the boy, give him to me."

From the other side of the camp, Black Widow and Quartz dragged the teenagers Doria and Straus toward the middle of the camp and threw them down at Legion's feet. They were slightly beaten and panting for air, but no worse for the wear.

"Hey, watch it!" Straus said.

"Master, the prize you have been searching for," Black Widow said.

Legion grinned at his new captives, their faces were a blend of anger and fear.

"Who in the hell are you supposed to be?" Straus asked.

Legion looked down at the boy with a devious smile. "Why, didn't your friend Clover talk about me?" Legion received no response and his sinister smile grows. "I'm astonished because we go way back. I'm the demon that escaped from what your society considers Hell." Legion laughed and turned to two of his servants. "Prepare the children for the journey."

"Master, what about the rest of them?" Quartz motioned to the other humans.

Legion looked over at the humans then back at Quartz. "Kill them all and burn the camp to the ground. I want Clover to understand his grave error. Make sure several charred bodies lay in the middle of the camp so he can find them."

Quartz gave his master a look of confusion. "But Master Legion, what will that—" He stopped midsentence, fearing Legion's wraith. "Yes, Master. As you command."

Legion walked away. In the distance, screams could be heard as the humans were slaughtered. Then the camp was set ablaze.

CHAPTER 12

Clover climbed over a dune and peered down into the valley of sand below. There it was! They had finally had arrived at their destination. The San Francisco Bioengineering Laboratory owned by the Corporation sat a mere one hundred and fifty paces from them. Their journey had taken them through some of the roughest terrain the Wasteland had to offer. The farther they had traveled west the harder the terrain had become and the steeper the dunes of sand which seemed to rise to meet them. Only small portions of the Sierra Nevada had survived the onslaught of nuclear bombardment and, later, the nuclear fallout in the form of acid rain, which slowly disintegrated both natural stone and any remaining artificial structures. Looking down on the building where Doctor Sergei Peterovitch and his staff had done their initial research for the famed project, Clover could sense the enormous size of the once-great entity known as the Corporation.

Before the war, the building had been a humongous place. It had towered over everything around it. It had once had gorgeous landscaping, with amazing California sycamores lining the perimeter creating a lavish courtyard setting. The building had once had a shining exterior that seemed to match the outside landscape, the metal and plaster combining to create its unique exterior. The lab had many personnel working at it and just like the secret moon base, the lab was kept so secret that security, rumor had it, was tighter than the famed Area 51. Its visible areas displayed a normal biology lab like the ones found on college campuses, but the work was kept behind thick blast doors and mounds of concrete for secrecy. The building's façade masked the real lab work and the extreme security that had once protected the lab's secrets. Now only hollow structures were buried deep under the sandy surface.

As they approached the tomb-like building, with nothing surrounding it but thousands of tons of sand and no trace of life anywhere, Clover thought it looked more like a crashed spacecraft, with its nearly covered structure embedded deep into the sandy ground. It seemed so far removed from the pinnacle of its majesty, much like the society it mirrored. The vision the facility created inside Clover's mind was nothing like what sat before their eyes. It was like the occupants of the lab had switched off the lights and simply abandoned the structure. There wasn't even a hint of a security shed among the ruins. The place's aura was of gloom and death, a post-apocalyptic haunted house.

The complex could barely be seen from the surface and only fifteen percent of the complex remained above ground. Dunes that had developed from decades of powerful storms coming out of the Wasteland shielded the complex's existence from approaching parties and covered most of the first three levels of the building. A singular side entrance, which was only partially visible to the naked eye, was exposed on the west side of the complex and accessible to the weary travelers. This side hadn't completely disappeared under sand drifts, allowing them to spot its location.

Clover's team approached it with extreme caution, with Clover at the point. He kept a tight grip on one of his katanas, holding it out in front of him, protecting the team from being exposed to a frontal attack. Zeus brought up the rear of the group and, using his military training, scanned the horizon for anything that might attack from above.

Tigerous turned to Schmidt. "So is this it, the complex you mentioned. This is the place Preist lives?"

Schmidt backed away from her a little, afraid of being struck again.

The soft feline features on her face transformed as her mouth tightened and her tiger-tattooed skin compressed closer to her eyes, as if she were ready to attack some prey.

He shook his head. "Yes, this is the one."

Clover responded with a slight tone of disappointment. "I was expecting a lot bigger place." He looked at the door much like he would an assigned target. "The way you went on about it made it seem like much more than what we are seeing now. It feels drab and desolate and we haven't even gotten inside yet." Clover looked over at the rest of his travel companions, gauging their reactions to the place. The party had halted very near the facility's structure. The place expressed its humongous size now that they had got much closer to it. Before, it was barely visible to them, but now Clover realized that there was much more to the place than met the eye.

"Relax, everyone," Schmidt said. "Most of the complex is buried underground. Trust me, you won't be disappointed once we are inside."

The group slowly approached the humongous gray weather-beaten metal door. The door's exterior was ravaged with rust and in spots the paint had completely peeled away, exposing the material underneath. It was brown from extended periods of oxidation and the rest of the exposed structure seemed to be heading in the same direction, like a snake shedding its skin

"How are we going to gain access through that thing?" She asked.

"Look for a keypad or something," Clover said.

They all searched around the door, but there was nothing they could see that would facilitate their access to the structure's interior. The large metal structure just sat there like it was hiding some secret and refusing to let them in. Its exterior seemed to guard their path like a rust-covered behemoth.

Zeus turned angrily to Schmidt, grabbed him by his collar and threatened to choke the life out of him, like he had on their first encounter. "How did Legion gain access to the building when you were with him?"

The slave shrugged his shoulders. "I don't remember, it has been a while since I have been here."

Zeus struck the slave with his massive hand, sending him to the ground, tossing up sand. Schmidt rubbed his face, which stung from the strike and still had a big handprint on it. He gave the giant gorilla a look of detest.

"Okay, okay. Just give me a moment." Schmidt sighed. "Preist always had the doorway open by the time we arrived," he said. "He must have the controls inside the lab, close to him."

"Maybe the controls to the door were moved from to the inside of the structure for safety purposes," Tigerous said. "That will cause us more work."

"Do you think he is that paranoid that he didn't want Legion to be able to have access to the lab anytime he chose?" Clover asked.

Zeus pounded his chest. "Legion is quite manipulative. It would keep him from dictating to the scientist when he could gain an audience and when he had to announce his presence. It would reverse the roles of power, for once."

Maybe this is where the journey was meant to end. Maybe I wasn't meant to meet with Preist. Clover shook off the notion and kept looking for a way in.

Zeus moved to the giant door and Clover watched with intrigue as the massive apelike creature carefully ran his hands over its surface. Zeus pressed his weight against the structure and started to grunt as he strained against the immoveable object. It was an awkward dance between their new colleague and the stubborn rusty door.

Tigerous looked at Zeus. "What are you doing?" she asked.

Zeus turned to her with confidence. "A lot of these large blast doors are mechanically operated. With enough force we might be able to lift the door."

Tigerous looked at Zeus perplexed.

"Are you insane? That door has to weigh more than fifteen hundred pounds."

"It probably weighs more than that," Schmidt said smugly.

Zeus knelt, placing his hands on the surface of the door, his palms flat on its surface. He grasped it forcefully and gave a loud growl as he pushed on the door. Slowly, inch by inch, it started to rise. The door creaked its displeasure as Zeus pushed it open. The struggle between Zeus's superior strength and the door's dead weight was comparable to two behemoths in a death match. The question was, which one would give way first?

The mechanical sprockets that operated the door moved in protest, along with the door itself. Their clanking made Clover wonder which noise was more painstaking. They needed maintenance and clearly hadn't been used for a very long time. Tigerous wasn't sure what she hated most, the rusted protest of the door itself, or the mechanical devices that operated it.

Zeus issued another loud roar and the door moved even more. His superior strength shifted the door and soon light emerged from the structure's interior.

Schmidt looked at Zeus, astonished. He couldn't believe his eyes. "Damn! You go, Zeus!"

Finally, the door was lifted high enough that all of them could get inside the building. Once everyone was safely inside, Zeus let go of the huge door and it came down hard. The crash echoed through the building's interior, penetrating the darkness.

A force halted Clover in his tracks. He could hear what was going on around him, but something had a hold of him. Something inside of the deserted lab wanted his undivided attention. Then someone spoke to Clover, a voice only he could hear.

"Clover!" said Preist. "Welcome. I have been awaiting your arrival for some time. I am anxious to speak with you exclusively. I know you have many questions. Come, I am waiting for you."

"Wait, Preist," Clover's voice reverberated through the deserted lab facility.

"Are you alright? Were you just speaking to someone, Clover?" Tigerous said.

Clover shook his head. "No, it was nothing."

They continued farther into the lab, not sure what to expect. Each party member lit an illumination stick, a device much like a glow stick filled with phosphorus, famously used during the early twenty-first century, but these lighting devices were electronically driven. Clover shone his illumination stick toward a far wall. Despite its ruined state, the nuclear blast hadn't destroyed it completely like so many other structures he had seen.

These walls must have been fortified from within. The builders must have taken extra precautions when constructing this place's walls or they would show much more wear.

The building appeared to have been deserted for a long time. Dust and sand particles floated in the air but there was no evidence as to where the sand was seeping in. The place was dingy and ill-kept but in the section, they now had entered. It was as if someone had taken care to make this portion of the building livable, despite how it looked. Even decades of neglect would bring on the smells of dampness and mildew, but there wasn't any.

Clover looked around, searching for something specific but not finding it, even with his nocturnal vision. He sniffed the stale, warm air and despite all the stench coming from other parts of the building, he could still pick up Preist's scent.

"This place is way too large for us to search it room by room. I think it may be beneficial if we split up and sweep through each section. We can report back in—let's say an hour or so?—and exchange intel."

"Do you think that's wise? It's hard telling what lurks in the shadows of this place. It gives me the creeps," Schmidt said.

"What's wrong, little man? Afraid of the dark?" Tigerous bellowed out a high-pitched laugh which echoed throughout the adjacent hallway, leading down a dark, uncharted path.

"Come on, let's take that hallway and see where it leads, human," said Zeus. He grabbed Schmidt by the arm and dragged him down the dark hall.

They split into two groups to cover more ground. Clover and Tigerous headed westward, along the wall closest to them and toward the rear; while Zeus and Schmidt moved eastward toward the rear of the complex.

As Clover and Tigerous progressed, they could tell this place used to be home to number of different scientific projects. Numerous types of equipment, some neither had ever seen before, looked foreign or old. They passed inspection tables, testing equipment, slots for x-rays and many other types of dust-coated lab equipment which, in Clover's opinion, had seen better days. It was clear the equipment hadn't been used in a while.

Tigerous passed one of the inspection tables, stopped abruptly and leaned over. She picked up an item laying on the table and lifted it to her illumination stick. It reflected the light and she turned to Clover, shocked.

Tigerous looked at Clover with a frown, one that made Clover think she was about to cry. He had never seen this exotic young thing shed a tear, not that he could remember, but he had been known to be wrong before.

"Were all of us made like this?" she asked.

She showed Clover the shackles attached to the examination table. Dried bloodstains and strands of hair were stuck to both the shackles and the table, like something had died on it. She couldn't tell if it was animal fur like her own or human hair. The shackle was rusted and seemed fragile in Clover's hands. Anger flashed onto Tigerous's face, her jaw muscles tightened and her lips forced back, exposing her sharp feline teeth protruding as if they were about to sink into a helpless victim.

"The humans must have been monsters and treated these poor souls—may they rest in peace—like ravaging beasts. Who is the real animal to be feared in this whole plight I wonder? Maybe Legion is justified in his hatred of them after all," she said.

Clover went over to Tigerous, placed the shackles back on the table and consoled her.

"I don't think all humans were like this. I think with all species there are good ones along with the bad. We just have to take them as individuals not the whole society," he said. "I've learned though my assignments that not all humans are evil, manipulative and deceitful."

They continued through the dark corridors of the complex. Much of the lab building seemed to be in shambles. In their exploration, Clover and Tigerous discovered many items like the shackled table. But, unfortunately, none of the artifacts they discovered gave them any idea what had really gone on in the facility or any clue where to find Preist. The air became cooler and had a staleness that didn't exist in the other parts of the wing.

After what seemed like hours of exploring, Clover and Tigerous reunited with Schmidt and Zeus. Like most of the abandoned buildings of this world, the lab was dingy, dark and appeared to be as deserted as the rest of the building. The only light that illuminated the room was a fluorescent and dangled from the ceiling by its wires. It flickered in a unique beat, off and on, like a digital spotlight illuminating a performer on stage.

They took a few more steps into the room and scouted it for any clue that might give them the information they had been looking for.

"Did you find anything on your tour of this place?" Clover asked.

"It appears that our side of the building housed a berthing section and a galley. I think most of the other sections are underground like the main lab," Zeus said.

"What gives you that idea?" Clover asked.

"We discovered a large portion of the wing we explored had numerous holes in the floor," said Schmidt.

Clover and Tigerous looked at each other. "Holding cells under the floor?" she asked.

Zeus shrugged. "Furthermore, there was a massive hole in the middle of the floor that these smaller ones interlinked with. There must be some type of tunnel system connecting them that was hidden from our view. It's the only logical conclusion," he added. "We also discovered underground storage compartments. We explored one. It had a massive door that had fallen off its equally massive hinges. It was as dark and dry, so our little lighting devices didn't reveal very much, but I doubt there was much to see anyways."

"Underground storage compartments?" Tigerous said.

"For food, or something more sinister." Clover was getting a vibe from Schmidt. The human was becoming less at ease the farther they ventured into the complex.

"Yes, the compartment we explored was big," the slave said. "Large enough to contain the room we found Zeus in. I can't fathom what they needed with storage space so large, and maybe more labs connected to the storage compartments, as well as to the holes in the floor," he said. Schmidt looked around the lab they were standing in.

"I think the humans had our brothers and sisters in these holes, like the cages humans used before," Zeus whispered to Tigerous.

Tigerous's expression transformed into hatred. "I thought you told us that this research assistant lived here. Was that another lie?" She struck Schmidt across his left jaw with such a blow that it sent the human off his feet. He landed on his backside, slightly dazed from the attack. His face was numb. Trembling, he started to crawl away from his captives.

"Trust me, Tigerous, I have not deceived you. He did live here, once, but it has been a while, maybe even years. I have lost track of time since my captivity under Legion. Maybe he got tired of Legion's persuasive scheming and left."

"Why you little—" Tigerous started.

"And go where," Zeus asked. "This whole landscape is dead and desolate, he couldn't have migrated anywhere—or have you not noticed, little man?"

Clover cut off his companions. Someone was watching them. "He's not lying. Someone else is in the room with us, I can sense his presence."

Clover's traveling companions searched the lab, but discovered no one.

"Then where is he?" Tigerous asked, frustrated.

From the dark shadows of the lab a voice boomed, accompanied by a steady series of claps. "I'm impressed, Clover. You have become everything Doctor Sergei Peterovitch ever wanted you to become. Even more, I believe."

The group spun in the direction of the visitor lurking in the dark. Clover couldn't see him, despite his nocturnal eyesight, but he could sense the presence of the one they sought.

A tall figure, clothed in a dingy gray cloak covered with dirt and sand, approached the party. He was a lean individual and wore a tan robe underneath his frayed, weather-beaten cloak. He had long fragile limbs and an embedded crucifix on his forehead. He possessed the ability to blend into his environment and that made him difficult to trace.

"It is very nice to finally meet the infamous Clover in the flesh. The one our kind calls the demon of the darkness." The man looked Clover over carefully, as if inspecting a newly manufactured piece of equipment.

"Preist, I presume?" Quizzed Clover. "You shouldn't get into the habit of entering someone's mind without their permission." Clover moved slowly toward Preist.

Preist smiled crookedly. "I'll keep that in mind for future reference."

Clover nodded. "Preist, we have come—"

"I know why you have come and I know what you seek," Preist said. "And yes, I am the one they call Preist. But embedded within my DNA is Doctor Peterovitch, father of us all."

Clover and his companions looked on, astonished, and unsure of how to respond.

"Tell me, my friend," Preist said, looking directly at Clover with his diamond-shaped eyes. "What will you do once you get the information that you have been searching so long for?"

Clover shook his head, confused. He was still stuck on Preist's declaration that he knew who they were, why they had come and what they were searching for.

Clover shook himself. "Preist, I don't know what I am. I desire to understand this very thing. But Legion must be stopped before we all become extinct, not just the humans he terrorizes." Clover paused a moment then looked at Preist with a renewed vigor. "I'm going to kill

Legion and that's all I know. That's the only way to stop his rampages."

A smile grew on Preist's face. "I've been waiting for one of our species to have the nerve to proclaim just that. I knew all along you would be the one to step forward and challenge his existence." Preist reached in his cloak and pulled out a vial. He tossed it to Clover. "Fair enough, my friend." He pointed to the object in Clover's hand. "What you hold in your possession a sample of your DNA. You're part wolf, which gives you advanced scent abilities. You're part hawk, which gives you your hunting skills and night vision. Finally, there was a missing element that even the former Doctor Peterovitch wasn't totally sure of. Only the good General knew the last part of your DNA code. He wanted it that way so neither the doctor nor himself had the total DNA code, for security purposes. You can understand that, right?" Preist took a deep breath and then continued. "Clover, the most important thing you must understand is this: you're the origin of our species."

Clover peered down at the vial.

Tigerous looked at Clover a moment, then at Preist. "So, we all have human DNA after all? The ones we are made to kill could may be our blood relatives after all."

Preist responded to her without altering his tone. "It is possible, that's one way to put it. But"—Preist looked from one visitor to the next—"there is some missing from

Clover's DNA coding and I still haven't discovered what it is. The rest of us had human DNA substituted for the missing code. It was a corporate decision. They weren't willing to hold up the process to discover the deceased doctor's hidden ingredients. I have no clue what Doctor Peterovitch used in the early stages of the project." He turned to Clover. "I do know, however, that the genetic code was humanoid. That much I am sure of."

"Why do I have this strong connection with Legion? Why can I sense him so much?" Clover asked.

Preist folded his arms back into his grungy robe. "You and Legion are the first of our kind. You share some of the original DNA. That's why you both have a strong connection."

"Well, I guess there is only one thing left to do then." Clover closes his hand over the vial. "We have to stop Legion and spoil his master plan. We can't allow him to of kill off the humans. We can't lose that part of ourselves forever."

Tigerous smiled. "That's my boy. But how do we stop him? He has that impenetrable armor built into his skin, remember."

"He's not indestructible," Preist said.

In a deserted cave, far from the buried lab in San Francisco, the Shadow Agent was entrenched in a virtual conversation with his superior. A blueish-green glow came from the holographic communication device held in his dark palm.

"Yes, Master," the Shadow Agent said. "Clover and his party have arrived in San Francisco and should be at the one they call Preist's abode. As far as I can tell he has possession of the Monoarc Stone."

The holographic figure paused, as if the contemplating what it was being told. "That doesn't matter now," the Shadow Lord said. The menacing creature's image flickered briefly. It was gauging the dark assassin's response—or lack thereof.

"What about the mission directives? Don't we need the stone's energies to complete the final preparations?" asked the Shadow Agent.

Another moment of eerie silence from the Shadow Lord.

"Our master no longer needs the stone. He has ordered all agents to return for the pending siege. Everything has been set into motion, Shadow Agent. You are ordered to return immediately."

"What about the duel with Clover!" the agent argued. "That's why you created me in the first place—to take him out. That's why I was kept secret all this time. It's my destiny. It's my right!"

"That will be left for another time. The siege of the master's army is the priority, not your vendetta against the Corporation's prized creation. This is not up for discussion, understood? Return immediately."

The image disappeared and left the Shadow Agent holding the communication device speechless.

Preist led Clover into the lower level of the lab. It was even darker than the previous areas and had a smell of mildew about it, even with the absence of moisture. *It must be left over before the environment became corroded with the radiation that now poisons the air*, Clover thought. The sound of creaking, busted pipes rattling without a water source emanated from the darkest part of the level.

Preist turned toward Clover. His eyes shone in the darkness with a silvery essence that made Clover think of an owl's eyes watching for prey scampering through the night. He didn't think that Preist would give him a "hoot" but it wouldn't surprise him if the odd figure did.

Clover looked away from Preist with an eerie feeling. "g. They were horrible things. Killing people, assassinating leaders—I feel that we were murderous thugs."

Preist shook his head and walked toward a shadowy corner of the room. Despite his keen vision, Clover had trouble making out what Preist was doing. The man had a way of flowing like a spirit. His host reached down for something.

"Clover, the Corporation, or I should say General Reinhart, wanted a solider that could morph its skin into a suit of armor."

Clover looked beyond their current location; something drew his attention, but it was more like a sense of déjà vu. He could recall seeing his brother morph into his suit of armor without worrying that Clover saw him do it.

"Doctor Peterovich and his team struggled for a long time on this," Preist said. "They couldn't come up with any solutions to the problem at hand."

Preist reached into his safe and pulled out a small wooden box. Clover could smell the slight scent of the pine that made up the box's construction. It made him curious about the box's contents.

"The elemental's outer layer of skin could not be penetrated by any weapon known to man. That's when Peterovich's team came up with the idea to use its DNA to fill in the missing code," Preist said.

Clover stared at Preist and shook his head in disbelief. "That's just obscure, Preist. Can you hear yourself? Now don't get me wrong, I've seen Legion morph into his suit of armor, but it can't be some form of unknown DNA I've never heard of before? And what the hell is an elemental anyways?"

Preist's expression didn't waver. "I'm dead serious about this. From the little knowledge I have of them, an elemental is a race of superior beings that live a long time ago. I don't joke about the possible end of our entire species at the hands of a warped madman."

Clover sighed. "Okay, if I am to believe you, what you're telling me is that Legion is part elemental?"

Preist nodded. "Only the part of his DNA that morphs his skin into the suit of armor. The scaly outer surface of the Omnipresence was almost impenetrable and the DNA was difficult for them to retrieve. The origin of the creature is still unknown. All that data was lost in the crash."

"Impenetrable, you say?" Clover said.

"Or that's what they wanted the rest of us to believe. This could be why he seems to possess a lunacy within himself. He isn't as immortal as he believes himself to be." Preist unwrapped the item in his grasp.

Clover leaned in to look. "What do you have there?"

Preist kept the object in the pine box covered, not revealing it to Clover yet. "Patience, Clover," he said. "You see, Legion's armor may seem impenetrable. But all suits of armor have their weaknesses, even his."

Preist held out an amber-colored jewel It shone brightly despite the lack of light in the room. As soon as Clover saw the jewel in Preist's hand, he became mesmerized.

"You see, Legion's armor has invisible seams that you can use to access his internal body. What I hold here is a

Monoarc Stone. The purest form of power known to us in the galaxy." He handed the gem to Clover. "Place this inside his armor, and embed it into his DNA. As the stone dissolves, it will devour the demon portion of his DNA and his armor will dissipate. Then will be just like those he hates."

Clover looked at the gem with awe, then back at Preist.

"Legion has been searching for this stone forever. He feels it can give him immortality. He has been hounding me about its location for a long time," Preist said. "I kept him thinking that I didn't know where the doctor had hidden it, but I had it all along."

Clover looked at Preist, trying to gauge if he was being deceived or if Preist was telling him the truth.

"Well, can it make him immortal?"

"I don't have any idea if it could or not. It was best kept out of his hands either way," said Preist.

"But you want me to give him the opportunity to take it from me," Clover said skeptically.

"No, I want you to insert it into him. That's why I'm offering it to you. It's what you must do."

CHAPTER 13

While Clover was busy with Preist discussing the destruction of Legion down in the lower part of the lab, new, unwelcome guests had arrived unannounced. Preist had not realized that Legion had discovered an alternative route into the lab which didn't include going through any of the traps Preist had set up. Clover, however, sensed the newcomers' presence instantly. He quickly looked at the ceiling above. Preist reached out to the assassin. *Clover*, Preist's voice entered Clover's mind, *what has your attention?*

Clover replied with a muted, angry look, one that told Preist right away that they had uninvited guests. Preist knew who had arrived and looked at the Monoarc Stone in Clover's hands. "Hide it. Don't allow him to steal it from you."

Legion was escorted by only a few of his trusted followers including Black Widow, Momentuim and Quartz, along with Legion's mentor, Master Reinhart. The rest of Legion's entourage had been sent back to Demure. Momentuim shoved a piece of lab equipment, knocking it over, sending dust everywhere. The lab equipment's collision with the floor rang throughout the lab, alerting the lab's occupants of their arrival.

With the ruckus being made by Legion's raiding party in the main lab, Clover and Preist rushed up the short flight of stairs to aid their friends, who had already arrived to meet the invaders.

Legion mocked his adversaries' lack of attention. "Look, Master, they decided to throw a party without inviting us."

Master Reinhart acknowledged his protégé's jape and gave a chuckle, one that bordered on the sound of dying frogs bellowing their last croak. "Yes, I can see that, Legion. You are quite observant."

"Now, that's a shame. I always enjoy a good throw down," Black Widow said. She gave her master a slight smile with her usual sinister twist. "I am truly heartbroken."

"That's okay, we brought party favors anyways," Quartz said. He cracked his knuckles. It sounded more like jagged glass being scraped across smooth pavement or an old chalkboard, making a screech sound.

Clover had to cover his ears; the sound made his sensitive ears ache and he staggered for a moment before he recovered.

Tigerous gave them an angry look. One that made her nose scrunch up to expose her sharp teeth. Even her thin, furry tail swung madly back and forth.

"What are you doing here?" she asked. "You're not welcome here, so I suggest you hit the beaten path before things get ugly for you."

Zeus puffed out his chest, and beat on it as he roared mightily, exposing his massive teeth. He moved forward, placing himself between her and their uninvited guests.

Legion pointed at Zeus as if to command him. "I can see you'll keep all types in your company, brother. I notice you like to collect rejects among you, especially this one. I'd keep your dog on a leash before I have to discipline it."

"What have you come for, Reinhart?" Preist asked.

Master Reinhart slapped his hands. Clover noticed a shift in Preist's demeanor—from calm and subdued to dissatisfaction and protest. Preist folded his arms together and disinclination settled in his expression. No words were exchanged between Clover and Preist, but none were needed. Clover thought he heard Preist mumbling to himself in a foreign tongue, but he couldn't decipher the words.

"Oh, my dear friend, Preist. We haven't joined company in a while. I was beginning to think you were avoiding us. Now, that wouldn't be the case, would it? That would be such a hurtful thing to do to your friends," Reinhart said.

Clover saw Preist tense with built-up anger. "That's because you maim and murder your own kind like cattle. You do even worse to the humans."

Reinhart chuckled in amusement. "To tell you the truth, I have come here to give you a chance to join us. Soon you will be looking at the one that will be ruling the entire globe," he said.

Preist's eyebrows sank. "You're human and you treat them like a delicacy for your pets to devour. That's not the company I desire to keep."

Legion placed his massive hand on Reinhart's shoulder. "Yes, but it's not who you think it is. There is someone else you should be fearing." Legion peered down at the old wrinkly man he had considered a father. "Don't take what I'm about to do personally, old man. I do adore you for what you have taught me."

Legion grabbed hold of Master Reinhart's neck with his enormous hands and squeezed. A crunching noise emerged from Legion's hands and he broke the old man's neck in two. Reinhart's fragile body hung limp like a rag doll in Legion's mighty grasp.

Legion tossed the body away and looked around the poorly lit room. "I've come for two purposes, one for you to worship me as your god."

Tigerous spat at Legion's feet. "You got to be fucking kidding me, you ugly bastard."

"We will never bow down to you, Legion," Zeus bellowed. His eyes were steamed with rage and he had balled up his fists, ready to pounce on any of Legion's goons.

Legion's devilish smile turned into a look of disappointment. Clover knew now what his brother was about to do. It was the only option left and it wouldn't be joining his brother's ragtag gang. No matter who he had in his company, those that stood in Legion's path would perish by the tyrant's hand.

Clover stepped toward Legion. "What's the second reason?" Clover demanded.

Legion turned to Clover. "Preist knows, ask him. Or has he already told you?" Legion stared intensely at Preist. "Where is it, Preist? I know you have been negating my efforts to find it." Legion looked around the devastated lab. You have been hiding it all these years and have been sending me on a goose chase, haven't you?"

Preist walked toward Clover and Legion, nodding as he did. "Yes, I know what you have come for. But there is no way in hell I'm giving you the stone. It's somewhere safe from your tyrannical grasp."

Legion looked down, feigning rejection, then his sinister laugh started again, echoing in the hollow lab. He motioned to his posse with a forceful gesture.

"Kill 'em all. Leave none of alive to tell the tale of their destruction." He looked straight into Preist's gray eyes. "If you won't give me the stone, I shall pry it from your cold, dead grasp."

Legion transformed his skin into his suit of armor. The suit was hard, with jagged edges over its entirety. It reminded Clover of something being enflamed with small jagged edges protruding from the suit at its small seams while larger protrusions amassed on his torso, chest and legs. It appeared that Legion was on fire or had maybe even become a solid piece of crystal. Only Legion's demonic eyes penetrated the horrific façade.

Legion didn't hesitate or hide his transformation, but did it with a sense of pride. Instead of the behemoth that had just been standing right in front of them, boasting about his future conquests, there stood this thing, one that would scare any opponent of Legion's half to death simply by its appearance. Legion had never tasted neither a warrior's honor for battle nor defeat, and his arrogance shone through even with the suit's extravagant design.

Black Widow grabbed Schmidt and pressed his frail body up against hers. "This is for your betrayal to us. It will only hurt for a moment, my dear." She stabbed him with her stinger shaft. The needlelike protrusion pumps her deadly toxin into his bloodstream. The deadly poison that eats the victim from the inside out, corroding and dissolving every organ and vein in its path, much like sulfuric acid. Foam emerges from his mouth and ears and flows to the ground.

By the time his body struck the floor, Joachum Schmidt was dead.

She peered down at her victim with a quaint smile. "We no longer need assistance from humans, so your contract has expired," she said.

Both sides prepared to dual each other like raging beasts assigned a death match. The first to engage each other were Zeus and Momentuim. They raced toward one another and their behemoth bodies crashed, sending the walls and the floor of the lab shaking. They struggled with each other like giants on a battlefield, each pushing the other with all their might. They maneuvered all over the lab, knocking things over as they went.

Momentuim growls at Zeus. "Don't you realize you can't stop me once I get started? You have no chance to win, my hairy friend."

Zeus returned the sentiment, but took it as a challenge and scowled at his nemesis, displaying his massive canines as his furious jaws tried to clamp down on Momentuim. "Then I guess I can't let you get started then, can I?"

Zeus shoved Momentuim off him and his adversary stumbled clumsily into an adjacent wall in the lab, denting the metal structure. Momentuim leaped at Zeus and attempted to strike him, but landed poorly and stumbled uncontrollably. While he was off-balance, Zeus struck Momentuim in the face with a massive, hairy fist and sent him crashing into the wall behind. The collision created a large crack in the foundation and the entire lab started to shake. The foundation could be heard starting to crumble under the two giants' struggle.

Frustrated, Momentuim shook off his collision with the wall; his body wasn't quite ready to reengage Zeus, but Momentuim did anyway. He ran toward Zeus in an attempt to catch Zeus off guard. The giant primate leaped into his opponent and they collided again, the force sending each adversary in the opposite direction, dazed.

Zeus shook of the after-effects of the collision.

Instead of giving Momentuim a chance to generate energy, making the enormous creature unstoppable, Zeus ran towards Momentuim, trying to eradicate any opportunity his opponent might have in becoming indestructible. Zeus and Momentuim collided and trying to prevent the juggernaut from fully recovering, Zeus began to squeeze his adversary with all his might, not letting him escape. He knew that if he allowed Momentuim to generate enough energy, his adversary would become unbeatable. Momentuim screamed in agony, he could feel Zeus's mighty strength crushing his bones in on themselves. He had misjudged his opponent and hadn't allowed his body to recover totally from the first collision. In the end, Momentuim's massive bones crumbled under the furious pressure of the once-great master-at-arms.

Black Widow was still hovering over the slave's body. Tigerous was not about to make the mistake of underestimating the black witch and allow Legion's she-bitch to inject her poison into Tigerous. The feline warrior decided to wait for her opponent to strike first and catch Black Widow exposed. Black widow threw a slew of roundhouses wildly at Tigerous, but close combat wasn't Black Widow's strength and she missed in nearly every attempt. Tigerous slapped Black Widow on the side of her head. The attack left a deep gash on Black Widow's unblemished skin.

Black Widow touched her wound, furious with Tigerous. "You little bitch! You scarred my face."

Tigerous smiled mockingly at Black Widow. "It makes you look more presentable. Gives you some personality on that rather dull-looking face."

Black Widow recovered and tried to pull Tigerous in close, hoping to use her deadly weapon. Tigerous kicked Black Widow in the chest and danced away from her, just avoiding being stung. She retrieved one of her razor-sharp claws and flung it at Black Widow. The claw split the air so quickly that Black Widow didn't realize what was upon her until it hit her. The attack struck Black Widow in the shoulder and she fell in agony, clutching her arm.

"This is for treating your pets like shit. And for all the humans you have killed," Tigerous yelled.

Tigerous retrieved another claw, leaped onto Black Widow's chest, and forced her knee into Black Widow's chest, not allowing her to recover. Tigerous rammed the claw up, inside of Black Widow's skull, and dug it deep.

She didn't relinquish her thrust until she heard a crunch. Black Widow gasped and closed her eyes. She had fought her last battle and Tigerous was glad she was the one to take the evil witch's life.

In the dark corner of the lab, Quartz approached Preist. Preist didn't let Quartz get too close to him. He knew what would happen if Quartz got his greasy paws on him, so he kept moving, keeping an equal distance from his opponent to prevent Quartz from turning him to a statue.

Quartz pulled up his sleeves and attempted to touch Preist but couldn't with Preist's sudden movements.

"Come here, Preist. We have never been truly introduced properly," Quartz said.

Preist vanished into the darkness and Quartz couldn't discover where his robed adversary had vanished to. It sent him into a wild rage.

"You fuckin' piece of shit, Preist. Come face me like a real man and stop using your stealth like a coward."

"No thanks." Preist's voice bounced all around Quartz, frustrating him even more. He couldn't pinpoint where Preist's voice was coming from. "I think I want you to keep your paws to yourself. You have a nasty habit of giving people migraines."

While Quartz had his back turned, Preist reappeared and kicked him, sending the man to the floor. Quartz reached to his belt and retrieved a long dagger. He attempted to hit Preist with it, but only managed to throw it wide. Preist had once again disappeared into the receding shadows. The dagger struck the wall and clanged to the floor.

Preist appeared behind Quartz again, but this time he didn't taunt him. Instead, he grabbed Quartz by the throat. "I know that if you can't concentrate on me, then you won't be able to crystalize me, like so many of your victims." Preist whispered into Quartz's ear.

Quartz tried to wrestle free from Preist's wiry grasp, but the ghost slit his opponent's throat from ear to ear.

"You have been cleansed of your demons, my son," Preist said.

Finally, the two brothers faced one another. Clover and Legion squared off. Legion's suit reflected off one of Clover's drawn katanas. The assassin held it directly in front of his face, prepared to deflect any attack from his brother.

"So, you have come to die, brother," Legion said.

Legion lunged at Clover with his massive great sword, which was covered in a similar material to his suit. The hulking, serrated blade edge, hissed through the air, missing its intended target by mere inches. The substantial blade slammed into the ground, causing it to quake under its vigorous collision with the earth.

Clover gracefully stepped out of the path of the attack and tapped Legion's helmet playfully with his katana.

"Little anxious to get this over with, Legion? I thought you liked to savor your victories," Clover said.

The two warriors reestablished their positions, circling one another to gain control of the battle. Then, just at the right moment, they engaged. Their swords clashed together, making a loud crash that echoed through the desecrated structure. Each struggled to gain leverage over the other. With their skillful training and abilities, neither warrior could gain the advantage.

"You can't beat me. You never could, and you never will." Legion stared deep into Clover's nocturnal red eyes.

With all his great strength Legion pushed Clover and sent him tumbling to the ground. Clover reached for his back, making sure the stone was still in his possession. Once he confirmed he still had it, he regrouped himself for another round.

He waited for another attack from Legion, which didn't take long. Legion had never been a procrastinator when it came to battle, and Clover had anticipated his brother's impatience. It was his key to the fight. Legion swung his heavy great sword at Clover in a slow, ungainly motion. Its ungraceful, time-consuming transit permitted the assassin to wait until the last possible moment to maneuver out of the massive weapon's path. It was his lightning-fast dexterity that had always gained Clover the upper hand in any confrontation and this conflict with Legion would not be an exception. Clover vaulted his body over the sword's downward swing; it passed directly under him—a near miss. Clover landed on his feet, directly behind Legion, and unscathed.

Legion couldn't believe how much faster Clover was, but they also had never fought face-to-face like this before. The upper hand had always been on Legion's side, but that was with a multitude of distractions he had employed to keep Clover off-balance. It was a tactic he used consistently to distract his opponents before striking them down.

"New move, Clover?"

Clover stared at his brother playfully as Legion slowly spun around. "I've been practicing," Clover said. "But you still possess the same moves as you have always had. Way too predictable, and I've grown accustomed to them."

Legion let out a massive roar and charged Clover. Their swords collided with a fury neither warrior had experienced, nearly knocking both over. After struggling to gain control, Clover pushed the attack away, separating them both. Legion stood, stunned by the move. Clover leaped up like an acrobat and kicked Legion in his arm plating, sending the elite warrior off-balance and stumbling backward. While still in the air he reversed his momentum and kicked Legion in the chest, forcing bits of the skin suit off its master and slightly damaging it. The attack sent Legion crashing against the wall behind, causing it to collapse in on itself.

Legion threw off the debris from the collapsed wall in anger. He glared at Clover and ground his teeth. Clover could hear the heavy, uncontrolled breathing coming from inside his brother's helmet. Legion grasped onto his great sword even tighter than before but, for a moment, seemed frozen on one knee, not having the willingness to attack. Clover couldn't decide if Legion's hesitation was him trying to comprehend what had just taken place or if fear had truly set in.

Does he fear that he now is vulnerable to my speed and agility?

"They don't make skin suits like they used to, do they?" Clover mocked with a shit-eating grin.

The collision shook the foundation, much like Zeus and Momentuim had. Legion shook off his disillusion and weariness from Clover's retaliation. Clover realized the real Legion had returned and the hell if he was going to let Clover win the day—at least, not quite yet. Clover stood, ready to continue their battle, his katana draped over his right arm, inviting Legion to retaliate. This enraged Legion even more. Legion looked around and, without warning, stopped.

"It appears that today isn't the day either of us should perish." Legion's sinister voice boomed throughout the room.

Realizing that this wave had been lost, Legion sheathed his weapon and exits without turning his back to Clover, his demon eyes of fading into the darkness of the unlit lab.

"Trust me, brother," Legion said. "We will finish this soon enough. But for now, I must say adieu." There was a brief moment of silence. "Soon I will come seeking our ultimate confrontation. Until then."

Legion retreated out the lab doorway and all that could be heard was his gargantuan footsteps fleeing.

Tigerous approached Clover from behind.

"I've never seen Legion yield to you like that before," she said.

"He knows the game has changed. The stakes are higher than they have ever been—for the both of us."

CHAPTER 14

After the confrontation with Legion, Clover and his comrades collected their wits, the battle had taken a lot out of each of them, mentally as well as physically. Clover knew that it wasn't the final battle. His job wouldn't be complete until Legion was dead at his feet. He felt for the hidden Monoarc Stone to make sure it was still secure. Clover's fear was the confrontation with Legion had made might have forced the stone to move from its hiding place. It was right where he had placed it and, satisfied with its security, he focused back on his companions and their recovery.

Tigerous was cleaning her nails and seemed satisfied with having killed Black Widow. Zeus labored slightly, his chest heaving in and out, showing the fatigue of battle. Clover wasn't the type to show much sympathy toward individuals, his design as an assassin didn't come with a sympathy manual. But he cared for the big hairy beast.

He cared for them all in some form or another, they were comrades in the same fight.

Clover saw Preist's shadow from the corner of his eye and turned his attention to their only lead. He could get over that Preist was once the renowned Doctor Peterovich, the father of them all. He was leaning over, covering Schmidt's body with some type of blanket. *He gives the deceased human dignity. Maybe this figure can be trusted after all*, Clover thought.

"You are a unique individual, Preist. One that astonishes me by each moment."

Preist looked up at Clover with a calm and collected manner. "Still don't trust me?" Preist shook his head. "You have become way too jaded from your past. You have the capacity to be compassionate, I have seen that with my own eyes, but you still struggle with your very nature. Haven't I proven myself by not giving Legion the stone, even though I had plenty of opportunities to do so? I waited to give it to you because you are the one who can end it all. Let me prove to you I will be one of your greatest assets in this war."

Clover sensed something approaching. At first, he wasn't sure who or what it was but his keen vision and sense of smell soon allowed him to focus on the figure. The figure was staggering out over the dunes and coming slowly toward them. Finally, a voice rang in his ears like an echo bouncing off a cavern wall. It was low and hoarse but still recognizable. The unknown figure approached the lab. An eerie feeling crept into Clover's companions as they watch the figure nearly collapse face-first in the sand several times. Finally, the stranger lost its struggle with exhaustion and passed out merely meters from the building's exterior.

Zeus carried the wayward figure to the lab and lay it on one of the lab's examination tables. The group surround their new visitor. It was Ruphus, one of King Rue's leading sergeants. The Wolf Pack member looked as if he had been thrown from the sky. Cuts, bruises and damaged tissue covered his fur.

Blood ran from every orifice of his canine body. There was no stopping it. Occasionally he spat up blood from his battered snout and onto the inspection table. What was left of his face was trying to clot the oozing blood, but in the end there were too many wounds on his face.

"Ruphus, what happened?" Clover asked, worried.

Ruphus looked over at his old friend and reached out for Clover.

"My friend, it was a tragedy." Blood slipped from his noise and ran down onto his mouth.

"What was a tragedy, my good man? Speak clearly, we can't understand you," Tigerous said.

Ruphus looked between Clover's comrades with a sad expression, one that was desperately attempting to apologize to Clover.

"Legion, he attacked the camp." Ruphus coughed loudly and tried to recover before continuing. "Right after you left. King Rue sent me to warn you Legion would head your way." He looked around sadly. "I fear I am too late though."

"Lie back and rest," Tigerous said.

"Legion did what?" Clover asked. "Why would he want to attack the refugee camp?"

Ruphus shook his head in confusion. "I don't know, but no one survived his slaughter." The dying canine grabbed for his stomach, clearly in great pain.

"No one survived?" Preist asked.

Zeus's face contorted with frustration and he displayed his primordial teeth in anger. He let a loud roar and struck his massive chest rapidly with both fists. "I knew he was a monster. He has been planning a total annihilation—even while I was in his army—but this is uncalled for."

Ruphus's bloodied hand grabbed Clover's. "He killed everyone in the camp, including all the humans living there. But there is one thing you must know," Ruphus said.

Clover leaned in close so that Ruphus could whisper to him.

"What is that, my good friend?" Clover asked.

"Legion took two prisoners. The young boy and his twin sister, the ones that you brought to the camp."

Contempt and rage flooded Tigerous's.

"He took both as his prisoners?" Tigerous asked.

"And what of the rest of the family?" Clover asked, his usual cold, stern expression on his face.

"Dead, like the rest of the camp's inhabitants, I suppose," Ruphus said. He closed his eyes. Clover watched as his former pack mate began to lose his battle with death. Ruphus's chest slowly heaved in and out. His breaths shortened and Clover could hear the air escaping Ruphus's lungs, like a tire rapidly leaking air. It seemed to Clover like eternity, but it didn't take the doglike creature long finally lose the battle. He died on the metal exam table without speaking another word.

Preist looked down in shame. The others understood that he was sorrowful for the Wolf Pack member's death and the slaughter of the humans in the camp. Preist shook his head. "This is just as much as my fault as it is Legion's."

Tigerous went to console Preist. "No, it—"

"He's using them for insurance," Preist said. "You know that, Clover. He wants to make sure he wins the day, he wants to keep your mind distracted and not focused on the final confrontation."

Clover gave Preist a determined look. He was prepared to do anything to rescue the teenagers and defeat his archnemesis.

"He wants this to be the endgame," said Clover. "So be it, the endgame it shall be."

"This is an unfortunate turn of events," said Preist. He looked at every one of Clover's crew with a tranquil, but solemn stare. It was like he had practiced this look for a while and Clover and his comrades saw Preist wasn't about to waver in his stance. "But it doesn't change what must be done, it only heightens the need to end Legion and his reign. I will stand at your side and assist you in any way I can, Clover."

Clover hadn't waited long after Ruphus had passed on. He was so determined to get the children back from Legion and to end Legion's terror that he was already in the process of sharpening his katanas. He pretended not to hear Preist's comments. His grasp tightened around the handcrafted, ancient sword hilt as his anger slowly built.

"There is no way Clover can do this on his own," Tigerous said. "He can't take on Legion and rescue the children at the same time, he will need our help." She turned to the rest of the group for support.

"I can't ask any of you to do this. It has to be your own decision," Clover said.

Preist was the first to respond. "She is right, Clover. We will all need to do our part for this to work."

Zeus moved forward to address the group. "Preist, how are we supposed to rescue the children when they will be heavily guarded? Knowing this is all a trap for Clover, how do we get around the town's protective shield?"

Preist smiled at the question. "That's a wonderful question to ask, my friend."

Preist patted Zeus on his hairy arm and moved toward a table in the middle of the room.

"Clover and my faithful comrades; take a hard look at what I have to show you. I have a plan that should be successful at this task." Preist reached under the round table and flipped on a holographic three-dimensional map of the town of Demure. They could see the above-ground and below-ground levels. It displayed the area surrounding the town. Preist pointed at a space just above the town. Lines moved like an air current.

"As you can see here the outer perimeter of the town, for about two miles, is protected by the energy shields Zeus mentioned. The generators that operate the shield are two miles underground," Preist said.

"So, we have to go deep underground to turn off the shields?" Tigerous said.

"Yes, but I have an alternative idea. Why risk trying to deactivate the town's shields? Deactivating the energy shields will only draw unwanted attention, bringing down the rest of Legion's faithful in a wrath of fury. No, what I'm suggesting is, why not go around the defenses altogether?"

Clover gave Preist a mistrustful glance. "What do you mean?"

"What I mean is, I know of an underground entrance into the city, a hidden sewer system that was once the answer to all human waste in Demure. It isn't used any longer and none, even Legion himself, know about it. One of us, meaning me since I know the town like the back of my hand, can get into the city nearly undetected. We'll need a quality diversion, though. Maybe Tigerous and Zeus could draw out a few of the remaining members of Legion's posse, giving me less to deal with once I get inside Demure. I can rescue the children and get back out of Demure virtually unnoticed."

Tigerous and Clover looked at one another, not sure how to take Preist's proposed plan.

"Once you're inside the town, I think I know where they will have the children imprisoned. Legion uses a pit to punish those that fail him. It's the most obvious place," said Zeus. "While serving under Legion there was this large container, I think it once held oil, before the world collapsed. Legion used to put undesirables in it until he was ready to deal his special brand of justice. It's near the center of town, but very close to his own living quarters. That is the drawback."

Preist extended the map by sliding his pale hand over a portion of the hologram to show the land farther out from the town.

"Why should you be the one to do something like this?" Clover asked. "And why should we trust you to do it? You have nothing at stake in rescuing the children."

Preist shook his head. "You still don't trust me, do you? I want to aid you in your efforts, and you know how badly I want Legion's death. I may want it at least as much as you. For all our sakes, it needs to happen, so let me help you. You can trust me. Remember, I have the father of us all inside of me and I care for all of us." Preist looked down, then back up at them with a hardened stare. "We won't wavier, and we will win the day—if we stick to this plan. It's not foolproof, but it's the only viable choice when we don't have many options at our disposal."

Preist looked at every member of their team, studying each face for rejection. He received none, not even from Clover himself. The assassin had chosen to trust him when he could easily have denied Preist's wish to be involved in the plan. Preist wanted to prove to Clover that he was worthy of the trust given to him and he wanted to prove that he could be an asset and a quality ally to them all.

"Perfect. Our plan would strike two birds with one stone. Drawing out needless posse members will act as a diversion." Preist looked at Tigerous and Zeus with a sly smile. "They still have one more that we'll need to deal with who resides inside Demure."

"Deselation," Zeus said. There was fury in his eyes and it laced his voice. He had not forgotten Deselation or forgiven him for exiling Zeus to the arid prison. The two warriors had been at each other's throats since their creation.

"What do you need from us?" Tigerous asked. "Me and Zeus, that is."

Preist gave them both a malicious smile. Clover recognized the response and he now truly saw his maker within Preist for the first time. At that moment, he knew they could trust Preist.

"If you can draw him out into the open, I can deal with the humans that still serve under Legion's command," Preist said. "That will make rescuing the children a lot more manageable." Preist looked over at Clover. "Clover knows what he must do."

Clover nods without saying a word.

Tigerous pulls Clover aside and whispers to him. "Are you sure we can trust him?"

"I don't think we have a lot of options at this point. I don't think Preist will lead us astray. It is apparent he hates Legion as much as we do," Clover said.

Approaching the town with caution, Tigerous and Zeus stayed aware of any ambush that may be awaiting them. Zeus looked skyward to see if they were being watched from above. He knew all about Oracle's flying friend and didn't want to be caught off guard by an aerial attack, but the blazing sun kept him from seeing anything above.

"Get ready, they should be coming to meet us very shortly," Tigerous said.

Zeus grunted in acknowledgment.

"Zeus, watch out just in case they try to flank us from behind."

"Tell me something I haven't already thought of, Tigerous. Remember I used to be a great military leader myself."

✝

Tigerous and Zeus slowly approached the town, fighting through a dust storm which had cropped up suddenly from the west and obscured their vision. If anyone approached from the town Zeus and Tigerous would not see them until they were right on top of them. Whoever came to greet them would also be in the dark until the parties engaged each other in battle. It had become too eerie and with the silence and the sand blowing all around them it felt like an old western. Tigerous was waiting for some corny music to start as they got ever so close to their destination.

Soon four ominous figures started to move away from the town, toward Tigerous and Zeus.

As they got close to the party, Tigerous could see it was Deselation and three unfamiliar figures who she had never seen before. Deselation's eyes glowed through the storm and smoke rose from the horns on the top of his head. The welcoming party stopped twenty feet from

Tigerous and Zeus and the two groups stood and stared one another down.

Geez, thought Tigerous. *This is becoming so anti-cliché. Where are the rolling tumbleweeds? I will pull my hair out if he gives a moronic gesture to the old west.*

Deselation was blowing smoke through his nostrils, making him look like an old steam engine from the nineteenth century. Unrest shone from his demonic eyes.

"So, you have both come to perish at my feet."

"I think you've got it wrong," Zeus said. "It's you who will be dying today at our feet." Zeus puffed his massive chest out.

Tigerous prepared a few of her claws for the upcoming battle. *Great, I'm surrounded by testosterone. If the battle doesn't kill me, their egos definitely will.*

"It's time for your wickedness to subside, Deselation. Prepare to die," Zeus said.

Zeus let out a massive roar, as if it aided him to release his built-up energy and prepare him for the confrontation. He catapulted himself toward Deselation.

"Zeus, wait! We should attack him together," Tigerous cried out.

She reached out her hand but it was too late. Even if she could grab hold of Zeus's arm, his momentum was too great for her to halt him.

Tigerous shook her head. "Men, I swear. They are all glory hounds to the death."

Deselation and Zeus collided creating a clash that echoed for miles and shook the ground.

Zeus grabbed Deselation's horns and wrestled with Legion's loyal servant. He contorted Deselation's massive head sideways, but it only aggravated his opponent. Zeus pressed down harder on Deselation's head, but the minotaur-like creature had too much strength in his neck and stopped the massive ape's attempt dead in its tracks.

Deselation let out a loud roar, deafening and disorienting Zeus.

Smoke protruded from Deselation's nostrils, temporarily blinding Zeus. His eyes watered and tears flowed from them, making it even more difficult to see. Deselation took the advantage, striking Zeus in the face with his stony fist.

"AFFFHHH." Blood spurted from the corner of Zeus's mouth and landed on the ground, staining the off-color sand.

The attack sent Zeus off-balance, but his massive strength and his grasp on Deselation's horns tightened and he kept himself from falling to the ground. He looked Deselation square in the face with his stern face.

Zeus laughed and mocked Deselation. "I hope that wasn't your best attempt. If so I would say you have gone soft in the service of your greedy master." He struck Deselation in the face, which sent Legion's loyal servant soaring into the air. He landed away from Zeus, sending dust and sand in every direction.

The three human servants moved in on Tigerous, surrounding her. Tigerous looked from one side to the other. She was gauging who was the bigger threat. The first attack came from her right. He moved quite slowly. Unlike the speed and agility of the designed species, humans were much frailer and less agile. Before he could reach her, Tigerous flung one of her claws and struck the human in the chest. The man fell to the ground, dead before he even landed. Blood oozed from his wound.

The two other humans approached her, but with much more caution than their comrade had. Tigerous looked from one to the other and gave them one of her catlike smiles. One man made his move. She waited for the attack to get deep into the action before she spun out of his way. He missed her completely and she kicked him, sending him soaring away from her, out into the dust storm. Screams of terror could be heard; something else had found the slave and was making a meal of him.

"One less human for Legion to manipulate." She smiled to herself.

The final human squared off with Tigerous. He retrieved a long-bladed dagger from his pants and flashed the jagged blade at her. The blade was dull and looked as if it hadn't been sharpened in a long time.

"Is that supposed to scare me off?" Tigerous asked.

"I'm going to slice that pretty little face up," the slave said.

Tigerous pulled out a claw and held it tightly in her grasp. She maintained a panther stance as the two of them circled one another. The human swung violently at Tigerous but missed. Tigerous coaxed the human to lower his guard by faking an attack. He lowered his weapon to block her blow and Tigerous swung her razor-sharp claw toward his head. It sliced his throat, cutting a neck artery. He bled profusely and fell to the ground.

"You make the human-race look incompetent." Tigerous laughed.

She knelt, lifted the bleeding man's head and rammed another of her claws into the man's skull. Blood foamed from his mouth and nose, and his eyes turned glassy. She let him go, and the slave's body fell back to the sand.

In the battle between Deselation and Zeus, the action had intensified. Deselation had recovered from Zeus's attack and the two engaged each other again.

Their massive strength pushed each other in the opposite directions but still each of them struggled to gain control of the other. The earth shook as the two warriors struggled to keep their footing. Deselation forced his elbow into Zeus's lower jaw and then struck him in the ribs, sending the mammoth gorilla to his knees.

Deselation roared, thinking he was about to win the battle. His premature celebrating was short-lived.

While Legion's most trusted follower was being occupied by Zeus, Tigerous used her catlike quickness and stealth to sneak around the two warriors, stalking Deselation's meaty backside. Tigerous hesitated only briefly, knowing she had to choose the right moment to strike. If her timing was off, even just a bit, she would be knocked aside by the battling brutes. She removed one of her poisonous claws and held it like a knife.

She could see the back of him in greater detail than she ever wanted. Deselation's back moved in odd curve, looking like a mountainous heap with steep inclines and massive indentations. His massive upper and lower back muscles protruded through his attire, flexing constantly as the two massive creatures battled.

The closer Tigerous got to the two battling warriors, the more she became entranced by the struggling beasts. She had never seen such a battle for supremacy between two foes before. Maybe that's because she never bothered to observe, she was always the one to react. Deselation's hooves started to slide backward as Zeus gained the upper hand. Deselation attempted to regain his footing, but he only managed to toss sand and dust into the air.

Tigerous spotted blood trickling down one of Deselation's hoofed legs. *He has been injured*, she thought. It must have happened without him becoming aware of it, otherwise he would have at least acknowledged it.

Deselation looked deep into Zeus's dark, primordial eyes. He saw his own reflection, with his nostrils flaring rapidly—blood trickled down the side of one. "Zeus, you have served our kind well but it is time to put this old warrior to his resting spot. I'm the superior soldier now, one like you were years ago."

Zeus shook off Deselation's strike. "Don't start the party until the fat chick starts her chorus, Deselation," Zeus said.

Deselation gave Zeus a bewildered expression. "Do what?"

From behind, Tigerous struck Deselation in the shoulder with one of her claws. The pain was excruciating and numbed his right shoulder. He screamed in pain and hit Tigerous across her face, flinging her far away from him. She landed unconscious on the sandy ground.

Deselation screamed in pain again as he slowly pulled out the claw from his shoulder. He tossed it to the ground and it was still sizzling with his acidic blood when it landed. Blood streamed from his wound.

"It appears that the young lady has wounded you," said Zeus. "I believe it is time to finish you off."

Deselation issued a demonic yell at Zeus.

He attacked Zeus, but Zeus maneuvered around the attack, flipping Deselation and sending him harshly to the ground. Zeus moved in for the killing blow.

"I think it's time to close the circle of Legion's terror for good this time. No one will come to your aid as before, Deselation." Zeus grabbed Deselation by the throat and started to crush his windpipe.

Deselation grabbed Zeus's wrists and attempted to pull the massive hands from his throat. His loss of blood had weakened him and Zeus's strength was too mighty. Deselation's throat collapsed.

Zeus leaned in to Deselation, watching the last bit of his life fade.

"Goodbye, demon," he said.

Deselation's body went limp and dangled from Zeus's mighty grip. Zeus tossed the body aside and rushed to Tigerous.

"Are you alright?" he asked.

Tigerous started to come to. She opened her eyes and looked around. Tigerous looked at Zeus. "Is it over? Have we won the day?"

"Our task has been completed," Zeus said. "Deselation will not terrorize this world again. It's up to Clover and Preist now."

CHAPTER 15

Near the east end of Demure, no one was patrolling or observing. The entire town was too occupied with the ongoing distractions from Clover's allies. It afforded Preist the opportunity to sneak up to a patch of desert brush undetected. He was wearing his familiar dingy white cloak, making him appear like a demented banshee moving along the surface. There was an object very few knew about lingering close to the town, hidden in plain sight.

Under the rotted, dead brush, Preist uncovered the access point to the sewage system which led to the town. It would give him access to an underground passage which would lead him into the heart of Demure itself. Dead weeds, sand and other useless debris stood in his way. They would have to be removed before Preist could enter the dark tunnel which would lead him to the human children.

After tediously removing the useless debris, Preist pulled on the heavy, dense cover. It was one of the few things left from an older time. The cover, and the sewer it allowed access to, was like a time capsule. It made the once proud and so-called civilized society seem ancient and archaic. He struggled to move the heavy cover. In his first attempt, it didn't move at all. He became red in the face and the muscles in his neck protruded from the strain. He took a minute to catch his breath but, like any great warrior, he wasn't about to give in. Neither Preist nor the cover gave an inch. He didn't remember it being so heavy in the past, but to his recollection he hadn't tried to enter this secret dungeon for a long time. He hadn't had any need to sneak into the town for ages.

Preist scolded the sewer cover. "You're a heavy bugger, aren't you?"

Preist continued to struggle but as before failed to move the lid at all. He was forced to abandon the effort and took a moment to catch his breath. "I don't ever remember it being this hard getting into this sewer before. But it has been a while since I tried to use it." He looked down at the sewage cover in mounting frustration.

"How did I access it in the past?"

Then something dawned on Preist.

Preist looked around but couldn't find uncover what he had remembered using to access the sewer entrance. His efforts soon seemed fruitless. His normal calm demeanor was being replaced by anxiety and he could feel his heartbeat quicken. His head began to spin and Preist wasn't quite sure if it was the vigorousness of the solar heat beating down on him, or if it was the adrenaline rushing through his body making him delirious. Preist wiped the sweat from his forehead and continued his pursuit.

I will have to go back to Clover and admit I have failed him—that I failed them all. He began to walk away but kicked something in the sand. He discovered a T-handle with a hollow middle buried partially under the sandy surface. Preist picked it up and inspected it. It were as if his prayers had been answered.

"There you are my enduring agent."

Preist measured the handle and the device made its tortoise-like movement magnetically toward the heavy, rusty sewer cover. He was unable to halt the device's progress and it slammed into the cover with a loud clang.

Preist, in his astonishment, looked around diligently, making sure no one was observing, then started to lift the cover off the sewer entrance. His veins protruded from his thin, chicken-like neck, much like his first attempt, but this time the massive cover slowly shifted.

Inch by inch, the cover came off its iron perch, exposing the entrance to the sewer's dark interior. With nearly every ounce of energy left in his tired body, Preist tossed the cover to the side. After catching his breath for the second time in a matter of minutes, Preist climbed down into the sewer. The smell of decay and disease lingered. The sewer had been dried up from years of no use but the remains of the once dominant human society still lingered within. The ladder leading into the dark abyss was encased in rust and Preist struggled to maintain his grip during his descent.

Since he didn't possess the nocturnal senses of Clover, Preist was forced to pull out a light stick to illuminate his path. It only had the ability to illuminate a small area around him, so he moved at a slow and methodical pace as he made his way down the service ladder and into the depths of the massive sewer. When Preist reached the bottom, he looked up. The light from the surface had become minimal, making him feel like a small animal locked down a decrepit hole. He continued to struggle along as he made his way through the sewer's congested path. Preist moved toward the middle of town. He was not certain he was headed in the right direction. He understood the maze of sewer pipes ran in several directions and his senses were out of their element in this dark, desolate place.

I must remember where Legion placed his degenerate acolytes when they did undesirable things or questioned his leadership. I remember Legion saying something like a Lazarus Pit. But what could represent such a crude prison within the confines of the city?

The deeper into the maze of darkness Preist ventured, the wetter it became. He splashed through small puddles of water no more than an inch and a half deep. The stench that lay about the sewer had become thicker as he moved farther in, like a thick fog hovering over a city. He wasn't sure if he could endure the overwhelming aroma until the end of his journey. The closer to the center of the town he got the stronger the stench was getting.

Preist started to become woozy from a strong aroma coming from deep within the subterranean tunnels. *Wow, that horrid stench is getting stronger as I move on deeper into this maze. It's like something died down here long ago. Maybe something did.*

Preist kept looking behind him. He felt as if he were being tracked. His paranoia wasn't unfounded, but his foe refused to reveal itself. Unsatisfied but unable to discover anything, Preist continued on with his journey. He quickly became fatigued by his trek through the forsaken remnants of the abandoned sewer. Between maneuvering through the waste and the vile stench that hovered in the air, something else wore him down. Something came to Preist, alerting him to a sinister presence. He was not alone, but Preist couldn't pinpoint the source. Things that should have dissipated or passed on long ago still lurked deep within the confines of the sewer.

This place holds a powerful essence. It must have trapped an overabundance of immensely powerful energies before humanity abruptly ended. Several times he spun around, shining his light in an effort to see behind him but, like his entire journey through the sewer, he sees nothing. Whatever it was that followed him was still there, lurking in the distance. After a moment Preist returned to his descent into the sewer's abyss.

The puddles of water that collected along his path became deeper the farther he ventured into the dark, musky sewer. Echoes of unusual sounds bounced throughout the sewer like remnants of dead souls long forgotten.

He continued on, looking upward trying to gauge where under the town he was, but he still had no clue. Preist briefly closed his eyes and tried to imagine the surface above, hoping he could figure out his current location would be if he were on the surface. Interference from the elements in the sewer was disrupting Preist's normally heightened sense of concentration and he was having difficult pinpointing his location. Some noise from above penetrated through the cracked, porous concrete of the sewer. It sounded a lot like laughter. Preist shone his light up toward the ceiling of the sewer. For a moment he is filled with paranoia.

More noise echoed from the direction he had come from. The noise was getting louder and louder and Preist turned his light back the way he had come. Yet again he failed to see anything. Preist started to jog through the sewer, not paying any attention to what was following him. The teenagers were depending on his rescue—if they were still alive. Clover was also depending on his success, too.

He reached a section of the sewer separated by a large concrete, half-demolished pillar. It looked to Preist that it had once held a door; he could see holes in the concrete that once held the giant hinges. On the other side of the pillar, Preist ran into water deep enough to submerge his ankles. The deeper puddles slowed him considerably. Preist looked behind him, trying to see if whatever had been trailing him was still back there.

He stumbled and fell headfirst, disappearing into a much deeper pool of murky, nasty water. When he reemerged from the mucky water he was forced to spit some from his mouth just to breath. He had swallowed some of the stale water and had to do everything he could to prevent himself from throwing up

The little light that shone down on him, came through the cracks in the sewer to unmask the surface of the pool he had fallen into. Gray and filthy, small objects floated on its surface. He stood up and the water level reached his waist.

Preist lifted his illumination stick. Water dripped from its polymer shaft, the hazy film clouding the light and making it difficult to see into the pool.

Something grabbed tightly around Preist's waist and forced him to drop the stick into the pool. It hit with a *curplop*.

Preist and his adversary struggled against one another. The thing that held him tightened its grip. Its slimy arms seemed to tighten every time he tried to pry them free. Preist struggled to breathe and was nearly thrown into the pool's depths once again. He moved for his closest weapon, an electric device that could send over 150 volts of static electricity from its tip. He was unable to reach it—the creature had Preist's arm pinched against one of its tentacle-like arms. Preist also possessed an explosive device known as a Fireball grenade, but he was in no position to retrieve it from his stained tunic. Even if he could reach the device, he had no desire to use it at this point. He liked being alive too much and not disseminated across the entire sewer.

The creature threw Preist down again and the two disappeared for a moment beneath the pool's surface before reemerging. Preist spit up more dirty water and tried to breathe. He attempted to speak, but it came out in incoherent patches.

Preist struggled to get free of the creature's slimy grip, but the creature continued to force him in and out of the water. *I . . . have . . . to get . . . this thing . . . off . . . me . . . before it drowns me.*

He tried for his tool again and this time managed to wrap his hand around it. He tightened his grip on it, trying to keep it from falling out of his slippery grasp.. He struggled to keep his arms from submerging the tool in the filthy water, raising it high. He measured carefully before counterattacking the creature that gripped him.

He jammed the tool into the beast's leathery side and switched it on. A short burst of electrical current rages into the creature's midsection and his adversary let out a head-pounding roar. The creature became limp. The jolt of electricity temporarily forced Preist to the water's surface, disorienting him. He recovered quickly, knowing his fight wasn't over yet.

Fearing that the town's occupants would hear the creature's screams and would come rushing down to them, Preist glanced upward. Once he heard nothing, he jammed the tool into the creature's midsection again. It screamed much louder this time. Preist's attack loosened the beast's tentacles and they slipped from Preist's shoulders.

Now free, he is able to see his attacker's face. It was a hybrid squid with legs, which explained the footsteps he had heard, and squid-like arms with deformed fingers. He pushed the thing away from him and it splashed into the pool and sank into its depths.

With his remaining strength, Preist pulled himself out of the pool and rested for a moment against a half-corroded pillar as the remaining water drained from his clothes.

Convinced that he had recovered enough strength to continue, Preist started to move again. More sunlight penetrated the massive cracks and deformed portions of the concrete. There were even sections of the concrete foundation that had started to crumble away from the rebar.

"I have to be getting close to the middle of Demure by now. The town square should be directly above my head."

Preist looked up as if searching for something in the dilapidated concrete above.

The crumbling concrete floor dried out completely and soon he was walking on smooth dry pavement, without any impedance. A large source of light illuminated the entire section of the sewer he stood in. He thought he saw the skeletal remains of deceased animals and, once, something that resembled human remains.

He discovered a ladder which led him to a sewer cover like the one he had used to gain access to the sewer itself. He began his climb out of the dreadful place, hesitating a moment, making sure the cover wasn't booby-trapped. The rotted iron seemed foreign to his grasp.

Preist emerged from the sewer soiled but alive and carefully scanned the area for any guards. When he was sure the coast was clear, he climbed out of the sewer and onto the dry, arid surface. None of Legion's security forces where moving about. The streets were nearly deserted. He had emerged from his long trek through the sewer and had surfaced into the middle of Demure.

He knew he had to be cautious. It was likely that Legion had placed the town on high alert after the incident back at the lab. *He might even be anticipating a rescue attempt*, Preist thought, *I know I would.*

Preist scrambled behind the wall of a half-collapsed building, trying to avoid being spotted through holes in the wall. He looked out into the street; no one was moving in this part of town either, but in the distance he heard voices echoing. The voices quickly passed without noticing the town's new visitor.

Preist confirmed the coast was clear and continued onward, but with more caution. This part of town, much like where he had emerged, seemed more like a ghost town than anything else. Demure had changed since he last visited it. Everything was falling apart. The buildings were collapsing, there were corpses lining every street corner and the streets themselves had reverted to their origins. They were no longer paved, but dirt, and as he moved along his feet stirred up the dust, making stealth virtually impossible.

Preist discovered a structure which appeared to be mostly buried underground, but its top protruded from the ground like an ugly wart. It was in a similar condition as the rest of the buildings in the town, but seemed quite out of place. It was massive in size and shaped like a Roman coliseum. Despite the structure's size, there were only two sentries guarding it. One patrolled the perimeter, while the other one was stationary. Preist concentrated on the structure itself. *Why would such a massive structure have only two guards protecting its perimeter?* Preist wondered. Then it dawned on him. *Legion's commando ranks just be severely diminished due to the multitude of operations he has going on. Tigerous and Zeus's diversion has had a bigger effect than I anticipated. This might end up an easier task than I envisioned.*

Preist's focus turned back to the massive structure. *That's gotta be the place Legion has the children imprisoned.* He looked around to see if anyone was approaching from either side of the massive structure, then lifted his hood over his head and vanished. He moved swiftly across the street, hesitating for a moment as he waited for the roving guard to disappear behind the large metal structure he was approaching. When only one guard remained, Preist made his move.

The guard was whistling and not paying much attention to what he was doing. Preist lunged at the guard and wrapped the wire around the man's thick neck. He pulled with all his might, and the guard struggled, swinging his arms wildly. Finally, the guard's life gave out and Preist dragged the dead body out of sight.

Preist examined the interior of large metal structure before him. It had an elliptical shape to it but, to Preist's disadvantage, he couldn't see anything through the structure's darkness. He couldn't tell whether the children were inside or not but knew he didn't have any time to waste, so he yelled into the darkness, hoping to get a response in return. His voice bounces off the metal structure and returns to him as nothing more than an echo.

"Damn it!"

Preist moved back to the dead guard and searched him. He found an emergency flare that could light the structure's interior, then returned to his previous position. As he was about to light the flare, someone snuck up from behind.

"What the hell!" the second guard yelled out. He struck Preist on the back of the head, knocking him to the ground. Preist lie on the ground motionless; his body appeared limp to the examining guard. The guard had never seen the likes of Preist before.

"Who are you and what are you doing snooping around my duty station?" The malcontented guard hovered over Preist and jabbed the barrel of his weapon into Preist's supposedly limp body. The guard used the tip of the weapon to push back Preist's cloak and reveal the intruder's identity. The only thing the guard managed to accomplish was to move around the cloak's material. To the guard's feeble mind, the intruder had vanished into thin air.

The guard's frustration mounted, his face shifted to a shade of red which made him look like the blazing sun which rained down thermal radiation every day. He slung his weapon onto his shoulder and clenched his fists until they turned white. The guard punched at the cloak, hoping to force his intruder to reappear.

"What the fuck!"

Preist took the opportunity to strike back. He launched himself at the guard's midsection, knocking them both to the ground. Preist discovered the guard was stronger than he had anticipated, but the man was still human. While the guard's attention was diverted, Preist grabbed for the guard's weapon.

"That wasn't a very friendly thing to do," Preist said angrily. "You have a serious anger issue that I will have to eradicate." Preist struck the guard and leaped to his feet like a cat.

The two figures danced around one another, each attempting to possess the guard's weapon, which had fallen from the guard's burly shoulders to lie between them both.

"I don't believe you deserve this thing. It's obvious you don't understand how to use it, so I must remove it from your possession, my friend," Preist said.

The guard looked at Preist scornfully. "Like hell you will."

Preist positioned his legs just how he wanted them and kicked the guard in his chest, knocking him over. The guard tumbled away from Preist and his fallen weapon. He lay still, seemingly dazed.

"I am sorry I must end your life, my friend. I need to access this structure and you will hinder me and my mission's objective. Don't take this personally, because it isn't."

Preist retrieved the assault weapon, gripped its synthetic handle and pressed the trigger. The assault weapon ignited, spraying its villainous ammunition as Preist struggled to control his aim. He hated crude weapons, but even with his lack of skill, the weapon's wild firing hit everything in close proximity of them both. The guard's body wasn't spared; ammunition ran all over his fleshy body, damaging every vital system in it. When Preist finished, the guard's body fell to the ground. Blood spilled from every hole, natural and newly inflicted. Preist threw down the weapon in disgust and retrieved the fallen flare.

"What a dreadful weapon that thing is," he said.

Preist rushed to the edge of the structure and tried to peer into the darkness. He couldn't see anything through the darkness of the interior, so he struck the flare and shone it down into the metal structure. He called out for the children.

"Doria, Straus! Are you down there?" His screams echoed in the dark, oil-drenched structure.

He heard something move below, and he leaned over the pit's edge to shine the flare in the direction of the noise. The metal structure was coated with slimy oil giving it a glaring, reflective surface. Preist moved his flare farther across the pit. The twins were floating on a large flat surface.

Doria saw the flare's reflection bouncing off the pit's side and waved in a mad attempt to get Preist's attention.

"Help us! Please, my brother is injured," she yelled.

Preist waited for his vision to adjust to the darkness of the pit. "Hold on a moment, child." Preist knew he had to stay calm, but he wasn't sure how much time the children had—or how much time he had. Would someone come along and interrupt his rescue attempt? How long could the twins last in this dark, smelly pit? What other things might be lurking in the darkness for him and the children?

Preist ran back to the second dead guard and searched his body for anything that might aid him in rescuing the two human children. He dug through every pocket in the guard's uniform but found nothing. In the guard's knapsack attached to his service belt, Preist finally found a tethering rope with a metal clasp at the end.

Preist returned to the structure and attached the line to the pit's edge.

"Please hurry, Mister." Doria's voice echoed up through the structure; her young voice was laced with anxiety and distress.

"Relax, child. I am working as fast as I can," Preist said. He was working diligently on preparing the rope but Doria's anxiety was making him flounder.

When he was absolutely sure the rope would hold his weight, Preist started to descend into the dark, unaware of the obstacles he might find on the way down to the children.

Doria looked up as Preist descended toward them in a slow and scrupulous manner. He attempted to keep one eye on the steps he took, while keeping the twins in his sight. While his attention was drawn toward his descent, a noise came from beneath the oily surface directly below. The oily sea started to bubble and the platform Doria and Straus were stranded on began to move in unison with whatever was emerging from the liquid beneath.

"I don't mean to aggravate you, because I appreciate your rescue," Doria called. "But is there a way you could get us out of here any quicker? I think something is alive in here."

Another sound emerged from the oily surface and a split second later, an oily bubble burst on the surface, spraying residue in every direction. Doria shielded herself and Straus. Preist knew he had run out of time, so he accelerated his descent. *Whatever the hell created the air pocket is about to surface.* If the bubble was any indication, whatever made it wasn't on the small side. As he descended more rapidly, the rubbing from the line burning his raw hands; he had no time to let something so insignificant stop him now.

He finally reached the twins. Doria dragged her brother's body toward Preist, trying not to capsize the object they were adrift on. She struggled with her brother's weight, and slipped a number of times, nearly capsizing them into the oily abyss below. The children had been floating on an elongated piece of cold metal in the shape of driftwood. The end the twins were at was the widest section while the opposite end was narrow and ended in a razor-sharp point.

"Give me your hand, child," Preist said.

Doria shook her head. "No. Take my brother first. I believe he is seriously injured. He is unconscious, and he may have a dislocated shoulder from being thrown down here. He definitely won't be able climb like you or I can."

Preist grabbed Straus's limp body and threw it over his shoulder like a sack of potatoes. Despite his adolescent size, Straus had packed some weight on his body. Preist instantly realized the extra weight on his shoulders would make for a slower ascent. He looked back at the human child he was about to leave behind, defenseless to whatever was surfacing. *I hope I have enough time to rescue them both.*

"I'll be back for you as quickly as I can."

The treacherous terrain made it difficult to ascend at a rapid pace. He continuously kept losing his footing and his journey to the top seemed to take all day. Despite his slow progress, Preist continued to be cautious. He did not want to drop the boy into the oil below. If he did, he would never be able to live with himself.

Preist made it part of the way up and slipped, losing his grip on the rope for a moment, nearly sending him and the boy tumbling into the oily abyss below. Eventually he recovered, restoring his grip and halted their descent. He swiftly renewed their climb.

From the oily depths emerged a set of demonic eyes, a mouthful of razor-sharp teeth and muscular tentacles which reached for the young teen.

"Oh shit!" Doria squealed.

The creature slowly moved across the oily surface toward her. It was covered completely from the oil beneath the platform and had a piercing glance which didn't waver at all. All the massive creature could do was concentrate on its target, its next meal. The monstrosity leaned on the flat platform and started to pull it, along with the girl, to an oily grave. Doria stood as the creature started to move the jagged metal platform but quickly fell and only the palms of her hands kept her from bouncing off the lubricated metal. Preist started to panic, not sure what to do. He and Straus were only halfway up the structure's wall.

"I can't save both. I barely have this one to safety!" Preist looked around for a safe place to set Straus and noticed a catwalk running alongside the adjacent wall. He looked down at the receding platform to see Doria sinking toward the monstrosity.

"Okay, here goes nothing." He launched Straus toward the catwalk in one fluid motion and watched the unconscious child's flight toward what Preist hoped was safety. The boy's body moved closer to the platform but his approach didn't seem quite right. Preist realized his mistake.

Shit! I'm going to lose both children from my own stupidity, he thought.

Straus nearly reached the catwalk, but just as he was about to land safely on the platform, he struck the side of the railing running along the catwalk. Preist held his breath. There was nothing he could do to help Straus at this point. Fortunately, the boy struck the railing with his thighs. Preist winced, imagining how the boy's body felt. Fortunately, Straus being unconscious and motionless allowed his body to fall limply over the rail, onto the catwalk's platform.

With one child safe, Preist released the safety latch on the rope and rapidly descended to the sinking platform. Doria was so close to the creature and so near death, that Preist could taste her agony. There was barely enough time to react. Preist swung down and slid across the oily platform toward the creature about to devour Doria.

"Hang on, kid!" Preist said. He reached out and grabbed Doria's arm and started to pull her toward safety. The creature became furious and opened its mouth wider, displaying all its razor-sharp dagger-shaped teeth. Doria whimpered. There was a second layer of teeth, much smaller than the upper layer, but just as deadly. The monstrosity exposed a massive elongated tongue which reached for them both. The furious creature let out a deafening roar, spraying them with dark saliva.

Preist and Doria moved up the sinking platform. The two of them would never outrun the approaching monstrosity at their current speed. He wrapped the line around Doria.

"Climb as fast as you can," he said.

Doria didn't know how to respond to the kindness, but did as she was instructed. Preist started to slide back down the platform, toward the creature and its teeth.

Doria yelled at Preist as the line retracted. "What about you?"

Preist waved the girl on without looking back. His concentration was on the monstrosity before him. "Only one of us can use the rope at a time. Move swiftly, before this creature gets us both."

Preist approached the oncoming monstrosity which scooped him up with one of its large, leathery tentacles. It moved him toward its mouth, ready to devour the bio-engineered genius. *This is going to hurt a lot, I'm afraid.* Preist started to chuckle a little at his own wit. *I always felt dying would be more graceful than being one of Legion's pet's meals.*

The last remaining essence of Doctor Sergei Peterovitch within Preist spoke. *You still have a fire grenade left. Use it to exterminate this beast.*

Preist gulped and responded. *You know that will be a one-way trip, right?* There was no response from Sergei's essence. *Well, here goes nothing then.*

The tentacle tightened around Preist's midsection. He tugged at the small round explosive device and ripped it from his pocket. He stared at the creature, watching as its mouth closed in on him.

"You and I are going out with a bang, big guy."

Preist depressed the activation switch and the device started to beep loudly, echoing all around them. He threw it toward the opening mouth and the creature devoured it. At first nothing seemed to happen—Preist could only see the monstrosity chomping on the device. *Damn, it didn't work,* he thought. Then Preist started to smell burning flesh. Smoke began to emit from the monstrosity's flesh. At first it was only a small blotch on the creature's rubbery skin, but quickly the red mark increased in size. The fire from the device was devouring it. It let out a cry and exploded in a ball of flames. As it disintegrated, it sank beneath the oily surface.

The explosion catapulted Preist high into the air. Everything moved in slow motion, as if he were experiencing his flight to death from outside of his body. Preist watched as his body flew limply through the air. He wasn't sure if he was already dead or merely unconscious. Tumbling back to earth, the fall shielded his vision and he couldn't see which direction he was heading. Finally, he landed hard on the ground and knocked the wind from his body. He had landed just feet from the edge of the metal structure. He was groggy and briefly disoriented when he finally came to his senses. He slowly tried to stand but could only manage to get to his knees. Doria climbed over the edge with Straus clinging tightly to her back, still semi-unconscious.

"That was one hell of a trip," she said with a welcoming smile. "My name is Doria."

They shook hands.

"They call me Preist."

CHAPTER 16

At the southern outskirts of Demure, Clover approached from the west. He moved at a methodical pace; his hybrid coat blew in wind from the approaching storm, but he didn't waver in his steadfast approach. It was like every western shown on the Sunday matinee. All that was missing was some eerie showdown music to set the otherworldly mood. Legion's unseen spies carefully monitored his approach from afar. Clover sensed the spies' movements, but didn't retrieve his throwing weapon. He welcomed their shadow reconnaissance, it meant it would only be a matter of moments before his brother appeared.

A figure awaited his arrival near the southern entrance. It was Legion. Morphed in his full battle gear, making him look like a humongous ancient demon from the netherworld in shiny steel, Legion watched Clover move toward the town. The seemingly invincible warrior gripped his battle sword tightly in his massive hands.

"Come, brother, let us unite our souls one last time," Legion called out.

Preist's voice spoke to Clover, an echoing sound as he was preparing to engage in battle. *Legion isn't indestructible, Clover. There are weaknesses in his armor. Find one and place the stone inside of him.*

The tension mounted between the two warriors as they approached one another, each in their own way. Clover approached Legion cautiously, never letting his brother out of his peripheral vision. Clover's approach kept both warriors just out of range of one another. He tried to gauge the weak points in his brother's fighting style. He grasped his katana tightly, and circled his brother, closing in. Each time Clover came within striking range, he tested Legion's resolve, then backed away, taunting his brother into striking first.

Legion's fighting style was quite contrasting to Clover's. He observed Clover's antics, all the while grasping his great sword with such strength that his massive forearms became tense and swollen. Each time Clover moved into Legion's massive attacking range only to dart back out it enraged Legion further. He desired to clash weapons with his brother.

Clover gave Legion a mocking grin, and Legion issued a scream, forcing Clover to back away, nearly dropping the assassin to one knee. Clover thought that fire might be resonating from the eye sockets in Legion's helm. It was difficult to tell, with the intense blurriness within Legions Helm, whether it was just the glow from Legion's eye sockets or if it truly was fire.

Clover could taste the intensity that electrified the air. It seemed to be stuck on the edge of his tongue. The sensation was about to drive him insane, he knew the tension was mounting to a breaking point and the longer they waited to engage one another, the worse it would get. The levy would surely break with a force so massive. Clover swallowed deeply and prepared to engage.

"You came." Only Legion's glaring demon eyes and his near invisible smile could be seen through the façade of his morphed head. It was as if something had replaced his soul, if Legion ever had one to begin with.

"Yes, Legion," Clover said. "I have come to stop your reign and end this war you have started."

Legion laughed. "So, this is the endgame for one of us? I will truly miss our correspondence, brother."

Clover smiled back. "I'm sure you will."

"Let's make this a fight for the ages, one that will be talked about in folktales. Two gods who fought for glory," Legion said.

Clover nodded.

Both men prepared their weapons for battle. Clover quickly checked behind him to make sure the Monoarc Stone was secure in its hiding place.

The two warriors circled one another, and in one swift move engaged one another with such ferocity that energy exploded from their weapons as they collided. The steel from the swords ground against one another and both warriors struggled to gain an advantage over the other. Back and forth Clover and Legion exchanged blows, Clover's katana clashed against Legion's great blade, the sounds echoing throughout the deserted battle plain. The bombardment of was followed by a struggle of wills as each warrior pushed against the will of the other. Clover gained momentum against his brother, then the super soldier gained momentum against Clover. Back and forth they pushed and pulled against each other; both warriors struggled against the weight of the other, like a tug-of-war match where neither side gained the upper hand. As one of the warriors started to lose his footing. the other's hands started to sweat, the perspiration making the grasp on his weapon tenuous. Then, the momentum pushed back in the other's favor, while his opponent started to lose his footing. Finally, the force of the battle pushed both away from each other.

A sinister laugh emerged from under Legion's helmet that sent chills down Clover's spine.

"Excellent, Clover. This is going to be a lot more fun than even I have anticipated," Legion said. "I've been waiting for this, since our last encounter. This is immensely gratifying. You can't even begin to comprehend what this means for me, brother."

The two warriors reengaged one another as Clover moved in a little closer. Legion swung his heavy sword toward Clover in a wild and chaotic arc, as if the behemoth been struck with a deranged lunacy. Clover's agility and lightning-fast movements allowed him to maneuver out of the way numerous times. He felt the air split just above his right shoulder as the serrated blade passed by.

Each time Clover recovered, the adversaries would engage each other again. The ground started to crack open from the force of the powerful blows. The earth shook, and the cracked earth exposed a fierce heat which rose from the crevices as if the monumental cracks were aflame.

Both men shoved each other away using their weapons and attempted to reposition themselves for another attack. Legion snarled through the darkness of his helm and his grasp tightened on his great sword. Clover brushed himself off in a mocking gesture, as if their encounter was more a nuisance than a real battle.

"Looks like you have gotten a tad slow, Legion." Clover twirled his katanas in each hand.

They rushed one another, forcing their way through the slowly dissipating smoke from the cracked earth. Neither could clearly see the other as they closed the gap, leaping over the islands of charred earth that cluttered the pockmarked land.

Their weapons reunited in a thunderous collision that sent a shock wave of energy which shot out for miles, sending sand and rock debris flying. Even though neither warrior noticed, the earth started to move in a bizarre way. Portions of the ground started to push through the cracked surface, protrusions pierced the sandy, pale skin of the surface. Steam rose from cracks and each strike let off immense energy. The atmosphere had become electric and the air cracked, like a great thunderstorm was on the way.

"Clover, I'm going to kill you slowly. I want you to feel your life force fleeing from you as each blow of my sword falls."

"That's a little premature, Legion. You have to be able to land a blow first."

Legion maneuvered his massive blade back over his shoulder with both hands. Clover spied a small seam in Legion's suit. Flesh folded over flesh, like fabric entwined in an expertly sewn seam. There was his opportunity, his chance to insert the stone into Legion's body. *I need to find the other seams in the suit, but I doubt he will give me the opportunity to explore it up close.*

Legion's blade sliced through the air and moved toward its target. Everything happened in slow motion for Clover. Inch by inch he watched and waited as the serrated blade moved at a snail's pace toward him. One false move or miscalculation would mean his demise. He would wait until the blade had reached the peak of its momentous drive and on its decline, right before it reached the place he now crouched, he would duck the attack, leaving Legion exposed. But Legion did something different this time which caught Clover off guard—he swung his free arm and struck Clover in the chest. The blow sent Clover crashing to the ground, leaving the bioengineered assassin temporarily dazed.

Legion's momentum had thrown him far from Clover. Clover shook off Legion's blow and recovered swiftly. He knew Legion wouldn't stay off-balance for long.

I must find the right opportunity to insert the stone, Clover thought, staring at his overzealous brother.

Clover looked Legion up and down quickly before he attacked again. He shook his head to clear it and attempted to refocus on the task at hand. The two reengaged, the force of their attacks leaving them mere inches from each other, their faces just inches apart.

"Any last words, little brother, before I end you?" Legion asked.

Clover would need to allow Legion to become over-confident, to make him believe that he was gaining the upper hand.

"Nothing that you would understand." Clover smirked.

Legion raised his great sword for a killing blow, deter-mined to strike home this time. Clover let Legion's weapon come very close to his own body, but didn't allow the war-rior to land a fatal blow. The weapon nearly decapitated the assassin, but, like before, Clover used his swiftness to evade the blow. While Legion was still unbalanced from his own attack, Clover swept Legion's feet from out under him, sending Legion crashing to the ground.

Legion reached for his great sword and flung it in an act of desperation. The sword sliced through Clover's shoulder, leaving it bloodied and injured. Clover screamed in agony. The attack sent him to his knees in a moment of intense pain. He placed his hand over the wound to stop the bleeding, but knew he couldn't ignore his brother for very long.

Legion laughed. "I draw first blood, brother!" He retrieved his sword from the where it had landed. Clover stood back up, and Legion attacked, swinging his sword wildly. Clover struck Legion's armor between his brother's chaotic throws. All it managed to do is send sparks flying into the air.

Clover looked at his sword with dismay.

"Don't you remember, my suit is impenetrable!" Legion laughed.

Clover gripped his katana harder in frustration. He got back to his feet and their weapons met again. His sword moved down Legion's blade, and Legion kicked Clover in the chest with his hulking, armored leg and sent him flying. Clover landed roughly , covering himself in sandy debris.

Legion approached slowly, readying himself to issue a mighty killing blow.

Once again Preist's voice spoke to Clover. *Legion isn't indestructible*, it echoed.

Clover shook off Preist's voice. "Ya, but finding the weakness is causing me a lot of pain and will eventually lead to my death." He looked closer at Legion's armor as his brother approached. *There it was, in plain sight, just as Preist had said it would be. Just above his waistline a thin seam had become evident in Legion's armor.*

Clover stood up, retrieved the Monoarc Stone from inside his trench coat, and held it firmly in one hand behind his back.

With Legion still coming after him, Clover raised one of his katanas to eye level. He pinpointed the seam in the armor and waited for Legion to get extremely close.

Legion let out a terrible scream, raised his heavy battle sword for the kill, and with all his might, attempted to strike a final blow onto Clover.

Just as Legion brought down his sword. Clover maneuvered himself out of the way and Legion's sword collided thunderously with the ground.

Clover slid past Legion, striking him with his katana and sending sparks into the air. He passed over one of the fleshy seams in Legion's suit and in one fluid motion rammed the Monoarc Stone deep into his brother. The stone slowly dissolved in Legion's murky, acidic blood. Instantly it started to merge with the cells. Absorbed by the membrane, the stone's molecules became an integral part of the outer cell, and consumed the non-human elements. The process happened rapidly as the stone transformed the demonic blood.

Legion could no longer hold the structure of his suit in his DNA and it lost its impenetrable properties. His armor dissolved right in front of Clover's eyes.

Clover stopped his sliding attack and watched attentively. Legion looked back at him in dismay, not realizing what had just happened.

"My suit of armor is impenetrable," Legion said. "You can't harm me, little brother!"

Legion's blood fell to the ground. It was no longer toxic, and transformed as the air hit it. It was yellow and gooey, much like slime.

Legion looked down. "What the Fu—" He touched his wound and looked at the yellow fluid dripping onto his hands. He had never seen his own blood before.

Clover stood up and displayed his arm which was covered with Legion's yellow milky blood. "Well, it looks like I was never informed of that, brother."

"It can't be, I'm invincible. I can't die by your hand. I am a god! Don't you realize that?" A tear manifested in Legion's right eye.

Clover looked down and smiled as he wiped Legion's harmless blood from his arm. "We all have to die sometime, even those who think they are immortal."

Legion fell to his knees, as if he might faint. He raised his arms to the sky as if to pray to some mythical god he had never known.

"You know that stone you have been searching for? Well, it's now permanently a part of you," said Clover.

Legion looked up at Clover as the assassin circled to the front of him. Legion's form started to change. His morphed skin turned from the suit of armor that had shielded him to regular human skin.

"What the fuck have you done to me?" he screamed, reaching out with a bloodied hand.

"I've turned you into what you despise the most." Clover showed Legion his own reflection.

Legion raised his bloody hands. "Please, have mercy on my soul." He reached out to Clover.

Clover readied his sword. "I'll show you as much mercy as you have shown many others," Clover said.

With an enormous swing, Clover sliced through Legion's body. From the top of Legion's head, right to the bottom, Clover's blade sliced Legion's new humanoid form. The halves wobbled in place as if they were Silly Putty and, for a moment, Clover feared the two halves might force themselves back together. Instead, Legion's body fell in two and his gummy yellow blood oozed out on all sides and the two halves slithered to the sand ground.

"It's over now. The terror has ceased to exist," Clover said to himself.

✝

Clover disappeared into the raging sandstorm which was now in full force, blowing eastward across the deserted plain. It was already too late. Clover had merged into the storm like he had always done, just as he was programmed to do.

The faster the twins ran after him, the farther into the void their savior descended, vanishing from sight.

Straus screamed out through the wind. "Clover, wait! You don't have to leave, we want you to stay."

Deep into the emptiness Clover went, disappearing back into the heart of the Wasteland. Clover's cloak could be seen blowing in the immense wind as he disappeared.

Straus turned to Tigerous. "Why is he leaving? Where will he go?"

"His job is complete. He has given humanity a second chance," she said.

"His penance has ratified his existence. He has atoned for the sins of his past," added Preist.

"He will go back to his life of solitude," Tigerous said with a tear in her eye.

Preist nods his head in agreement.

EPILOGUE

In another dimension, one that separated the world Clover and his allies resided in, a set of eyes observed the only metropolis in sight. The holographic, three-dimensional binoculars picked up on a group of slaves being escorted by three heavily armed guards. A closer look at the spotted an insignia on their garb and the figure recognized it with dread. The figure ducked lower to avoid being seen. One guard had stopped and looked around, suspicious of his surroundings. He walked the perimeter of the slaves, as if protecting them from something in the distance.

Did he see me? Can he sense me?

The mysterious figure moved behind the boulder shielding his position and took off the goggles. He wiped sweat from his forehead with a rag he had hidden beneath his disguise. Preist continued to scout the area around him. Despite being alien to him, the ancient city of Rectour had a sense that made the ancient city quite familar to Preist.

The ancient city seemed to be built in a style reminiscent of Earth, but it screamed flamboyance and charismatic appeal. Scanning the skyline of the city, which had been unnoticeable just moments before under the exotic structures, Preist started to understand what the inhabitants of this once grandiose metroplex were about. The skyline held the curvature of the erect buildings in symmetrical form. Despite each structure's unique design, the entire skyline seemed to have a cohesive flow, like it had been born all at once.

Preist focused in on one structure that caught his eye. Its smooth, delicate surface shone like glass, but he could tell it was made of a composite material which made it durable as well. Despite the gray sky the structure still gleamed as if it were a bright day. Unique symbols spread down one side of the structure, some sort of alien script that showed up only on this structure and none others. The building looked newer than the rest, and the symbols seemed out of place. *I don't see any on the other ancient structures—not that I was paying much attention to them.*

He noticed who that seemed all too familiar. He placed the binoculars back to his strained eyes and took another look. Yes, the guards were leading the chained prisoners back toward the metroplex Preist had just escaped. In the distance, in one of the tall buildings that could be seen over the rocky horizon, lights began to shine and a mad scene unfolded before his eyes.

"That's not good at all," he muttered.

Tiny individuals emerged from the elegant structure, rushing to intercept the chained slaves. The first figure that arrived at the bound chain gang struck the lead prisoner and the prisoner fell to one knee. The officer gestured to the bound prisoners. Preist got the impression the officer was screaming at the fallen prisoner. Preist focused his binoculars on the prisoner and his tormentor. He saw a significant difference between the prisoner and his captor.

He spun around and looked away from the scene in shock. The bound prisoners looked very familiar, much like humans outside of their gray skin. Their captors, on the other hand, gave Preist a revelation he hadn't expected. He shook his head in disbelief. *No, that's impossible. There is no way . . .* Preist trailed off as a loud noise came from the street below.

Preist returned to position in time to see a pair of enormous metal doors appearing from under the ground. Gas hissed from mechanical struts lifting the massive ground upward and exposing the city's underground. Gigantic sprockets and other mechanical devices worked nonstop, like the massive innards of an oversized cuckoo clock. The prisoners are led quickly toward the underground entrance.

Preist refocused his binoculars, this time on the gears themselves. As the massive sprockets turned, he could see each tooth, which were larger than the individuals entering the underground passageway. A multitude of platform layers stacked on top of each other like a cake. Preist could see the constructed platforms in fine detail. He was perplexed by the purpose of the gargantuan plates. Each one's surface was different; some of the platforms had rocky textures, while others had cobblestone or brick surfaces.

There were platforms that seemed eerily familiar. *One of those platforms looks like the front walkway of the formal Kremlin Palace. I need to get back to Clover ASAP.*

He replaced the binoculars snuggly in his travel pack.

Flashback:
One hour ago.

Preist wore a disguise which allowed him to blend into the city's population. He didn't want to draw attention to his being an outsider. His mission was to be incognito until he had seen his contact. He had been corresponding via telepathic communication with his contact on this side. Preist wasn't sure who might be interested in their conversation or what they might do if he was discovered but his associate's tone had been filled with anxiety and he didn't want to do anything to heighten it further. He wore his typical gray cloak under his disguise and had draped the hood over his face. It was difficult to tell what authorities from this foreign place might do to him if he was discovered.

Several citizens passed Preist, only noticing his presence with a glance. He hid in a shadowy part of the market. The towering structures that protruded at each end of the market square provided significant cover which cocooned him in shadow. He was reluctant to speak to any citizens that passed by, in fear of revealing his alien accent. Doing so could lead to his capture. He was forced to wait impatiently for his escort's arrival. In his apprehension, he constantly looked toward one end of the plaza's long walkway. It seemed to stretch for miles on end. Down the other end of the elongated walkway was semi-dead underbrush. *It's like someone took great pains to make this place utopian, but forgot to tend to the foliage.* He looked up at the plaza's construction. It was tainted by age, the ancient stone masonry thoroughly weather-stained. *This venue must have been something to behold in its finest day, but now this place, the entire city seems to be a mortuary full of roaming corpses. Something cataclysmic must have happened—must still be happening.*

He wasn't used to being out in the open. He missed the confines of his underground lab, which kept him hidden from sight. He loved the seclusion it gave him. His patience was running out. *Where can she be? I hope she didn't get caught, I couldn't live with myself for endangering that girl by giving her such a dangerous assignment.*

The risks weren't Preist's; they were his contact's as well. He knew, by the tone of her voice inside his head, that numerous traps awaited them both, hoping they would let down their guard. If the authorities discovered their plot, she wouldn't be the only one in danger.

While his back was turned to the shadowy part of his seclusion, a young local woman snuck up behind him and lightly touched him on his left elbow. Preist jumped in surprise.

"Don't do that. You will give me a heart attack," he said.

She motioned with her petite hand. "Come, let's take a walk. I know a place we can converse without being seen or heard." The two of them walked a while in silence. Preist watched her graceful and elegant motions. In his disillusion, he discerned that the young woman levitated on thin air, instead of walking next to him. When he could bear the silence no longer, the young woman turned to him. Her captivating and hypnotic eyes had him lost in a daze. Preist's body became numb, as if his very soul had been encapsulated within her gaze. She turned and spoke, snapping Preist out of his semi-entrancement.

"My dear friend. My people are suffering and our oppressive captors don't care how many of us they slaughter. They are not like us in any way." Preist's escort looked at him with a sad, discomforting smile. "They seem to be more like your kind, my friend. Their former masters have long been deceased, but their tyrannies have been allowed to remain. We are in desperate need for aid and I didn't know who to turn to. You are our last hope for survival." The woman stopped and looked around to see if anyone was spying on them, like she had sensed someone or something mirroring their path. Preist noticed something enclosed in her hand. She looked away from Preist and slipped the device into his hand.

Preist looked at the device's cold black surface.

Before Preist could ask what was on the device the woman whispered to him. "On this data disk you will find all the information you need. Our people's history, the story of our oppressors and how we have become a near-extinct people. You will find that our species and your human creators coincide with a common linage." She closed Preist's hand over as to caution him to take care of the device. "There is something else on the device that Clover needs to know. View it and take to him. It has vital data that pertains directly to him." A tear formed in one of her sensual eyes.

Noises came from across the hallway. The woman spun toward the sounds as if she suspected them to be rushed by security personnel. She turned back to Preist. "You must go now or risk being caught." She spun and ran in the opposite direction.

Preist touched the cold metal casing of the disk and closed his fist around it protectively. He shut his eyes briefly, trying to imagine the beautiful Dragoniran woman in his head. *The things happening here are horrendous. I must stop this metal tyrant before he has the chance to unleash what he has been building here. Clover must learn about all of this, his destiny has changed and it is imperative that I get this information to him. Discovering who these tyrants have prisoner will not make Clover ecstatic at all. I will look after this disk like it was my own child. I will get it back to the others and give Clover the information he needs. I won't fail you.*

Preist stood, looked around to see if the group was still nearby or if any other interested party was watching, and then dashed toward his spacecraft. He knew he had to hurry back as swiftly as possible to Earth, but he needed to avoid drawing too much attention.

The sound of an explosion came from the distance. Preist replaced the binoculars to his eyes. A search party rapidly approached his location. Preist lifted his ship off the ground. The small craft teetered from starboard to port as it slowly rose to a low altitude. At this level Preist could see the city's horizon and the expanse surrounding it.

A ship hovered at a similar altitude and it was advancing it to his position. A portal opened slightly to his craft's starboard side and the other ship moved quickly toward the opening. The foreign spacecraft vanished through the opening leaving Preist in a state of disbelief. Had he dreamed the entire episode or had that craft moved at a much quicker pace than his own craft could?

Preist tried to come to his senses. "Who in the hell was that? Whoever he was; he was heading toward Earth, according to the ship's data computer. I have to get back and warn Clover. I must open my own portal to Earth." Preist looked at the disk he had been given. "I wonder if any of this has to do with this little thing?"

His position in the air had become compromised and he knew he needed to leave immediately. The small spacecraft danced in the air, swaying back and forth as he spun the ship around. He engaged the ship's thrusters and instantly the craft jolted forward violently, catapulting through the still-open portal.

The place had an eerie feeling. *There are too many shadows and places to hide*, Clover thought. Normally these were places he would gravitate toward, but in this unusual place he dared not. He scanned the horizon. There were no clouds in the sky, just a haze of gray hanging over his current location. Something watched him, he was sure of it, but a second scan of the area didn't provide any further evidence.

He approached a run-down building made of weatherboard. At a closer glance, Clover noticed wood rot all over the run-down building. Sand covered two-thirds of the walkway and shattered glass littered his path. He tried to look inside, but all he could see was some old chairs knocked over on the rotten floor. Something was drawing him to this place, but he couldn't decide what it was. It wasn't like the connection he and Legion had shared, it was a different feeling altogether.

The decision is this, the assassin thought. *Stay out here in the gloomy twilight that is making my skin crawl, or enter the unknown establishment with no knowledge of what lies inside.*

He decided to enter the building, despite his better judgment. He shook off the euphoric notion that was irritating him and took several steps toward the run-down building when a centipede scampered across his boot. Clover stopped for a moment to watch the insect scurry away under dead brush ten or so paces from him. *At least this eerie place isn't devoid of life.*

He moved onto the first steps and the rotting wood gave a detestable creak in defiance. There was no door, just an opening where one might expect there to be. Clover hesitated at the opening and sensed something staring back at him from within.

He scanned the room for existing life-forms and, discovering none, entered the building. Just as he crossed the threshold an immense pressure halted him in his tracks, preventing him from proceeding any farther. Something pressed down on his chest, stomach and shoulders all at once. He couldn't sense its origins. He inched his way into the main room of the building, still fighting against whatever had halted his progress.

Finally, he broke free of whatever had stood in his way and fell to one knee, gasping for breath and trying to recover. His lungs flexed in and out rapidly, trying to regain some type of control over his body. Dazed, his mind spun wildly. *Probably from the lack of oxygen*, he thought between long gasping breaths. When his senses returned, he was able to sense a figure in the room with him. This alarmed Clover, because he could sense the figure glaring at him intensely.

A clapping noise sounded in the dark. "Bravo, Clover. That's the spirit I have come to expect from a killer such as yourself. I am truly impressed, my friend."

Clover looked into a corner of the room which he had thought was void of life. Something flickered in and out of sight. It was like what little gray light that penetrated this dark place was exposing the figure—now clearer to Clover than before. Clover got up, still with a slight dizziness resonating in his head. He walked over the dusty, sand-covered floor and approached the shadowy figure sitting in the corner.

The ominous, dark figure sat on the other side of a round, decayed wooden table, but Clover could only make out its silhouette. His nocturnal vision wasn't working in this eerie place.

"What's wrong, Clover? Do you need a better look at me? Will that place you at ease in my company?"

Clover squinted, but his vision didn't improve.

"Very well," the ominous figure said. The figure leaned into the gray-tinted light exposing its identity.

Clover stared at the figure, speechless. It was like looking in the mirror. Clover and this ominous figure were nearly identical, outside of the dark camouflage color that made the figure's presence ominous and cryptic, and its charcoal-black eyes which refused Clover access.

"It's like . . ."

"Looking into a mirror?" finished the mysterious figure. Clover's near twin leaned in closer. "We are brothers, Clover, in an odd sort of way."

Clover was overcome with a series of emotions. He felt dismay, because this dark figure baffled him. Anger, because he still hadn't come to realize what he truly was and now there was a second version of himself sitting across from him. Fearful, because he didn't know what this figure was capable of. Torment, because he didn't know what to feel, or how to react, or even what to do. Clover was caught in a plethora of confusing emotions he had never felt before.

Clover attempted to shake the emotions from his mind. "Who are you? Where am I and why have I been brought here?"

The dark figure leaned back into the shadows and laughed. Clover glared at the dark eyes of the shadow figure. For a moment Clover doubted if the figure was going to respond to him. It was only when Clover thought he might be driven insane by the eerie silence that the dark figure spoke.

"Yes, my friend, I guess I owe that much to you." He tapped a playing card on the decrepit table. Clover looked down at it feeling the tension in his neck. "I'm known merely as Shadow Agent, but I prefer to be called Nightshade. It fits me perfectly, don't you think?" Nightshade watched Clover, noticing his attention was locked on his fidgeting with the playing card.

"We are the same, you see. No matter how you sugarcoat it, we are both contract killers, we just have different masters. If it smells like shit, tastes like shit, it must be shit, no matter what you do to disguise it. Right?"

Clover looked up at Nightshade. "That doesn't answer why I'm here and where here actually is." Clover crossed his arms.

"Very well. I thought we should see each other in person. Just to see the face of our vexations. It was inevitable that it would eventually happen, so I chose our first encounter to ensure it would be one without confrontation.

And to answer where we are, well, think of it as a thin fabric between realms—you could call it a void. Nothing will interfere without invitation. I filled it with familiar things so you wouldn't find it so nerve-racking."

Clover had to shake his head free from the ache in his skull. He was still confused by the entire encounter.

"Would you like to play a game?" Nightshade gestured at the deck of cards on the table.

Clover looked apprehensively at the deck. "What type of game?"

"It's called The Game of Death. Let's turn the card in front of you and you will learn it as we play." Nightshade flipped over the card. "The Hangman's Noose!"

The picture was of a hangman's noose, nothing more, but the image sent chills down Clover's back. Clover's face became stone gray and he couldn'tmove a muscle. It was like he was frozen in time. "What the hell does that mean?"

Nightshade chuckled again. "Oh, forgive my absent-mindedness, my friend." Nightshade gave shit-eating grin, like he had something to tell Clover but wasn't sure how. "I must congratulate you on your recent accomplishment."

Clover's facial muscles contracted inward like a dried-up prune. "Accomplishment?"

"Indeed! The annihilation of our nemesis, Legion. It was something that made many others ecstatic about," Nightshade said. "What's wrong, Clover? You look unappreciative of my comments."

Clover backed away from the table.

"Wait! We have only begun to play, you must not leave so soon."

"The annihilation, as you so call it, couldn't have happened without the stone, and Preist's help."

"Yes, the infamous Monoarc Stone. You shouldn't give Preist so much credit. If it weren't for my master guiding the great Doctor Peterovitch to find the powerful stone, you may never have had the opportunity to kill Legion."

"So, your master planned all this? Why?"

Nightshade waved his hands as if sweeping something invisible out of the air. "No, no, my friend. Never planned, let's call it more of a theory than a plan. Hell, I'm impressed it worked. Trust me, I have had a chance to tangle against that behemoth and know how defeat feels."

"You also have lost against Legion? Is that why your master placed the stone in our path?"

"Let's call it a test of whether there was a weakness in his DNA armor, and to decide if the stone would work or not. He packed a powerful punch. After that encounter, I knew how you must have felt every time you took one another on."

Clover leaped to his feet, knocking over the chair he had been sitting on. "Lies. All you tell me are lies."

"Let's continue our card game, shall we?" Nightshade said. He flipped over another card. A man in a dark cloak held a massive sword. "The Lord of Destruction." Nightshade looked at Clover somberly. "It is as I have predicted. We will clash blades, but not before we have been useful to one another. Our duel is inevitable."

"You think I will partner with you, just so you and your master can use me to do your own will? Just to await your blade through my very heart? You must be delusional, Nightshade." Clover stormed from the old building.

"You must understand it by now. A storm is on the horizon and heading this way. No matter what we do, it cannot be stopped. All will perish that stand in its path," Nightshade called.

Clover looked back with a calm expression. It hid the multitude of emotions stirring within him. "I *am* the storm. Take that back to your demented master and remember, we will always be at odds with another."

Until we meet again, Clover. Maybe then you will reconsider. Nightshade concluded.

AUTHOR BIOGRAPHY

Craig R. Smith is a Science Fiction & Fantasy author. He possesses a Master of Arts in Creative Writing from Southern New Hampshire University. Mr. Smith grew up in a suburban town just outside of Kansas City and has always had a passion for reading, especially science fiction. Before becoming a published author, Craig worked for many years in the Information Technology field. Craig's narratives work on all the audience's senses and question the true definition of humanity. Most of the characters in his work are unconventional, fun, relatable and keep audiences wondering what is coming next?

Some of Mr. Smith's published works are *Journey into the Dark Realm*, a riveting space opera epic told in three books and *Clover: An Apocalyptic Tale*. The first book of this original Post-Apocalyptic series.

www.ingramcontent.com/pod-product-compliance
Lightning Source LLC
Chambersburg PA
CBHW070932100726
47908CB00001B/183